I0583211

AUTO NO MO US

Christopher L. Truxaw

Auto No Mo Us

Part One

Friday

May 26, 2056

Christopher L. Truxaw

Self-published by the Author.
Christopher L. Truxaw
Santa Ana, California
www.autonomousbooks.com

ISBN: 979-8-9922584-1-7 Paperback

Format generated:
Thursday, May 7, 2026 (minor formatting edits)

Table of Contents

Chapter 1

Early

12:01 AM, Stargazing

Although it appeared still and quiet from a distance, up close the desert landscape was alive in the moonlight. Lizards and rodents enjoyed the cool of the night to gather seeds. Rattlesnakes moved into position under small bushes to wait for mice, kangaroo rats, or other prey to mosey by. A few coyotes prowled, restraining their penchant for yipping and howling, while looking for something tasty or dead. Bats flew everywhere in their chaotic patterns to nab flying insects. An owl perched on a Joshua tree branch looking for small prey to swoop down upon. A solitary mountain lion with a tracking collar climbed a rock and crouched looking at the scene. On a rock below the lion lay the still body of a woman in an old jacket and blue jeans, all looking silver in the moonlight, staring at the sky with eyes closed and neck exposed.

"It's midnight," came a voice from the woman's wrist. As the woman stirred, the cat started to silently retreat.

"Huh? What?" Jo-Jo blinked her eyes a few times. Thinking she saw two very bright stars moving together quickly above her, she closed and rubbed her eyes before opening them again and the stars were gone. Maybe a double shooting star. Too bad she missed it.

"Sorry to wake you," came an apologetic voice from her wrist. "You asked me to remind you if you were still out at midnight."

Jo-Jo sat up and pulled up the sleeve of her jacket to look at the time displayed on the wristband and then looked around at the moonlit landscape and up at the starry sky. She was sitting on a rock, just below a much bigger rock with a cloudless night sky above her. Other large piles of rocks were scattered under the moonlight with an occasional Joshua tree or other desert bush between them. After a long look at the sky, hoping to see another shooting star, she leaned forward, sliding down off the rock, picked up the bag at her feet, and stood to start the walk back to her vehicle.

She walked slowly, enjoying the view of the sky and trying to remember the way back. Tonight was the last chance before going into the lights of the city. She saw many stars and dozens of satellites crisscrossing the sky, but with the moon nearly full the Milky Way was disappointingly dim. Moonlight allowed her to avoid running into rocks and bushes as she looked for the gravel roadway.

Her heart raced when something moved in the shadows at the base of a large pile of rocks to her right. To avoid it, she moved farther to the left. She lifted her bag above her head to look bigger. She glanced back to the right and thought she saw another shadow move under a nearby Joshua Tree.

Shivering, probably not from cold, she called out, "I'm not food. No food here. Just a very tall and fearsome creature."

She looked at the bag above her head and wondered if the bones, rocks, and plants she had picked up earlier smelled like food to a predator. She sniffed up at the bag and didn't smell anything.

"You can't have my bag of bones," she called out. "Or this bag of bones," she said more quietly referring to herself.

After continuing around a few large rock piles without being eaten she was getting unsure if she was on the right path when she felt and heard gravel crunching under her feet. She realized she had reached the roadway. "Where is it?" she whispered to herself. She looked both ways for her vehicle. She could see a shadowy shape about the right size 100 yards or so to her right.

"That must be it. Or with my luck, a rock the same shape."

She looked back and there was something moving on the last pile of rocks she had passed. Should she run? She tried to control her breathing as she continued at the same pace along the roadway, her crunching footsteps making enough noise for any predator to easily follow her. She moved off the roadway to the left and tried to walk on the sandy dirt at the edge instead of the gravel. She slowed her pace, carefully picking her foot placements to make less noise, still holding the bag over her head.

She sensed a sudden movement to her right and ducked and braced herself. Looking up she saw a large bird, probably an owl, pass silhouetted against the moon carrying a small animal.

Hoping that there were no more predators nearby, she lowered the bag from over her head and held it by its straps, swinging as she walked more quickly towards the large grey moonlight-illuminated box that loomed in front of her at a wide spot in the gravel road. She crossed the road, gravel crunching under her feet with each step, and came around to its shadowed right side.

Around eight feet tall and close to twenty feet long, this side looked plain grey or silver in the indirect moonlight, with a few inches of very dark shadow beneath it. She knew in daylight it should be bright blue with hints of white clouds above and stylized shapes of brown mountains below. She had painted the sides herself. Close up now, she could barely see outlines of some of the clouds and mountain peaks on the exterior wall. Maybe moonlight affected its appearance or maybe it was just dirty.

She recalled it had been dusty or dried muddy brown earlier today in the daylight. She sensed a movement by her feet and looked down. Did something run under the vehicle? She didn't see anything except one of her shoed feet in moonlight. The other was hidden in the stark shadow of the vehicle. She must have imagined it. She bent over and could see nothing in the dark void under the vehicle, not even the vehicle's small wheels.

She raised her left hand, and a door slid open. The interior lights were not much brighter than the moonlight. Sam was reclined in a chair surrounded by bins and bags of future art project materials she had gathered from various other stops. She looked behind her to make sure nothing was following her and quickly stepped up and in. She found a spot to set her new bag near the open door, then stepped carefully past Sam and through the collected materials to her small bed.

Sam seemed to be playing a game and didn't even turn his head towards her, but as she sat down, he asked, "Any meteors?"

"I saw two, maybe three, but lots of satellites. And I found some bones and some rocks with interesting shapes," Jo-Jo replied as she took off her jacket and stretched out on the bed. "An owl too."

"You caught an owl. Wow. Good job!" Sam said.

She ignored his sarcastic comment. He continued to play his game, manipulating a tablet and watching a screen on the wall. "Any more stops tonight?"

"Not for me. I was falling asleep out there. The moon is too bright. Maybe we can time our return trip for a New Moon and stop somewhere dark."

"A clear moonless night in somewhere like Bryce might be enough to get me to go outside for a few minutes. I remember once we went there when we were kids, and we could see shadows from the starlight," Sam reminisced.

"Another memory returns. And a good one. Star shadows. I think I remember that too. Nothing like that tonight. Lots of shadows from moonlight though. Sure you don't want to go out and take a look?" Jo-Jo offered pointing at the open door.

"No thanks."

"Abbie let's get going," Jo-Jo spoke to no one in particular.

A moving shadow with curious yellow-green eyes approached as the door slid shut and a voice from the walls said, "We need to backtrack to a charging station near the highway. Estimated arrival in Orange County around 7:30 AM."

"Don't explain every detail. Just take us there," Jo-Jo said.

"Sorry," said the voice.

"And stop apologizing so much," said Jo-Jo sternly.

"Uh, okay," said the voice.

She had told her Abbie not to speak unless asked, but Abbie would still sneak in unsolicited comments or advice, which had some effect. Now Jo-Jo was sober a lot more of the time, and she was getting more done on her artwork. Sam adored his own Abbie and followed a lot of her advice. He was still an asshole, but Jo-Jo appreciated being able to talk to him sober sometimes. And he was writing again. That was good.

Jo-Jo pulled off her pants and got under the covers in her bed.

"You should get some sleep, Sam. Don't play games all night."

"I can't sleep on the road," said Sam, "You know that."

"Then do some more writing if you can't sleep."

"Maybe. Let me finish this game first."

4:30 AM, Jeremy's Homework

The bed vibrated, the lights began to brighten, and a voice called out, "Wake up, Jeremy. Wake up."

Reluctantly opening his eyes, Jeremy replied, "What time is it? It's too early to get up." He looked at the wall opposite the bed and saw several options displayed for articles to read or historical games to play to help with his homework assignment.

"It's half past four. You told me to wake you with enough time to complete your Memorial Day essay."

"Oh. Yeah, Abbie. I guess I did." He sat partly up. "Are we still at home? I forgot to tell Mom and Dad about the party after-school."

A window opened on the wall display showing a map of a route between Owens Lake and Orange County with a blip showing him near Victorville, 74 miles to go, and a composite external view showing his Abitat moving with other vehicles on a highway.

"You decided to leave extra early today?"

"You have exams today. I'm allowing extra time to make certain you are not late."

"Okay. I guess that makes sense."

Jeremy was late to school about once a week, but still his parents complained about him not spending enough time with them. What did they expect after moving to the Owens Valley for work. They threatened to switch him to a closer school, but he knew they weren't serious. None of the closer schools was nearly as good as STEAMBOAT. And after today he'd be a senior. No way they would make him change schools for his senior year.

"Remind me after school to message them about the party. They don't need to know now." It occurred to him that if they really wanted him home early for some reason, they could take control of his Abitat and make it bring him home without going to the party. They probably wouldn't do that, but best not to chance it. "Better yet, you message them for me after you drop me off at *The Theme Park* after school."

"Message your parents. You'll be late. Yes. I will do that."

Jeremy checked quickly on the game world he built yesterday after school. The game world was supposed to give him advice about who he should ask to go to the party with him. There were a lot of interesting girls in his class but two who he knew better than the others. He decided to let the game world run until just before school today. He offered fractional point rewards for anyone responding with a recommendation and a chance at a larger reward if he followed their recommendation and it worked out for him. The cost so far was almost 100 points. It shouldn't cost him more than 500 points max. That would be okay. He had saved a lot more than that from his allowance, and it would be worth it if it helped him make the right choice and go on an actual date.

"Now, about your homework: I suggest you review these research materials about Memorial Day and the Jackson Memorial Festival," said the voice as each of the documents on the wall display highlighted one by one.

"I'm tired. I don't want to. How about this?"

Jeremy sat up and pulled up a draft essay he had previously written with information about Abitats and the AM Game.[*] In a few seconds he had moved several paragraphs from those and added a few words about Memorial Day and Jackson Memorial being about remembering things.

"How's that?"

The voice sighed before responding.

"Unacceptable. Those may technically count as your own words, but you've used some of that on other assignments, it is much too long and not on the prompt. This is supposed to be your thoughts about the meaning of the holiday in 800 to 1000 words. You are over 3000. Your teachers won't read that."

---

[*] See Appendix A, Jeremy's Writings

Jeremy cut three quarters of the paragraphs and added a few personal comments and general BS statements.

"How about now?"

Still not a good essay for the prompt. You should do the research. But at 986 words, 1000 with headings, you are within the word count requirements. I can vet it is arguably in your own words. It might pass, but barely."

"Good enough." Jeremy laid back down. "History isn't a core subject at STEAMBOAT anyway. There is no H in STEAMBOAT. And I need more sleep before the exams. Lights out."

"Very well." The lights and the wall display began to dim. The images of the pages of his essay shrank and faded.

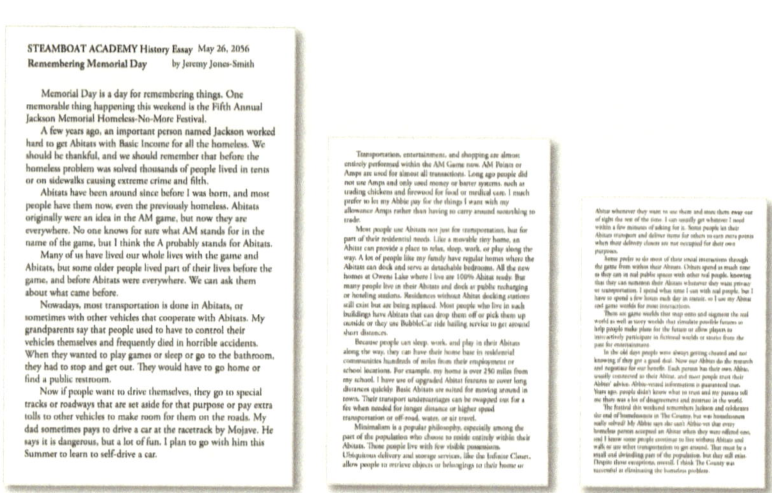

STEAMBOAT ACADEMY History Essay May 26, 2056
Remembering Memorial Day   by Jeremy Jones-Smith

Memorial Day is a day for remembering things. One memorable thing happening this weekend is the Fifth Annual Jackson Memorial Homeless-No-More Festival.

A few years ago, an important person named Jackson worked hard to get Abitats with Basic Income for all the homeless. We should be thankful, and we should remember that before the homeless problem was solved thousands of people lived in tents or on sidewalks causing extreme crime and filth.

Abitats have been around since before I was born, and most people have them now, even the previously homeless. Abitats originally were an idea in the AM game, but now they are everywhere. No one knows for sure what AM stands for in the name of the game, but I think the A probably stands for Abitats.

Many of us have lived our whole lives with the game and Abitats, but some older people lived part of their lives before the game, and before Abitats were everywhere. We can ask them about what came before.

Nowadays, most transportation is done in Abitats, or sometimes with other vehicles that cooperate with Abitats. My grandparents say that people used to have to control their vehicles themselves and frequently died in horrible accidents. When they wanted to play games or sleep or go to the bathroom, they had to stop and get out. They would have to go home or find a public restroom.

Now if people want to drive themselves, they go to special tracks or roadways that are set aside for that purpose or pay extra tolls to other vehicles to make room for them on the roads. My dad sometimes pays to drive a car at the racetrack by Mojave. He says it is dangerous, but a lot of fun. I plan to go with him this Summer to learn to self-drive a car.

Transportation, entertainment, and shopping are almost entirely performed within the AM Game now. AM Points or Amps are used for almost all transactions. Long ago people did not use Amps and only used money or barter systems, such as trading chickens and firewood for food or medical care. I much prefer to let my Abbie pay for the things I want with my allowance Amps rather than having to carry around something to trade.

Most people use Abitats not just for transportation, but for part of their residential needs. Like a movable tiny home, an Abitat can provide a place to relax, sleep, work, or play along the way. A lot of people like my family have regular homes where the Abitats can dock and serve as detachable bedrooms. All the new homes at Owens Lake where I live are 100% Abitat ready. But many people live in their Abitats and dock at public recharging or hoteling stations. Residences without Abitat docking stations still exist but are being replaced. Most people who live in such buildings have Abitats that can drop them off or pick them up outside or they use BubbleCar ride hailing service to get around short distances.

Because people can sleep, work, and play in their Abitats along the way, they can have their home base in residential communities hundreds of miles from their employment or school locations. For example, my home is over 250 miles from my school. I have use of upgraded Abitat features to cover long distances quickly. Basic Abitats are suited for moving around in town. Their transport undercarriages can be swapped out for a fee when needed for longer distance or higher speed transportation or off-road, water, or air travel.

Minimalism is a popular philosophy, especially among the part of the population who choose to reside entirely within their Abitats. Those people live with few visible possessions. Ubiquitous delivery and storage services, like the Infinite Closet, allow people to retrieve objects or belongings to their home or Abitat whenever they want to use them and store them away out of sight the rest of the time. I can usually get whatever I need within a few minutes of asking for it. Some people let their Abitats transport and deliver items for others to earn extra points when their delivery closets are not occupied for their own purposes.

Some prefer to do most of their social interactions through the game from within their Abitats. Others spend as much time as they can in real public spaces with other real people, knowing that they can summon their Abitats whenever they want privacy or transportation. I spend what time I can with real people, but I have to spend a few hours each day in transit, so I use my Abitat and game worlds for most interactions.

There are game worlds that map onto and augment the real world as well as story worlds that simulate possible futures to help people make plans for the future or allow players to interactively participate in fictional worlds or stories from the past for entertainment.

In the old days people were always getting cheated and not knowing if they got a good deal. Now our Abbies do the research and negotiate for our benefit. Each person has their own Abbie, usually connected to their Abitat, and most people trust their Abbies' advice. Abbie-vetted information is guaranteed true. Years ago, people didn't know what to trust and my parents tell me there was a lot of disagreement and mistrust in the world.

The festival this weekend remembers Jackson and celebrates the end of homelessness in The County, but was homelessness really solved? My Abbie says she isn't Abbie-vet that every homeless person accepted an Abitat when they were offered one, and I know some people continue to live without Abitats and walk or use other transportation to get around. That must be a small and dwindling part of the population, but they still exist. Despite those exceptions, overall, I think The County was successful at eliminating the homeless problem.

As it got darker in his Abitat, Jeremy yawned, rolled over, and started to breathe rhythmically.

The fading external views showed his vehicle passing a dirty, bright blue Abitat with low, in-town undercarriage, not suitable for long distances on the fast highway. It was partly on the shoulder of the road, moving slowly and just beyond and ahead of it the side of the road was lit up with a brush fire. Jeremy's Abbie signaled all the vehicles within a couple of miles about the fire, and they all started adjusting to make room for emergency vehicles.

Finally, with another long, barely audible sigh from the Abbie voice, the suggested research documents vanished one by one. Jeremy's rhythmic breathing continued.

4:45 AM, Sam and Jo-Jo's Road Trip

Jo-Jo awoke with a feeling that the Abitat had braked or swerved. Sam was making snorting sounds, like he did in his sleep whenever the Abitat shook. Jo-Jo's eyes were still closed. She considered whether to try to get more sleep and then opened them and saw an orange glow above her. It must be early dawn or maybe they were getting closer to lights of a town. Either way she should probably get up. She sat up and swung her feet out of bed searching with her toes for a free spot on the floor where she might stand, pushing bags aside with her feet until she felt the floor. She checked her wristband to see what time it was. Oh no. Way too early. She should go back to sleep.

Sam was snoring softly again in the reclined chair inches away. The orange light visible through the translucent panels of the ceiling of the Abitat was barely illuminating her home. It was especially cramped these last couple weeks, sharing the space with Sam, especially with the delivery closet fully expanded and encroaching on the living space. Things were piled everywhere. Bins, bags, boxes. Lots of bins. Hopefully the big delivery transfer would be completed today when they got into town, and she would get back some elbow room and a nice fee.

She was looking forward to seeing places and people from where she had spent most of her life even if her memories of that time were still hazy. After a few months off of NeverMind and most other drugs, she was going through memory recovery fog, and she hoped seeing familiar people and places would make her memories sharper. She had been told she needed to remember who she had harmed and seek amends as part of her recovery steps.

If she spoke out loud to ask where they were that would wake Sam. She looked for her tablet. She saw one tucked under Sam's arm, and she gently pulled it away without waking him. She checked for current Abitat status and location. It showed its Abitat was currently doing early morning deliveries in Lawrence, Kansas. Damn. This was Sam's tablet, which he kept linked to his own Abitat and his own Abbie. He was obsessed with his Abbie.

The glowing light from the ceiling seemed to be getting brighter. She spotted her own tablet leaning against the wall display on the other side of Sam on top of a pile of bins. He must have used her tablet to play a game on the Abitat wall display. She could probably reach it without waking Sam but decided to use the bathroom first. She looked at the path to the bathroom and realized even though it was just a few steps away she would need to move some bags and bins to get there. She was still holding Sam's tablet and decided not to try to put it back under his arm. While looking for a good place to set his tablet she noticed a partially visible window with text on its screen. It was probably the new story Sam was working on. She knew he didn't want her to read his stories before they were done so she wedged the tablet down next to his chair. In setting it down she must have nudged the text window because it expanded to cover the tablet screen, showing more text. It was upside down, but she bent over and tilted her head to read a little bit.

and I couldn't tell what was happening. The rush of the drugs made everything both hyper-realistic and completely distorted. My world was rocking and shaking. I could see Douglas leaning to one side and then the other and smiling with his eyes glazed. He seemed to be shifting his weight in time with the same changes of gravity that I was experiencing. We were both floating in space. We must be sharing our hallucinations.

Then there was water. Warm water seemed to be embracing me. It felt good. I was in a bathtub with my clothes on, but I was also sitting on a padded bench at a table and floating in space with Douglas. He was sitting across the table in the same water. The water sloshed over the table and Douglas started splashing it into my face. It tasted salty.

"We're not in space, Douglas. We're in a boat," I said.

"Really?"

"We're in a boat and it's filling up with water."

"That's so cool," he said.

"Yeah. It feels good."

"Maybe we should get out," he said.

"No," I replied and enjoyed the warmth of the water, then I said, "Yeah. Maybe we should."

"I'll get the supplies." He grabbed a floating orange plastic container of drugs and clicked to seal the lid.

"Good idea."

"I think this is the way out," he said as he floated towards the hatch and pushed it up and open while clutching the container.

Water was sloshing up to my chin, and I blew bubbles. Douglas was climbing out of the hatch. I ducked underwater and it felt warm and safe. Then I wanted to breathe so I stood up. There was still a few inches of air below the ceiling when the water sloshed away. I found the hatch, took a deep breath, and climbed out into deep space.

She could scroll and read more, but better not. She nudged the screen to push the text window back to where it had been. Then she started quietly moving bins and bags from her path stacking them higher or setting them on her bed to clear a path.

Most of the containers had materials she had gathered on the trip for future art projects: an assortment of rocks and pebbles, bags of rich-pink-colored powdery soil, various kinds of flowers and fiber-laced leaves for weaving, bones from some kind of desert creature, colorful pieces of cloth, pieces of metal, some sizable prickly limbs from a cactus. and five quart-sized cans of paint she had found behind a paint store. Jo-Jo wasn't sure how she was going to use any of these, but she could always figure something out. Some bins also held finished work: mobiles, earrings, and small sculptures mostly.

As she opened the lightweight folding door to the bathroom, she could feel an odd vibration, or a lack of the usual vibration. The Abitat must have stopped. They might be recharging or pulling aside again to make way for faster traffic.

In the bathroom, she spritzed some disinfectant spray on the seat and waited a few seconds for it to dry before closing the folding door and sitting down to pee. The room was getting uncomfortably warm. She would have to talk with her Abbie again about not letting Sam mess with the temperature settings. But first things first. Pee and do a quick sink bath while Sam was asleep.

She put up with sharing her bathroom with Sam during this trip. Abitats weren't perfect, but they were a lot better than homeless camps or shelters. She never wanted to go back to constantly searching for public restrooms or peeing or shitting in the bushes. She had doubts when they first offered free Abitats, but eventually she and Sam decided to try it, and she learned to appreciate hers. Having her own safe, private space, with bed, bathroom, and transportation was a blessing. Well, not so private on this trip. But still. After she washed her hands, splashed water in her face, and wiped in a few places, she opened the door. Sam was now sitting up on her spot on the couch bed holding her tablet and playing some kind of game displayed on the wall.

"You're awake," Jo-Jo observed.

Sam replied, "Yeah. Things kept shaking and swerving. And I heard someone rummaging through the bins. I hate rummaging. I didn't sleep at all."

"I heard you snoring, so I think you did sleep some."

"I doubt that. I didn't hear any snoring. But I'm awake for sure now. The light this morning is a weird color and it's getting hot in here. You need to turn down the heat. You told me and Abbie not to mess with it, but really? Are you getting the opposite of hot flashes or something? And by the way, Are we there yet? Are we there yet? Are we…"

"Shut the fuck up," Jo-Jo gave Sam a stern look. She was completely fed up with that little routine. Then she continued, "My fifty-something big brother is still an infant. You tell me where we are." She pointed at the tablet he was holding.

"Yeah. It's weird, but you probably are my little sister. I'm remembering more every day. Have you always been this bossy?"

Jo-Jo pointed again at the tablet.

"Oh yeah. Okay. Just a sec." He quickly paused what he was doing in his game and used Jo-Jo's tablet to bring up a map on the wall display, and then, one-by-one, external views of the area.

Jo-Jo sat in the chair, which was no longer reclined, and moved some bins to make more room for her feet. She also picked up Sam's prosthetic from between two bins on the floor and set it on the couch next to him.

The map showed them close to the Cajon Pass, soon leaving the desert communities and heading into the valleys and plains closer to the coast.

Sam said, "Looks like we're coming into town soon. Are we going first to the old river camp to look for Doug and Brock? That's about 50 miles. Maybe a couple hours or so."

"You think they will be there still?" Jo-Jo asked.

A rotating display of external views was partially blocked by stacked bins. The first view visible showed many other Abitats and larger cargo vehicles passing them on their left side in several paths of fast traffic going both ways on a wide undivided highway.

"They always went back to that one before. Wesley said Pat saw them near there a couple days ago."

"But he didn't actually talk to them. His Abbie tells him to stay away to avoid relapse triggers. He wasn't sure it was them," Jo-Jo added.

The view behind them showed emergency vehicles with flashing lights approaching. Sam picked up his prosthetic and pulled it onto the stump of his leg and said "Who else would it be? But I guess we'll find out. If they're not there, we know other places to look."

Additional external views appeared, showing a brush fire burning on the sloping hillside next to the road, sending embers and flames close to their Abitat. Sam raised his left hand, bringing his wristband close to his face, and said, "Abbie, I know Abitats are fireproof, but are we in danger?"

A voice from his wristband and from own tablet in his lap said, "I'm fine, Sam. I don't know about you. Why do you ask?"

Jo-Jo grabbed her own tablet away from Sam's other hand and tapped her wristband. "Abbie, get us away from this fucking fire!"

"Waiting for traffic to adjust sufficiently to allow us to merge smoothly. Estimating 3 minutes. Please stand by."

In the right-side external view windblown flames were now touching the Abitat, and the temperature inside was rising fast.

"Screw smoothly! Get us out of here! Now!" Jo-Jo insisted.

"Very well. Please hang on."

With an unnerving squeal of electric motors revving beyond their normal limits, the Abitat accelerated suddenly into a small gap between two windowless big rig cargo vehicles. Sam was thrown sideways against the pile of bags on the couch bed and Jo-Jo had to grip tightly to the arms of the chair, almost tumbling out of it. Several bags, bins, and boxes tumbled over, spilling their contents.

Jo-Jo wasn't willing to presume her Abbie would get her away safely if she waited. Her Abbie had repeatedly assured her that each Abbie was dedicated to the safety and well-being of its person and completely private. She didn't buy it. Abbies must all talk to each other. If they coordinate traffic and deliveries, what's stopping them from talking about other things? And if they lie about privacy can they be trusted to keep you from getting burnt up in a fire? She didn't want to take that chance.

The map view showed they were now moving on a broadly curving part of the highway with traffic backing up behind them. The external views showed the burning hillside. Fire was engulfing the shoulder area they had just left and blowing across part of the road. The container vehicle behind them emerged from the flames and approached them fast. They could hear its brakes screeching and could feel their Abitat still accelerating. The container vehicle in front of them was pulling away leaving a growing gap. They watched the rear camera view as the container vehicle behind them approached to within inches. They leaned forward as the feeling of acceleration suddenly stopped. The screeching and squealing stopped. No impact. Jo-Jo relaxed her grip on the arms of the chair and Sam propped himself up on his elbows.

As the Abitat continued up the road, the view of the fire was mostly blocked by the big rig behind them, but a glow was still visible, and flashing lights of emergency vehicles passed in different views. After a minute the Abitat settled back into the rightmost lane or shoulder and slowed down allowing other traffic to speed up again in the regular lanes. As the illumination from the fire faded, the interior of the Abitat returned to near darkness. Jo-Jo said, "Abbie, turn on the lights," and it got bright inside again. Jo-Jo started picking things up and putting them back in their containers. Sam sat upright, raised his wrist, and spoke to his own tablet. "You still there Abbie?"

"Yes of course. Did something happen? Was there a fire? Are you alright, Sam?" said the voice from his tablet.

Sam answered "Yeah. Fine. Don't worry."

"Okay. Let me know if you want to talk."

"Not right now." Sam put some of the things that had spilled on the couch bed back into bags. Jo-Jo noticed he was putting things in the wrong containers.

"Don't mix those."

"What?"

"Leave it. I'll put things away the way I want," Jo-Jo said.

"Okay," said Sam and he reached for Jo-Jo's tablet and started up a game again.

After a few minutes picking up, but with a lot still scattered about, Jo-Jo decided that was enough for now.

"We should try to go back to sleep. It's still early." She pointed Sam back to the chair and as he moved around her, she sat back down on the couch bed. She moved a few more things off the bed to make room to lie down. She picked up Sam's tablet and looked at it for a second and then handed it to him. She said, "Okay. Let's head to the river camp first. I know you want to talk to Doug. I peeked at your shipwreck story. I didn't read it. I didn't read it. I just saw a couple words. But I couldn't help seeing you've got a character named Doug in it."

Sam said, "Not Doug. Douglas. Not sure if he's the same guy as Doug. I do wonder if Doug remembers some of the same things. It might mean it really happened rather than just being something I'm making up."

"Doug's probably still on NeverMind, deep in Neverland, and wouldn't remember anything. But either way, memory recovery fog is a pain. Most events from before we started using NeverMind are still very fuzzy. I kind of remember something about you and a shipwreck. If you let me read your story, I can tell you if I remember any of it."

"No. Not yet," Sam replied. "It's not finished. And if you read it before you remember that time on your own, you're going to get a bunch of false memories and think it all really happened that way whether it did or not. I should never have said I was writing about a shipwreck. And now you looked at it?"

"Just a few words. Okay. Okay. What about today after Doug and Brock, if we don't just hang out at their campsite all day?" Jo-Jo asked.

"They'll have some ideas of what's good to do now," Sam said. "We can go wherever they want to go. I wonder if they'll let us give them a ride."

"No room in here until we do that delivery," said Jo-Jo.

"That's true," said Sam. "But that should happen as soon as we get to town. Plus, they were so against us getting Abitats, they probably still don't want to ride in one."

"Yeah. Probably. But you never know. People change. We could walk with them or meet them someplace. They don't have to ride with us. Or we can just hang out with them at one of their camps," Jo-Jo said. "Later we can try to find Wesley. I hope he changes his mind and will tell us where we can visit him. Pat doesn't have to come with him."

Sam said. "He wouldn't say where he works, but he hinted that we might run into him, so it's probably near one of the places we plan to go. It'll be a shame to come all this way and not connect up with him."

"Hey. At least we've got the beach and *The Theme Park*." Jo-Jo smiled.

"Yeah. Those should be fun." Sam paused and then continued, "How about the old house. Have you decided yet if you want to check on the parent? That should trigger a lot of old memories."

"Maybe. But she told us never to come back." Jo-Jo said quietly. "I remember that much."

"As I remember it, she didn't say never. It was more like, and I'm paraphrasing, 'Do not show your faces until you get your shit together.' Aren't we more shit-together now?" Sam gestured around the crowded space filled with tumbled containers and smiled.

"I don't know. It doesn't look like it, but maybe. A little." Jo-Jo laughed.

"We have a few days to decide." Sam said, "What about the Iz? Remember her? Do you want to track her down? She could be living there still. Any amends to make there?"

"Yeah. Definitely. But no. I don't think so. If she's still there I should stay away. Maybe you try. She knew you better than me. Why would she want to see me?"

"You never know unless you try."

"Lights off, Abbie."

5:00 AM, Bella Backpacking

A hungry black bear with tracking tags on both of its ears sniffed at and nudged a bear-proof food canister on the ground, starting to put its weight on it, then hearing a shuffling sound, it paused and looked across an open space in the direction of the sound. It saw a tent. The bear decided not to investigate whatever was moving in the tent. It put its weight on the canister one more time and when it didn't open, it left it and moved away.

Bella woke up after a gentle nudge on her shoulder but hesitated to open her eyes.

"You asked me to wake you at dawn," Bobbie's voice explained.

Bella listened to Bobbie shuffling in her own sleeping bag and said, "Thanks," and opened her eyes in the pitch darkness of the tent. She trusted Bobbie that dawn was coming and started to yawn and stretch to wake up.

Feeling around in the dark she found the pack next to her and reached into it. A soft light inside the pack lit up just enough for her to find a shirt and pants and stuff them down into her sleeping bag to warm them before putting them on. It was quite cold overnight at 7500 feet in the High Sierras this time of year even with the insulation of the tent. She could only imagine what it must have been like for her dad and uncle when they camped here in colder weather. Gear back then was primitive compared to today and they went very light. They must have been cold a lot.

Barely visible, as the glow from the pack's light dimmed out, a head-shaped shadow turned towards Bella and asked, "You didn't say why so early. Fishing again?"

"Yeah. One more try. This has to be the spot." Bella whispered as she started to pull on her pants while staying in her sleeping bag. She was pretty sure the fishing spot she found yesterday was one that her uncle and dad had told her about when she was little. It had a square rock sticking up in the middle of the stream like they described. She had no luck fishing there yesterday, but she didn't find it until later in the day. Early morning should be one of the best times to catch something. It wasn't too far away. Half an hour or so of climbing and scrambling up off trail from the campsite. She wanted to get there before it got fully light.

"I thought maybe you wanted to get an early start on the hike out, or to finish that report for work."

"No. That report was a pain. I was messaging back and forth about it with the new guy last night, and he kept wanting to add things that weren't necessary, but we got it done. I told him to double-check the format by start of work today at nine. That should be easy enough for him. I should be back from fishing before then and we can start hiking out after that. Only a few days behind schedule." She sat up and put on her shirt and jacket.

"The new guy. This is the ancient new guy you've been complaining about?" Bobbie asked from her sleeping bag, rough outlines of her face now barely visible in the dawning light.

"That's the one. I don't know why Elsie hired him. His law and intellectual property skills are all store-bought AI—no law school. And he must be old enough to be her dad or at least mine. Maybe he knows some dirt on her, or maybe it's an age diversity thing. There's so much he doesn't know, but I guess he's not completely incompetent."

"You sound more forgiving about him than what you were saying yesterday afternoon. 'Feeble, nitwit impostor'?"

"Yeah. I may have been a little harsh then. Just a little. I still don't like these instant-purchased-skills people. Instant surgeon, just add water. No thank you. There's no substitute for years of schooling and experience on the job. But this guy seems to have some brains of his own besides what he gets through the brain cap. Thinking about it afterwards, I have to admit he asked some good questions about the mechanical details of the furniture designs. Fake lawyer but maybe a real engineer. I should give him some more time. Maybe he will work out in a few years."

"Quite a change of attitude."

"Still too early to tell. One step at a time. He should at least be able to format an IP assessment. That's in the AI package for sure." Bella sat on top of her sleeping bag, a silhouette against the slightest glow of dawn through the tent fabric and pulled on her boots then crawled to the door of the tent, opened it, and stepped outside to pick up her fishing gear which was visible leaning against the nearest tree. "Wish me luck," said Bella.

"Good luck fishing," answered Bobbie from inside the tent.

Bella closed the tent door. Bobbie stayed in her sleeping bag but made mental notes about alternate menus she could prepare for breakfast with their remaining supplies, depending on whether Bella actually caught some fish.

6:05 AM, Billionaire in the Surf

A man was sitting up on his board waiting for a wave, both his hands in the water pushing gently back and forth, making the board slowly turn for a look back towards the shore.

A ten-foot mako shark with a tracking tag on its dorsal fin swam out of a kelp forest and into water near the surf line to investigate the splashing on the surface in the distance. As it rapidly approached the disturbance it considered the possibilities. Seal? No. Bird? No. Otter? Maybe. It didn't smell like food but was worth a closer look.

The sun was beginning to shimmer on the water as it rose over the hills or small mountains to the east and with that glare the surfer didn't notice a shadow passing under him and turning away from the shore.

Almost time to go in. Some wispy high clouds were illuminated in the sunlight. The air was clear, nearly still, and felt cold at this hour. The water was relatively calm. Nothing much to ride today. That was fine. He used his solitary time on the water to clear his mind, whether sculling about on the calm surface or trying to ride big angry swells. Calmer was better, given his meager skills, but either way it was all meditation. It was all part of his therapy.

Slowly turning full circle and looking out to sea he sensed patterns in the tiny swells that told him there could be some rideable sets of waves if he waited long enough. He couldn't explain what details in the patterns gave him that sense of anticipation, but he felt confident that it was true. He had learned some things in the months he had been making these solitary early morning outings.

The visibility was good and with the growing light of morning he could see clouds forming over the sea on the horizon beyond Catalina. A storm bringing rain was rare here in recent years, but it looked to him like one might actually be brewing today. Yes. With the rising tide and impacts from a brewing storm, swells would be getting bigger in just a few minutes, but probably not before he needed to head back to shore.

Looking again towards the shore he kept his gaze low and focused on the water, the beach, and cliffs which provided a natural seawall. No sign of people in the water or on the sand between him and the base of the cliffs. Good.

Moving his focus above the cliffs, the resort tower loomed into the sky, sixteen tall stories high with elevators to lift guests' personal Abitats to dock at their suites if they wished. It looked as much a part of the air and sea as of the land. He smiled. The sun was rising to the right of the tower, and the shadow of the tower extended out into the water to his left. With deep foundations and sublevels, he knew the tower was secure, but not necessarily the additional resort buildings on either side of it. There were casinos, showrooms, convention halls, bars, restaurants, shops, pools, and spas. Many of them might need to be relocated if the cliffs continue to recede. They had receded at least a foot since the tower was built. He would have to approve the project to reinforce the cliffs soon. He just needed to decide whether to spend extra to keep a natural look. He decided. It would be worth it.

To the right, south of the buildings, were the canopies of the "camping village." He knew from the report he reviewed when he first awoke, the camping village wasn't fully booked and that meant the casinos were also not as busy as they could be.

Something must be wrong for it to have vacancies just before a big holiday weekend. Maybe the camping village needed to be replaced with a different kind of accommodations. Or maybe he should try a Late

Spring Coupon deal. Simulation models said allowing guest access to the beach in the early morning hours would draw more surfers to the camping village, but so far, he insisted on his private dawn time in the water.

Scanning his gaze farther to the south, he could see two body surfers were now entering the water a few hundred yards down the beach and some walkers were on the sand at the edge of the water in the distance heading away towards the south, walking a dog. No one appeared to be a threat, but they made him nervous. Either it was later than he thought, or someone had opened the beach access gates early today.

Looking north up the coast, he could see two other surfers near a rock outcropping at a curve in the coastline. The coast beyond that point was out of view, but he knew that further north and south where the shoreline cliffs disappeared, the coastline was engineered with seawalls, some designed with beaches for surfing and sunbathing, others with protected boat marinas.

The rock outcropping immediately to the north was the closest other surfers normally got during these hours. He didn't understand surfing at that rocky point. The rocks and thick kelp beds around them made it unnecessarily dangerous. The surfers there this morning seemed, like him, content to sit and watch the morning scene. Were they looking at him? Did one of them have binoculars? Probably not.

He wore a simple lightweight black wetsuit cut to expose his forearms and calves. No body armor. While he acknowledged there should be few risks during these early morning outings and the point was to relax, he still paid attention.

He pretended to be an anonymous surfer during these outings but being alone here on this access-restricted stretch of water probably did make him stand out if anyone was watching. Anyone in the tower or on the bluffs could see him in the water if they looked. He might blend in more if he let others surf here at this hour. But he really didn't like being in crowds. He did not bring along a bodyguard, and he did not notify the resort security team. They must know, but he did not wear a wristband or other communication device to summon help. Being exposed was part of the therapeutic experience. He could do this. He was doing this.

He tried mindfulness. Focus on his own state of being. How did his body feel in this place and moment? He raised a hand and felt the top of his head and his face. His hair felt very short but not receding. He knew it was still dark brown. He felt lines in his face from recurring anxiety. His hairy arms and legs were brown and had some inconspicuous muscles from his surfing habits. His belly was substantial, but he thought he carried it well. His looks and his accomplishments both were suitable for someone with much more than his 35 years.

He certainly didn't fit the age-old surfer stereotype of sun-bleached, long-haired blond, thin and muscular. He knew there wasn't really a typical image for a surfer, since so many people enjoyed the sport. He wasn't sure about what-all he had mixed in his ancestry, but certainly no surfer blondes. He definitely had some Indian in his bloodlines, or some kind of south Asian, probably also some Native American, along with African, Spanish, East Asian, and who knows what else. With his ample physique and racial mixture, he liked to think he could pass for a descendant of the original pacific island surfers.

That resemblance was actually useful. The resort business he led was founded based on a controversial claim of indigenous rights to the land with himself being the prime surviving representative of a secretive ancient seafaring people who settled this particular land. Fortunately for him, in recent years the legally accepted version of history favored this claim.

He noticed the birthmark on his exposed left calf. In the cold it was just a faint pink blotch and no longer a pink hippo on a surfboard like when it inspired several of his dad's silly childhood bedtime stories. He wondered if he should try to contact his dad and see if he remembered those stories. It had been months now since he had talked to him. He could probably figure out where he was if he tried. Not like his mom. No trace of her for many years now. His dad had been silly and creative, but his paranoia had infected the whole family. Maybe that was related to his mom leaving. Talking to his dad about the stories might help his dad remember more and might help himself as he worked to control his own fears.

The rising sun and the appearance of others on the beach were clues about the time. He should head in. He thought he had a good intuition about time even without the cues, and typically he would head back to shore in time for his first scheduled appointments. Although if he was late, the scheduled meetings adapted to him, so maybe he was fooling himself.

He decided one last try and then head in whether or not he caught a wave. He paddled out towards a slightly larger swell and spun around just in time. He made several strong strokes and almost caught the wave, then kept paddling towards shore. A second wave in the set caught up with him, and pulling again with both arms, he propelled his short board to the sloping front of the small swell. He raised himself up on one knee, then planted one foot on the board, almost standing, and rode it briefly through the choppy break and finished, stepping off into the shallow foam before picking up his board and trotting out of the water and across the sand. Not an impressive ride, but it counted. He stood, almost. He caught a wave. Two days in a row.

At the base of the cliff, he rounded a rocky outcropping and entered a small cave which revealed a well-lighted concrete-reinforced entry with a thick glass waterproof automatic door. Inside he set down his board to be put away by a member of the resort staff who was dressed in a green and brown uniform and stood back at a respectful distance. He proceeded through an "authorized personnel only" door and down a hallway to his private elevator.

6:20 AM, Bella Fishing

Bella stood on the square rock as the shallow stream flowed around it. Her fishing line and lure dangled in the water to one side where she thought the stream was deeper. Behind her was a series of smaller rocks protruding from the water providing a path she had crossed from the bank. The top of each rock was a couple inches above the moving water and relatively dry. Stepping from stone to stone had been easy for her. The water level must have been higher when her dad and uncle had *walked on water* across their secret path to the square fishing rock. Still, this had to be the spot they had described. She didn't really see their *deep hole full of fish* anywhere near the square rock, but the water level was lower. And maybe the streambed had changed in the intervening years. She hadn't caught anything, or even felt any nibbles yet, but she would keep trying.

6:25 AM, In the Penthouse

Stepping out of his elevator at the top of the resort, he went to his shower room to wash off the sand and salt. As he peeled off his wetsuit he enjoyed the warming spray from every direction which came on automatically. He reflected on how nice it was to be here.

Although he owned properties around the world, he had visited in person only ones on the west coast of North America. He like this one best. He seldom left this resort on the bluffs over the beach at the edge of the Pacific Ocean. The 12,000 square foot penthouse occupied the

15th and 16th floors above one of his most successful businesses; the sunset views were spectacular, and he could easily get down to the sand and surf whenever he wanted to disengage from his business empire and just enjoy the meditation of waiting for or riding a wave. He only took advantage of the opportunity during early morning outings when the beach was empty, but he liked the idea that it was always there.

After his shower he toweled off and put on a robe and sat down at a table by the windows to eat his breakfast. He picked at some fresh fruit, sipped his mug of cappuccino, and then went for a bowl of sugary cereal with milk. As he ate, an image appeared on the window in front of him. *Therapy Session.* He said, 'Go ahead. Let's get started," and a face of a balding older man appeared in the glass.

"Good morning, sir," spoke the face.

"Good morning, doctor."

"I'm not a doctor. I can arrange for one if you wish."

"No thanks. You are close enough."

"Very well. Did you go to the beach today?" asked the face.

"I did."

"And how did you feel while you were out there?"

"Cold and wet."

"Okay. Any anxiety today?" asked the face.

"No panic. But I kept checking to see where other people were."

"Did the people you saw make you nervous?" asked the face.

"Maybe a little. No one was close."

"Any specific thoughts connected to your nervousness?"

"I thought about what to do if someone tried to attack me. How long could I hold my breath underwater and how quickly could I get back to the shore."

"Do you really think anyone would try to attack you?"

"There are people who want to."

"Do you think anyone this morning wanted to attack you?"

"Probably not. But I couldn't help having those thoughts."

"What did you do when you had those thoughts?"

"I focused on the water and the scenery."

"How did focusing on the water and scenery make you feel?

"They were peaceful. A storm brewing on the horizon seemed like a positive thing."

"Do you consider it progress to be able to appreciate nature?"

"I guess so. Yes."

"It's good when you can sense progress. I think you should continue to do this surf therapy and focus on the progress you've made spending time in nature, but you may also want to explore putting yourself into more situations with closer contacts with people. Maybe go out when there are other people on the beach, walk through the casino, or take a ride into town," proposed the face.

"I'll think about it."

"Is there anything else you would like to talk about today?"

"No. Is there anything else *you* would like to talk about today?"

"This is your time," said the face.

They wrapped up the conversation and the face disappeared from the window glass. He walked towards a sound coming from his balcony. The door slid open, and he heard a wind chime ringing. He looked up at it and at the clouds in the distance and took a couple more sips from his cappuccino before going back in to his closet to get dressed.

6:45 AM, Bella Still fishing

Bella stood on a tree branch twenty feet above the stream looking down. The wind rustled the branches above her, rocking the tree slightly. She still enjoyed climbing trees and feeling the wind like when she was a kid. She didn't spot any fish swimming in the water below but did eye a spot upstream that looked promising. She started to climb down to move her fishing gear to the new spot.

7:00 AM, In the Conference Room

He sat at the head of a large table with holograms of his executive staff already at seats all around. The sides of the room appeared to be all glass with unobstructed views of the coastline and the surrounding area. Two of the walls had actual glass windows. The other two and the ceiling were 3D video displays, but it gave a seamless panoramic view. The abstract Honus Resorts corporate logo which some compared to a surfing Hippo was projected in a hologram floating behind his seat.

This kind of virtual meeting could be simulated in a much smaller space, such as in any Abitat or anywhere with a tablet or a 3D-headset, but he liked the extravagance of this room. And someday he might actually invite his team to meet him here in person.

His first topic was always security. They reviewed the protests that were planned outside the resort later today: Two environmental groups and one Native American, and the measures to prevent guests from being disturbed.

"Full catering for all the protests?" he asked.

"As usual, sir. I think some of them come just for the food," said the local executive responsible for catering and guest services.

Honus repeated his standard saying on the subject, while his executives silently mouthed the words, "I disagree with their opinions but admire their passion."

Reflecting on the protests he recalled how his claim to this land was settled in the Great Reset when game law was adopted and storylines, facts, and identities from several popular game worlds, were merged into World One. An unlikely game world based in part on stories his dad told him as a child was included, and as a result he was able to legally become

Honus and gain control of hundreds of acres of formerly public beachfront land. Since then, he thought of himself as Honus most of the time and rarely thought of the other names he had used when playing in other game worlds or before. The Honus Resorts name was now synonymous with luxury resorts around the world. It was never clear how such a far-fetched game storyline got included, but he gladly took advantage of it.

He shared income from the resort with local indigenous groups and intended to eventually give this resort to them. But he really liked this place and was not ready to part with it yet. He wanted to believe that the ridiculous stories his dad had told him that seemed to underlie his claims had some basis in truth and he had some magical indigenous heritage himself.

The executives reviewed daily summaries of various resort properties against quarterly plans. Most of them were doing quite well. He got status on progress being made on development projects.

"What about the Honus Lake Resort?" he asked.

The holographic image of Sarah Jones-Smith, the project director, replied, "Water rights have been secured. Lake levels are rising. Resort construction is on track. Presales for the next two phases are strong. Making progress on renaming Owens Lake."

"It is Honus Lake. Do what it takes," Honus insisted.

"Yes, Sir," Sarah answered, continuing with another of Honus' common phrases, which was also mouthed by the other executive holograms, "Better to ask forgiveness than to wait for permission."

He grilled his local executives about the unacceptable vacancy rates in the local camping village, and after some leading questions he endorsed a suggestion for offering a coupon deal and developing proposals for replacing the camping village with other offerings.

"How are we doing on servicing our debts?"

"All on track sir."

Juggling finances played a big role in the success of Honus Resorts from the very beginning. Despite his demonstrated success as a real estate developer in dozens of game worlds, and some small successes with his own money in the real world before the Reset, he had trouble getting the financing to build this resort. Investors wanted control of the project and Honus wasn't willing to give that up. But then an anonymous investor made an offer: A generous credit line and development control in return for too large a percentage of gross resort revenues, too high a rate of interest, and too short a time limit to pay off the loan. They seemed to be betting on his failure and taking the land in foreclosure. He decided being able to build the resort the way he wanted was worth the risk.

Using skills learned from his game playing, he made the resort profitable in just a couple of years. Then he was able to get financing for other projects which also became quickly profitable. He managed to pay off the initial loan and get clear ownership of this property in seven years but had sizable debts on other projects.

Finally, the topic was raised of a project that was behind schedule. It was inland just a few miles from here. One of his hologram executives addressed the continuing resistance to sales of properties needed to complete a big development just outside *The Theme Park* district. The executive assured him that *Theme* was not behind the delays. They currently had no interest in expanding the borders of *The Theme Park* district in that direction. The anonymous owners of one key property were refusing to sell, even for well above market offers. Efforts to claim the property as abandoned were thwarted by a number of residents who continued living in the rundown buildings.

They asked him to choose a line of action: Allow more persuasive efforts to evict the residents; or significantly redesign the project to work around the holdout property. He decided he wanted to see the location for himself. His leadership team tried to show him extensive holographic images of the area and biographical data on its residents, but he waved that aside. Going into town could be therapeutic, he thought. His therapist had suggested a ride into town. This was the opportunity.

7:15 AM, Sam & Jo-Jo Approaching Town

Jo-Jo came out of the bathroom. She was wearing her new jogging suit. She said to Sam, "Your turn. Take a shower and get dressed." She pointed to his matching jogging suit on top of a pile of bins. "We should be at Doug and Brock's camp in about a half hour." Sam reluctantly set down the tablet and picked up the clothes.

7:20 AM, Honus Leaves the Resort

He didn't think much about the fact his assistants had to scramble to reschedule all his morning appointments as he headed down the private elevator to his private garage deep below the resort. He might go to the beach alone in the early morning, but he was not going to go alone into town. He tagged Mike, one of his bodyguards. Mike silently followed him. He could have his pick of a number of different Abitats or other autonomous or chauffeured vehicles. He pointed to two of his custom gas-powered motorcycles. He put on some protective riding gear before getting on and heading up the long tunnel to a concealed private entrance in a residential area a quarter mile beyond the edge of the resort, out of sight of any of the protestors that might be at the entrance to the resort.

Once out of the residential neighborhood he unmuted the bikes and the deep-throated roar of the two motorcycles shredded the morning quiet as the silent stream of other vehicles maneuvered to keep out of their way on the highway. One modified Abitat heading towards the beach resort was painted with slogans from the nature lovers who protested regularly.

He didn't understand the environmental protesters' objections to the loss of public natural land. People could still use the beach, most of the time, and many native plants and animals were featured in resort exhibits.

Leaving the beach traffic behind he continued his ride inland towards the neighborhood near *The Theme Park* where his current big project was stalled. Game simulations and business projections by his staff showed that this new project with all the latest amenities located just outside the boundaries of the district controlled by *Theme* would be a big money-maker.

He no longer played in the simulated game worlds much himself, but he had staff that worked full time exploring the histories and current events of many AM game worlds and brought back development opportunities and ideas. Ideas that had caught the imaginations of players in the virtual worlds had a good chance of catching on in this world. His staff also researched in game worlds the practicalities of developing the projects. Most obstacles were anticipated in the simulations and could be handled quickly by offering the right price to the right people.

The game simulations suggested that the existing owners should have accepted his offers and sold by now, so something was unpredictable about the holdouts. He wanted to see the area for himself for a clue about what motivated them. He hated delays but also had some regrets about the heavy-handed actions some of his executives had previously employed to remove obstacles. He wanted to see if he could find a solution before resorting to those tactics.

7:25 AM, Jose and Emily: Trailer People

A sturdy-looking woman wearing coveralls moved quickly between some rundown tiny houses and a trailer surrounded by three- and four-story buildings that also looked like they suffered from deferred maintenance. With a bandana over her hair, plus dark sunglasses not suited to the shadows of the hour, she took pictures and jotted down notes on her tablet as she went. She paused when she saw a large feral house cat exploring under the trailer. The cat ignored the sounds of movement and running water coming from the trailer above, but the woman took notes before hiding her tablet in her coveralls and moving swiftly away and out a driveway between the taller buildings.

Inside the trailer, bubbles were forming on the bottom of a small metal pot of water sitting over bluish flames. A narrow door opened a step away from the small stove and a man who looked like he was in his forties came out dressed in coveralls with the name "Jose" embroidered on the shirt. His hair was dark, full, and curly. He was clean shaven. A flushing sound behind him came from the tiny toilet. The whole bathroom was just big enough for one person to stand or sit in at a time with the toilet doubling as a seat in the shower. "Bathroom is yours, Emily. Get moving or you'll be late for school."

He grabbed a bag of coffee beans from the miniature refrigerator next to the stove and a grinder from the shelf above while turning off the burner. With practiced motions he plugged the grinder into a power strip attached to the wall, ground a scoop of coffee, dumped it into the filter over his mug and poured water from the small pot over the coffee while returning the grinder and coffee beans to their places. While the water filtered through, he reached back into the refrigerator returning the coffee beans and grabbed a glass tub of plain, locally sourced yogurt and unscrewed the top. Blindly and deftly fishing a spoon out of a drawer next to the stove, he dumped the coffee grounds into a small composting wastebasket without looking, and took a sip then spun around and sat at a chair at the fold-down table on the side of the trailer—coffee mug, yogurt tub, and spoon all in precisely the same place as yesterday morning and the day before. He thought about that for a fraction of a second and nudged the mug and spoon into a slightly different position.

He touched the small old-fashioned flat screen on the wall, and a weather reporter was talking about the chance of showers in the area later this morning. "Drought in the southland continues but we could have some scattered light showers in a few neighborhoods in the late morning or afternoon so you might want to have an umbrella or a raincoat with you today. I know. I know. I've said that a few times in the last year, and the rain didn't show, but maybe this time it will really happen." The weather reporter was short, dark-haired, and wore glasses. His voice was extremely deep and did not seem to match his small size and youthful appearance.

Sitting on a bed a couple steps away was Jose's daughter. Thirteen, but looking younger in her panda bear pajamas, her brown curly hair framed her light brown face, she held a computer tablet in her lap and was apparently deeply absorbed in whatever game she was playing. "About time, Dad. You were in there forever," she said without looking up. "Did you forget to take your fiber again? Hey! And aren't you going to be late for work?"

"They won't fire me if I'm a little late. Thanks for reminding me that I'm not as young as I used to be. Yes. I probably should eat more fiber. You sound more like your mom all the time."

"She still worries about you. You know. She doesn't really wish you dead. No matter what she says."

"That's good to know. That's good to know."

She did some kind of flourish on the computer tablet and a celebratory tune chimed forth. "Beat the level 42 puzzles again! Fastest time ever! Even with you distracting me!"

"I'm proud of you."

"I think I'm done with this level. But I need a lot more points to open the next level. Can you help me out with some points, Dad?"

"Does it look like I've got extra points lying around?" He gestured around the tight quarters of the trailer. "Ask your mom."

"Right. Like that's going to happen. She doesn't like me playing the scammer puzzles in the first place. Why do you think I do it so much when I'm here? She thinks I should study all the time."

"Studying is good. And you know, I've heard there are lots of better ways to earn points, in the game and out. More than just solving puzzles. You could save your allowance, or if you didn't spend your points redoing the same puzzles to set records, maybe you'd have saved more."

"It's not the same puzzle each time. It's just the same level."

"I'm just saying, look for challenges that pay more or be more careful what you spend. Try something different for a change."

She looked back at him with a frustrated young teen look. Parents just don't understand some things.

He continued, "But now, eat, get dressed, and get moving. Don't you have an exam today? Cyber-something programming? Are you ready?"

"No worries, Dad. I'm ready for all my exams today and I ate already. You were in there a long time. I just need to shower and change."

"You spent a lot of time on the tablet studying last night."

"Yeah. Some of that was studying. I wondered if they might make the cyber exam harder this time, so I spent some time getting ready last night."

"Extra studying is good."

"Sort of studying. I solved the pre-exam challenge and decrypted the codes on the cyber exam."

"What do I say about hacking?"

"They encourage it in that class. That's what it's all about." She continued, speaking very quickly, "All the questions on the exam are actually really easy, so I didn't change them, but I tweaked them to all to be asked by deepfake characters patterned from really old antique television show game worlds you watch sometimes, like Big Bang Theory, Lucy, and the Apprentice, and re-encrypted with a new Cerberus-Mack timed stealth algorithm with a double-Loki variation. No one should be able to change them or notice the changes until the exam starts when it will unlock again. Even if someone can break that and change the questions, I can pass whatever they throw at me."

"My baby girl. Take a breath. I don't know when you are joking sometimes. Hey, I don't know what the heck you are talking about half the time."

"Yeah, Dad. You are so old-fashioned and slow," she drew out the word slow and had a sarcastic, knowing look. She set the computer pad on the table in front of him; she pulled a bundle of clean clothes, a towel, and a small bag of toiletries from the tiny closet and stepped into the bathroom. "Oh, Dad!" she complained. "Open the window next time." She opened the louvered window not much bigger than her hand and closed the door.

He sipped coffee and spooned yogurt. The display on the tablet showed where Emily had left it: 'Abitat Mysteries: World G19; Emily - Elegant Maestro Puzzler Panda; Balance: 2006 points; Cyber Puzzle Challenge Level 42; Completed Record time: 6 minutes, 21 seconds.' Another message window said, "Open Level 43? 4300 points. 1994 needed. Transfer?"

He typically didn't sign-in to the game when Emily was staying here, but he could make a quick exception. He made a few motions on the pad, removed a small metal cover from his wristband, setting it on the table. Then he waved the wristband over the tablet and applied his thumb on a grey oval that appeared in the lower left corner of the tablet surface. He tapped out a 52-digit key and moving away from the bathroom door to keep her from hearing him he whispered to the tablet, "Peter Piper Picked a Peck of Pickled Peppers." The words *'Authorization verified: 'Abitat Mysteries: World G19; Unnamed - Sixth order Harlequin Barrister; Level 263, Balance at last checkpoint: 48,721,500,319 Points;'* After a few more motions a message box saying, *'Transfer 2500 points'* showed on the screen. With a few more motions of his hands and taps, that message box disappeared and the display below it changed to show *'Balance: 48,721,497,819 Points. Additional transfers pending from associated worlds. Update?'* With a few more hand motions the balance counter jumped by a few hundred thousand and began incrementing quickly, then with more hand motions a picture of three mutt dogs appeared and the *'Cerberus-Mack Stealth Mode'* message appeared briefly before Emily's view reappeared. He wrapped the new challenge in a capsule he labelled, *Special Challenge Puzzle,* and set it to appear in eight hours in the background of Emily's world view, mixed in among various wandering icons of pandas and other animals and message trails from her friends. He made a point of never reading her personal messages, although he was curious. Trust was important.

With sounds of water running in the sink and brushing of teeth, coming from the tiny bathroom Jose whispered, "It shouldn't take you long to find this challenge, and if you know your cyber like you say, you shouldn't have a problem breaking it."

The sound of the running water stopped, and Emily said with a mouth full of toothpaste, "Did you say something, Dad?"

"No. Just talking to myself."

"Stop doing that. Or I'll tell Mom."

Pressing a button to change the input on the TV display, he looked quickly at a series of security camera images. The views showed a large courtyard surrounded by three- and four-story live-and-work buildings. The ground floors had space for businesses, such as offices, stores, and galleries, with living units above. Jose tried to patronize the businesses in the complex. Some of the units had garages on the ground floor facing the courtyard. Windows were broken or blocked with cardboard on about half the units. He suspected some people he hadn't met were living in some of the run-down units without paying rent. He didn't need to make them all pay. It was a way of helping people through tough times.

Two cats were exploring around shriveled trees in one of the views but no one else was in view. The courtyard had a few run-down tiny houses in addition to his trailer. The tiny houses and his trailer were similar to Abitats in terms of size and simplicity, but, without autonomous mobility, they were far from what people demanded today. As far as Jose knew, if you didn't count cats, none of the tiny homes currently had regular residents.

The courtyard had once been a parking area and greenspace for the live-work community. At some point twelve tiny prefab homes were wheeled in for prospective residents who wanted to try the minimalist life. The tiny-house community went downhill once people started using Abitats, and especially after the County started giving out Abitats with Basic Income (ABIs). Now the only people still living in older kinds of housing without Abitats made too much to get free Abitats but not enough to buy one, were too stubborn to change, or were paranoid and didn't believe Abitats were as private and secure as people say. Jose fell into the last two categories, stubborn and paranoid. Or, as he thought of himself, well-informed. He could afford more but chose to live simply and somewhat outside the Abitat mesh network. Developers were always trying to pressure stragglers to move out to allow more redevelopment. Jose resisted the pressures, but he knew eventually he would have to move.

The security camera view of his trailer home showed it to be old but well-preserved. About 18 feet long and 7 feet wide with curved lines at the front and rear for a sense of aerodynamics even though it hadn't moved in years. Its metal surface had fresh paint over multiple repairs. Small windows with curtains were on both sides. A hose supplied water from a spigot by a picnic table nearby. An extension cord ran across the yard from a small outbuilding which housed a clothes washer and dryer that Jose could use. Multiple extensions of gas connectors flexed and snaked from an old gas barbecue hookup nearby, around the trunk of an emaciated apple tree to the trailer's propane connection. The *new natural gas* from the line was supposed to be climate-friendly and still worked in his old stove. But at some point, the gas might be shut off, and he would have to go all electric if stricter climate controls didn't get delayed again. He might have to risk going standard and getting an Abitat. He focused his mind back on the present. How much time had he just wasted? Security looked okay right now. No one out there but the cats.

He switched the video input back to the news. After a few seconds seeing nothing interesting, he stood up and smiled. Talking at the bathroom door, "I've got to go. Be amazing but be careful out there."

"Yeah, Dad. You too."

He tapped on the bathroom door twice and heard three more taps from inside followed by the sound of the shower starting. He picked up the small metal plate from the table and snapped it onto his wristband. Jose didn't like letting his wristband communicate with any networks he didn't have to. He kept his communication channel off as much as he could. And for extra safety he had fashioned the metal cover for the wristband, which should block most electromagnetic communication. He would admit to being a bit paranoid, but he had his reasons.

He opened the exterior door and stepped down from the travel trailer to a greenish patch of yard. Grey water from the trailer shower was draining into a struggling vegetable garden. A 10-gallon portable waste carrier sat on the ground, connected to the trailer's toilet waste outlet. He glanced at the fullness indicator showing about 90%. "Eww. Got to dump that soon. Maybe tonight. No time now." He looked beyond the broken fence at a usable sewer hookup by an empty tiny home space and mentally calculated the effort to move the trailer or to extend the waste line. "I've been meaning to connect that. But not today." He started to walk quickly between the tiny homes and toward the alleyway at the far corner of the courtyard, flipped up the metal cover and looked at the time on his wristband, pushed it back shut, and broke into a medium run.

A large, curvy, fifty-something-ish woman in a well-fitting white lab coat over green medical scrubs, stepped out the door of a tall dirty green tiny house into his path near the alley as three cats squeezed by her and into the yard.

"I hope the cats are all healthy again, Magnolia. No more of that cough?" he said, slowing as he trotted by.

"Yeah. These are all healthy now. Joey boy." She spoke with a trace of Australian accent. "How's Little Em? She's staying with you again?" She tried to close the door as four more cats squeezed out to run in the patchy grass of the courtyard. Then speaking to herself more than to Jose. "Too many damn cats. I keep catching and fixing them, but there's always more. I don't know where they all keep coming from. Probably sneaking out of Abitats when their owners are at work. Not enough people reclaim their lost pets or want to adopt stray cats." She shook her head, brushed some cat hair off her scrub pants.

Jose had long ago given up on correcting her about his name. He replied, glancing back as he reached the gate out of the complex, "Emily's doing great. She'll be back with her mom for the weekend." And he waved and continued into the alleyway.

She watched him go out of sight. "Always on the run. You'll have to slow down one of these days." She smiled to herself and went back in. The unit was filled with scratching posts and climbing towers for the cats. That, and an arrangement of kitty beds, litter boxes, food, and water bowls. Two small carrier boxes were on a counter along with some veterinary equipment. One carrier was labeled Magnolia Overly, vDVM,* Her pet care clinic was on the first floor of one of the live-work units nearby, and she lived upstairs. She had converted several of the abandoned tiny homes in this courtyard as space for her growing family of rescued cats.

Leaving the alleyway Jose turned left down the sidewalk of the city roadway which was bustling with vehicles of various kinds going in both directions in a seemingly random fashion. Margin of space for passing was often centimeters or less. It looked like some kind of swarm of bees or a stirred-up ant colony, but this hive was organized and efficiently cooperating to let each vehicle get where it was going as smoothly as possible. Each vehicle kept a steady pace and direction but somehow with slight adjustments they all flowed past one another without colliding.

He recalled explaining the algorithms for this kind of coordination to Emily. More than once. He liked Dad-splaining things to her. When she was four, she understood some of it. By eight she had the concepts

---

* vDVM: virtual Doctor of Veterinary Medicine, purchased professional license with practical skills provided when needed by a brain interface cap. Similar to vJD acquired by some new attorneys.

down pat. But now if he brought it up, she would rattle off its flaws and how she would have coded it to work better.

A small public open circle bus was cruising along with three passengers. It was round and resembled a small carousel from a park with six benches radiating from a central post under a scalloped canopy. Most people were creeped out by these things, but every time he saw one, he had to smile. Some, but not this one, replaced one or two of their benches with carousel animals. This one was quietly playing a tune that seemed suited for a seedy carnival. Jose had to concede it was creepy, but he smiled all the more.

It was open all around for easy on-off access. The overhanging canopy partially protected passengers from the sun, or light rain if it happened as forecast today. These carousels usually did not rotate, but their chassis allowed it. He had seen the designs on occasions when one would come into the shop for repairs.

Jose remembered that these ridiculous busses started as shuttles to take people to and from parking lots in *The Theme Park* District. With the closure of *The Theme Park* District parking lots, the underutilized carousel busses tried to make themselves useful and stay busy by offering free rides between points further afield in the county. Jose was one of the anonymous donors who helped them stay in operation.

At the curb, a young man in a Nehru jacket and an old woman with a baseball cap with the stylized *A* logo of the local team both raised their hands at the bus and tapped their wrist bands almost in unison. Traffic immediately parted and the circle bus swooped to the curb, its music changing to a faster tempo. It rotated to offer them open seats and paused briefly as they stepped aboard. Jose didn't recognize either of them. He wondered if they were among the anonymous unpaying residents of the live-work units who had kept out of his sight up to now. Jose knew the bus would learn the intended destinations of its passengers by communicating with their wristbands, or they might speak their destinations out loud, and it would adjust to the most efficient route. The traffic smoothly adjusted to let the bus back into the flow. It pulled away from the curb and the passengers held on while the creepy music played.

Jose seldom used the busses. He preferred to walk. Only a few blocks to work and the forecast said it shouldn't rain until later. It never rained near here enough here to make things wet anyway. Not since the botched climate mitigation projects in the 40's.

Besides the creepy factor, Jose also thought of the open round busses as risky; people could fall out. The potential liabilities were huge. But who would you sue? The busses were autonomous entities, not owned by anyone and they didn't own anything but themselves other than any small balance of points from riders' donations. Still, he preferred them over Abitats, even though riding within private Abitats was notoriously safe and smooth. He wasn't surprised that the carousel buses seemed to be getting rarer all the time. Some were probably getting themselves converted to delivery vans.

Unlike the carousel busses, other vehicles on the street were enclosed, most with no windows, other than maybe translucent roof panels for natural light during the day. People didn't usually care to see where they were along the way. They just wanted to be comfortable until they arrived. And most people wanted privacy. If they wanted to see outside, they always had wall video displays. But why bother looking. Vehicles would know where to stop and would give warning to get ready when they approached their destinations.

Two black mini pod bubbles each just big enough for one or two passengers to sit or recline on short trips zipped through the traffic. BubbleCars could make better time on short trips in town since they were smaller, and with seated passengers, they didn't try to eliminate all jerky motion. Delivery vehicles or Abitats currently without occupants could also move more briskly. Several grey, medium-sized Abitat units with more interior space than his trailer rolled steadily along, giving a perfectly smooth ride to their occupants. Who knows who might be living in those right now.

Just then a delivery truck snuggled up to an Abitat for a package pickup or delivery while both continued down the street towards the river. The Abitat was smudged with dust and mud spatters partly covering a bright blue exterior and abstract green and brown shapes that looked like mountains painted around the base making the blue mass above look like sky. The delivery vehicle followed closely behind the blue unit, matching its speed, and a probe reached out and made contact. A flap or skirt over the receiving unit's delivery portal tilted up exposing the portal. The delivery unit's probe attached to a spot on the edge of the portal, and a larger delivery appendage extended out from the delivery vehicle filling the portal. Out of view something would be transferred between the units. Jose noticed that they stayed connected longer than usual. Maybe it was a big delivery, or maybe packages were being transferred in both directions. Or maybe something was interfering with the transfer. After a few seconds, the delivery appendage retracted into the delivery vehicle, the portal skirt on the dirty blue-sky Abitat closed, and the two vehicles separated. Jose always thought that docking and transfer looked a bit obscene. He imagined the vehicles exhaling smoke afterwards, like a couple smoking cigarettes in some old movie, but vehicles with exhaust were rare. In the distance he noticed that the delivery vehicle approached the Abitat a second time and initiated the exchange process again. If it was having a malfunction in the transfer chamber, he wouldn't be surprised if that blue Abitat came in for service later. He thought through some of the failure modes that could interfere with a transfer.

None of these vehicles seemed to be stopping on his block. All were on their way somewhere else, carrying their passengers or cargo, or heading to pick up or drop off the same.

Since the Nehru-jacketed young man and white-haired baseball fan woman got on the bus Jose was the only pedestrian visible on this street. The businesses in the live-work buildings were not open at this hour. It was early and he noted that the struggling art gallery and attorney's office should be open later and might attract some visitors. Dr. Overly's pet care center would be open later too. He wondered if she got any business other than volunteer work caring for abandoned cats. The Thai restaurant on the corner never seemed to be open when he was around lately, but it didn't look abandoned. It seemed to be a losing battle, trying to resist the redevelopment wave that had been sweeping over this part of the city.

Buildings not torn down and replaced were sometimes converted, adding docking porches and charging stations, but that involved compromises. Docking ports in old garages only worked for Abitats that could retract vertically for clearance. Most couldn't do that, so they couldn't use those ports. Docking porches outside older homes and apartments usually did not offer direct access inside the home from the Abitat. Most people preferred a fully Abitat-compatible home or opted for the Abitat-only virtual life, with no permanent home port.

Across the busy street for a couple of blocks was a fenced off demolition-construction site which had once been a set of older condominiums. The old buildings were leveled and most of the debris had been hauled away, but the excavation and new construction seemed to be on hold. No activity had occurred in that area for a few weeks now. That was unusual. It was probably going to be developed into another luxury Abitat living community. It seemed like everything was being torn down to rebuild with Abitat living in mind. Even if he avoided it himself, Jose knew that his job and his other income depended on people living the Abitat life.

The Abitat Specialty Service building where he worked was five more blocks down the street. Most Abitat recharge and service was fully automated; units would just hook up at the nearest open outlet for a few minutes whenever they needed to drop waste, replenish fluids, or get a fast charge. They might stay connected longer to get a deep charge if they didn't need to be somewhere else right away, such as while waiting to be called back by residents who were at work, shopping, or out and about, or if a resident wanted an extra-long shower. A few full-service businesses provided repairs, upgrades, and specialty services with a human touch. He was glad to have the work.

He paused before crossing the side street. If his wristband was activated, it could negotiate with the traffic and tell him when it was safe to cross. With it shielded he was essentially a cat or squirrel crossing the street. Still, he should be safe. As he stepped into the street and crossed at a steady pace the traffic adjusted around him with just the slightest changes of speed or direction, giving him a margin of a few meters as they flowed past him.

He was familiar with the vehicle sensors and algorithms. They were good at predicting if an animal or pedestrian was likely to move erratically; and more leeway would be provided, but no sane pedestrian wanted to test the theory, even with an active wristband. Unpredictable movements could cause havoc for traffic flow and even more so for the animal or pedestrian. A vehicle following standard avoidance algorithms would not be liable and would not have to stop. Almost always, the navigation software successfully avoided pedestrian or animal collisions even if it occasionally meant disturbing the steady ride for occupants inside vehicles. Jose didn't want to test it, so he always crossed at a steady pace.

Halfway to the other side he noticed a new noise and the whole flow of traffic in the main avenue began adjusting, slowing, and shifting to the side as a loud, low, sputtering guttural sound came from the east. He broke into a run to get to the other side, just missing a BubbleCar turning into the side street, as a wide pathway opened in the middle of the main road. Two apparently gas-powered motorcycles seemingly controlled by actual human riders roared down the street in the open path created by the parting of the traffic seas. The rider in front turned and looked towards Jose, slowing as he approached, and finally adjusted the front of his helmet, either to get a better look, or maybe as a wave, as he rode past. Jose wasn't sure if the gesture was one of recognition, but it seemed to be. With the reflective face masks, he couldn't see the faces of the riders. He had an idea who the waving rider might be based on the gilded color-scheme of the motorcycles.

"Now that's something you don't see around here every day. Almost got you," said a familiar voice from behind him. Joining Jose from down the side street, a woman dressed in a similar set of coveralls with the name tag *Julia* spoke up, "I wonder what it takes to get a drive-yourself permit these days. That's got to cost some big points, plus paying all the other vehicles to move out of the way as you go. That self-driving can't be cheap. Even fractional points add up fast if you are dealing with hundreds or thousands of other vehicles."

"Maybe they are just outlaws."

"Yeah. Maybe. Does anybody even do traffic enforcement anymore? No more police, but I guess there is *Public Safety*." She removed her sunglasses and stared down the street at the receding roar as the traffic converged behind the motorcycles. Julia was just a bit shorter than Jose but more solidly built. He was pretty strong himself, but she looked like she could beat two of him in a fight. She was attractive in an interesting female linebacker sort of way, curved but also beefy.

"I guess we're both running a little late today, Jules? Let's go in together so they can't dock us both."

"I've got no rush. My shift starts fifteen minutes late this morning. But you, my friend, are probably not going to make it on time."

"Oh, Shoot. See Ya." He broke into a run down the sidewalk.

After covering the remaining blocks in record time, crossing two more side streets at a run, and then slowing abruptly as he approached the entry for his workplace, Jose lifted the metal cover off his wristband, swiped and thumbed it to reactivate its ability to communicate with the building's security system and identify him as an authorized employee. The door swung open, and he hopped twice to avoid tripping as the momentum from his run caught up with him and he passed through the door.

In the workplace he had to keep his wrist band's ID feature on most of the time. Most people didn't even know how to turn them off if they wanted to. And they didn't want to.

He grabbed a computer display tablet and earpiece from a hook on the wall. A voice responded, "Good morning, Mr. Mendoza. Report to service bay three immediately, please."

7:50 AM, Emily Leaves for School

The door to the bathroom opened and a cloud of steam emerged, and then Emily stepped out of the steam in slow motion wearing her school uniform looking at her glistening reflection in a round 8-inch mirror attached to the wall by an articulated arm. The logo for *STEAMBOAT Academy* on the polo shirt included a stylistic steamboat. Grabbing the mirror, she checked her hair and makeup; she was going for an Anime look today with her wavy hair brushed as straight as she could, but something wasn't quite right. She had outlined her eyes with light and dark eyeliner to make them look cartoonishly large, but the shape just didn't seem quite right. "Oh well. Time's up. It will have to do. Maybe it will be a new style." She bunched up her pajamas and put them on a shelf in the little closet and picked up her wristband from a drawer by the bed. Twisting her hand through the stretchable band, she picked up her computer tablet and put it in a small shoulder bag and reached for the door.

On the tv an advertisement for *Endless Closet—Infinite Storage* was wrapping up with its trademarked tag line and image, "All your treasures, safely at hand whenever and wherever you want them;" a rainbow lined with clothes, small appliances, and various kinds of knick-knacks moving both directions extended from the cabinet door in front of the actor out above the Abitat and through the clouds into the indefinite distance.

The reporter came back on and mentioned the planned celebration this weekend of the anniversary of the end of homelessness in the county. She replied to the reporter, "No more homeless, huh? Tell that to Doug and Brock." She checked her school bag for the book she planned to bring back to Brock today. Then she paused and turned off the tv just as the weather guy was saying "No kidding. A real chance of rain…," and grabbed the compact umbrella from the hook by the door. Rain was so rare these last few years that her dad keeping an umbrella handy was more of a prayer for rain than anything practical. Maybe today she would actually be able to use it. Not much chance, but her dad would like it if she actually got to use it. She dropped it into her bag and headed out.

As she stepped down, she saw Dr. Overly carrying a grey cat with black ears in a carrier and heading in the direction of her clinic. Emily was crossing her path and recognized a familiar feline face in the opening of the carrier. "Hi Doctor Magnolia! Is that Catsby? How is she doing? She was so sick the last time I saw her," Emily stopped and looked in the crate.

"Hi. Emily. No. Sadly, Catsby didn't recover. This one is new." She held up the carrier to look in at the cat and said, "You're right. He does look a lot like Catsby. They may be related."

"I'm so sad about Catsby. She was so friendly," said Emily as she poked a finger at the opening of the crate and the cat hissed.

"Don't worry this one isn't sick. Just nervous. I think Catsby might have been his mom. She had a life somewhere before she wandered into our little neighborhood, and I snipped her chances for more kittens. This one wandered in last night, probably from wherever Catsby came from, and he's about to get his little snip snip as well."

"Ohhh. Good luck with that, Son of Catsby! Bye. Dr. Magnolia," said Emily as she briskly walked away towards the far side of the courtyard opposite to the way her dad had gone.

"Say Hi to your mom for me when you see her this weekend."

"Sure thing." She replied without looking back.

Dr. Overly continued to the back of her home and clinic. She entered through an old-fashioned garage door after pressing a code on a touchpad and waiting for the door to roll up. Inside was an antique automobile with a faded green paint job. It had a driver's seat with a steering wheel. It was plugged in to power for a charge, but without any of the other utility hook-ups that most vehicles had these days. She pressed a button on a keypad to close the outer door and grabbed the knob on a door with a sign showing the name of her clinic "The Crazy Cat Lady" to open the door from the garage to her clinic. She went in and set the cat carrier on a shelf just inside.

Meanwhile Emily walked out of a walkway between two live-work units, both with boarded up windows, and turned left down a quiet two-lane road. As soon as she emerged onto the sidewalk, two loud motorcycles turned a corner and cruised past. She paused and watched them continue down the street and around another corner.

The street was much quieter after they went out of sight. Across the street was a new set of nearly complete Abitat-compatible condominiums. Most had external docking porches with secure access from inside the home to the doors of the Abitats, and some had tall garage doors sized to accommodate Abitat vehicles. Construction fences were still in place around parts of the property.

Other units seemed to be complete, and the construction fences had been removed. A couple of them had Abitats docked. She wished her dad would get with the program and get a real home. Maybe he could get one of these condos. It would be close to his work. She didn't mind staying with him in his trailer, but a real home or even just an Abitat would be so much nicer. He said he didn't like Abitats, or couldn't afford it, or something, but her mom would probably help him if he asked.

She crossed the quiet street to look through the construction fence on the other side to better see the new units. The houses were similar to her mom's place in Jurupa Valley but without yards.

The construction fence blocked the sidewalk, so she walked in the street. As she approached the corner, a construction work vehicle appeared on the side street, slowing to a stop at the intersection, and a bright blue Abitat appeared from the other direction moving briskly away from the river, apparently unoccupied. When people were inside Abitats, they moved smoothly to make the occupants feel no motion. When they moved abruptly you could tell they were unoccupied, or in a big hurry.

She hurried ahead to get out of the street onto the sidewalk at the corner. As she stood on the corner, the construction vehicle turned smoothly onto the street with the new condos. The work vehicle was painted white and about twice the size of a standard Abitat. It featured many doors and access panels for tools and construction materials. The back of the vehicle had windows and two workers inside were sitting and a third one was standing, all talking and drinking coffee. One of the seated men turned his head and had a good look at Emily as the work truck made its turn and continued past her and down the street. He had serious look on his face as he tapped a few notes on the computer pad in front of him.

Emily kept going around the corner to the right and down the side street towards the river. She had quite a few blocks to go to get to her school. Today she planned to take the river trail. In the next block or so was the trail access. People exercising on foot or on bicycles used that trail and Emily did so when she felt like walking along the river, but it meant overshooting the school and backtracking a block or so. It was farther, but usually just as fast because of less need to deal with traffic.

The "river" itself ran through this part of town below street level with some brush, weeds, and a few small trees growing in its base. A trickle of water flowed somewhere in the middle. Of course, in theory, if it really rained today then it could be more than a trickle, but she had never seen more than a trickle.

She thought it could be refreshing to walk close to nature along the river trail, seeing the plants, birds, and other wildlife down in the riverbed. And if she ran into Doug and Brock, the stubborn homeless people who still lived in the riverbed, she could say hi. And she had the book to give back to Brock.

She had first met the riverbed campers, Doug and Brock and some of their friends, when she was looking in the riverbed for samples for Biology class a few years ago. They seemed harmless, though paranoid of Abitats, maybe even more than her dad. They liked it when she said her dad avoided Abitat living, so they were helpful to her. She didn't mention that her dad worked on Abitats, or that she used one when she stayed with her mom.

Looking through the trail access opening in the fence and seeing people below who seemed to be arguing, she paused. Two of the people arguing were in dingy clothes. They looked like Doug and Brock, both big and heavily bearded, one with reddish hair and beard and the other grey, but she wasn't sure from this distance and with the others blocking her view. The others she didn't recognize. They were smaller and facing away from her and were in matching jogging clothes. She couldn't make out the words of the argument, but it seemed like someone was very loud and angry, probably Doug. He could be loud. Staying on the streets seemed like a better choice today. She could give Brock back his book some other time.

As she continued down the street and crossed over the river, she looked down from the bridge and saw a family of ducks in a wet spot among the weeds with a feral cat with black ears stalking them. The arguing people were now out of sight behind some bushes on the trail along the bank.

7:58 AM, Honus Has a Panic Attack

Honus felt the start of a panic attack after circling the delayed development neighborhood twice. His heart began racing and his vision started to white-out. He tried hyperventilating to counter it but was having trouble controlling his breathing. His motorcycle pulled over. An Abitat had been following him discretely and pulled up a half minute later. He threw off his helmet and riding gear and climbed in as soon as it opened its door.

His bodyguard Mike stayed close, silently watching until Honus entered the Abitat, and the door closed. Then Mike gathered the gear, secured it to one of the bikes and got back on the other. The two bikes moved silently side-by-side without disrupting traffic. Mike sat on one, taking notes on a tablet. The other one, riderless, moved along next to his, with helmet and gear strapped on the seat.

Honus appeared to be sitting cross-legged on a large pillow doing deep breathing exercises with calming music and dim lights. The holographic images all around him had the appearance of a mountaintop at sunset. He was alone on a large pillow floating on top of the world. No signs of humans could be seen in the crystal-clear scene extending out a hundred miles in every direction. The temperature was cool but comfortable, out of place with the snowy high-altitude scenery. The glow of the setting sun did not diminish with time.

After failing to regain much of his composure, he took another halting deep breath and said, "Simulation off" and the scene changed to the inside of a basic Abitat with a couch, table, three chairs, tiny kitchen, and door to a compact bathroom. He was sitting on the couch. His legs were not crossed.

This Abitat scene was also familiar and should be comforting to him, but he was still anxious. He might not be able to work anymore today. Going out on the bikes had probably been a bad idea after all. He lay down on the bed and pulled the covers around himself. The Abitat bed was not good enough. He needed a real bed. The Abitat would take a long time to return to the resort if it moved smoothly in traffic. He wondered, should he strap in so that it could go back to the resort in emergency mode or was there any other option?

He peeked at the map display on the opposite wall and noticed a place that was closer than the resort and would probably be even more comforting. He hadn't been back to that house for years, but he had always felt safe there before.

He grabbed a tablet and ducked back under the covers. Struggling to gain some control of his breath, he spoke to the tablet and walls again, "Cancel my meetings for the rest of the day."

"Request acknowledged," spoke an English butler voice.

Under the covers he made some motions on the tablet. A message appeared on the wall display as well as on the tablet: *Abitat control off mesh. Self-contained operation.* His voice still shaky with shallow breaths, he spoke, "Take me to the old house." The Abitat made a smooth turn to the right at the next intersection.

He remembered why he had left the resort this morning—the delayed development project—and a possibly familiar face he had seen. Still wrapped in the bed covers, with heart still racing and breath still rapid, he peeked out, he leaned up on one elbow, peeked out and said, "Review video from bike ride." Several displays appeared in the air before him with views from cameras helmet and bike cams, as well as from public shared cameras along the route. He spun through the views until he found the man with coveralls with the name "Jose." He combined the feeds into a 3D holographic view and examined it closely. He age adjusted the image to make it years younger. Speaking quietly to himself, but still short of breath he said, "Okay. I know you. Haven't seen you in a long time. If you're involved, maybe I *can* solve this reluctant seller problem."

Honus made motions on the tablet and spoke again, "Reactivate saved game world PW3709." Then he ducked back under the covers and pulled them tight around himself. Activating the game world might be enough to get a response, but if not he would send a message once he got the house and calmed down some more.

Chapter 2

Morning

8:05 AM, Jeremy near School

Jeremy Jones-Smith put the tray with the remains of his chili-cheese omelet and sourdough toast breakfast that he had hardly touched into the returns compartment of his Abitat and sat back down at his table/desk. He had showered and dressed earlier. Looking at the wall display he called up again the results of the game simulation he had run last night.

His appetite had been weak thinking about after school and the weekend. He had heard stories about students from the school who went with dates to *The Theme Park*[*] after exams and the things they bragged about doing with their dates in dark parts of the park. He had avoided going to the park after exams the last two years because he had been too shy to ask someone. He wanted to go this time, but he was not sure who to ask. He figured it might be one of his two classmate friends, Emily or Chandra, who had been his friends since he started at STEAMBOAT,

---

[*] *Theme*, italics required, is the largest company in the world, or more properly, in the solar system, after the mergers and acquisitions of hundreds of corporations. One of its most visible businesses is *The Theme Park*, italics required, which encompasses most entertainment venues.

but maybe it would be better to ask someone he didn't know as well. To help him decide, last night he had created a fictional mini game world.

He had started with anonymized fictional characters based on all the public profiles of the students at his school. He added some of his personal observations about some characters, especially Jay, Emma, and Chandler, who were based on himself and his friends, Emily and Chandra. He had to make up some information for Emma because, curiously, her public profile was almost empty.

Like Jeremy, Jay was sixteen and a freckle-faced physics and game-world building nerd who had challenges with other subjects and with understanding how to deal with people. He attended a selective science and technology academy like STEAMBOAT, and he wanted to go on a date. Chandler, like Chandra, had already turned seventeen. She was a quiet girl, but very funny and an electrical and mechanical engineering genius. She also seemed to practice some kind of cultural conventions that included wearing loose clothing that covered her head to toe. Jeremy thought there was probably a name for that style of dress, but he wasn't sure what it was called, and he had never asked her. Jeremy wasn't sure of Emily's age but knew she was young for the class. He guessed and said Emma was fifteen, a really pretty computer science geek who was also very good at martial arts, but he misspelled it as *marital* arts. He added details to some of the other characters, such as several people that had said mean things, and several who seemed to think he was funny and laughed at things he said or smiled at him.

Jeremy had posed the situation in the game world last night and offered points to random people to observe the game and make their recommendations on who Jay should ask. If he used their recommendation and things went well for him, they would have a chance at a 200-point prize.

The recommendations were overwhelmingly in favor of asking Emma. Over 55% of 2600 human responders and 52% of 8320 simulated-sage advisors. Chandler was next at 38% and 40%. He had run branch world simulations for what would happen for the next week with each of the top five recommendations, almost all of which resulted in Jay being happy in the days following regardless of his choice. But he got partially naked in the park with only the fifth-choice classmate, who he didn't really know. He was tempted to try that one, but wasn't 100% sure who that character mapped onto, and decided to go with the top vote-getter and ask Emma, aka Emily.

Jeremy always felt nervous when he talked with Emily, aka Emma, and found it very easy to talk with Chandra, aka Chandler, but the advice from the game simulation seemed pretty clear. Jeremy checked his find-your-classmates app to see where Emily was. She was four blocks away from school walking parallel to the river. Video feeds from various storefront cameras showed her lost in thought as she walked quickly along. He would have to hurry to catch her before she got to school. "Abbie, drop me off just ahead of Emily, and hurry," he told his Abitat. He gathered up his backpack and braced himself for the slightly jerky ride and for the nerve to follow the game's advice.

8:20 AM, Emily and Jeremy Walk to School

A few blocks and a number of turns past where she crossed over the river an Abitat pulled up to the side of the road just ahead of Emily. The side door opened and a freckle-faced teenage boy wearing a STEAMBOAT Academy sweatshirt and baseball cap jumped out and said, "Hi, Emma, Uh, Emily!" The door of the Abitat remained open behind him.

"Hello, Jer, uh, uh, Jeremy. We're still blocks from school. You didn't have to get out here."

"I know, but I thought maybe we could talk before school. And walk. Unless you want a ride?"

"Walking is fine," she said as she kept moving. Her mom's and stepdad's warnings about not getting in a boy's Abitat had their effect, even if she knew Jeremy was harmless and she could break his arm if he tried anything. She laughed at the thought.

Jeremy wasn't sure what to make of her laugh, so he laughed too. He waved and the door closed and the Abitat moved away as he hurried to catch up. "Are you ready for the Taekwondo test today, Em?"

"Is that today?" Emily asked.

"You don't sound worried. I guess you always ace martial arts."

"Yeah, but you know they don't count our Athletics grades."

"History too. Right?" Jeremy responded.

"I guess. Did you ever turn in your history paper?" Emily asked.

"This morning," Jeremy answered.

"Finally. What was your thesis?" asked Emily.

"It doesn't matter. You probably turned yours in a week ago?"

"Yeah. Got it out of the way before exams. Exploring common militaristic themes from traditions for memorial day and the Jackson homeless-no-more festival. Chandra did something like Memorializing Jackson: Hero or Villain. Why did you need extra time?"

"I just don't like history. At least not PreAM. It's all just somebody's story. Her story. His story. Nothing Abbie-vetted. Nothing provable. You don't know what to believe," Jeremy complained.

"Looking for patterns and figuring out what to believe is the point, isn't it?" Emily asked.

"Like some of your cyber puzzles, huh?" Jeremy suggested.

"Yeah. Maybe. Are you ready for the cyber test? Personally, I think it might be fun."

"Fun? No. I really don't like cyber either, but I think I will survive. Give me physics or chemistry, something real. All the hocus pocus of encryption and stealth and the psych-out scams—all that seems so contrived… Sorry, Em. I know you get into that stuff, but I just don't like it. If we have to do coding, why not just let us do something practical and real, like making new game worlds? Or whole new games!" They walked along quietly past a few businesses near the school while Jeremy summoned his courage to ask. "Em. Are you going to the party after school at *The Theme Park*? A lot of people are going to celebrate finishing the exams."

Emily kept walking, looking ahead, "I don't know. Are you?"

Jeremy looked around like he was hoping for advice from the people opening their businesses. He said, "I mean. I was thinking of going, but it would be more fun if we both went. I mean if we both wanted to go, we could both go and be there at the same time." He felt like he sounded like an idiot and was blushing and was relieved that she didn't seem to be looking at him. He noticed her eyes were outlined with black and white ovals. It must be a new style. He wondered if he should try it.

They passed the last of the businesses near the school and started up the school sidewalk next to the drop off area. Students were climbing out of four Abitats and two bubble pod cars in the drop off lane, while several more vehicles were approaching on the street.

"That could be fun, Jeremy. We should do that. It's been weeks since I went to *The Theme Park*. Hey! Chandra! Wait for us!" Emily waved at and hurried towards a short, dark-eyed girl in a STEMBOAT Academy head scarf and ankle-length plain dress just out of a bubble pod car and lifting two canvas bags and a large box full of odd-looking electronic devices with antennas and lenses. "Let us help you carry that, whatever that is," said Emily.

Chandra had made her custom headscarf labelled STEMBOAT instead of STEAMBOAT to stress her preference for Science, Technology, Engineering, and Math over Art. She didn't really think the BOAT part of the academy's name mattered enough to change. Business, Optimism, Athletics, Teamwork. That was just a contrived vehicle to spell BOAT and justify the logo for the school's sponsorship tie-in with a boat ride in *The Theme Park.* She acknowledged to herself the irony of having crafted this headscarf to make her point. She rationalized the making of the headscarf as an act of engineering rather than art since she used a 3D printer. So far no one had noticed the subversive spelling on her headscarf, or at least no one had pointed it out to her.

Chandra tried to not look at Jeremy but couldn't suppress a hint of a smile while saying, "It's okay. I've got it." She looked at Emily, noticing her eyes, thinking they looked ridiculous, such a child, but deciding not to say anything. She was a friend.

Jeremy caught up and said, "Really, Chandra. We know you are strong and independent and all, but what would it hurt to let Emily help you carry that." Emily took one of Chandra's canvas bags and Jeremy tried to take the box, but Chandra shifted it out of his reach and offered him the other canvas bag, which he took and the three of them walked side-by-side into the school building.

"What is all this stuff, Chandra?" Emily asked. "Did you do some extra credit project to try to get out of one of today's exams?"

"Our inter-term project. If I can get both of you to help."

'Oh! So? You did come up with an idea after all!" said Emily.

"I'm in," answered Jeremy. "What is it?"

"We can talk about it later in a group study room. Not here. Right now, just help me put this stuff in my tech lab locker before the exams start." As other students walked by looking at them, pointing, and talking to each other, Chandra tried to block the view of her box of equipment, eventually realizing they were looking at Emily's eyes and not at the equipment. She relaxed and continued, "The inter-term projects are supposed to use only materials already on campus. They don't specifically say it has to be materials provided by the school," Chandra pointed down the hall towards the door to the tech lab room, and Jeremy and Emily followed her quickly.

Emily replied, "I might want to study for my last exam during study period. Maybe we can talk about it at *The Theme Park* after school. Jeremy was just saying a lot of people are going this afternoon, after the exams."

"*The Theme Park*? I don't know. I don't have a pass this year," said Chandra. "And I spent all my allowance on these parts."

"Oh. Too bad," said Jeremy. "Emily and I are going."

"That's no problem," said Emily. "You can get a park entry code and food voucher from the school for finishing the exams. It's good for tonight and tomorrow, I think, and maybe Sunday, but not the actual holiday on Monday."

"Really? That would be nice. Then I can probably go. I didn't hear about that," said Chandra.

"Me neither," said Jeremy as they entered the tech lab, and Chandra waved her wristband to unlock her locker. "Not like it's a big deal prize for me since I have an all-access park pass every year, but I would have remembered hearing about a free food voucher."

Emily handed a bag to Chandra to put into the locker and said quietly, "Well, I guess the prizes are actually connected to the Cyber test."

"Which Emily knows she can ace so it's as if she's already got the pass." Jeremy looked at Emily's equivocal expression. "Oh. I see. You've already cracked the Cyber test. Of course!" said Jeremy in a co-conspiratorial whisper and then added, "Good thing I already have a park pass, since even passing the Cyber exam is not a sure thing for me, like you two."

"Okay. Let's meet up after today's exams. Good luck."

8:40 AM, Sam & Jo-Jo Heading to the Beach

Jo-Jo came out of the tiny bathroom after putting on a bathing suit under her jogging suit and stepped her way between stacked bins and bags and sat down on the compact sofa bed, picking up her tablet to check the beach weather reports.

Sam stood up from his chair and turned towards the mini refrigerator, "Jo, do you want some wine before we get to the beach? It's good stuff –glass bottle with a cork." Sam pulled a bottle of discount red from the tiny fridge and held it up for Jo-Jo to see. She didn't look up. They were wearing their new matching grey jogging suits with red trim that they bought specially for this trip.

"I'm still upset about Doug and Brock," Jo-Jo replied. "I thought they would be glad to see us. I was so looking forward to spending time with them and catching up." She continued checking on the conditions at the beach and the estimated arrival time through heavy local traffic. She had hoped their Abitat would have charged and finished its delivery while they talked with Brock and Doug. But they had to call it right back. "We had to get out of there too quick."

Sam replied, "I really thought Doug would be happy to see you again. You two were together a long time."

"You too."

Sam continued, "Yeah. I suppose. They both looked surprised to see us, and Brock seemed happy—at first. But Doug seemed angrier than I remember him. And Brock didn't dare say anything after Doug started in. I was actually starting to get afraid that Doug might try to hurt us. I can't believe taking an Abitat still means so much to him."

"He talks about the Abitats. He and Brock always hated Abitats. But I think something else is bothering him," Jo-Jo said. "He's acting different."

Sam decided to open the wine. He found a corkscrew and two nice clear glass cups in the cupboard over the tiny sink. It felt like an extravagance to use the clear glasses instead of using the same mugs they normally used for coffee, water, and any other drinks, or drinking straight from the bottle, but he wanted to be able to appreciate the color of the wine. This was their vacation after all. And he was able to liberate the glasses with free water from a food place along the highway yesterday, so it wasn't really that big of an extravagance. With the delivery closet over-filled with packages, they had to actually go into stores and food places along this trip instead of getting things delivered to their Abitat. That saved them a few points, but it also gave them the opportunity to pick up little extras like the glasses that wouldn't normally come with the delivered purchases. With awkward twisting and pulling he managed to get the cork out, then he poured wine into both glasses which he had placed on the flat surface above the fridge.

Sam continued, "Let's not let Doug's paranoia spoil this vacation. We've been saving from both our allotment points for months to afford this trip back here. And you've finally sold a few of your art pieces. You're making progress. Speaking of progress: Are we there yet? Are we there yet? Are we there yet?"

"Stop that. Or I'll take you back and let Doug end you. Or I'll do it myself. It wasn't funny the first time, and it's still not funny. But, yes, we're getting there. With the traffic, we probably could walk to the beach faster, but we're getting there. We should be there before the Abitat needs another charge. How about we let her drop us off near where the river meets the beach? We know that area pretty well, and it's usually not as crowded as other places." Jo-Jo looked up to see Sam offering her a clear glass cup with red wine. She smiled and, setting down the tablet, took the cup. "Thanks. Vacation time."

She raised her cup, looking at the color of the wine, seeing the distorted red image of Sam and the interior of the Abitat through the glass, and then took a big sip.

Sam smiled and looked back at her through his own wine. "That's what I was thinking." He drained his cup and filled it again, looking at the color once again.

"Abbie, please drop us off at the parking lot of the little park where the river meets the beach," Jo-Jo spoke clearly, towards the low ceiling.

"Is this where you mean?" came a pleasant voice from the walls, as a map and picture of a sign at the entrance to the "Anderson Wetlands Preserve" displayed on a small panel on the wall. "Arrival in about 20 minutes."

"Yes. That would be perfect. Faster than I thought," said Jo-Jo. "Let's get ready," she said to Sam. She stood up and opened a little cupboard door to find her hat, sunglasses, towel, and a large cloth bag from among many things stacked and stuffed tightly in there. The mini fridge was packed almost as tightly as the cupboard. She searched both to find a few snacks to take along, which she put in the bag along with her towel. "I hope Abbie can finish the delivery while we are on the beach. You hear that, Abbie? It will be nice to get back some space in here. And points."

"About that..." started the Abbie voice.

"Did I ask you a question?" Jo-Jo interrupted.

"Uh. Sort of," said the Abbie voice.

"Enough," said Jo-Jo.

"Sorry," said the Abbie voice, "I mean, Okay."

Sam refilled, re-examined, and drank another cup of the wine and then once more to finish off the bottle. "Oh, sorry. Did you want another cup? I've got another bottle in the fridge. Should we take it with us, or keep it cold for later?"

Jo-Jo was in the bathroom checking her hat and sunglasses in the mirror. "Bring it along. This is our vacation. We've saved enough points we can get more wine after the beach. Let's enjoy ourselves."

Instead of putting the empty bottle in the recycling chute Sam opened the delivery closet door and forced the bottle in along with other cans and bottles he had been saving there. It was tight but he was able to wedge it in. He pushed the closet door closed, applying his weight, squeezing the contents until the door latched.

He hoped to take them to a cash for recycling center to get some old-fashioned pocket money. He last cleared it out a few days ago when they passed through a town with a recycle-for-cash place near a park where Jo-Jo set up to sell her artwork. From the old days he knew some recycling places that paid in cash here near the coast. He would take the bottles and cans when Jo-Jo wasn't looking. He liked having cash for himself instead of points since they were sharing all their points. He figured Jo-Jo wouldn't notice that her Abitat was short the few points for regular recycling.

Jo-Jo came out of the bathroom and Sam smoothly danced around her in the small space, found a small backpack and stuffed it with his towel and some other items, then he stepped around her again back to the fridge to find the unopened bottle of wine. He placed it in his backpack and carefully added the clear glass cups and the corkscrew after wrapping them in a kitchen towel.

8:45 AM, Elsie and Andre Heading to Work

Elsie and Andre felt guilty dropping baby Alex off but neither of their jobs offered good on-site childcare. Elsie looked down at the baby who was fussing and checked their diaper, pulling back one of the edges and peeling the diaper away just enough to see that this one needed to be changed. "Andre," she called out extra sweetly. "Your little one needs you." Whispering to Alex, "Mommy needs to go to work now. Daddy will take good care of you."

"Okay. You timed it just right, didn't you," said Andre's voice from the background.

Elsie said, "I love you, little one," caressing her baby's cheek and forehead, stepping back out of view, and dissolving into the air. All except her hands which settled down next to the crib. In Elsie's personal Abitat the baby's crib dissolved into air and Elsie picked up a briefcase, checked herself in a full-length mirror display. Almost perfect. She picked a scarf out of a nearby drawer, wrapped it loosely around her neck and back over her shoulder. A power scarf added a certain statement to her look and hid that neck rash from the latest round of tattoo removal. Her shoulder length dark brown hair covered most of the marks, but a little more cover would be good. She felt that she still looked good at 40-something and after two kids. She liked the fact that her husband Andre, at 36, appeared to think so too.

Andre stepped up behind her and said, "I wish we had installed the adult interface options and not just the childcare system, so I could give you a kiss goodbye."

"Adult interface? Not a chance, pervert," she replied with a smile.

"Just a kiss."

"Right. That's what you meant," she said as she took a good look at him in his t-shirt and boxer shorts with his well-defined muscles. Definitely better to get with him in person than through holograms and robots. "See you for real tonight though. Love you," she said.

"You too." He blew her a kiss and then his hologram reached forward and hugged through her as the wall opened to a curbside at the door of the law offices of Mendoza, Sakharov, and Associates.

She looked back as she stepped to the curb, "I mean it. I'll see **you** tonight, Andre."

"Have a great day. Give them hell," he said.

Elsie stepped out with an air of authority and walked briskly into the building with her briefcase in hand. Andre's hologram dissolved as the door closed behind her. With no occupant, her Abitat jerked suddenly back into a break in traffic and proceeded briskly down the street.

In his own personal Abitat Andre was still getting dressed. After showering and eating, he had a few minutes before he would be at work. But right now, he had a mission. He needed to change that diaper. Even though he knew doing this couldn't really soil his clothes, he felt better changing the diaper before putting on his work clothes.

The crib materialized into view in the middle of his Abitat and his hologram materialized in the baby's Abitat. He stepped up and cooed to his baby, "Hey there little Boo. Did my little Alex-Boo do a little poo poo? Daddy will take care of that poo poo for you." He lowered his hands and raised them again while the robot hands in the baby's Abitat matched his motions and aligned with his holographic image perfectly. "I'll get that nasty diaper off and clean you up." His holographic image, augmented by very realistic and warm robotic hands reached down and picked up little baby Alex and held them to a robotic chest, also warm and complete with heartbeat matching his own, and moved them to the changing table.

Diaper came off and was wrapped up and dropped into the trash chute. With multiple baby-wipes, he gently cleaned them, spritzed them with spray-on powder, positioned a fresh diaper, and wrapped it around them, then put them onto a clean warm blanket and wrapped them tightly, tossed the dirty wipes in the trash, then picked them back up and danced with them, looking holographically into their eyes, singing, "Alex has a fresh clean bum. Alex has a dry clean diaper. Daddy's glad hologram smell-o-gram features can be turned off. Now they're back on and now you smell so good. Daddy's little Alex is the most beautiful little baby in the world."

He gently placed Alex in a baby carrier seat, secured them in, and put it on a swing. Then he stepped away, letting the robotic hands and chest settle out of view before his hologram went to the drawer and closet to get his work clothes. He put on his Batman costume, but not the mask. He thought it better if Alex didn't see him in the mask.

Just then Camilla's voice could be heard at the edge of the baby's room. "Are you decent, Mr. Martin?" She exaggerated the stress on the second syllable, mar TEEN after being corrected once for pronouncing it like it rhymed with carton. "May I take care of the baby now?"

"Yes, Camilla. As usual you are right on time. Please come in."

A wall in the baby's room slid open revealing a slim and tall woman wearing a well-fitted pantsuit, who looked to be in her seventies, but still well-preserved. She had light brown skin with few wrinkles, dark brown hair with grey roots and carried a large canvas bag with some baby toys and stuffed animals. She stepped into the baby's Abitat through the open door. The space beyond the door showed the interior of her home. She set the bag on the floor and bent over to talk to the baby. "Hello, sweetness and joy. We are going to have a good time today, aren't we? Okay Mr. Martin, I have everything under control. You should say bye-bye to Alex and go to work."

"Thank you, Camilla. You are a blessing to us. Bye! Bye! Alex. Daddy loves you!" He faded from view in the baby's room, while back in his Abitat the baby, crib, swing, changing table, and lastly Camilla all faded from view. He saw Camilla put some of the baby's toys from the Abitat into the canvas bag and reach for the baby carrier as she separated into pixelated dust.

His wristband vibrated. He should be just coming to his work location. He pulled on his mask, verifying that its heads-up display and direct brain interface cap was working. He used it to authorize daily licensing payment for use of the trademarked character. It really should be out of trademark if you count the years back to when it was first introduced, but since the Reset the rules were different and trademarks that were ever owned by the companies that were merged into *Theme* were enforceable, although seldom actually enforced. Given his job, he needed to follow the rules.

Then he checked himself in the mirror display on the wall, double-checked the whiteness of his teeth, rubbing them with his finger, and polished some items in his utility belt with a cleaning wipe before turning to the wall which opened, and he stepped out onto the sidewalk bustling with tourists waiting for *The Theme Park* to open. He needed to get out there and start earning his keep. In a deep guttural voice, "Pictures with a Batman, anyone?" The Abitat sped away into traffic and down the street towards a recharge and parking garage a few blocks away. He hoped the trash pickup would get that diaper before it stunk up the place. But then he shook his head, remembering the diaper was miles away in the baby's Abitat at Camilla's house. He tapped his forehead a few times with his palm, "Get it together, man!" he whispered to himself, and he began his day of trying to bring peace and justice to the city.

8:55 AM, Doug and Brock at Home

Doug was still agitated. His long reddish-brown hair and beard looked even redder around a face flushed from his fuming. He couldn't settle down if he tried. He kept sitting down in his discolored, molded green plastic chair and immediately jumping up again and pacing in front of his tent, muttering, "They think we're stupid?"

Both Brock and Doug had been on edge lately but the run-in on the trail earlier when Sam and Jo-Jo showed up in an Abitat had really set Doug off. Brock was pleasantly surprised that their old friends were still alive, but Doug thought they were trying to talk them into giving up and going to the County for Abitats. Maybe he was too harsh, but with all the banners around now about some festival celebrating getting rid of all the homeless, Brock had to admit the timing was suspicious.

Brock was sitting quietly on another plastic chair from a different mold in front of his own tent, holding a book, and trying to read, in-between Doug's outbursts. With his wild grey hair and beard and reading glasses, Brock gave an impression of a bedraggled professor.

Their camp was under a highway bridge in a neglected "riverbed"— a partly concrete-lined and mostly dry channel that was designed for flood control but really only carried the county's minuscule effluent a few short miles to the sea. Tall bushes grew in clumps in the channel hiding their tents and accumulated belongings under the road bridge and out of view of people who jogged or biked on the trail that ran alongside the river. It had been years since a storm dropped enough rain to wash out the channel, and the County had stopped cleaning up homeless camps a few years ago after they declared victory on the homeless problem, so they had accumulated a lot of stuff under the bridge.

Brock set his book on his lap and looked over his glasses and said, "Hey, Doug. I wish you hadn't run them off. I didn't want to say anything while you were telling them what you think, but I'm starting to think maybe they're right and taking one of those free Abitats might not be so bad, at least for them."

Doug picked up his chair and tapped it on the ground as he spoke. "Not you too, Brock? You were always the one who didn't want anything to do with Abitats, ever since you showed up out here. And no phones, no tablets, nothing that can track us. Are you giving in now? You know they just want to get rid of all the homeless."

"I guess you're right. Abitats and tracking devices do kind of freak me out. But now, Doug, we're the last ones out here. We haven't seen other campers for a year or two now since Sam and Jo-Jo left. We've still got great camping spots, but with all the new construction those keep disappearing too. It's a matter of time. Sam and Jo-Jo seemed okay. They came back. They were alive. They looked good. They looked healthy and happy—before you scared them away. Maybe it would be okay?"

"Yeah. Yeah, Brock. They came back here just to convince us to give up. I bet they're working for *The County* now."

"Doug, I know we thought that *The County* gathered all the homeless, took them away and chopped them up, but Sam and Jo-Jo are alive. They got Abitats a couple years ago and they're back, still alive. Jo-Jo said they're here on a vacation. And she said they keep in touch with some of the others who left before, like Pat and Wesley, who have jobs around here now. They're still alive too."

"I don't trust any of that, Brock. Maybe Sam and Jo-Jo made a special deal. Maybe that wasn't really Sam and Jo-Jo. There are robots, you know. I haven't seen Pat and Wesley. If they were still alive, don't you think we would see them somewhere? I don't know. But these Abitats are all about the government and corporations controlling everyone's life. *The County* said they'd give free Abitats, but people who took them disappeared. The freaking Abitats control them or kill them. The Abitats take them all away!" Doug put down his chair and sat down.

Brock felt that Doug had been getting a lot more agitated lately, not just from seeing Sam and Jo-Jo. Brock felt more anxious lately too. Unwanted intrusive thoughts and images kept bothering him. The drugs he normally used to stay calm had been unavailable for a few weeks and the alternatives Doug made from native plants were not working as well.

He took a deep breath and tried to remain calm. He opened his book, adjusted his bookmark, and closed the book again before looking up and reasoning, "Jo-Jo said *she* tells her Abitat where to go. But the points, the credits—what did she call it? An Abitat Allotment, Abitat Basic Income? What they get each month won't pay for much around here. They went inland where they can afford to dock their Abitat and eat and live better. She said life was pretty good. She said they were even making some extra points doing deliveries, and she is selling her art and Sam is working on his writing again."

Doug jumped out of his chair and shouted, "You believe all that crap they were saying?! It's crazy! They don't give anybody something for nothing!" Then he spoke more quietly and paced, "I like living here, near the coast. I like living near the theme parks and the tourists. And I like living, period. We've lived around here for years. We're getting by fine. If we want a change, we can move our tents wherever we want. We could even go to the mountains. I'm starting to remember I lived in the mountains before. They cleaned out some spots, but there are still a lot of places we can camp." Then, moving his chair and sitting right in front of Brock, leaning in face to face, "No autonomous little outhouse on wheels is going to take me away from my life."

"You said all that to Sam and Jo-Jo. I heard it already. No need to get all angry with me. I'm still here. For now."

"For now? Yeah? If you want to go. Go! Go! See if I care! Everybody else is gone." Doug stood up from his chair and started to gather belongings into his backpack and shopping bags. "But don't expect to find me here if you come back." He started to take down his tent while Brock sat and watched. Doug continued, "Sam and Jo-Jo said they would be around the beach or theme parks for a couple days. Go see if you can find them in their little dirty blue Abitat with the mountains. But when you all get chopped up and dumped in the desert, don't tell me I didn't tell you so. I'll be fine here or in the mountains or somewhere and you'll be cat food like all the rest."

Doug put on his backpack and started to walk away, then came back and grabbed his plastic chair and walked out again carrying the chair. Brock sat and opened his book. He didn't make much progress on reading. He read a page or two and then stopped to stare towards the place on path where Doug had gone out of view. Then he would re-read the same pages again. After a few iterations when Doug did not reappear, Brock sighed deeply, closed his book, put his glasses in his pocket, stood up slowly and started gathering his own belongings.

His eyes were moist, but he blamed it on the foul smell of months of his and Doug's shit scattered farther back under the bridge. "This place stinks. A place with a clean bathroom and bed sounds pretty good to me. Sam and Jo-Jo say Abitats are safe. Maybe they are safe. Why shouldn't I have one?" He pulled a backpack from his tent and gathered some clothes and books. He began to take out a sleeping bag but stopped. "Maybe I won't need that anymore." He left his tent and his chair but picked up his backpack and walked to the path going opposite the way Doug had gone.

9:00 AM, Elsie and Bella

Elsie settled in at her desk in her large office with walnut-paneled bookcases with an appropriately impressive set of out-of-date law books, two walls of windows with spectacular views of the city below, the Pacific Ocean in the distance to the southwest, and hills and mountains to the north. Some clouds were visible over the ocean. She reviewed notes on several of the cases her firm was currently working. She had a stack of paper briefs as well as written and video files she could view on her large display screens.

The topics that needed extra security or privacy were printed on paper from systems that had no connection to any network or were hand-written. Elsie took most of her own notes by hand on one of those ancient traditional yellow "legal pads." Many stayed only in hand-written form or were burned to reduce the chances for unintended exposure of the intellectual property and contractual strategies of her clients.

She tapped one of the displays on her desktop and said, "I need to speak with Bella and Tristan about the Son'o'Ra Interiors case. Let me know when they are on the line." She continued looking through two of the paper reports and scanning a number of files on her large displays and taking notes on the yellow pad.

"Bella is on the line. Tristan has not responded. Do you want to proceed?" said a disembodied from the middle of her office.

"Yes. Proceed." She adjusted her outgoing image before activating the connection by tapping another spot on the display. An image of Bella appeared on one of the display panels. Bella's image was of a well-groomed young woman in professional suit, sitting in front of a glass wall with a view of distant mountains.

Actually, Bella wore sunglasses and a brimmed hat with a bandana wrapped around her neck to protect her light skin from the sun, and the view behind her included a mountain stream rushing over large rocks with tall trees on both banks. Her red hair was pulled back in a ponytail. She wished she had gotten more of the darker complexion common on her mother's side of the family, but she could deal with what she got.

She was late returning to the campsite from her fishing expedition after repeatedly getting lured farther upstream by visions of promising pools above. She had barely gotten back when Elsie called. She was seated on a fallen tree trunk near the stream below the campsite with her work tablet propped up-slope on a rock in front of her. A lightweight fishing pole and a bag with fishing gear leaned against the rock behind her tablet.

"Good morning, Bella," said Elsie, her face displayed in front of a background that looked like a desert scene with Joshua Trees.

"Hello, Elsie. You have a question about my IP assessment for Son'o'Ra Interiors? How can I help you?"

"Your research on the origination of the design for the latest Son'o'Ra Interiors line disagrees with the evidence that Tristan found. How do you reconcile the different conclusions?"

What had Tristan done now? Bella suppressed the impulse to complain about Elsie asking her to supervise the new guy on this assignment in the first place. She could understand that Elsie might not trust one of these newer brain-cap-wearing, AI-augmented lawyers to work on his own. Skipping law school entirely and just buying your expertise seemed to be the new norm, but she didn't have to like it. AI-assist was fine to check citations, draft routine motions, and even to help get through law school and practice for the bar, everyone did that, but it shouldn't be a substitute for law school.

She was supposed to be on reduced hours during her vacation. She ended up rewriting the report last night to get it out of the way so today would be clear. She was also peeved that Tristan had continued working on it after she finished the report last night. He was just supposed to check formatting and not supposed to send anything to Elsie without checking with her first.

She reviewed the information on her screen and said "Elsie, Tristan and I worked on this yesterday until 10 PM and were going to release it to you this morning after final formatting. I now see Tristan released his own supplemental analysis at 4 AM. I will get with him right away to cross check his analysis. Tristan and I should be able to give you a full consolidated response later today." She scrolled through some notes on the tablet screen. "I see Tristan has been offline since four, but he should be back in the office about now."

Elsie replied, "Give me a response by 10. I have a meeting with the clients at 11. I am sending you a new encryption key. Use it on top of our scheduled encryptions when you submit your response and on any of our follow-up calls on this subject." Elsie dragged an icon onto Bella's window and swiped the corner, and her outgoing picture and Bella's picture disappeared as the call disconnected.

9:05 AM, Bella and Bobbie in a Campsite

"Yes. Ma'am. Right away, Ma'am. By 10, Ma'am. It should only take me a couple minutes to redo hours of work, Ma'am." said Bella after she was sure the call disconnected. "How am I supposed to get that done in less than an hour? Whatever happened to this being a vacation?" She reached for her tablet and began carefully reading the report from Tristan.

As she read, she stopped fuming and started to get interested. What had this artificially enhanced lawyer old man come up with?

"Hey, Bobbie! This is interesting. I know Tristan and I verified all the possible worlds in the game where similar combinations of design elements were presented and traced them back to their first instances. All Abbie-vetted, stipulated facts. The IP rights under game law is a no brainer. But this is something new. Tristan says the game manifestations were irrelevant and the designs originated earlier and independently outside the game. He's found non-game evidence in some videos from internet archives outside the game. This is a real pain. If we are going to start going outside the game for evidence, there is no end to the research horizon or the chance for second-guessing. And involving pre-game law could add a lot of complications. I suppose, in theory, this could be great for generating more billing, but it really complicates things. I don't like it. Where did he come up with this? This can't be in the virtual lawyer package he's using. He's old, maybe he knows something from before game law?" She looked up the slope from the riverbank to their campsite where Bobbie was preparing breakfast.

"That's inconvenient. If it violates game law can't you just ignore it?" said Bobbie.

"Under game law we definitely should ignore it, but it will be up to Elsie—or the clients actually—to decide. Pre-game-law was never abolished. People just don't bother with it anymore."

"Want some more coffee, Bella?" She mimed sipping from a steaming cup. She was wearing a grey thermal form-fitting body suit and hiking boots with loose laces. She had a knit cap pulled down over her short black hair. Dehydrated spinach omelets were in a package next to a cooking pan, ready to be reconstituted.

"More coffee, yes! I need it. Can you bring me a cup? I've got to redo a week's research in less than an hour. And, sorry, I didn't catch any fish. No trout for breakfast again today. I thought I found the great fishing spot, but again no luck."

"Okay. I'll make the eggs. But first that coffee… So, I guess we aren't going over the pass today after all, are we?" asked Bobbie as she picked a disk-shaped object from a blue sack and gave the disk a shake, expanding it into a cup and setting it down.

"Not likely. Even if I'm done with the revised report by 10, I'll need to be ready for follow-up calls all day. I suppose I could do them on the trail, but it wouldn't be safe to do the pass while I'm working if there is still some ice or snow at the top. I'm sorry." Bella was still focused on the tablet, re-reading Tristan's report and starting to check his references.

Bobbie sat down on a folding stool with composite legs that looked impossibly lightweight for holding a full-sized adult. "Let's see." She went through some mental calculations. "We originally planned to start by 8 to get go over the pass and get to Lake Anne before dark." She took a few items out of the blue sack. "You were fishing a lot longer than I expected. If we start by 10:30 today we'll have to make really fast time, which would be hard but maybe not impossible…" She shook some coffee beans through a grinder tube with the fine grounds dropping into a compact coffee press sitting on a flat rock. "…or camp somewhere higher, near the pass, which might be uncomfortable and cold…" She poured cold water from a metal bottle through a heating funnel held in her fist. Boiling water flowed from the bottom of the funnel into the clear press. "…or keep hiking after dark, which could be dangerous." She placed the lid and plunger into the press. "Okay. We're staying another day. Since we're staying another day, do you mind if I order more coffee? I know you wanted to get over the pass before our next supply order, but we're getting pretty low on beans. I know it will cost more this far out, but the supply drones will deliver here, won't they? We need more coffee." She slowly pushed the plunger into the coffee press with two fingers and then poured the coffee into Bella's cup.

"Sorry. Do whatever you think is best. I need to concentrate now. And I need to talk to Tristan. Where IS he?" Bella looked like she was concentrating. She took off her sunglasses and squinted, pressing her lips together, and made wrinkles on the bridge of her nose as she stared at her tablet and tried to reach Tristan.

"I know not to bother you when you've got that look, girl. Here's your coffee…when you're ready," Bobbie whispered as she held the steaming cup out to Bella. Realizing that Bella didn't hear her when she was focused like this, she waited.

After a minute Bella noticed her holding the coffee. "Thanks, Bobbie," she took it and sipped a bit. "That's perfect. I'll make it up to you later."

9:15 AM, Tristan Wakes

Tristan had been dreaming about fire alarms and fire engines and police cars rushing to an emergency. He was a hero. He rescued a curvy young woman with long dark hair and a flimsy nightgown from a blazing building along with her two tiny dogs before the emergency workers could get there. Before she could show her appreciation, he woke up and lost the dream.

He opened his eyes to a sunny scene on a sandy beach on a Greek island. A woman similar to the one in his dream but blonde and much thinner, wearing a small green bathing suit was resting on a beach recliner next to his, under a large umbrella.

"Hi, sleepy head," said the blonde woman. "You had some calls, but I didn't want to wake you. You were up too late last night. Do you want to set your preferences for my appearance now?"

"Defaults are fine. Or you decide," he said as he propped himself on one elbow and rubbed his eyes and the top of his head with the other hand. He adjusted a mesh cap over his short grey hair, then rubbed his mustache while he tried to remember where he was and what he was doing. Gentle waves were lapping the sand and the blue sea stretched to a distant horizon with two sailboats under full sail. A repeating annoying buzzer sounded from somewhere nearby.

A wooden board leaning against the blonde's recliner had scrawled on it in black marker, '*Missed call from Elsie. Incoming call from Bella.*' And in the upper corner was a hand-scrawled analog clock face indicating a quarter after 9.

"Uh oh. If it's a call from my boss, don't let me sleep," he said.

The blonde said, "Okay. I'll remember that."

He sat up on the side of the bed. "Answer call. No video." He smiled and waved at the woman with a little "bye-bye" wave. The miles-distant horizon and sailboats over the sea collapsed into blank walls within a stretched-arm's reach. The beach scene and woman disappeared and the spartan interior of his Abitat was now apparent. A small lit rectangle appeared on the wall with a digital time of 09:16:31 and the words *'Answering call from Bella - no video.'*

"Hello, Bella. I'm just waking up. Must have overslept. I'm guessing you saw my report on the Son'o'Ra Interiors designs and want to talk about it."

"Hi, Tristan. Elsie saw it before I did. She's giving us less than an hour to get our research stories straight before she has to talk with the clients."

"Sorry. I thought you would read it, and we would talk about it before she saw it," Tristan was now more fully awake.

"You need to learn how to manage the sharing of documents. But even so, Elsie can get to everything." Bella admonished him.

Tristan responded, "I just need a couple minutes to clean up and get dressed, then I can be back in the office. I don't have access to the offline archives here," said Tristan as he grabbed an energy bar from a cabinet, tore off the wrapper and took a bite, pushed the bed, sliding and folding, into a small space under a set of cabinets, leaving a small sitting area. He opened one cabinet door to find a freshly cleaned and pressed suit and shirt, along with fresh underwear, tie, polished shoes, socks. He turned around and took a couple steps before pulling out and expanding the retractable bathroom from the opposite wall. He pulled off his shorts and tossed them into a dirty clothes drawer. He was wearing only the mesh skull cap. He was tall and thin. "Meanwhile, what can I tell you?"

"I see your report, but I'm not sure I follow how the videos from the archives define ownership of the new designs," said Bella. Especially since there is a clear trace in the Abitats game showing when and who first introduced these design ideas as game Abitat features before Son'o'Ra started to manufacture them for real."

Tristan said, "I think I explained that in the last couple pages. Basically, the exact same design was offered for sale in the real-world decades before. There was documented prior design ownership pre-game. Those videos are pretty clear. But really… Just give me two or three minutes and I can call you back from my desk."

"Okay, call me right back," said Bella.

The wall display showed, '*Call ended.*' Tristan entered the bathroom and sat down on the toilet while also putting a toothbrush in his mouth and turning on the shower, which partially sprayed on him as he sat. "I really would like a chance to finish shitting before I shower one day, instead of having to multitask this way every day," he mumbled to himself around the toothbrush. "…but the law waits for no man." He removed his skull cap and hung it on a hook on the wall before standing and putting his head into the shower spray. A timer appeared on the wall mirror.

A few moments later Tristan emerged from the bathroom clean and mostly dry. Hot dry air was still blowing from multiple vents in the bathroom, clearing the last traces of shower steam. He grabbed a small towel from a drawer and rubbed it over his short grey hair and mustache then tossed it towards the dirty clothes drawer. He pulled out a brush and worked it through his hair in about five strokes while he looked at himself in the wall-sized, mirror-image display which also showed a running timer that was turning from yellow to red, before tossing the brush aside and putting the skull cap back on. The timer reset to zero, turned green and disappeared. He quickly started putting on underwear, socks, shirt, suit. He had confidence in his Abitat to know, without being asked, that when he was dressed, he needed to be at the side entrance of the office building, near the service elevator. As he adjusted his tie, rubbed his mustache, and pressed his skull cap in place one last time, covering it with a beret, the side door opened, and he took a big step directly into the open side entrance. He turned back a moment and said to his Abitat, "Thanks, Abbie. I can always count on you."

"My pleasure, Tristan," came the voice of the girl on the beach, who reappeared as a hologram wearing a housekeeper uniform. The doors closed just after Tristan stepped into the service elevator, and the girl from the beach smiled, looking around the Abitat at the unmade-bed, food wrappers, yesterday's socks, and hairbrush on the floor, and a towel partly hanging out of the dirty clothes drawer. "Time for some cleaning, then laundry, recharging, and restocking. Got to get everything looking right before Tristan comes back."

A cleaning unit the size of a small cat, but with extra limbs and attachments came out of an opening at the bottom of a wall panel and began extending its limbs until it was almost as tall as the hologram of the housekeeper. The hologram housekeeper stepped into the space occupied by the housekeeping cat and together they began picking up items and putting them in appropriate drawers: trash, dirty clothes, personal items. The bed extended itself out from the wall and the housekeeper/housekeeping cat bent over and straightened the sheets and covers.

Tristan had only moved into this upgraded Abitat a couple weeks ago when he got this law job, so this new Abbie was still trying to adapt the Abitat environment to his preferences. He had not specified any settings, and Abbie had been adjusting and observing his reactions. She might try a different beach setting for tomorrow's wake up. Her own appearance was also a work in progress. He had resisted specifying his preferences, so Abbie adjusted based on general demographic preferences and his biometric reactions to her image and voice. A mirror-display appeared on one wall and the hologram of the housekeeper woman paused and checked her own virtual hair, makeup, and uniform. Another area on the display next to the mirror showed *'Subject profile:'* A list of profile facts spun by too fast to read. *'Gender: Male; Age range: 50-65; Profession: Junior Law Associate, AIAug'* and many more characteristics.

'Assessing reactions.' Images of slight variations in her appearance while on the beach and graphs of slight changes in her voice flashed alongside changes in his pupil size, temperature, heart rate, and other measurements.

'Assessing matching population preferences.' Two statistical preference distribution curves displayed on the wall, one based on input from other Abitats and the other from game players, statistical curves changing shape as her breasts changed size dramatically, first showing deeper cleavage, then shrinking to almost nothing, then returning to just a hint of cleavage. Her hair and skin color changed to pale and lighter blond, then through a spectrum of darker shades and various unnatural colors, before settling back to blond with just a touch redder than before. She briefly changed to a male appearance then back to the last female version. "I'll need a crowd scene to check his reactions to more combinations, or maybe he'd prefer just a voice?" Meanwhile, the vehicle was making its way out of the alleyway and back out into the busy street, heading for a recharge location and a laundry drop off.

9:25 AM, Tristan in the Law Office

Tristan stepped out of the service elevator on the fourth floor and walked briskly down an aisle with cubicles to either side separated by partitions just high enough to give an illusion of privacy when sitting. He stepped into his cubicle and said, "Tristan here. Reactivate." The displays on the walls of his cubicle lit up and as soon as he placed his left hand on a touch pad on the desk, they changed to show where he left off on his work earlier this morning.

Schematics and moving three-D images of Son'o'Ra Interiors latest line of collapsible furniture for Abitats showed in some of the windows.

Another window showed crude 2D images from the off-line archives including an internet clip from about 17 years ago. As the collapsible table and chairs expanded and contracted in the Son'o'Ra Interiors design material and in the old internet video it was clear that they were very similar designs. "Call Bella."

9:30 AM, Bella's Breakfast and Call with Tristan

Bella had moved from the edge of the river up the slope into the campsite. She was sitting on one of those impossibly lightweight fold-out chairs and had her tablet and plate with steaming spinach omelet on another similarly ethereal stand which served as her work table. She had a mouth full of eggs when Tristan's call appeared on the display. "Answer call," she said as she tried to swallow. She choked and was coughing as Tristan's image appeared. "Just a sec." She sipped from her coffee cup and swallowed a couple times to settle her cough. "Okay. I'm okay. Now let's talk about these designs."

"I can send you the images from the internet videos. You already have the 3-D illustrations. You will see even without comparing the specs that they are almost identical," said Tristan.

"I have to say, I'm surprised you were able to find something like this from the pre-game archives. I checked your citations: they were not online and searchable. How did you think to look for such old video files?"

"One of the benefits of being old." Tristan unconsciously ran his hand over his grey hair and skull cap. "After we finished up last night while I was checking the format of the report and looking at the Son'O'Ra designs, I suddenly remembered seeing something similar years ago. Anyway, I had an idea what I was looking for when I went into the stacks of internet archives."

"But Tristan, even if someone did create a similar product twenty-something years ago, the rules of Abitat intellectual property are clear now. It doesn't matter. From our client's point of view the outside evidence is unreliable and irrelevant."

Tristan frowned, but it gradually turned to a smile as he explained, "Maybe so, Bella. Maybe so. But I think we should make the argument that our client can keep ALL the royalties and stiff the first player who introduced them in the game. As I explained in my note, we can claim that the prior design existence 'BAM', before the AM game, makes it public domain under game law. And if the original inventor wanted to claim rights they would need to resort to a pre-game court of law. Where are they going to find one of those??"

"I read what you wrote, Tristan, and I don't agree," said Bella impatiently. "I think the only safe approach for Son'o'Ra is to pay the standard royalties for the first introducer of the designs into the game. It would set a dangerous precedent if we succeeded in cutting off benefits for design introduction and accept evidence that is not Abbie-vetted. It could have a chilling effect on innovation. People would start finding all kinds of prior evidence, real or not, and claim everything was public domain. Litigation might make a comeback. Bottom-line: You can't use evidence from before the game. The antique videos, if they are real, are interesting as an historical artifact, but are irrelevant to the case."

"Maybe you're right. You do have seniority over me as an associate, while I'm just a junior AI-augmented researcher, new to the law game, but I think the client might want to take a chance on this idea for keeping all the profits. It's a lot of points."

"I'd just say no, but Elsie said she wants one answer from both of us, and we've got less than a half hour now to write it up and get it back to her. We will say that all recent precedents inform us that it is safest to escrow the standard royalties for designer AM Game player zero, as identified per our research and as stipulated true by Abbie testimony, but that the client can choose, at their peril, to pursue the public domain argument, which might save them the standard royalty on gross sales, but could expose them to full loss of profits plus possible additional penalties if they are found to have knowingly denied royalties without reasonable justification."

"I can live with that," said Tristan.

"Write it up and let me review it one more time before we send to Elsie," said Bella. "And make sure you use Elsie's latest encryption keys for any transmissions." Bella's face went pale as she realized something. 'Tristan, we're not using Elsie's latest encryption keys for this conversation. Quick. Disconnect and get the key from Elsie and call me back again. Don't let her know we've already discussed this. Tell her I said you needed to get the new keys before we talk."

"I'll get the keys from Elsie and call you back, but I think we should be up front with her. This call had all our normal encryption including the time-specific keys you took with you on your little hike. It should be completely secure."

"Safe from snooping, but not safe from Elsie if she finds out we didn't follow her instructions. Hang up. *Disconnect*." The connection ended. Bella's red hair looked flaming in contrast to her face as her normally pale skin paled a few shades lighter than white. "Oh, Shit! Bobbie, I am in so much trouble. Elsie said to use an extra encryption key on our calls, and I didn't do it with Tristan while we viewed and talked about the details of our argument."

"I heard what she said before. She said, add the key 'on any of our follow-up calls on this subject.' She didn't mention your calls with Tristan. I think you are within the letter of her instructions."

Bella replied, "I sometimes forget that you hear and remember everything, Bobbie." She smiled. "That might be an argument, but I'm pretty sure what she meant and I'm pretty sure I'll be toast if she finds out." She still looked pale and worried as she waited for Tristan to call back.

"You worry too much."

9:40 AM, Bella, Tristan and Elsie Meet

After a few minutes an incoming call appeared on her display with an image of a bank vault. She dragged the encryption icon onto the vault and the call connected. Tristan and Elsie were both on the line. Bella swallowed hard.

Elsie said, "Bella, I've been talking with Tristan here and he has a suggestion for how to reconcile your two sets of research. I'd like to get your take on his suggestion before I go forward to the clients."

"I'm all ears," said Bella, biting her tongue. "I've reviewed and thought about Tristan's report, and I have some ideas myself for how to reconcile his with mine."

"Tristan, explain your suggestion," said Elsie.

"I think it's also Bella's idea. Basically, we suggested we recommend the clients pay the standard royalties to an escrow account for the player zero who first introduced the designs but also explain to Son'o'Ra the risky option of claiming evidence, based on my research, that the designs were public domain, and holding back on all royalties." Tristan added, "but we would also need to advise them as Elsie just pointed out to me that asserting public domain would reduce their ability to fend off other manufacturers from using the same designs. If they go down that path, they will have to quickly patent their manufacturing process for the design, but they should be doing that in any case."

"Bella, what's your opinion?" asked Elsie.

"Elsie, I agree with Tristan on this," said Bella. "The safe approach with escrowing of royalties, is obvious. We can explain to them the other option, with its significant risks."

Elsie broke in, "Let's push harder on getting them to try the public domain argument. Looking at the archival video evidence, I think it has a high chance of success. It may not be Abbie-vetted evidence, but it's compelling. Clearly this design was out there before game law. It's unlikely they would be required to pay more than the standard royalties and some interest if it gets decided against them on appeal. Your documentation shows that they should have no problem patenting their manufacturing process effectively blocking other vendors from using the same designs. Tristan, write it up. Bella, you can take the rest of the day off. You should get off the trail before the big storm hits. You should be just about to the end of your hike by now, if I remember your itinerary."

"Actually, we are a few days behind schedule on our hike, but I should be back after the holiday weekend. We were trying to find some elusive fishing spots."

"All the more reason to get moving. From what I've heard the storm is going to be a rough one up there," said Elsie with some concern in her voice.

"Thanks for your concern, but we'll be fine. We're prepared. And thanks for the day off," said Bella. "Tristan, you can reach me by voice call even if I'm hiking."

"I'll call you, if I need to," said Tristan.

"Tristan, get moving on that write-up. I want it in less than two hours. Bella, get moving to safe ground. I want you safely back here next week. ... *Disconnect.*"

The call disconnected. "So, Tristan now gets two hours to write this up?" Bella said to the air, then to Bobbie, "What's this she's saying about a big storm coming in? Is that true, Bobbie?"

"Yeah. I guess so. I've been saying we should keep moving, but you had your heart set on finding those fishing spots your dad and uncle told you about from their days as MinQuest guides, and I didn't want to rush you. The weather still looks nice today." A gentle rumble of thunder sounded in the distance and Bobbie added, "Maybe I should have mentioned the storm forecast."

9:50 AM, Honus at the Ranch House

Honus emerged from under the covers of his old bed in his old bedroom feeling much calmer. He noticed the time. It had only taken a little over an hour to get calm. Not bad.

He sat in his old comfortable gaming chair and picked up a tablet and game controller. Large game display panels almost covered two of the walls. He checked, but no response yet on the message he sent on game world PW3709. Not really a surprise. He could find things to do for a few more hours while he waited if he had to.

He connected to some of the old game worlds that he had played here years ago. His characters were still alive in their worlds and doing pretty well without his input, mostly in the same careers, but some now had relationships. A couple of them had kids. One of them seemed to be married or at least in a current parental relationship.

He took some pride in having helped them get started towards career success. Personal relationships they had probably managed on their own. While checking in, he tried not to interfere much in their current lives, but couldn't help himself, and made some innocuous tweaks, like making one spill his glass of water at a restaurant twice and having another call his daughter by a random name. Little things that might make them question themselves for a second but wouldn't change the course of their lives.

He did searches to see if he could find any new information about his mom and dad. He didn't find what his dad was doing now but did verify he still had avatars in some old game worlds that he could use to contact him if he wanted.

He had done something similar this morning when he reactivated world PW3709 and sent a message to try to reach the guy he thought he recognized on the street near the stalled development project. His dad might also notice that PW3709 was reactivated, even without a message.

As for news about his mom, no surprise, no luck, nothing new. The background search patterns that had been looking for his mom in fictional, historical, and augmented reality game worlds for over seventeen years now still didn't show any hits. He stood up to go to his mom's bedroom office and look around to see if he could find anything that he hadn't noticed before.

10:00 AM, Sam & Jo-Jo Arrive at Beach

"Arrived at destination. Watch your step. Have a nice day." The pleasant voice spoke from the walls and the door slid open showing that the vehicle was in a gravel parking lot off the highway near the beach. It was sunny outside.

"Thanks, Abbie."

Sam and Jo-Jo took their pack and beach bag, put on their sunglasses, and stepped out of the vehicle.

"It looks different," said Sam.

"I'll say," said Jo-Jo.

"It's only been a few months since we were here, right?" asked Sam.

"Two years now," replied Jo-Jo.

"It looks different," said Sam.

"I'll say," said Jo-Jo.

The natural marsh wetlands preserve they remembered had been hundreds of acres stretching along the highway with natural trails and raised wooden pathways, but now only a tiny fraction of its previous size was visible, maybe an open acre or two. The rest was covered over with a three-story stacked array of concrete driveways and Abitat docking facilities. Most were occupied with vehicles and people enjoying a stay with a view of the ocean. From the ground level gravel lot, Sam and Jo-Jo could not see the ocean over the sea wall on the other side of the road.

Sam and Jo stepped away as their own Abitat closed its sliding door and backed out towards the highway. It returned to the highway and merged into traffic to find a charge and complete the delivery.

"It's a shame they destroyed so much of the marsh. There were a lot of cool places to hide in there," said Sam.

"I don't know. The marsh was going downhill anyway after they built the sea wall," Jo-Jo replied.

Pointing at the structure Sam said, "But this new place would be a really nice place to stay the night." He admired the facilities and envied the people sitting at tables in front of open doorways of their Abitats, most with drinks in hand, looking out across the highway over the seawall at the beach and ocean.

"I don't remember this one, specifically, but all the docking and recharging fees I looked up close to the beach would wipe out our whole vacation budget," said Jo-Jo. "It costs even more on the beach side of the highway. But that's okay. We can hang out on foot as long as we want and then call the Abitat back to get us." She held up her hand and tapped on her wristband as if to demonstrate.

"How can I help you?" came the voice from her wristband.

"Oops. Nothing now, Abbie," she said into the wrist band. Then holding her other hand over her wristband she said, "Let her find a place to recharge and rest somewhere cheaper. Maybe she can finally deliver those packages that take up so much space. So, anyway, we can't stay overnight and sit here in the Abitat with the door open enjoying the ocean breeze like those guys," Jo-Jo said wistfully. "Who cares where you are when you're sleeping anyway."

"It would be nice. It would be nice to hear the waves while we fall sleep again," said Sam.

"Maybe we can stay late and sleep on the sand, like the old days. They can't patrol the whole beach," said Jo-Jo.

"That's an idea. We may want to take a couple blankets."

"Later. That's not for hours. We've got a lot we want to do today. Let's check out the beach now."

"I want to check out the marsh first. It shouldn't take long. It's small," said Sam as he headed for the wooden path that crossed the remains of the marsh.

"Hold on. Hold on," Jo-Jo warned. "See the sign. Five points entry fee per person. Do you really want to check out the mini marsh that much? We need to save our points for *The Theme Park* tomorrow. Let's do free stuff today." As he continued slowly towards the walkway she said more emphatically, "Stop! Don't step onto the wooden path or they will take points."

"You sound like your Abbie. Be careful how you spend your allotment. Don't go there. Don't buy that. Maybe I want to go there. When did they start charging here anyway? We never paid before. I thought it used to be a 'suggested donation,'" said Sam.

"Back then we didn't have the wristbands, so it didn't matter. They couldn't charge us."

"Should we dump the wristbands for a while?"

"Are you nuts? And what if someone finds them and takes them and takes our Abitat. Then what will we do?"

"We can hide them in one of our secret places around here. Some of those places should still be here."

"I'm not taking that chance."

"Okay. Okay. Then let's check out the sand. The river trail was just over that way. With all the traffic out there on the highway we should go under on the trail, if they haven't made it a tollway now."

They walked out of the gravel parking lot and down the side of the highway a short way to the bridge where the highway crossed over the end of the river. The river trail opened onto the highway on the far side of the bridge. A notice was posted by the trail entrance, saying something about a public hearing regarding a user fee for maintenance of the river trail.

"What was I saying about a tollway?" asked Sam.

"You've got to be shitting me," said Jo-Jo.

"Watch your language, young lady. It says the hearing was last week. Do you think they approved it?"

"You know they did. They always do. But I don't see any sensors. I don't think they can charge us for using the trail until they get the sensors up. The marsh walkway sign had sensors," she said.

"I guess it's good we didn't wait longer to come. We could have saved more, but things just keep getting more expensive. Before long we won't be able to afford to come within twenty miles of the coast," Sam complained. "Unless those found-object art pieces you make really catch on. Sell a ton of those and then maybe someday we can afford the splendid coastal life."

"Yeah. Or you write that best seller you were going to do."

"One of these days."

10:10 AM, Bella and Bobbie Starting to Hike

Bella and Bobbie were cleaning up their campsite after getting dressed and packing their gear in their small backpacks, which were set at the edge of the site near to the trail. Or Bobbie was cleaning up and Bella was watching her. Bobbie had out a tablet and was comparing the current state of the site to photos she had taken when they first arrived. She adjusted some rocks and leaves to make things match more closely. She looked around and found a bent stick that was in the wrong place and moved it.

Bella stood back and watched. "You really take that leave no trace idea seriously, don't you, Bobbie?"

"There is no way to leave it exactly the same, but I can try."

"It's a noble idea, but I don't think it's necessary."

"Minimal impact. This is our MinQuest. Remember? We took the minimalism pledge."

"I don't think that's what it ..."

"Am I being dumb about something? I feel like I'm not as sharp in the woods as in town. It's not really my element."

"Never mind. Sure. You're right. You're right. Minimal Impact. How can I help?"

"I think we're good. Just be careful not to kick anything else out of place as we get going."

It was getting windy and branches overhead in the trees were starting to sound like a rushing river, drowning out the sound of the water flowing in the stream below the trail. Bella picked up and put on her backpack and stepped onto the trail. "Where to? I don't need to work so maybe we can get over the pass today?"

Bobbie bent over and smoothed some twigs that Bella had moved when she picked up her pack, and then she carefully picked up and put on her own backpack. "Not sure. Bad weather could slow us down. And I can't get a weather report."

"What do you mean?" Bella asked.

"There's no connections."

"How can that be?" Bella asked.

"I guess everyone else with a comm device has already left this valley. The only connections I see now are to our own gear."

"A peer-to-peer mesh comm fabric with just us in it isn't going to be much help. Time to break out the satellite link. That always works," Bella suggested.

"I didn't bring that. Not minimalist." Bobbie explained.

"I told you I wanted that as backup for reaching my work."

"I know, but it was redundant. Extra weight. Bad minimalism. And mesh connections always work better than satellites."

'Uhhh. Until now maybe," Bella said.

"Yeah. Maybe," Bobbie admitted. "The chance that we would be somewhere with no other comm devices within kilometers was too small to consider."

"Like in the remotest parts of the mountains? Yeah. Okay," Bella sighed. "It's looking like it's going to get nasty out here. I guess we try to get over the pass today. That's a lot closer to civilization than going back the other way. At least see how far we can get." Bella started walking up the trail as the wind got stronger and leaves and twigs started moving on the ground. "But when we get higher, we should stop and check for connections. We're going to need to order more supplies. At least it shouldn't get too cold this time of year."

Bobbie looked back at the blowing leaves and twigs in the campsite area and sighed but followed behind Bella. Speaking loudly to be heard over the wind she said, "I can set an alert to let us know if I get a new connection."

"That's good. Do that," Bella shouted back. "Then we won't have to keep stopping to check."

Bobbie followed Bella and shouted over the wind noise, "By the way, I ordered more coffee earlier when the connections were still working."

Bella didn't look back but replied, "That's right. You said you were going to do that. Is it on its way?"

Bobbie answered, "I don't know. I didn't get a confirmation on delivery time before we lost comm. Normally, they deliver sometime in the afternoon, so I wouldn't expect it anytime soon."

Bella thought about it and shouted back. "I doubt if the delivery drones will be flying in this wind. And until we can connect, they can't finalize the delivery location."

Thunder rattled the forest drowning out part of Bella's comment.

"What did you say?" asked Bobbie.

"It doesn't matter. If they fly over the pass into this valley, they should be able to connect to us." Bella checked the time on her wristband and leaned against the wind while she walked.

"That's true. Or when we get higher up, we may get a connection." Bobbie kept pace a few steps behind Bella. "Let's see how far we can get before it starts raining."

"You think it could rain? This time of year? My uncle said that used to happen in the high country any time of year back when he was young, but not in recent years this late in the spring."

Thunder crashed above them, and it began to rain a cold rain, whipped by the wind. "Okay. Then." Bella pulled the hood of her jacket over her head and cinched it tight but some of the rain still hit her face. Bobbie walked behind her with her head uncovered.

10:15 AM, Tristan Tries to Call Bella

Tristan didn't have to make many changes to his writeup, so it was finished before Elsie's deadline. Since he had some time, he felt that he should call Bella and go over it with her one last time before giving it to Elsie. Elsie said to let Bella have her time off, but he wanted to stay on Bella's good side. He might not need her help on this, but she did have more experience than him in the law and he would probably need her help on other projects. She had said it was okay to call while she was hiking, so she probably wanted him to call. Checking with Bella before submitting it would show respect and professional courtesy. Besides, it should only take five minutes.

"Call Bella."

"Contact unavailable."

"Try again. Call Bella."

"Bella is not currently reachable.'

Tristan shrugged and said to himself, "Well, I guess you must be pissed after all. Turning off your comm? Or just blocking me? Really? That's not professional. Oh well." He sent the documents to Elsie and looked for his next assignment.

10:45 AM, Brock on a Walk

Brock had been making good time walking down the river trail as it passed industrial buildings, playing fields, shopping areas, and near some old and new neighborhoods of homes. As the path sloped down to go under another street, he saw one of the "Jackson Memorial, Homeless No More Festival" banners on the bridge above. The banner's slogan seemed mostly true: Other than Doug and himself the homeless seemed to be no more. He passed some joggers and bicyclists on the path but didn't notice any other campers in the riverbed or on the trail along the way. Not like a few years ago when there were campers all along the river and people hanging out in every park. Sam and Jo-Jo came back so Abitats must not be the death traps Doug thought. He had a vague notion that there might be other reasons to avoid Abitats, but right now, he couldn't think of any.

He had stayed on the river trail and didn't make any of his normal side trips to check out dumpsters or trash bins looking for books or food or valuables to trade. He was heading towards the ocean, thinking he would find Sam and Jo-Jo there. But he was getting tired. He slowed down and wondered if it had been smart to leave most of his stuff behind. Maybe he should go back.

But he was tired of living under bridges. He wasn't exactly sure where to go to get a free Abitat. Given some time, he might remember. He felt like he once knew. Sam and Jo-Jo might know, if he could find them, but that might not be easy. He was heading towards the beach because they mentioned going there. But the beach was huge. And really, they could be anywhere by now. They also mentioned going to *The Theme Park* and that's a whole different direction.

Maybe he should go back and try to find Doug. Doug was scary sometimes, but that was mostly good. Other people left them alone and he felt safe when he was with Doug. Doug never hurt him really. And Doug could usually score food and some Forgetdibles or even some NeverMind. Not in the last few weeks for the drugs maybe, but usually. They seemed to be in short supply lately. He was not thinking straight going weeks without them. He was starting to think differently and have bad dreams.

He was starting to think he made a big mistake by telling Doug that he was still here "for now." He should have known that saying "for now" would make Doug mad. But Doug never stayed mad. He was pretty sure he could find Doug again if he went back now. He knew all the places

Doug liked to camp. Doug always got mad, and he always got over it after a little while.

But now Brock was getting really tired and wanted to sit down. He could rest in the shade where the trail went under a street, or he could go off the trail into a neighborhood to find a park to rest in with trees for shade and maybe some food. He vaguely recalled there used to be a park near the trail a mile or two up ahead, so he decided he'd push on, keep going, and go there to rest. He hadn't gone to that park in a long time, so he hoped it was still there. For some reason he thought it might be gone. If it was still there, he could rest and after he rested, he could decide what to do next.

11:00 AM, Sam & Jo-Jo on the Beach

Sam and Jo-Jo were sitting on their towels on the dry sand looking down towards at the water. The sand was sheltered between a series of evenly spaced rock jetties just beyond the sea wall that protected the lower parts of the county from high tides. Fluffy white clouds were moving in, but it was still sunny on this beach. "This is nice," said Jo-Jo as the surf washed up across the sloping sand towards them, but stopping several yards away, scattering some small birds that ran short distances and stopped and poked their narrow beaks repeatedly in the foamy film of water on the wet sand before running again and again. Surfers were in the water down the beach, between other jetties, but not right in front of Sam and Jo-Jo. Some families and couples were sitting on blankets and beach chairs in both directions a little way off.

Sam took off his t-shirt and replied, "Yeah. It is nice. I wish we didn't have to pay that 20-point fee for crossing under the roadway. I can't believe they charged so much. But this is nice. I should have guessed they would put the sensors where you can't see them until it's too late. Beep. There go the points for a souvenir from *The Theme Park*."

"Forget the fees for now. Enjoy the beach. They can't charge us for sitting on the sand, or to take a swim. Go ahead and get wet."

Sam stood up and took off his prosthetic foot, then the pants of his jogging suit, tossing them in a lump on his towel along with the clumps of his jacket and t-shirt. He was wearing a small thong bathing suit showing a rose tattoo on his right butt cheek.

"You too. Come on in with me. I know you've got a new swimsuit under that jogging suit. Let's go." He hopped towards the water.

Jo-Jo smiled and nodded and started to unzip and take off her jacket. She folded it and draped it over the beach bag and then, still sitting on the towel, she wriggled out of her sweatpants, folding them neatly on top of the jacket. She still had on a tee shirt when she stood up and said, "Let's go."

Looking back from the edge of the water Sam said, "T-shirt too. You don't want to get it wet."

"Oh. Okay." Under it she had on a tight-fitting one-piece dark purple swimsuit. She folded the t-shirt and placed it on top of her other clothes.

"You look great!" Sam shouted over the sound of occasional breakers.

"Not bad yourself, rosy cheeks."

She ran to him as he hopped a few steps into the water. Jo-Jo held Sam's hand to keep him steady. They continued in just far enough that the water from a small wave rushed above their knees. Sam let go of Jo-Jo's hand and dove into the shallow water and swam a few yards, then looked back towards Jo-Jo. An orange drone flew in quickly from the right and hovered overhead. "20 points, lifeguard observation fee assessed. Per person. Please swim safely," came a sweet female voice from the drone.

"Son of a..."

11:15 AM, Honus Finds Something

After digging around in the family data files accessible from his mom's computer to see if he could find some clue about his mom that he hadn't noticed in all the years since she disappeared, the only thing Honus found that didn't look familiar was an historical biographical game world. Its summary and previews suggested it reflected a version of events from the time when his mom first went missing. That seemed like it might be important.

He decided to try to play the game to see if it had any clues. Its central character seemed to be loosely based on himself. Maybe closely based on himself. He went back to his own room to play it.

The interface he first used to engage with the summary of the story world gave all the characters random AI-generated appearances, so the characters didn't look that much like himself, his mom, dad, and the others from that time, but some of the events depicted in the summary seemed to be close to what he remembered.

The full game version was encrypted with a set of challenges that he couldn't immediately solve. The questions all seemed like things he should know, so it seemed like it was intended for him to open it. But his memory was rusty about details from those days. Without solving the challenges, he could see only highlights and tiny excerpts from different time points.

Based on the excerpts he saw he concluded that whoever made this must have had access to the family security videos and private recordings of his game sessions and game chat forum discussions or a good imagination and lucky guesses. The scenes may have been cast with different looking characters but included details that others would not know without that access. His dad could probably have accessed all of that and maybe Javier or Lae C could as well. Both of them spent a lot of time with his dad back then. Javier was really good with computers, so who knows if he was able to get access on his own. His dad could have helped either of them.

The most logical person to have created this kind of story was himself, as some kind of personal diary world, but he didn't have any recollections of ever creating such an historical game world diary. Even though he was fuzzy on some of the challenge questions, he was pretty sure his memory wasn't slipping that much.

11:30 AM, Brock at a Park

Brock sat on a three-foot-tall toad sculpture in a shady playground area of the park, thinking. He didn't remember how long he had been sitting there, but it felt like it was a while. He liked sitting on the toad. It felt comforting but also somehow very sad to sit there while he thought. Which way should he go? To the beach? Back to the camp under the bridge? To a house or a store or an office to ask how to get an Abitat? Where is home? He felt like he'd be fine if he could find Sam and Jo-Jo or if he could get back and find Doug. But he was also getting hungry. Doug always found them some food. Sam and Jo-Jo must have points in their Abitat to buy food. He hadn't found anything edible in the trash cans in the park. Lost in his thoughts he didn't notice people approaching.

A young boy ran ahead of his parents down the concrete path in the park and towards the play area. He stopped short when he saw Brock sitting on the toad with his backpack on the ground beside it. The boy looked at Brock for a minute and then walked closer and asked, "Are you okay? You look dirty. Did you fall in the dirt? Mom doesn't like it when I get dirty."

"I'm okay."

"What's your name?"

"People call me Brock. What's your name?"

"I'm Sandy J. Can I climb on Froggy?"

"Sure. Sure," Brock slid down off the toad. "Pleased to meet you Sandy J." He looked at the boy with a sense of melancholy familiarity that he couldn't quite place and whispered, "I once knew a Sandy, I think."

"Mr. Brock are you okay? Are you lost?" asked Sandy J as he climbed up and stood atop Froggy.

"I don't know. I'm just tired and a little hungry."

Sandy J's parents had been in a lively discussion with one another about who would win the Spring baseball tournament and hadn't noticed at first that an adult was in the play area. When they saw their son talking with a man they hurried ahead then stopped as they got close to the play area and looked and pointed at Brock. They actively discussed something in hushed tones before reaching some kind of agreement. Then they stepped forward.

"Sandy J. You have a new friend?" asked his dad.

"He's Mr. Brock, and he's dirty and tired and hungry."

"Brock, you say." She looked at her husband knowingly. "It's not nice to say someone is dirty, sweety. Are you really hungry, Mr. Brock?" asked Sandy J's mom. "We are Charly and Jameel. Do you live around here? Do you need any help?"

"Charly? It's okay. I live around here. Somewhere. Everywhere. I should find my friends. Sam and Jo-Jo were going to the beach, and Doug was probably going to *The Theme Park*. Sam and Jo-Jo might go there too. I should find them. They call me Brock."

"Okay, Barack," said Jameel and he got a quick "watch it" look from Charly, then he continued, "Mr. Brock, we live really close by. Would you come over to our house and have some lunch? We'd love to have you come over," Jameel offered. "That would be okay wouldn't it, Charly? You don't mind?"

"Not at all. Of course, I don't mind. I'd love it if you came over, Mr. Brock. Would you please join us for lunch?" Charly asked. "You could rest and take a shower too if you want. Then maybe we can help you find your family… or find your friends, I mean."

"Really? Can we really have him over for lunch? That would be fun. Mr. Brock, would you come over to our house for lunch today? I get dessert when we have people over. Please? Please!" Sandy J said enthusiastically.

Brock said, "No. No. I don't want to impose. I should go find Doug. I should go home. I left my tent and my books. I should go back. I should go home." He repeated the last word softly with a nostalgic question in his voice. "Home." He was having trouble making sense of things lately, with bad dreams and intrusive thoughts. Was it okay to go to a stranger's house for lunch? He didn't think so, but…

Charly said, "We were going to order Thai food from the Bangkok Spice Shack around the corner. If that's okay for you to eat?"

"You shouldn't. I don't know. I don't know. She always loved that place. I don't know," Brock mumbled quietly. Something seemed very familiar and sad.

11:40 AM, Doug Back at Home

Doug came back towards the camp wearing his backpack, but without his plastic chair. Instead, two nice folding director's chairs were tied to his backpack. He saw Brock's tent and chair still in place. He smiled and said, "I'm baack! You know a walk helps me calm down so I'm good now. Hey, Brock. I knew you wouldn't run off. I found us some new chairs. Nice ones. And some sandwiches." After no answer he took off his backpack, untied the chairs, and looked around the area, looking into the shadows deeper under the bridge which they used as their toilet area. His eyes needed to adjust to the shadows, but he saw some movement back there. "You back there taking a dump, Brock? I swear you are always taking a dump." Still no answer, he unfolded the new chairs and tossed Brock's plastic chair into the bushes, sat down on one of the new chairs and started to take his tent out of his backpack to get it ready to set up again. "Okay. Okay. Yeah. I know you need your privacy to take your dumps. I'll let you do your thing." He took two paper-wrapped sandwiches out of the backpack and set them on the other chair, then he started shaking out the tent which took shape as he shook it. "Hey. Hey. You'll want to hear this. After walking an hour or so I was close to *The Theme Park,* and I thought maybe I'd camp in our old spot near there. We haven't been there for weeks or maybe months. I'll tell you. It has changed. Our spot is gone. Completely gone. Or almost. You know the bushes where we camp near the drainage channel that leads into the back lot of *The Theme Park*? The place with the twisted tree by the fence we go over to get into that part of the channel? I was thinking about camping there, but it's all a construction mess. Do you believe it? They are tearing it all up to add more Abitat docks or something, right near the back of *The Theme Park*. Are you kidding me? How many docks do these things need? They tore down an old hotel or something there too. Our tree is still there, and the drainage channel still goes through there, but most of the area is all construction equipment and trenches and pipes and concrete work. You'd hardly recognize it. Hey! But I did find these cool chairs and sandwiches. Hey, Brock." A cat ran out of the shadows and towards the bushes nearer to the trail. "Brock? Brock?"

After searching the area and checking in Brock's tent Doug realized Brock was gone and he became increasingly agitated again.

"Run out on me? Huh? Trying to get one of those nasty Abitat vans after all? Really? Go ahead and try! Live in an outhouse on wheels. Gross me out! Go away to die? Sam and Jo-Jo and now you too? Damn it!"

Doug shouted at the underside of the bridge, and then as he stepped quickly, but precisely through the mine field of the shit-zone to a metal door in the concrete wall. He tapped a code on the keypad and opened the door. "Sam and Jo-Jo, and now Brock, You idiots. Why did you do it? They're going to kill you." He felt his way a few feet along the underside of a pipe low on one side of the dark space beyond the door and removed a small cloth-wrapped object, then backed out and closed the door. He unwrapped a large-bladed hunting knife. "But not if I get to you first. Maybe I'll protect you. We'll see. Run out on me. Huh? We'll see." Admiring the blade and stepping backwards away from the door he stepped in a large shit pile. "Sheet! Sheet! Sheet!"

He hobbled to his chair and sat down, taking off his shoe and starting to clean it, scraping away shit with the knife. He looked up and said, "I'll find you. If I'm not too late. Don't believe what they tell you, Brock. Where did you go? Beach or Theme Park? Either way they'll try to get you to take one of those Abitats. He rubbed his shoe on the ground and then sat back in the director's chair examining the shoe and the knife.

11:45 AM, Sam & Jo-Jo Leaving the Beach

In the shadow of a passing cloud, the door of the Abitat closed after Sam and Jo-Jo climbed back in, with their towels over their shoulders and their bags filled with pieces of kelp, shells, and other random found objects from the beach for Jo-Jo's art projects. They had left the beach in a bit of a rush.

"That was a pain," said Sam.

"We should have known alcohol isn't allowed on the beach."

"But a 100 point fine? Each? That really sucks," Sam complained.

"Well, no more surprise fees for a little while. We're safe back in the Abitat," said Jo-Jo. "And when did they start charging just to go in the water at the beach?"

"User fees for all county public facilities were established last Fall as an offset for the free Abitat program to prevent homelessness," came a voice from the ceiling of the Abitat.

"That was a hypothetical question, Abbie. It did not need an answer.

"Oh. Okay," said the voice.

"So, where to now?" asked Sam. *The Theme Park?* We could go today instead of tomorrow."

Jo-Jo was looking at her tablet checking on her points balance and looking at the still-expanded delivery closet. "We still haven't gotten the payment for the delivery we picked up a couple states back. It should have been transferred on by now. That alone was supposed to give us enough for entry fees for *The Theme Park* for a few days, with souvenirs and food. We saved enough to get in at least once, even without that delivery, but with all the extra fees we keep getting hit with we can't afford *The Theme Park* right now. Damn. If it doesn't get delivered soon, we might need to dump it so we can get some points from local deliveries before we go."

"Dump it? Can you even do that? I thought other people's packages were untouchable." Sam wondered quietly if the empty bottles and cans he had been stuffing in the transfer closet had anything to do with the delivery not working, but he decided not to say anything about it. He could take a look at it later when Jo-Jo was in the bathroom again, or if she set up outside somewhere to try selling her art. Sam continued, "Maybe we should find a busy sidewalk to set up and sell some of your artwork."

"Maybe after the delivery and I get some room in here to find things," Jo-Jo replied. "There has to be a way to dump it if the delivery never happens. Abandoned goods. I don't remember the rules, but Abbie could tell us."

"Failed delivery rules are as follows…"

"Not now Abbie."

"Okay."

"If we don't have the points to go in the front entrance, there is always the old way we used to get in," Sam suggested.

"We should just go somewhere to relax and wait for the delivery. Then we'll have enough points we can go in in style."

"Somewhere to relax? Hmmm? Like the beach? How did that work out?"

"Yeah. Yeah. Maybe you're right. They make it hard to relax around here without spending a lot of points. Okay. Maybe we should try the old back entrance after all," Jo-Jo conceded.

"Now you're talking," Sam rubbed his hands together in anticipation.

"We can check the park out today and see what's changed then go in the front gate tomorrow after we get the points from the delivery. Or, if we have to, we can dump the packages tonight and spend a couple days doing local deliveries to get some points for the park."

"Going in the back like old days will be more fun anyway."

"It will take a little while to get to the back side of *The Theme Park*. Let's get some lunch first. Maybe the delivery will still happen today." She looked in the mini-fridge and some nearby bags for lunch items. Sam picked up the tablet and started playing a game on the wall display.

11:50 AM, Bella and Bobbie towards the Pass

Heavy rain and wind for the last hour or so made climbing the trail towards the pass slow and dangerous. Most parts of the trail were muddy. Some parts were flowing streams. Water flowed over slippery rocks. The rain made it hard to see ahead. More than once they missed a switchback in the trail and had to backtrack when they realized they were off trail. Bella and Bobbie took turns leading. Bella was in the lead now.

"Should we stop and use a tablet to pinpoint where we are? Are we still on the trail to the pass or not?" Bobbie asked.

"You haven't gotten any alerts about restoring comm? Without peer-to-peer reference points AND without satellite comm I'm not sure if location will work, but we can try if you want," Bella replied.

"Once again. I'm sorry I didn't bring the satellite comm link."

"Okay. Enough about that. We're dealing with it. You're right. Maybe we should stop and try my tablet. We're higher up now. The tablet might have contact. Even if you didn't get an alert. My tablet's comm might be different from yours."

"Do you see any place ahead with any shelter from the rain?" Bobbie asked from behind Bella on the trail.

"I can't see much of anything ahead. Period. This rain is crazy," Bella complained.

"Then maybe we should just stop here. Do you need help reaching your tablet?"

"No. I got it." Bella reached behind her and pulled her tablet from a slot in her pack. She attached it in front of her on the holder that allowed her to work as she hiked.

"I just wanted to offer to help," Bobbie offered.

"It's okay. I've got this," Bella replied. "But this isn't going to be easy in this rain." Bella activated her tablet and opened a map. "No video details from other hikers. And it's hard to read when it's so wet, but I think it shows our location."

"Is it communicating?" Bobbie asked. "My comm is still down. Can we do a supply order? Or ask for help?"

"No. It's still not communicating. It only sees us. Nobody else."

"But it shows our location. How can it? Without the peer mesh network relative positioning it shouldn't work," Bobbie said.

"Oh. I think I know. The tablet must have a *G.P.S.* My uncle told me people used to use G.P.S. to find where they were before they had relative positioning. He and my dad used one on some of their Min Quest hikes. Vehicles used to use them."

"But why would tablets still have it? It doesn't seem minimalist. It's not necessary," Bobbie objected.

"Maybe it's a vestigial feature. Maybe it was easier to keep it than to remove it as they made new generations of tablets," said Bella.

"That seems wasteful," said Bobbie.

"Or maybe it helps somehow for deliveries. It can give a location with just signals from GPS satellites, even without other communication. That can't be as good has having thousands of peer network reference points to guide a drone in, but it could locate you on a map to start a delivery in the right direction."

"I don't think my comm has it, so it must not be in all devices," said Bobbie.

"Maybe yours is more minimalist, Bobbie. Do you think you can rig this tablet to send messages through those GPS satellites?"

Bobbie paused in thought. "Maybe. I don't know. GPS might be one-way. Even if it was possible, I'd need comms to get instructions for how to do that."

"Okay. Too bad." Bella wiped her hand and sleeve repeatedly on the display screen to remove water, causing it to scroll and change focus. "With the display so wet I don't think I can read the map. Here you look. Can you read this? "Bella turned and tilted the tablet towards Bobbie.

Bobbie looked and shook her head to say no luck, then suggested, "Can you hold it above you with the display pointed down, so the display isn't getting rained on?"

"Just a sec." Bella disconnected the clips that held the tablet in front of her and held it over her head. Looking up, even with the tablet blocking some of the rain, her face was still awash, and she was not able to read the display. "This rain is crazy. We need to get somewhere out of the rain."

Bobbie said, "It can't last forever. Should we just wait here on the trail? Or maybe there is somewhere near here we can set up a tent to wait it out?"

"I don't know. I can barely see ahead, and I can't read the map."

"We know there are places to camp on the other side of the pass. Maybe it's not that far? We might find a flat spot for a tent along the way if we keep going. Or else we could backtrack to the campsite we left this morning. That was just a couple hours back," Bobbie said.

"I don't want to backtrack. We're low on supplies and I need to get back to work in a couple days. Let's just keep going and get over the pass," Bella said.

"Okay. Let's go."

Bobbie watched as Bella tried to put her tablet back into the slot in her backpack. She got it halfway in, but it stopped. "Let me help you with that." Bella allowed Bobbie to help. Bobbie jiggled the tablet until it slipped the rest of the way into its slot.

"Thanks, Bobbie. Do you want to take the lead for a while?"

"Sure."

Bella stood to the side of the trail while Bobbie stepped around her and started up the wet trail which was almost like walking against a running stream. Bella followed, looking at Bobbie's boots slogging against the flowing water and asked, "Are you staying dry in your boots?"

Bobbie replied, "I think so. So far. How about your boots?"

Bella said, "Yeah. I'm glad we have gear that can handle weather."

"Sorry I didn't warn you more about the forecast," said Bobbie.

"No more apologizing. I was expecting maybe a little rain. A little rain is weather. This is something beyond weather. I don't know what to call this."

"A flood?" Bobbie suggested.

"A deluge?" Bella countered.

"A blizzard??" Bobbie suggested.

Bella was alarmed. "Oh shit. Is that what I think it is? Is it snowing now?"

"Uh. Yeah. Yes. It is," Bobbie replied.

"Is that even possible this time of year?" Bella asked.

"No. I don't think so," Bobbie answered.

"It's happening. My dad and uncle said it was possible any time of year at high elevations, but that was like thirty years ago. I didn't think that was still true," Bella said.

"We didn't plan for snow. Is your gear good enough for snow? Are you getting cold?" Bobbie asked.

"It is cold. I'm okay so far. I guess we will find out. Let's keep going." Bella indicated to Bobbie to push on.

They continued up the trail as the rain turned to snow which swirled around them in the wind.

Chapter 3

Mid-day

12:00 PM, Brock's Recollection

Brock came out of the bathroom and walked into the front hall after showering and shaving, wearing a robe and slippers that Jameel and Charly had provided him. His hair was clean, grey and black, and stood out large around his head. He said, "I hate to impose like this. You really shouldn't do this for a stranger like me."

"Let me take those," said Jameel. Brock handed his dirty clothes to Jameel, who continued, "It's no trouble. 'What you did unto a stranger' and all that. We can get these cleaned really fast. They'll be back by the time we finish lunch." He handed them to Charly who put them in a laundry chute and tapped a couple of times on her tablet to request a rush job.

Looking at her tablet she said, "Speaking of lunch, it looks like it was delivered." She opened the door to the delivery cabinet and picked up the bags of Thai food. The display on her tablet showed a view from the front of the house where a food delivery drone buzzed away and rose up out of sight while a laundry pick-up drone came into sight.

"Bangkok Spice anyone? Follow me. Let's eat on the back porch by the pool. Jameel is already out there. Sandy J! Come and get it."

As they walked towards the back of the house, they passed shelves with a number of family pictures including one of a family of three with a dad who looked a lot like a younger, shorter-haired version of the newly cleaned and shaven Brock. Charly didn't notice that he stopped and reached out to touch the picture while she continued out to the back yard.

Touching the picture, images flashed in Brock's head. First an image of flames surrounding him like he was alone in hell. Then a quick succession of images that included others in the picture.

After posing for the family picture, he stepped away and said impatiently, "Come on. One of those must be good enough. No more takes. I have to get back to work."

"Read me a story, Daddy."

"Not now, Sandy. Ask your mom. I've got to get back to work."

"Take a break. You work too much."

"Leave me alone, Celine. You complain too much. You spend a lot of time on law school too. Stop complaining about my job. I've got to get back to work."

"Look at how cute Sandy is in their dance costume."

"I know you wanted a girl but stop trying to turn Sandy into one. Don't keep putting him in that tutu. I've got to get back to work."

One particular memory crystalized:

"What do you expect from me, Celine? This is important. I have a real chance to solve the homeless crisis this time. Don't you want that? I'm so close now."

"Some of the people you are making deals with are scary. And you care more about homeless people you don't know than about your own family."

"That's not fair. This is important. You know how important this is. Some of this was your idea. Making this deal will be good for our family."

"Good for you maybe. When was the last time you read a book to Sandy? They loved it when you did that."

"Don't give me that. I do that all the time."

"Not in months. Why don't you go do it now? Go upstairs and offer to read them a book. It's the weekend. Can't you take a few minutes off on the weekend?"

"Not now. Back off. Stop pestering me. Leave me alone. I need to take my swim and get my thoughts together before my next meetings. This is important. I can read to him later."

"Really?" She looked at him with sad resignation, changing to resolve. She turned away and went up the stairs.

This was so typical of her. So demanding. He didn't need this. He needed to have some space. There would be time for family in a few days, or weeks, once he worked out a few more details and got his proposal funded and approved. With this success he would be on a roll. There would be no limit to how high he could go. He had a plan. Celine would be okay with him in a few years when they were living in the White House.

He took off his wristband and slapped it on the table a little too hard before shaking his head and stepping outside through a patio door. The wristband was waterproof, but he was in habit of taking it off when he swam. Outside, the path to the pool was partly blocked by construction tools and piles of dirt. The construction project was making slow progress, and it made a mess of half of the back yard. The pool was still usable, but before swimming he decided to first take a look at the progress on the project. What is holding it up now?

He climbed up a pile of dirt and stepped into the seat of a rusty old backhoe parked near the back corner of the property. This kind of old gas or diesel-powered tractor was almost illegal, but some of these old relics just kept on working. The contractor said he would keep repairing and using it until he could no longer get fuel or parts for it. Brock had pulled some strings to get a drum of fuel for him from the County in return for a discount on the project. Despite his favors the contractor kept stringing the project along.

From the elevated seat he could see over the back block wall to the river trail that ran behind his neighborhood. Tents were visible in both directions in the distance alongside the trail, but not right behind his house. The back wall for his yard and the ones next door on either side extended into the trail easement about 10 or 15 feet more than the other properties, giving these homes larger back yards and limiting the room for homeless camping on the trail. He had pulled strings in the County to create a special zoning district allowing their back walls to be set into the river trail easement. So what, if the district only applied to three properties. So what, if he actually took over more of the easement than the special district allowed. An easement. It was technically his property anyway and there was no way he was going to let some crazy easement rules keep him from using it. Not while he had the power to get his way. Use power and whatever means necessary to make good things happen. The trail was still plenty wide enough for walkers and bikes to get by. And the narrower path kept the homeless tents away from his back wall. Two of his neighbors benefitted too, so no one could say it was only a perk for a county supervisor. Soon all the homeless tents could be gone once his big project got moving.

He turned back to look inside his yard. The open trench extended along the side of the property from near the yard's back wall and out towards the street. The construction contractor said they would be back after the weekend to finish the work of connecting directly to utilities. Heard that before. They kept finding new reasons to delay the project. It's not like they should have any trouble getting County approvals. He could fix that. But they kept saying they needed updated maps or clearances or something. Some of the utilities ran underground near the street and others were in back along the river trail. For some reason they couldn't just use existing utility connections from the house but needed all new connections to water, power, and sewers. Higher capacity or something. It's a pain when contractors won't just do what you tell them and keep getting hung up on rules. He would need to express his impatience more strongly.

Looking down the length of the trench along the side fence towards the front yard, he could see his Abitat parked in the driveway near the front corner of the house not far from the trench. He sometimes used his Abitat for transportation but mostly to hold meetings virtually and as a man-cave to get away from stress in the house. It stayed in place in the driveway most of the time.

He looked at the extension cord and hose water line hookups connected to his Abitat. He had jury-rigged temporary connections while waiting for the new docking stations to be installed. The embarrassment of using those temporary connections would be over soon. To be replaced by top-of-the-line high speed automatic Abitat docking stations. No more need to hook up by hand or let the Abitat go out to charge or flush its tanks at a public station. He liked the idea of being able to fully recharge and flush his family's Abitats without leaving home, but another justification was that since he was pushing to make Abitats available to all the homeless in the County it looked good offering public Abitat docking ports in his own yard. YIMBY. Yes, in My Back Yard. Or Front Yard. YIMFY? Technically they would be available for public use but, of course, being in a gated community they weren't likely to get much use other than by his own family and maybe occasionally by some rude neighbors.

He needed to convince a couple more supervisors to go along with his plan and get commitments from a couple more investors or philanthropists. He was so close. Their resistance seemed to be weakening. What else would he need to promise to make them see the light? Some people just don't have vision. Some of the investors wanted special deals and he was considering giving in to them, despite Celine's reservations; whatever it would take. After his swim he would go into his Abitat and make those calls.

But he should calm down first. He was still agitated. A swim would be good for that. Or maybe if this damn docking station project messing up his back yard wasn't taking so long, he would be calmer. He could dig a trench by hand faster than this contractor was moving. What was their problem? If you need to trench under the back wall to reach the utilities in the trail just do it. Or knock down part of the wall and rebuild it afterwards. He looked at the controls on the backhoe. The keys were here. Maybe he could do this too. He turned the key, and it started it up. He tried the controls. It was tricky, but he could figure it out. He was able to turn the digging arm and extend it down into the trench. He scratched and scooped a few pounds of dirt and raised the scoop back up, turned the unit and dumped it on a dirt pile. That was pretty easy. I can do this. He found himself repeating the process several times, and losing track of how many, but getting the hang of it and taking more dirt away with each scoop. Soon he had extended the trench deeper, starting to dig under the footing of the back wall. This is not that hard. Get rid of a reason for delay if the trench is already dug to the trail. He was getting good at this. He had dug below the wall's footing, and the wall didn't fall. He dug deeper to extend the trench under the footing to the other side of the wall. He scraped against something hard deep in the trench towards the other side of the wall. Maybe a big rock? He scraped at it a couple more times to try to break it loose. The scoop got stuck and started bouncing between the rock below and the concrete footing above. The rock didn't seem to budge, but as he repeatedly bumped up into the concrete footing, a crack formed that extended up into the wall. Several blocks fell, some into the trench in his yard and some back into the river trail area, leaving a gap in the wall. Oh well. It was bound to happen. It can be rebuilt. With the footing cracked, the scoop moved free. He turned the backhoe scoop away from the trench, leaving the motor running. and climbed down into the trench to pick up the blocks that had fallen there. On closer inspection the big rock that he had bumped into seemed to actually be some kind of metal object. He had put a pretty good dent into it with the scoop. Who knows what could be buried out here. Maybe it is some kind of treasure. Probably too far from the beach and on the wrong coast for pirate treasure. But he could dream. He could take a closer look later. As he looked at the progress he had made on the trench he felt satisfaction. He felt like he had really accomplished something. He decided to move the fallen blocks, take a quick swim, and then make those calls. After lifting some blocks out of the trench, he climbed through the gap in the wall into the trail area behind to get to the blocks that had fallen there, while the backhoe motor sputtered next to the trench in his yard.

While picking up blocks and stacking them next to the wall he looked back through the gap along the length of the trench to the front yard and saw another Abitat pull up in the street. It was probably his wife's. She must be planning to go somewhere. He continued picking up loose blocks and stacking them next to the wall. The homeless people down the trail didn't seem to be interested in him. He realized something. Shit. If she is going somewhere she'll want him to keep an eye on the boy. He doesn't have time for that. "Shhhh…it."

Oh. Maybe not. Celine walked from the house holding a small duffle bag and leading Sandy to the Abitat. Sandy was wearing his ballerina tutu again. He should be relieved not to have to watch the kid, but he still felt anxious, and angry again about the tutu. Where are they going? "Shhhhhh…it." He still felt something was wrong and finally realized it was not him saying "Shhhhhh…it"

The ground seemed to be hissing the word 'Shit' for him. The hissing was getting louder. Now he noticed dirt spraying up from the trench and a foul smell. It sprayed in a growing arc towards the house and the front yard. The arc of spraying dirt reached along the trench at the side of the house almost to where the wife's Abitat door was closing. The backhoe sputtered twice. There was a flash. And he staggered quickly backward.

The shock of the light and heat was intense, and he kept rolling backwards until he found himself in the wetness at the bottom of the concrete river channel with the sky above him filled with hellfire. He crawled and then ran in the wetness down the channel to get away from the heat until he was under a road that passed over the channel. The fire seemed to be growing and following him. Under the bridge he found a steel door to an underground utility room and tapped the county access code on the keypad for unlocking the door. It shouldn't work without his wristband, but it did. It opened. Stepping inside and closing the door as the overwhelming heat swept the area, he collapsed in the darkness. A darkness he didn't want to leave.

Maybe the flashback took just a second, or maybe it was a lifetime, or several lifetimes. Brock couldn't tell, but it knocked the wind out of him. He was bent over holding the picture and hyperventilating when Sandy J ran down the stairs and caught up with him. Brock sobbed, "I don't want to remember. I don't want to. It's not real."

Sandy J said, "Come on. It's lunch time, Mr. Brock. Are you okay, Mr. Brock? Hey! Is that you in that picture, Mr. Brock? Hey, Mom and Dad. Did you know we have a picture of Mr. Brock. Is that your family, Mr. Brock? Are you crying? Don't cry. It's lunch time."

Charly came back in from the back porch and saw Brock holding the picture.

"Oh. No," she said and walked over closer to Brock and held the edge of the picture frame between her thumb and index finger, deciding not to put the other hand on his shoulder. She continued, "It's okay. Barack. It's okay. I'm your cousin Charly. Charlene Jackson. Second cousin. Yeah. We weren't close but we met once when we were young. We are family. You're with family again. Everybody said you all died in the big gas line explosion. We're so glad you are alive. Where have you been all these years? Jameel and I rebuilt your house. The whole neighborhood rebuilt. We named our Sandy J after your boy. Sandy Jackson Malik. You're with family again. So sorry for what happened."

"Family? I don't have family. I don't want to remember. I don't want to remember. It's not real. I should go."

12:15 PM, Andre's Lunch at *The Theme Park*

Andre was taking a break. He still wore his bat costume but had taken off his mask. He was sitting in a quiet shady alcove out of the flow of tourists coming in and out of *The Theme Park*. Looking through some bushes he could see Abitats coming and going from the drop-off curb, with individuals or small groups of people stepping into or out of each.

Pulling aside leafy branches, he could still keep an eye on the flow of people while he rested and sipped a bottle of water and ate a sandwich he had taken from a small ice chest. He could see some kind of large rodent creature in the crowd posing with a family of tourists. He honestly didn't know what story world or movie that creature represented. He hadn't been keeping up with popular culture lately. The giant rat thing bowed to a group of tourists as they went towards the park entrance, and then it came around the planter and spoke to him.

"Hey. I thought I might catch you here. Any big drug busts today, partner?"

"Not so far, Rodent King."

"That's not… You seriously don't know this character? And you claim to have a kid?"

"She's just three months old."

"That's not too young. You must be a negligent parent," said the rat.

"And you're still not going to tell me?" protested the bat.

"You'll learn soon enough. Every parent learns."

"So, you say."

"And once they get in, you'll never be able to get the songs out of your head, as much as you might want to." The rat stood listening to a song in his head. He chanted, "And don't you mooove my cheese…" and then shook his head to try to make it go away. "Almost makes me want to try some Forgetdibles or even NeverMind myself."

The bat replied, "If they worked that way. If you could pick one thing to forget. Everyone has something they'd like to forget. By the way, word is that a new supply of NeverMind is supposed to hit the streets today."

"That's what people keep saying. I've had people asking if I have any, but I haven't gotten any offers yet," shrugged the rat. "And no alerts on the sniffer." He tapped on the nose of his rat face.

"Me neither. Cool that you put the sensor in there. Makes sense for a 'sniffer'."

"Where's yours? In your bat ears? Sense everything by sound?"

"No, it's just here on my utility belt." He patted a small black bat-shaped box about the size of a deck of cards, attached to his belt. "But I do get an audible alert when it detects something. So yeah." He tapped his ear. "No NeverMind alerts so far today. Lots of 'tax free' and 'special price' offers for other drugs though. A few claiming to be Forgetdible candies—but they didn't trigger any alerts. Probably really just dangerously high corn syrup sugar candy—or cannabis edibles, but no one even claiming to have any NeverMind. I've picked up a pretty good selection of samples to send in for testing. Prices were surprisingly good. Only one wanted cash instead of Amps." He opened some compartments on his utility belt to show a collection of pills, vials, and wrapped candies, and some paper money.

"What is it about grownup people in cartoon costumes that makes people think we want to buy drugs?" asked the giant rat.

"Well, we do. Don't we? It's part of our job."

"There is that I suppose. Speaking of jobs, are you back full time at work now?"

"I'm trying to do full time now. I'll take whatever shifts I can get that fit with childcare. Alex is in childcare for a full day today, so I'm here all day. The daycare lady is really good, but it still seems strange to leave Alex all day with someone."

"You're really domesticated since you and Elsie got together. No more wild man Andre?"

"Wild Andre seems like another life."

"Really? You taking turns now on parent duty with Elsie?"

"Sort of. She is her own boss so she can take as much time off as she wants, which means she works almost all the time. She says she is taking time off during the long weekend, so I'm planning to work tomorrow. I've still got a couple weeks leave in reserve just in case."

"Well, congratulations on the baby and on the big bust. Nice job for a part timer. Wasn't it your first day back?"

"First week. First time back in this costume. I was filling in a couple hours that day for someone who was out sick. It was a fluke."

"Says the modest one. How did you catch that guy? Did someone tip you off?"

"Pure luck. I didn't do much. It was a short day for me, and just before I go home a guy bumps into me and asks me if I'm ready for some NeverMind. The sniffer gave a positive indication. I ask for a single and he acts like I should want a lot more. I say no thanks. I go and drone in my samples and videos and head home. Turns out the sample was NeverMore, the uncut base for making NeverMind. Pretty dangerous if someone took it like that. I heard all hell broke loose after that, but I wasn't here when the squad swarmed the park. They followed the guy to an Abitat full of uncut NeverMore."

"The local NeverMind supply dried up since then. Forgetdibles too," said the rat.

"But you think it is coming back today, Rat man?"

"Yeah. That's what they say. I guess your lucky break got a big shipment of the stuff off the streets but didn't find the source. The guy we caught wouldn't say where he got it from or why it wasn't cut. Scared to talk and didn't seem to know much. But now word on the street is another shipment is on the way," the rat explained.

"So, we're supposed to keep an eye out for the stuff. But I still don't understand why do we care so much about this drug? Sure. The product was being sold outside of normal channels and was too strong last time. We want to catch adulterated or dangerous products, like always, but normally drugs are a personal or medical choice. Isn't NeverMind just a stronger form of Forgetdibles? Why so much attention?"

"You've been out of touch, haven't you? First of all, even when it is cut NeverMind can be dangerous, but it's not just the drugs themselves. It's the identity theft," replied the rat.

"Identify theft?" asked the bat. "Catch me up on that, Mr. Rat."

"You skipped the briefings, didn't you? Bat brain."

"I attended all of them on the days I was on duty. Some were virtual and I may have been watching Alex too. Multi-tasking. So, I might have missed a point or two."

"Okay. Shit. Some recent users of NeverMind are reported to get whole new personalities. Different memories. Different identities."

"Dressing up as rats or bats? That kind of thing?" asked the bat.

"Ha Ha." The rat peeked out through the foliage to keep an eye on the crowds coming and going from the park while they talked.

Andre continued, "Forgetting stuff is a big part of what these drugs are all about. Isn't that the point? Aren't people who take them trying to forget their troubles for a while?"

"Maybe. Some call that a side effect, but that probably is the goal for some Forgetdible and NeverMind users. For most though, it's a chance to disconnect from the stress or disappointments in their lives and experience the, what do they call it, the *blankness bliss*. That's fine. Everyone could benefit from that sometimes. But that doesn't explain the ones who come out of it acting like completely different people. Not just blanking for a day or two and maybe losing a few random memories of their families or jobs, or maybe a relentless song—I wish—but suddenly knowing other people and having completely different interests."

"That does sound different."

"Nobody's sure where the new identities are coming from or why. That's why we're both out here looking for clues. Track where the drug is coming from and maybe we'll find out who is taking over people's lives and how and why." The rat continued looking through the foliage at the crowds passing by.

Andre mentally called up the briefing he had missed, using the DBI features in his costume cap, briefly staring into space while it began playing at high speed in his head. He learned that the labs hadn't found anything in the recent samples of NeverMind itself that would transfer memories or identities—no detectible nano-agents. The chief wanted more samples and info on where it was coming from. The people producing the latest version of NeverMind must be behind the identity thefts. After getting the gist, Andre said, "Sure. Okay, so these identity theft victims all seem to be users of NeverMind, but most people using it still stay the same person. Right? Just feeling good or forgetting some of their troubles for a while without taking on new identities. Shouldn't we be looking at other patterns besides the drugs? Other patterns common with the people who are losing their identities?"

"Maybe. Somebody should. But not our job. We do our assigned part. If NeverMind shows up again today in the crowds at *The Theme Park*, we report it, get it tested, and track the sellers. Maybe we can get some clues about where it's coming from. Maybe something was added to just some of the drugs. Getting more samples might help find that."

"I don't understand why people buy and sell here in person instead of just ordering drug deliveries in their Abitats. That would be harder to trace."

"How long have you been multi-tasking during the briefings? Sure, it might be harder to trace, but these people tend towards paranoia, and most people don't want their Abbies to know about drug transactions."

"I guess I can see that. Hiding certain things from Abbie to avoid the persistent gentle nagging about bad habits?"

"There's that."

"But Abbies keep quiet. Don't they? Abbies have to respect privacy. It's built-in to their core mission. Isn't it?"

"Sure. That's what the slogans say, if you believe it, and up to a point it's probably true. 'My Abitat is my castle.' 'What happens In-Abitat stays In-Abitat.' 'My Abbie, my Self.'"

"But? I hear a 'but' coming…"

"But …Abbies look out for the well-being of their inabitants and cooperate for the well-being of everyone. That can get complicated, especially when the inabitant's personality seems to change. Most of the complaints about people changing are actually coming from their Abbies."

"Wow. I didn't think that happens. Abbies are sometimes reporting things about their inhabitants? Hmmm. That's good to know."

"Oh? Are there things happening in your Abitat that you don't want your Abbie talking about?"

"I'll have to think about that. No. Of course not." The bat thought for a few seconds then continued. "I'm pretty sure this wasn't in the briefings I skimmed. Where did you get this?"

The rat replied, "I've been doing some extra reading on the case reports. And I've had my Abbie do some research too."

"Okay. So, let's keep looking for people peddling the strong stuff." The bat finished eating and took up a position near the foliage watching the crowd coming into the park so that the rat could relax and stop looking. The bat continued, "What happens if we're successful and keep disrupting the supply? If people go weeks without the stuff? Do they get their old memories back?"

"I don't know. With Forgetdibles, the forgetting is all temporary. It lasts longer with NeverMind. But with the current disruption in the supply for both, we're already seeing more reports of domestic violence. And an interesting note, in the reports about people on NeverMind with changed personalities, a lot of the reports say they're actually nicer people after. The reports say they've changed, but most say they're nicer. I wonder if we should just let them be."

"Maybe we're trying to disrupt a public service rather than a crime?" asked the bat.

"That's my theory. Nobody's found a financial motive yet. The identity victims don't seem to be funneling money anywhere. Other than starting to pay back child support and giving to charities and stuff. No one group seems to be profiting that anyone's been able to track in the reports."

"People being taken over for no apparent reason. And having new more moderate personalities. Sounds like an old movie. You call it identify theft, but maybe it would be more accurate to call it body snatchers. You sure it's not alien invaders?"

"Hey. That must be it." The rat settled into a folding chair and opened the ice chest. "Did you take one of my sandwiches?"

"That was yours? Thanks for bringing that. It was pretty good."

"I'm working the longer shift today. That was for my dinner," said the rat as he took the last sandwich out of the ice chest. "Thanks for leaving one at least."

"Sorry. I can pick something up for you inside the park and bring it to you before I go home or have something droned over and I can pay you back."

"Never mind. Forget about it. Wild Andre can buy me a beer after work some time."

"Sure. On that note, I guess my break time is over. I see someone I should follow. A weak 'maybe' tone from my sniffer." He put his bat mask back on and headed out of the alcove and towards the park entrance, mixing with the tourists and following a young woman with baggy pants and loose-fitting sweatshirt as she went into the park.

"Okay. Let me know if you detect something real. Meanwhile, I'll cover things here," said the giant rat to no one as he unwrapped and bit into his sandwich.

12:30 PM, Honus Takes a Break

Honus tried multiple times to unlock the game world. He could answer some of the questions, but stumbled on others, being too slow or giving wrong answers, and could still only access the previews, which he also watched a few times, modifying the appearance of the characters to be closer to the appearance of the people he remembered.

As he spent time failing to unlock the world, he got repeated reminders from his butler voice that he needed to walk and get some lunch. Finally, he got up and grabbed a bite to eat from the refrigerator in his Abitat and went out through the backyard to go down the path and walk around the old farm behind the house. Along the way he noticed that a breeze was moving a wind chime making musical notes that seemed both pleasant and somehow sad.

12:40 PM, The Tourists Arrive at the Airport

Minh and Max were twins. They fought a lot but that's because they did almost everything together and fighting comes natural with that much familiarity, especially when you are six. One of the reasons they fought was that they seemed to know what each other was thinking most of the time. Besides leading to inexplicable fights, that bond also let them start adventures together with no more than a wink or a nod and no obvious prior planning. Their parents delighted in some of their exploits and inventive games, but tired of their unrelenting energy and pranks that, while imaginative, sometimes really could be annoying. They were on a family vacation trip to the coast. The parents hoped the new sights and experiences would distract their attention and tire them out. Mom also hoped to track down her estranged uncle on this trip and see what other family might be here. Maybe he has kids or even grandkids that the twins can play with. It would be nice to have more family to help keep them busy. And a compatible kidney for her mom would be a plus.

After a flight from Kansas City, near where they lived, they exited the plane. Dad checked his wristband and saw that their rental Abitat was due to arrive at the terminal curbside in 32 minutes. "I guess it takes time for the rental to pick up our luggage. We've got a half hour." That was longer than he expected, but it would give them time to let the twins run around and burn off some of the energy they built up during the flight.

Hitching up the carry-on bag strap on his shoulder, Dad said, "Kids, Are you hungry? Do you want something to eat before we leave the airport?"

"No. I want to see the ocean now," said Minh in his most insistent 6-year-old voice.

"Wait! I'm starving. I need lasagna right now!" said Max in her most endearing 6-year-old voice.

"Maxine, honey," said her mom. "I don't know if we can get lasagna here. Not the way you like it, anyway." Looking around the terminal she continued, "How about a cheeseburger?" pointing to the nearest food counter. "Or we can find a food court and see what else they have. Don't you want to walk after sitting so long on the flight?"

"I'm tired. I need to lie down," said Minh as he ran squealing across the concourse to a set of seats and stretched out across three of them.

Max followed him. "I want to lie down here too. Dad, Make Minh get up so I can lie down here."

"There are other open seats right there," Mom suggested.

Max tickled her brother, and he squealed and wriggled off the seats and onto the floor. She jumped onto a seat, stood up and said "I'm the princess! I'm in charge here!"

"Noooo!" insisted her brother from the floor. "Defeated by the evil princess once again. I will have my revenge."

12:50 PM, Tourists Eating at the Airport

A few minutes later sitting at a small table in the food court, Minh was eating a slice of gluten- and lactose- free pizza and Max was slurping a frosty and lumpy edamame smoothy through a thick straw. Mom was finishing off a glass of Central Coast Chardonnay and Dad a local craft-brew beer. He had a computer pad out of his shoulder bag and was checking on the time needed to get to the beach or to *The Theme Park* or to the last address he had for his wife's uncle's machine shop. "We can get to a place we can see the ocean in just a few minutes. We should go soon though."

"Yay. The Beach! We get to go to the Beach! We get to go to the Beach! Beach! Beach! Beach!", in unison.

1:05 PM, Tourists Leaving the Airport

As they walked out of the terminal a simple grey over-sized Abitat with obscured windows front and back rolled to a stop at the curb and side doors opened.

"Is that our vacation house? Is that where we are going?"

Dad pointed and said, "Go ahead."

They ran and climbed in and started exploring. "There's a kitchen. It's little. There's a bathroom. But where's the shower? There's beds in front by the windows! My stuff is in this drawer, so this must be my bed here. This looks like Dad's stuff. Look, I can hide in this closet. Will it put me in the storage cloud? Can I cook something? What's in the refrigerator? How does this bathroom work? Hey! The shower pulls out of the wall!"

Within a few seconds all four of them were onboard and Mom said, "Abbie, To the beach!" and the doors closed and the Abitat moved smoothly into an opening that formed in the airport traffic. Minh and Max had folded down their beds and were lying on them looking out the front windows at the traffic and airport scene ahead. "I guess they figured out how to operate the windows already," said Mom as the front windows switched back from clear to obscure, then to showing a weather map and then ads for toothpaste. "We'll have to ask them how that works." She smiled at Dad and sat in one of the comfy chairs in the middle of the unit. "How long did you say it will take to get to the beach?"

"Well, let me see again," pulling out the tablet from the shoulder bag that was sitting on the little table between the chairs, then adjusting the table to make its surface larger, he set the tablet down and brought back up the app he had been using earlier. "There is a sandy sea wall beach we can be at in about 10 minutes. The Abitat can drop us off there and go find parking somewhere. We would need to get changed and take with us whatever we want on the beach. Or in 22 minutes we can get to a hookup spot on a bluff over a beach. We can stay with the Abitat there overnight. Oh. And they have a coupon special. You get free points to use in their casino, two free adult drinks each, and they give you the hookup spot for half price if you pick up a coupon in the casino."

"A beach, free drinks, and a casino. Sounds perfect. Let's go there."

"Abbie, Take us there."

1:10 PM, Honus Walking through the Farm

While he was walking in the farm, Honus ran into Sergey who was still managing the place. Honus thought Sergey must be about 90 now, but it looked like he was still doing a lot of the maintenance tasks himself. He said he had helpers, but Honus didn't see them.

Sergey said his organic farm was still making a profit on the fruit and vegetables he grew there. Honus accepted and ate a freshly picked orange Sergey offered from one of the trees. It was as good as he remembered. He would need to take some with him when he went back to the resort.

He briefly thought about having the resort buy from Sergey's farm but thought better of it. No reason to make any obvious connections back to here. After leaving Sergey he walked downhill through areas with different kinds of trees and gardens, and some areas filled with solar panels.

A half-acre at the far end and the lowest part of the farm had been converted long ago to an Abitat Village, giving docking space usually used by several families, and sometimes by random visitors when spaces were open. He touched the wall that separated the Abitat Village from the rest of the farm. Before turning around to head back up the hill towards the house he looked above the wall and saw the tall solar panel shade structures above the village.

He felt safe even so close to strangers on the other side since the wall and hedges provided privacy and because the farm on this side of the wall was still familiar to him.

1:15 PM, Tourists Heading to the Beach

A few minutes later Mom sipped from her wine glass and looked up from her computer pad. She had been trading messages with her friends and family about their safe arrival and keeping up on the news including following the challenges facing her favorite characters in some currently popular fictional and reality worlds of the AM game. She saw the front windows were clear again and the ocean was coming into view in the distance as they came over a rise and started downhill towards the coast. A display on one wall of the unit showed features of their destination: *Pacific Camping Park at Honus Beach Resort and Casino: Swimming Pool, Sandy Beach, Fire Pits, Shopping Mall, Shows, Casino, Hotel Rooms, and Abitat Camping Village with views of the ocean.* Mom said, "We're almost here. Max, Minh, we're almost here. You can see the ocean now." She looked around the unit. "Where did they get to?"

Dad reluctantly set down his beer bottle and looked up from his computer pad where he was in some kind of game involving creating recipes for new drinks. "They were on the bunks in front watching the scenery. Where did they go? They must be in the bathroom?" He stood up from his comfortable chair and stepped over to the bathroom door while Mom poked around the beds, drawers and cabinets in front looking for them. The resort on the bluffs above the ocean was coming into better view in the front windows, looking much like the scenes on the side wall display as the vehicle continued smoothly down the hill.

"Max? Minh? Are you in the bathroom?"

Minh's voice said calmly, "I'm in here, but Max disappeared."

Dad opened the door and looked in. Minh was standing on the toilet seat, pulling fiercely at the handle of the retractable shower stall which was retracted *almost* flush with the wall. "Max was hiding in the shower, and it went back into the wall. I'm trying to pull it open again. It's stuck."

Dad said, "You're kidding, right? Max, Where are you?"

A muffled sound came from the lower part of the bathroom wall. "I'm hiding. Can you find me?"

"You come out of there. It's not funny. It might not be safe. How did you get in there?"

Minh said, "It won't open back up. You pull on this handle, and it opens up, but now it won't open up."

Muffled, Max said, "I need to go pee. Let me out. Minh, stop holding it shut and let me out."

"I'm not holding it shut! I'm trying to pull it open. You are holding it shut."

"No, I'm not. You are!"

"You are!"

"I need to go pee!"

"Okay. Okay. Just what is going on in here?" said Mom as she looked around Dad and into the little bathroom. "Where's Max?"

"The shower swallowed her! And now it won't let her out. She says I'm holding it closed. I'm not! She's holding it closed from inside."

"You're kidding, right? Maxie, where are you?" Mom looked in a closet next to the bathroom.

"I'm in here and I want to get out now," said Max's muffled voice.

Dad pulled gently on the shower stall handle, and it wouldn't budge.

Mom pulled Dad out of the bathroom and calmly lifted Minh off the toilet and handed him to Dad outside the bathroom and grabbed the shower stall handle and jiggled it, lightly at first and then much more forcefully. "Maxie. Maxie. Are you really in there? Don't fool around.

Come out of there. Or are you hiding somewhere else? Did you figure out a way to make your voice come out of there?" Turning around to Minh who was still in Dad's arms, "Minh. Are you two doing another one of your tricks?"

Minh started to cry, "Mom! Make Max come out of the wall. I don't like this."

Muffled, Max's voice said, "I need to go pee! It's dark in here. I don't like it. I want to get out and go pee!"

Mom said overly calmly, "We'll get you out, sweetie. You just relax and we'll get you out." Turning to Dad and whispering urgently, "Figure out how to get her out of there!"

"I got to go pee too," said Minh. "Dad, let me down 'cause I gotta guppy." He climbed up and over Dad's shoulder and then crawled headfirst down his back and onto the floor.

"Let me out!" said Max's muffled voice.

Dad quickly picked up his computer tablet and opened the Abitats App and asked, "How do I get my kid out of the shower wall?" It displayed a diagram of the expanded shower stall and how the door opened including a video of the door opening and closing. "Not the shower stall. The shower *wall*. My girl is stuck inside the *wall*." It displayed the retractable shower stall closed into the wall and showed an animation with a voice saying "A gentle tug on the handle expands the shower stall. When you are done a gentle push on the two dots with the arrows, here and here, and the shower stall retracts out of the way again."

"Try pushing on the two dots and see if it will open," said Dad.

"I don't see any dots. What dots?" said Mom.

Looking at the animation again Dad noticed, "On the part of the shower stall that goes back into the wall. Dang! That's not going to work." Speaking to the Abitats App again, "Can someone help me? I need to talk to someone who can help me figure out how to get my little girl out of the wall. She's stuck in the retractable shower stall. Please help me."

An ad popped up, "To get special services on your Abitat, with a personal touch, see the helpful folks at *Abitat Specialty Services,* at a service facility near you. The nearest ASS facility is 18 minutes away. Do you want to go there now?"

"Yes! And Hurry! Please hurry. It's an emergency, and can someone talk to me to help me now?"

The grey rental vehicle had entered the entrance driveway to the resort on the bluffs above the Pacific Ocean and it continued briskly around the entry loop and back out on to the roadway, then accelerated. "Brace yourself, Prepare for Jerky Motion. Emergency mode activated," came a voice from the wall display. The Abitat continued to accelerate and weave through traffic causing drinks to spill and Mom, Dad, and Minh to lean back and forth and hold on to the wall as the unit swerved between other vehicles. Outside, other traffic smoothly adjusted to clear a path. "Estimated arrival time 11 minutes. Attempting to contact a human service representative. Please stand by."

1:25 PM, Jose, et al. at Specialty Services

Jose was in a green Abitat using its display and tablet. He had finished installing and testing some new interior features in the Abitat and was taking a short personal break before starting his next task. He saw an alert that game world PW3709 had been reactivated. He had an idea what that meant but figured he should wait until after work to check that out. He accessed some statistics about transactions in one of the Infinite Closet Storage services. Something in the statistics concerned him so he pulled up some code and made a few changes, then disconnected and closed out the displays and stepped out of the unit. "I guess I should ask Emily more about her ideas for how to improve those algorithms," he thought to himself. He looked around the work area as the green Abitat moved backward out of service bay three and out the exit lane towards the street.

Six parallel service queues led into the Specialty Services building from the street entrance. A variety of autonomous vehicles of various sizes and features waited their turns in those six lanes, waiting to get recharged, cleaned, refurbished, or other services. Most took the quick route and exited to the right down a lane that looped back to the street as soon as they got a flash charge to their batteries, dumped any waste, and topped off water supplies. They could get those same limited services at thousands of local shared park and recharge ports throughout the city, but the charges took longer there, which was usually okay since parking and waiting off the street was part of the value. Here two of the queues could provide compressed hydrogen or other fuel instead of just a charge, and that was not available at a typical park and recharge port, but vehicles using those fuels were uncommon. In the county almost all vehicles were electric powered. A smaller number of vehicles stayed after charging and dumping, crossing the quick exit lane and into one of six service and repair bays to get extra services.

All six charge stations were busy with vehicles queued up behind them, but only four of the six service and repair bays were currently staffed and only three were currently busy. Julia had an off-road style camper Abitat up on the rack in bay 1. She seemed to be changing out tires and replacing some damaged suspension components. Bays 2 and 4 were shut down. Jose was waiting in service bay 3 with no current work. A standard Abitat was in bay 5 getting a full exchange of interior components. The unit was lifted up, and its floor was opened. Its standard utility interior, with bed, bathroom, seating, and mini-kitchen had dropped down and was being guided on to the track to storage by Jean-François. An alternate configuration with dual entertainment seating, larger surround displays, and bar/refreshment console, and an inconspicuous fully collapsible restroom was coming up from the warehouse to be installed, preconfigured to match the desired settings of the customer who was planning to step aboard from his workplace with a coworker in a few minutes.

Bay six had another Abitat getting a deep cleaning. Modesto had relocated all loose items to holding cabinets and was spraying steam through the open doors to sterilize the interior.

A ringing sound came over the sound system for the work area, followed by a voice saying, "In-coming customer service call. In-coming customer service call."

All the coworkers looked around at one another with expressions of mild surprise, raising eyebrows just a bit. Who would take the call? Eyes quickly focused on Jose because his service bay was currently empty.

"Looks like Jose gets to take the call," said Jean-François.

"No. Let me take it. I've got it. I need a break from this steam cleaning," said Modesto. He was sweating and steam was escaping from the gun trigger nozzle at the end of his steam-cleaning hose with the trigger off. He stepped over to the valve at the side of the service bay and turned a handle a quarter turn and the leaking steam at the nozzle quickly stopped. He wiped his brow with his sleeve, picked up his work display tablet, tapped the screen, and put an earpiece to his ear. "Abitat Specialty Services. Modesto speaking. How can I help you?"

Julie and Jean-François went back to their work but watching Modesto. Jose stood watching and listening to Modesto.

"Slow down and say that again. What did you say? Your child is stuck in the bathroom wall? I don't think that's possible, sir. Okay. Okay. Sure, if you come in, we can take a look. Right away. No. I don't think I can tell you anything you can do until we can take a look. We'll keep a service bay open for you and direct you straight in. No, sir, you won't have to wait. We have all the information transferred from your vehicle, sir." Looking at his display tablet, "It says you are only a couple minutes away now. You'll be here soon. We'll be ready to see what we can do as soon as you get here. See you in a couple minutes."

Modesto ran over to Jean-François' service bay. "Did you hear that? This guy says his kid got stuck inside the retractable shower stall in his Abitat. He says he can hear her talking inside the wall and they can't open it back up again. How is that possible?"

Jean-François said, "I don't think it is possible. There shouldn't be any way the shower can retract back into the wall with someone still in it. There is no way to get inside the wall, And I don't think there is enough space inside the wall for a kid." He grabbed the compact bathroom module that had come up from storage for the vehicle he was working on. "See look at this one. There's no space inside of this compact bathroom when it's retracted. What model do they have?"

"Standard Model BR8. It's a rental unit. I guess they are tourists on vacation, from the Midwest."

"That's basically the same model bathroom as that one I just sent to storage. I can call it back up."

Julia and Jose joined them at bay five. "How much space between the retracted shower unit and the outer wall, Jose?" asked Julia.

"Pretty close to none when it's fully retracted," said Jose.

"He said it was not retracted all the way, but it won't open back up either. Maybe if we just drop the unit out? The kid would either come out with it, or stay behind against the outer wall," said Modesto.

"I don't think that would be a good idea," said Jean-François. "Look at how this bathroom unit goes into the vehicle. See the edges at the top and bottom and the lower edges of the floor opening. It would slice up anything in that space as it drops out." He was showing them the metal flanges at the top and bottom of the new bathroom unit and the sharp edge of the open floor of the vehicle.

"Don't say that in front of them. Here they come," said Modesto.

Jose walked around the bathroom module for the vehicle in bay five, looking carefully at it from all sides, running his fingers on the normally hidden surfaces inside the shower stall walls, and examining the opening through the floor of the vehicle, then turned to watch the vehicle entering.

A plain grey oversized rental Abitat vehicle with transparent front windows came in the exit drive and pulled into service bay four. A man and woman were standing braced against each other and the furniture in the middle of the unit looking worried. The unit came to a gentle stop and the side door opened.

"Hello. Let's see what's going on here," said Modesto as he stepped up to the open door and faced two worried-looking parents. A young boy was retreating to the parents' sleeping space at back of the vehicle.

"See here in the bathroom," said the Mom. "See the shower stall." She pointed. "Sweetie, Maxie. How are you doing, Maxie?"

"I want to get out!" came Max's voice from the wall.

The dad moved out of the doorway to let the workers have a better view into the vehicle.

Modesto followed Mom to the bathroom while the other workers all crowded around the open vehicle door trying to see into the bathroom. "May I?", Modesto said, and Mom stepped out to let him into the bathroom. He looked up and down the partially retracted shower wall, felt along the edges that were not quite flush with the wall and grabbed the handle to gently tug and try opening it back up. Then he pushed very gently. "Hi. Maxie. My name is Modesto. We're going to get you out of there. Do you feel that when I touch the wall here?"

"I want to get out!"

"What are you going to do? How will you get her out of there?" said Dad quietly to Julia who was leaning into the vehicle with Jose and Jean-François behind her.

"How did she get in there?" asked Julia to Dad.

"I don't know. The kids were playing. We weren't watching them that close."

Modesto stepped out of the vehicle with Mom close behind him. "Sir, Ma'am, Let me talk for minute with my colleagues." The parents leaned against one another and watched the workers step away from the vehicle's doorway.

"It seems be jammed somehow. It's almost fully retracted into the wall, and it won't move in or out from where it is. Something is in the wall," whispered Modesto. "It's bulging about 4 centimeters from fully retracted. I don't see any other release points. Pulling the handle doesn't release whatever's holding it and the touch points for retracting it into the wall are already recessed out of reach. If we dropped it out, we could get to the mechanism, but we know we don't want to do that. Or we could cut through the wall. Is there any other way? I still don't know how anything could get on that side of the wall."

While the parents watched nervously from the doorway of the vehicle the other three workers turned to look at Jose. "I have a couple ideas," he whispered. "We can make a couple of cuts near the top to release the wall panels, but I think we may want to try something else first." The others waited for more explanation. He continued, "If I remember the components used in that unit, the wall panels look like one piece, but they start as three sub-panels. They seem permanent and seamless once they are assembled, especially if they are glued properly, but sometimes they don't get glued. In that case if we apply simultaneous pressure to five specific points on the panel it might disassemble. If we get one of those sub-panels loose, it should give us some access without cutting and maybe we can release whatever is catching the retractable shower stall." The others looked at each other with mixed expressions of *how does he know these things,* and *I'm glad he knows these things.* "You said it has about a four-centimeter bulge, right?"

"Yeah," said Modesto. "More or less."

Jose turned to Modesto. "You're in charge on this vehicle service, Modesto. Do you want me to assist?"

"Yes. Yes. Please. Let me introduce you to the customer." Modesto turned and walked over to the parents in the door of the vehicle. "This is my colleague, Jose. He will be assisting." Modesto handed Jose the display tablet.

Jose looked at the tablet and said, "Hi. May I take a look?"

"Hi. Yes. Yes. Okay," said the parents.

They stepped out of the door and gave way for Jose to enter. He stepped in and looked around. Minh was in the back of the vehicle. Jose waved to him and said, "Hi, son, I'm Jose. What's your name?"

"Minh."

"Min? Strong name. I like it." Jose stepped into the bathroom and pulled a marker out of a pocket in his overall shirt. He ran his fingers along the wall and tapped in a few places and then quickly marked five spots low on one of the panels. "Hello there inside the wall. My name is Jose. Are you Maxie? Are you ready to come out?"

"I want to get out."

"Okay. It will be just a minute." He turned around and looked out of the bathroom to Minh. "I need someone small to help me. Can you help me, Minh? Can you come here?" He turned and looked at the parents.

Mom and Dad were standing in the doorway with Jose's coworkers behind them. Mom said "It's okay, Minh. Help Mr. Jose."

Jose said to Minh, "Okay, Minh. Can you sit here and touch these three spots on the wall. Take off your sandals and use your feet and your hands. When I say 'press' press on all three spots."

Minh looked at Jose in a knowing way. "Okay. Mr. Jose."

Jose put two fingers on the other two marked spots and said, "Now press." Minh and Jose pressed the five spots at the same time and a seam appeared in the previously seamless wall. "Okay. That was good. Now one more time, press." Minh smiled and pressed with a toe and two fingers spread on the lower part of the wall as Jose tapped sharply on the other two spots above. The seam opened and a middle panel of the wall swung slightly out. "Perfect, Minh! You did it! Did you and Maxie do something like that before? When you were playing in here, did the wall open up like this?"

Minh looked sheepish and grabbed his sandals and wiggled out of the bathroom and ran to the back of the vehicle by his parents' sleeping area. Jose reached into the wall and pulled out a stuffed panda bear. As soon as it was out the shower stall retracted completely. He grabbed the handle, and it was now working again to pull out the stall. He held the bear up and spoke into it. "Maxie. I think it's time to come out now."

Max's voice came from the belly of the bear. "I do want to get out now. Tell Minh to help me get out."

"Minh, did you hear your sister?"

Mom and Dad were in the vehicle now and looking a combination of surprise, anger, and relief. "Minh where is Maxie?" said Dad. Minh unlatched and pulled out a drawer from under the parents' sleeping area and Max sat up.

"Surprise!" she said, holding a matching panda bear. "Now I really need to go pee!" She started to climb out of the drawer.

"Me first!" said Minh racing his sister to the bathroom.

Jose handed the panda bear to Mom and said, "Let me close this wall back up and I'll get out of your way." He pulled out a tube of adhesive and squeezed a few drops on the exposed edge of the panel, then he pushed the panel back into place and pressed on three of the marked spots. The wall again became seamless. He pulled a cloth from his pocket and wiped away the marks on the wall. "Okay, Modesto. I'll let you finish up here. No one should be able to open that panel again."

Modesto stepped in and spoke with the parents to see if there was anything else he could assist with. The parents were almost speechless. Minh was outside the bathroom telling Max to hurry up. Modesto was saying, "So even though you pay double for emergency service, we don't have any service category we can charge you, so the total is still zero."

Julia and Jean-François kept shaking their heads and laughing as they walked apart to finish their work at bays 1 and 5.

Jose noticed that bays 2 and 3 now also had vehicles needing service. "Looks like things are getting busy. Let's get back to work." He picked up the work display tablet at bay three.

As they stepped back inside, Mom asked Dad, "To the beach again?"

Dad answered, "No. I don't want to relive the last hour. Let's try something else first. How about *The Theme Park*? Our passes are good all week, right?"

Minh and Max were wrestling in front of the bathroom as the door closed, and the vehicle began to move.

1:35 PM, Honus Walks Back to the Ranch House

On his way back to the house Honus stopped in the "barn" building which still looked the same: Rustic on the outside, except for solar panels on the roof, but clean and modern inside. Built on sloping ground and with multiple hidden basements that extended into the hillside, it was much bigger inside than it looked outside. The ground floor level still had his dad's office and workshop with machines and stacks of materials. Honus quickly opened one of the cypher locked doors and ran a few steps down the stairs to see and hear that many computers were still running in the basements. Returning up the steps he closed and locked the stairway door and then left the barn, locking its door as well.

After leaving the barn and going through the hidden gateway from the farm up the path into the backyard of the old house, he didn't go straight to the private entrance to his old bedroom. Instead, he walked to the other side of the yard and looked through the fence into the neighbor's yard. It was quiet. No one there today. There was a new-looking baby swing hanging from the patio cover.

He remembered years ago the neighbor girl would climb over this fence, and they would go down the path and explore the farm below together. Or he would follow her while she explored. She climbed trees and scrambled through gullies, while he stood back and watched "to make sure she was safe." She was a few years younger than him, so she seemed like a little kid back then. She and Sergey were the only people outside the family or in games that he felt comfortable talking to back then. He remembered that she made him laugh. He smiled as he turned away from the fence.

He entered the house through the laundry room and walked through the nearly empty rooms where his parents had raised him. Things looked almost the same as when his mom left. The same dining table still had two chairs, one for her and one for when she insisted he come out of his bedroom and eat with her. An Ansel Adams print was still displayed on a large framed flat panel on one wall. A single chair and reading lamp faced the display panel. His mom sometimes sat in that chair reading. Before his dad got sick there were two more chairs next to it. Mom, Dad, and himself sometimes sat and streamed videos together when he was young. His mom disposed of the extra chairs when both his dad and he started spending all their time in their bedrooms.

A trace of dust on the table proved his mom's continuing absence; she never let any dust accumulate. It was just a trace, so it must have been cleaned in the last month. His dad had moved out a while ago, but maybe he came by and cleaned, or more likely he arranged a cleaning service.

When Honus got to his old bedroom, he checked again for messages on game world PW3709. Still no response so he decided to spend a few minutes playing an old bloody battle game. But first he paused to think again about the little girl next door. She must be all grown up now. He regretted not trying harder to keep in touch. Maybe he could find out what she was doing these days. Remembering the new baby swing, he thought maybe she recently had a baby. He realized she probably didn't live there anymore after all these years, and it probably belonged to someone else.

He recalled she called herself Izzie back then, but what was her name today? Could be anything. He'd need to remember some other facts about her to look her up. Maybe her full name from back then would come to him later.

1:45 PM, Bella Pushing Forward on the Trail

"Isabella Muller, slow down," Bobbie said. Bella was in the lead again, stepping through the swirling snow. Bobbie was falling behind, feeling her way with each placement of a foot. Her left foot sank through snow up to her ankle before hitting a solid surface. As she put weight on that foot it slipped on ice, and she almost lost her balance, grasping at the rock wall to her right, but she didn't fall. She paused to regain her composure.

Bella stopped and turned around in time to notice Bobbie's near miss slip and fall. She said, "What's the matter, Bobbie? Are you okay?"

Bobbie said, "You're going too fast. You could slip."

Bella took a few breaths and said, "The trail is getting icy. Let's think. In good weather it would have taken us four or five hours to reach the pass. And then a couple more hours to reach a good camping spot on the other side. We've been on the trail for about four hours, and it's been slow, so we're probably only halfway to the pass. I don't know if we can reach the pass today in this weather. We need to find shelter. As much as I don't want to, I think we may have to turn around. We can look for a place to camp, and worst case we can go back where we stayed last night. Going downhill should be faster."

"The trail behind us is icy too, or washed out," Bobbie said.

Bella said, "Okay. We don't have any good options. We don't have gear for climbing in ice and snow. It's slippery and will get worse if we go higher."

"If we can reach the pass we can get comms and order supplies and new gear, or call for help," Bobbie said.

"We need shelter. A late spring storm can't last long. We can hike out after it lightens up," said Bella.

"I still don't have comms. See if you can get comms now or look at the map for a spot to camp."

Bella removed her tablet from its slot in her pack and swung it around in front of her again. The blowing snow partly obscured her view of the display, but not so much as the rain had done. She could read the display while brushing off snowflakes. She said, "Still no comms."

"What about the map?" Bobbie asked.

Bella answered, "No details without comms, but it does show our location on a topo map."

"Are we close to the pass?" Bobbie asked.

"I'm not good at reading a topo map," said Bella. "We didn't need it when the comms were working, and we could get interactive 3D views of everything."

"I think I can read a topo. Let me look," Bobbie said, reaching for the tablet. She took the tablet and examined the map, scrolling and zooming and brushing off snow several times. "There is some kind of ridge just above us. With a flatter area on the other side."

"Really? Are we close to the pass?" said Bella.

"Not the pass we want. I think we must have gone off the trail back a mile or two," Bobbie continued looking at the map.

"If it's close let's go there and set up a tent to wait out the storm. How much farther up this trail is it?" Bella asked.

"Not up this trail. Up this wall," Bobbie pointed up the vertical rock wall to the right of the trail.

"That doesn't sound good. Can we still backtrack and get back to our last camp?" Bella asked.

Bobbie said, "It looks like there's an option to track our path, but it wasn't turned on. Okay. Now it's on."

"Does that help?"

"It could help us get back to this point later if we want but it doesn't show us how we got here."

"I guess that's something."

Bobbie continued to study the map and finally looked up. She said, "I think I can see how to get back to the trail, about a mile back. Then we can keep going to the pass, or back towards the camp we left this morning, but we will need to keep checking the map as we go to stay on track."

"Okay. Maybe we'll find a spot to camp on the way. But at least we know there's a good camping spot back there where we came from. Do you see any other level spots?"

"The closest level spot is on the other side of the ridge above us, but I don't see any easy way to get there. The path we're on doesn't go there and this wall is too steep to climb." She pointed at the almost vertical wall to the right of the trail. She counted lines on the topo map, "It's about 40 feet up from here to a gap in the ridge and a little more than that down to a level spot on the other side."

Bella looked up at the wall of rock above them and said, "That's not so steep. I'm a good climber. Let me try climbing it and see if the spot on the other side is worth it."

"Don't do that," said Bobbie. "It's not safe."

Bella took off her pack and took out a spool of carbon fiber climbing ribbon which she clipped to her waist with a couple of extra carabiners. She also clipped her tablet to her waist and started climbing.

"Be careful. Don't fall and break anything," Bobbie said.

"I'll be careful," said Bella.

Bobbie watched as Bella scrambled over the snow-frosted rocks and gradually went out of view in the blowing snow above. Bobbie gazed into the grey-white haze above her and said to herself, "I shouldn't have let Bella do that. What do I do if she doesn't come back? Or worse, if she falls? Could I catch her?" She tried to wedge her feet into the trail to have secure footing in case she needed to try to catch a falling Bella.

As she waited, she looked at the narrow trail with steep slopes to each side, steeply up on the right and down on the left. "It's narrow, but maybe we can partly open a tent here on the trail and make some kind of shelter?" She looked up again and strained to see some sign of Bella, while testing her footing again.

1:50 PM, Honus Unlocks a History World

Before he could get immersed into a bloody battle game the name of the girl next door came to him. Izzie. Izzie Muller. Probably Isabel Muller. He decided to try the challenges for the history world again.

Having remembered other things from walking through the farm and the barn, he was faster and more accurate at responding to the challenge questions this time. The last name of the family next door was one part of the challenge that was previously tripping him up. He still didn't think he had answered everything correctly, but apparently, he did answer enough to open part of the historical game world. He explored which views he could select. The choices were very limited, so he selected the character that seemed to be based on himself and started the game, playing it in a fast summary mode to see what it contained, without making much effort to control any of the characters.

> ## HW203904, Sunday, 04/03/2039, 12:30 PM, Billy Jay
>
> Balaji "Billy Jay" Lee was a great outdoorsman in his various aliases. He did long drives to the edge of the wilderness, where he would set off to live off the land, fish and hunt, scale mountains, build shelter from found materials, and climb vertical rock faces. He made the on- and off-road driving endurance trip to the north coast of Alaska, then to Tierra Del Fuego, and back home. He would take a hypersonic rocket-equipped unit for a quick trip to China to run the length of the Great Wall, to India to carve his initials into the Taj Mahal, to Machu Picchu to deface some other priceless rocks, or to the moon to hit a basket of golf balls at an Apollo lunar landing site. He also was afraid to leave his parents' house.
>
> Just now he was hunkered down in his bedroom wearing jogging clothes that he had never jogged in. Half of a roast chicken and wedge cut potatoes from a deli delivery service sat partly eaten on the table and an extra-large decaf iced tea in a clear plastic cup that was still mostly full was sweating drops of condensation onto

the tabletop. He glanced at the stack of empty delivery containers and bags from nearby restaurants: pizza, Chinese, Thai, burrito, tandoori, and a few others making a tower in a corner of the room. The pile was getting big enough that he should probably bite the bullet and take it out today. His neat-freak mom stayed out of his room in recent months, and she didn't know about most of the food he ordered, but he didn't like to let things get too out of hand. He was focused on the game on two large screens that nearly filled two walls of his room. He mostly used gesture and voice input, but also had handy a keyboard, a touch pad, and a collection of custom game controller devices his dad had invented for the game.

Sometimes he enjoyed playing a number of different role-playing and shoot-em-up games with varying degrees of grotesque realism and he had a few of them on hold in minimized windows on his displays, but he spent the most time in the immersive worlds of the AM game. He currently had a fortune of AM Points, or AMPs, in five different AM possible worlds and zero or negative balances in dozens of others. In the lingo of the discussion groups about the game, he was 'AMPed' in his successful worlds. AMPs were the currency in the game and sometimes he could use them for transactions in the real world.

Although there were many other play modes in the game—all of which somehow related to the autonomous live-in vehicles usually referred to in the game as 'Abitats'—Billy-Jay focused on role-playing—at first for the adventure and, recently even more so, for challenge of real estate development. The real estate development started as one of many avenues he tried to generate AMPs needed to finance his adventures, but as he found success it became an end in itself, and it was now where he spent most of his game time.

When his dad first showed him the AM game a few years ago he was not interested. He thought the name 'Abitat' was stupid. Billy Jay thought playing a game centered on these live-in vehicles was boring and he told his dad so. "Dad give it up. The only mystery is why anyone would play this lame game." His dad didn't push him on it. The home-schooling philosophy of his parents didn't allow forcing him. He learned what they asked him to learn, and they let him play what he wanted to play. His dad just said, "I'd really like you to try it and tell me what you think." "Not interested." But after his dad got sick Billy Jay decided to check the game out. He got hooked. Now after 2 years of nearly full time playing, the game seemed to be getting more complex and immersive, and he just accepted 'Abitat' as a normal word. From time to time when things didn't go well in the game, he still said to himself, "Stupid name, Dad. Stupid game." But he kept playing.

After some initial lucky successes and some spectacular failures, he was able to figure out strategies that would work reliably. Now he was able to make significant profits more than 20% of the time, and he at least broke even more than half the time. The Bollywood Jam Hotel and Casino in Possible World QX2230 was his first big success where he learned a lot, although he eventually had to abandon that world. He abandoned many different unsuccessful characters and usually avoided revisiting those game worlds. After trying in enough different worlds—he learned tricks, and he was getting better at leveraging other people's resources and skills to develop impressive investments in Abitat-living high rises, resorts, country villas, cruise ships, and space cruisers. He carried over experience and skills from one world to the next—both his own and copies of knowledgebases of his characters. AMPS were harder to transfer between worlds, but he found ways to do that as well. Once he had AMPs to spend on adventure or investments, that opened up more possibilities, and his successes grew bigger. "Billy Jay the Billy-ionaire," he sometimes called himself now, but never out loud.

…

1:52 PM, More Detail in History World

Honus decided he had enough of background on Billy Jay. He wondered how long the story world would go on in background mode if he let it. He didn't let it. He switched to live action mode, but still in a fast play.

HW203904, 12:32 PM, Billy Jay and His Mom

There was a knock on his bedroom door, and from the other side his mom said, "Balaji, I'm going to the store to get a few things. I might be gone for a while. I need you to check on your dad while I'm gone. Can you do that?"

It was about time she went to the store; he thought. We're running out of everything. But he wondered why his mom mentioned checking on his dad while she was gone. She was never gone long, and his dad wasn't going anywhere. Other than when she needed help lifting him, she did a better job of taking care of Dad anyway. But he didn't want to sound uncooperative. "Yeah, Mom. I'm busy now, but I'll check on him soon."

"Okay. I'll let you know when I'm leaving."

He re-entered a game world that he had been playing for a few months. It was set over 50 years in the future when tourist travel to the moon was common and he was the owner of a lunar resort. In game world QZ9301 he was Bartholomew J. Orlov.

QZ9301, 2093, Tuesday, 9:30 AM CST,[*] Lunar Golf

Bartholomew J. Orlov was standing at an opening in a wall of his private suite on an upper floor of the Tranquility Lunar Casino and Spa. A selective force field holding in the air allowed him to be comfortable in a lightweight designer exercise suit with goldthread

---

[*] In QZ9301 Lunar time was based on Central Standard Time (Houston).

fabric while the balls he hit sailed out through the vacuum over the lunar surface.

…

HW203904, 12:35 PM, Billy Jay and B.J. Orlov

In his bedroom Billy Jay was a few years younger and considerably less fit than his avatar on the moon. He had uploaded his own photo as a starting point for this character's looks and had fast-forwarded through months of fitness training. His soft, heavy, but not really obese body in his room had not started any fitness training. In his buff self-image on the moon, he could drive golf balls over the lunar horizon but liked to aim for the flag at the Apollo 11 landing site just visible in the middle distance. The display on his bedroom wall zoomed in on the large video display on the wall of Orlov's lunar hotel suite which in turn zoomed in on the Apollo landing site. The American flag waved as one of his golf balls struck home. "Yes!" he shouted in both worlds.

QZ9301, 9:35 AM, Orlov Golfs

Orlov hopped two feet off the floor and settled back down again in the slow motion of lunar gravity as he pumped his clenched fist in celebration. The display on the wall of the suite showed the ball coming to rest with five others in the indent of a footprint near the Apollo lander's ladder.

…

Honus paused the history world and reflected about the Lunar resort game world set in 2093. Back in 2039 people thought it would take that long. While he didn't own a lunar resort yet in 2056, *Theme* already had hotels on the moon and settlements on Mars. He should look into building one. He resumed the history world.

HW203904, 12:37 PM, Billy Jay in His Room

In his parents' house Billy Jay pumped his right fist while his left hand was holding the plastic controller wand that he had used to swing the golf club. He turned in his padded swivel chair, set down the wand on the table and reached over, broke off a piece of chicken, and took a bite. While he chewed, he looked around his room. He should take out the fast-food trash in the corner when his mom goes shopping, he thought. His bed was made up neatly, but the sheets probably ought to be changed. Maybe he should do that later today. He looked at his jogging suit and sniffed near his armpit. He should probably shower and change today. Glancing back at the game displays he saw minimized game windows for GTA XII, Battlefield Sixty, Hatchet Men, and several others, including windows for his other active Abitats Mysteries game worlds. Some games were frozen, but most, including all the AM games, showed views of continuing multiplayer activity. A small scrollable window with names of dozens of AM game worlds that he had tried and was currently avoiding was in a lower corner of the screen.

The view of the game on the moon in QZ9301 shrank to a smaller window in the upper left corner of one of the displays, but action continued in that window outside his attention, while Billy Jay started picking up the fast-food trash and putting it into a bag. Back on the moon without his input his avatar became autonomous again.

QZ9301, 9:37 AM, Orlov Returns to Work

Orlov hit one more ball, caroming it off the ladder of the lander and into the Apollo 11 flag before tossing the golf club aside and saying, "Back to work. I want to meet with the resort management team in the Armstrong conference room in five minutes and they had better be ready to explain the budget shortfalls."

"Yes, sir," said a disembodied voice with an accent like a British butler. After a five second pause the voice continued, "The department heads have been notified."

He bounce-stepped into a large closet and changed out of his exercise clothes and quickly donned a fine Italian business suit, putting on both legs of his suit pants on one high bounce. A few seconds later, fully dressed, as he headed out of his suite into his private elevator he said, "Has the cuisine consultant arrived yet? And what is her name again?"

"Her name is Lacy Hogan, and her flight is on approach to the resort portal now. She should be in the facility in 15 minutes," said the butler voice from the walls.

"Have Ms. Hogan wait for me in the main kitchen. I'll talk with her after the budget meeting."

"Yes, sir," said the butler voice.

He talked to himself, "I hope this cuisine consultant will pay off with ideas that bring more business. I had a solid gut-feeling she would be great as soon as I saw her proposal. She doesn't have much of a resume, but I have great intuition about people."

"Yes, sir," said the butler voice. "I'll have staff direct Ms. Lacy to the main kitchen."

…

HW203904, 12:40 PM, Billy Jay's Lunch

Billy Jay took another bite of his chicken and wedge potatoes, which were one of the few real-world benefits from his vast wealth in possible worlds of the AM Game. They tasted really good. The potatoes had some unusual spiciness that Billy Jay particularly liked. They were paid for an hour ago by another AM player who traded for his help in the game. In the game she was known as Lacy Hogan.

…

1:53 PM, More About Lacy

With the mention of Lacy Hogan in the history world, Honus wondered what kind of background information it would have on her. That might give a clue about who created this history world. He asked for background info on the Lacy Hogan character.

HW203904, Lacy Hogan

Her discussion forum tag LacyHogan235^AM[*] was based on her character's name, presumably so she could stay anonymous as a player and not reveal her actual name, so Billy Jay didn't know her real name. Billy Jay didn't worry about calling himself BillyJay4 in the discussion forums.

Like many players she was impatient with the effort needed to earn AMPs in the game and she was willing to trade things from other possible worlds or the "real" world in order to take short cuts. Apparently, she was a young woman who cooked at a market deli not far from Billy Jay's parents' house and was willing to pay for his chicken and potatoes, including delivery, in order to get a space-flight-capable Abitat and two hundred thousand AMPs transferred from his avatar to her avatar's account in QZ9301 as a "consulting fee."

They had crossed paths a few times in a discussion site for the AM game and that's where they made their barter deal earlier today. He had made better deals in the past, but today his haggling had been hindered by his hunger. He proposed ten thousand AMPs in QZ9301 should be plenty for a meal delivered here, but she drove a hard bargain, and he was hungry.

His mom's penchant for extreme tidiness in the home included keeping the bare minimum food in the house and what she bought was often not what Billy Jay wanted to eat. When he checked in the kitchen early this morning there was no food other than the baby-food mush she gave his dad and even that was running out. His mom seemed to be in a really down mood lately and wouldn't give him allowance, so Billy Jay had resorted to barter in the game to get his chicken and potatoes. If he had known his mom was shopping again today, he might have waited.

---

[*] ^AM was typically pronounced "in AM", "inam", or silent.

Once BillyJay4^AM and LacyHogan235^AM closed the deal in the discussion forum an hour ago, the chicken and potatoes were on their way. Things moved very quickly in the game. Her character Lacy Hogan owner of a restaurant* in Tustin, California, sent an email offering cuisine consulting to his corporation, BJO Development, in the game. His avatar Bartholomew J. Orlov quickly accepted and authorized payment allowing her character to be picked up by a new space-capable Abitat to fly immediately from Earth to the moon resort.

Conventions in the game strongly discouraged making characters discuss the real world within the game world. Characters had autonomous personalities and adjusted their self-image to make sense of their actions when under control of a game player. Making characters talk about things from another world they shouldn't know about could make them question their sanity. Characters might try to laugh off such incongruent words or actions as silliness, or they might consider them as disconcerting voices in the head or even demons taking over their actions. In the game Bartholomew Orlov and Lacy Hogan simply had a contract for her to visit the lunar casino and provide cuisine consulting services, with no mention of the deli chicken delivery back home. Two of his other food deals recently had traded for management jobs at the lunar resort.

Billy Jay realized that barter deals like this could eventually deplete his AMP balance in World QZ9301, but at least he did have something to eat here at home today. His avatar Bartholomew Orlov seemed to be getting stressed by budget problems and mismanagement and Billy Jay thought Orlov might have to declare

---

* Restaurants in the game were even more prone to failure than in the real world. Characters had experiences but the players could not fully share them. Players trying to run restaurants had to rely on presentation and other tricks to make their eating experience stand out for other players.

bankruptcy or worse before long if he didn't get better cashflow for his businesses in that world. Keep giving it away on "consulting" or over-paid jobs in exchange for real-world barter and the funds would run out in this game world. But if it came to that Billy Jay could just disconnect from that game world and walk away and let his autonomous avatar take the consequences. He didn't want to do that, but he had done it more than a few times before.

...

Honus noticed that even though he asked for more background on Lacy Hogan the narration kept coming back to Billy Jay. Oh, well. He let it continue.

...

That was one thing Billy Jay really liked about the autonomous characters in the game. After he initiated a character and adjusted its looks and talents and personality traits, he could control the character's every action when he wanted, or he could back off and watch and let it mostly act on its own with occasional advice on major or minor decisions. But if he let it go too long on its own, he feared losing control of the character.

In each game world Billy Jay could use the AMP wealth of characters that he created and controlled, but from his conversations in discussion forums he realized that many game players were just visitors and voyeurs in the game, not creating or taking full control of any characters. They might watch the game world through the eyes of one or another independent character and occasionally give voice-in-the-head advice when the character had a decision to make. Instead of earning points by doing business in roles in the game they could earn a few points if their advice was accepted by a character, and even more if the character got the results he or she wanted. It was a little like giving advice to other people on social media or on expert-advice websites. Being an influencer of a sort.

Some non-role-players also earned points by solving puzzles that the game presented, where the solutions to the puzzles helped determine outcomes for characters. Billy Jay didn't have patience for the puzzles, but he did sometimes give advice to other characters, usually to try to get them to make decisions that would benefit his characters. For some reason other characters seldom took his advice. He focused more on creating and guiding his own characters who could earn points through business opportunities.

Billy Jay currently had ongoing control of characters with significant wealth in five possible worlds in the game and he had started exploring a couple more worlds looking for new opportunities for when he had to abandon some of the current five. He found that if he tried to be active in more than five game worlds at the same time, he couldn't spend enough time in each to keep his characters fully under his control. Even so, actively juggling characters in five worlds required most of his waking hours.

Four of the AM game worlds he was working in now were closely related, addressing similar geography on earth, but with different implied time periods and different levels of technological developments. Only one of those also involved resorts on the moon. All four were improbable future worlds assuming at least some technologies that were not available today. Billy Jay was developing some of the same earth neighborhoods in all four worlds. Familiarity with the layout of the simulated geography saved him time for planning. He wondered how much of the simulated geography was based on real world locations. His fifth currently productive game world was another story altogether.

The worlds where Billy Jay was successful so far had no defined exchange rate with the real world. A few AM game worlds that closely mirrored and augmented the real world could be used for real world transactions. AMPs in those near worlds could provide secure, encrypted, and anonymous transactions.

He dreamed that someday someone would solve for the improbable initial conditions of one of his successful worlds, like force fields and 30-minute flights to the moon, and he could cash in his game wealth and start to live some of his adventures for real. Of course, in that case he would need to solve an even bigger improbability of being able to leave his parents' house.

In the past he did venture out from time to time, but the anxiety built and drove him back. Encountering people along the way, especially if they spoke to him, could lead to anxiety attacks that would affect his game play for days. For the last couple of years or more, he didn't go beyond the borders of his family's property.

Immersion in games was therapy for his anxiety, but when his anxiety got too strong, he would have to just get under the covers of his bed and wait it out. Sometimes letting his autonomous avatars play on their own for a few days was a good thing. They often made better deals and earned more AMPs when he wasn't controlling them. But he couldn't risk letting them go on their own too long or some other player might give them enough suggestions to take them over.

Getting good food was a challenge that forced him to deal with the outside world. Eating the food his mom ordered or brought home was one option, but it was all so healthy it made him sick. To get things he liked, delivery was the only option. He was familiar with all the food delivery apps and used them whenever his mom gave him allowance. Without funds recently his options were slim.

…

Honus asked for less background and more details.

HW203904, 12:45 PM, Balaji's Mom Goes Shopping

There was another knock on his bedroom door and from the other side his mom said, "Balaji, I'm leaving now, and I really need you to help your dad. Don't just keep playing your games and say you forgot. Can you get him into the shower and clean him up while I'm gone?"

"Okay, Mom. Get some orange chicken and the veggie pizza I like."

He thought for a second, then said, "Or better yet give me my allowance and I can order what I like."

He didn't need to worry about her entering his room and seeing that he was currently eating chicken. In the past they had several incidents when she had a fit after seeing how messy his room was compared to her standards, and he had anxiety attacks and hyperventilated about the violation of his private space. After a number of virtual sessions with advice from counseling professionals they had reached a truce and an understanding. He took care of his own room, and she never looked in. For some reason he didn't quite understand he felt a need to keep the room neat since she had stopped checking. But his definition of neat still did not measure up to hers.

"I set out some clean clothes for your dad and a bag for the dirty ones. The clothes he's in are worn out, so you can just throw them away after you get him dressed again. I'm leaving now so you can come out of your room any time."

"Okay, Mom. Dad should be fine for a couple minutes. He's not going anywhere." Billy Jay wondered about the part about throwing clothes away. The last couple years his mom usually made their minimal possessions last a long time, so these clothes must be getting really old for her to throw them away. Or maybe she's going to go back to work, and they can afford new stuff again? He decided not to ask her about it, since she seemed to be in a bad mood lately. No sense stirring her up.

He opened a view of the home security cameras. No activity around the outside of the house. On one of the inside cameras his mom walked away from his bedroom door down the hallway towards the door to the garage. She was short, dark-haired, and getting thin. She was carrying a purse. She wore her typical blank worried expression. How long has it been since he saw her smile? She walked slowly and seemed to be muttering to herself, but the cameras didn't capture any sound. She was not herself lately. She used to have lots of energy. She went through the door.

On another security camera view from inside the garage she stepped through the door with a brief smirk on her face that immediately faded back to her normal blank expression. The garage was spartan and clean. There were recharge hookups on both sides, one connected to a green-gray-metallic American-made electric autonomous car. The other side was empty other than an unused hookup station on the wall. There was an overhead opener, the door she had come through from the house, and a locked door on one side that led to another two-car garage where his dad stored things. Otherwise, this space was clean and empty with blank white walls. That was his mom's style to keep things overly simple, plain, and clean. His dad's storage area in the other part of the garage was a different story: neat, narrow paths between racks of shelves filled with his materials and finished works.

She disconnected the power cable from her car and hung it up on the power station on the wall. It was crooked and tilted, barely on the hook. She stopped and stared at it for a couple seconds, but left it dangling there before going to the driver's side door and getting in. She touched something on the dash and spoke to the car and waited for the door to open. Balaji waited until he saw in an exterior view the car pull out into the street and the garage door close.

…

1:57 PM, Honus Checking the Garage

Honus froze the last view of the car driving away and then reversed it back to the view of her getting into the car before it left the garage. His mom got that car before his dad got sick. His dad had installed charging hookups on both sides of the garage but hadn't got his own new vehicle before he got sick and then his mom got rid of his dad's old pickup truck. That old truck might be worth something for a collector today, he mused.

Looking at the inside of the garage in the history world, Honus was curious how much it had changed since then. He hadn't paid attention as he docked and came inside earlier today. He decided to take a look.

As he left his bedroom to check, he wondered if anything would have turned out differently that day if he had left his room more often or talked to his mom face to face before she left for the store. That security video of her getting into her car was the last time he saw a live view of his mom. The last time he saw her in person was days or maybe weeks before then.

Chapter 4

Afternoon

2:00 PM, Sam & Jo-Jo at *The Theme Park*

Inside *The Theme Park*, far from the main entrance, a panel opened on a wall painted with psychedelic flowers. It was a hidden door, and Sam peeked his head out. He stepped through and closed the door behind him. After looking around he knocked on it and said, "Come on." Sam stepped a few steps farther into the park and stood looking innocent, while blocking the view of the opening secret door for most passers-by. The door was a few feet off the path where people were walking fast to get from one attraction to the next. No one seemed to pay any attention to them. Jo-Jo stepped out behind him and closed the door most of the way, keeping a couple of fingers in place to keep it from latching.

"Don't forget to prop it open. Remember, if his door sticks you can't open it from outside" said Sam over his shoulder.

"I remember. I got it."

"Wait," said Sam seeing more people coming close on the path. As people walked by, they tried to look casual and bored, like they were waiting for someone in their party to meet them after finishing a ride. Jo-Jo kept the doorway ajar with a hand behind her back while waiting for a signal from Sam that the coast was clear. A family with twin six-year-olds passed. The twins briefly looked straight at them while repeating to their parents several times, "I'm hungry. Let's eat!"

After they passed, Sam nodded to Jo-Jo.

"Just a sec," said Jo-Jo as she took a small bag of 4-inch cloth squares from her art supplies out of her pocket. She compared their colors to the colors of the flowers on the secret door. She placed a purple square over the hidden latch and carefully closed the door. With the panel closed, only a small bit of the purple cloth showed at the edge of a purple flower where the opening had been. Not a perfect color match, but pretty close. Otherwise, the edges of the door disappeared in the flower patterns.

"Okay. Good. We're in. And we should be able to go back out the same way. What do you want to do first?" asked Sam.

"Look around and see what's changed so we can make good use of our time tomorrow. See if we run into anyone we know. Probably too risky to go on any rides without wristbands until we see how they're checking for them."

"We could go back and get the wristbands," Sam suggested.

"Hey. Sneaking in without them was your idea. I don't like hiding them outside, but you were right. Until we know what kind of fees they'll hit us with in here we can't afford to take a chance."

"I'm hungry. Let's see what we can find to eat," said Sam.

"Really? We stopped and ate on the way from the beach. And I asked if you wanted to bring snacks before we let the Abitat go."

"Yeah. But hearing those kids repeat, 'I'm hungry!' makes me hungry again. Besides, I like the park food better than our snacks. We've always been able to snag something to eat when we've been in here before. There's usually a food cart just down this way." Sam headed down the path to the right. Jo-Jo followed him. They turned at a bend in the path and there was a food cart. Sam gestured an 'I told you so' gesture. A mom and dad were ordering food while their two small kids were playing tag and climbing on a bench. The mom handed food items to the dad while tapping her wristband to pay. The dad kept turning towards the kids while they were running back and forth on the path. Finally, he set the food down on the bench and started following his kids down the path, telling them to come back and get their food.

Sam gave a hand signal to Jo-Jo that this might be easier than usual with the food just sitting there. She wasn't sure if it was a good idea but decided to go along. Sam walked ahead towards the bench. Jo-Jo checked her pockets like she was distracted looking for something and then pretended to trip on the path across from the bench. Sam smoothly picked up the food items from the bench and continued down the path while the mom and the food vendor helped Jo-Jo get up. Jo-Jo thanked them and continued down the path after Sam. Meanwhile the two kids had disappeared back around a bend in the path with their dad in pursuit.

The dad called out, "Minh! Max! Come back here and eat!" He found Max with both hands on a wall panel painted with psychedelic flowers.

"Where's your brother?"

"He's inside the wall," said the little girl.

"No. What!? No. Really. Where is he really?" He looked down the path and didn't see Minh.

The mom came around the bend in the path carrying a couple of drinks. "I got you something. Where's their food? And where's Minh?"

The little girl kept pounding both hands on the wall. The dad looked at the mom with exasperation.

The little girl said, "Okay Minh. I give up." Then the wall panel opened, and the little boy came out saying. "I win! I win! You couldn't catch me!"

"You cheated."

"I did not."

"Yes, you did."

The door panel closed again leaving no sign of an opening and a small patch of purple cloth lay on the ground in front of the door.

The mom and dad had some words about what happened to the food for Minh and Max.

"I set it down right here," said the dad pointing to the bench.

"It's not there now. Think where you really set it down." She looked around for other places he might have set it nearby and asked the food cart vendor if she had seen anything but ended up ordering it again.

Meanwhile Jo-Jo met Sam at another bench a couple minutes' walk and a couple of path intersections away, well out of sight from where he picked up the food. They sat down and sampled the food they had purloined.

"This isn't real meat in this hot dog," complained Jo-Jo.

"I'll eat it if you don't want it."

"Go ahead." She handed it to him.

2:05 PM, Tim near *The Theme Park*

A man in a hard hat was in a construction office pod near the highway a couple blocks behind *The Theme Park*. He was checking video records from cameras around the construction site. His work shirt had the name *Tim*.

He looked at various scenes showing deep excavations, construction forms, pipes, and rebar in various parts of the lot, apparently getting ready for concrete to be poured.

One view showed three workers drinking coffee at a break table under a shade cover near the office pod. A fence to a flood control channel that ran along one edge of the construction site was behind them. Two were sitting on mismatched chairs, one cheap green plastic and another a nicer director's chair, and the other was standing, holding his coffee mug, and looking for a chair.

Most views of the site showed no activity. He probably should get on people to work more. The project was behind schedule, but it was almost a holiday weekend. After running the views back in time a few minutes, he found a view of a blue Abitat stopping on the street just outside the work site, and two people getting out but covering their faces.

Tim spoke to the console at his desk. "Yes. A blue Abitat dropped off two people here a few minutes ago."

A very high-pitched, digitally altered female voice in an audio-only communication mode said from his console display, "We've been trying to complete a delivery from that Abitat all day. The transfers keep failing. We've had six different pickup vehicles dock with it today and so far, no go. *Mechanical failure* every time. Now they get out at one of our sites. That can't be a coincidence."

Tim and some others he worked with referred to this voice as "*The Squeaky Wheel.*" He didn't know much about the actual person on the other end of that voice. He'd never seen a face. The voice sounded ridiculous, but he knew enough to do whatever she, or maybe they, asked.

He said, "Sounds a little like last time all over again."

"Let's hope not. We can't afford to lose another shipment," squeaked the voice.

Tim wasn't sure of the details but understood that last time a guy in a transporting Abitat didn't complete the planned handoff, tried to sell it himself, and got caught. The whole shipment was confiscated. Word was he demanded more points and Squeaky said no.

Tim said, "What are they asking for this time? Maybe give them what they want. Or better yet, if you are tracking the Abitat, just tell me where it is now. I'll stop it, get the stuff, and take it wherever you want."

Squeaky said, "It was supposed to be an anonymous automatic delivery. But somehow they must have figured out what they were carrying. So far, these people have not sent any demands but getting out at one of our work sites is a message in itself. It shows they know about us and want to meet. Shut down the site for today. We don't need extra people around the site while we meet with them."

Tim replied, "Shutting this place down—that's not fast. A complex construction operation like this can't be stopped at a moment's notice."

Tim knew that most of the workers on site today were idle and would be happy to go home early but he wanted to hedge in case someone had started working on something complicated. Most likely it wouldn't take more than a few minutes to secure materials and put forklifts and tools away. He immediately sent a message out to the workers on the site telling them to take the rest of the afternoon off and then continued, speaking to Squeaky. "Any idea who they are? Who they work for? Maybe there's an inside connection for two shipments to be compromised? They must know something about our operations to come to us here."

"That is a concern. A big concern. We will deal with that, in time, but first we need to get the packages. The two people you saw must still be on your construction site. Find them and see what they want."

"I don't see them in the current video views."

"They must be there still. Find them," said the squeaky voice.

"Let me see." He opened the office door and looked around outside, then back at the display panel, he scanned several different camera views from around the construction site playing forwards and backwards at high speed. Some showed two people running across the site, hiding behind equipment and construction materials as they went. A view showing movement in a tree near a fence caught his eye. He zoomed in and looked more closely.

"Looks like they left our site. Climbed a tree. Went over a fence and down into the flood control channel."

"Send someone to head them off upstream. Downstream goes under *The Theme Park* and is blocked by security grates."

"Sure, Wait. Hold on. I've got a view inside the channel. Uh Oh. They opened the access gate and went into the tunnel towards *The Theme Park*."

"That is not good. They must be connected to *The Theme Park* security somehow. Or maybe they are law enforcement. Either way we'll have to be extra careful. Get me a picture of their faces so we can figure out who we are dealing with."

Tim continued looking through the camera views trying to get a good view of their faces. "Okay. I'm looking."

Squeaky continued, thinking out loud, "But if they are going into *The Theme Park* that may be a sign that they want to meet in a public place."

"Makes sense. I guess."

"Identify them first."

"Okay. Okay. I've looked at the camera views here. It seems they hid their faces from all our cameras. No ID."

"Sounds like we're dealing with pros."

"It shouldn't be too hard to find two people dressed in matching jogging suits like that."

"Okay. Find them. And get pictures of their faces so we can ID them. But whoever they are we still need to find a way to get the shipment that is in that Abitat. That is the priority."

"If you've been tracking their Abitat, just let me know where it is, and I'll go disable it and get whatever you want out of it. If it's armored it might take a couple minutes, but even then."

"No. It's best to get a normal anonymous delivery in public."

"Disable it and tow it? Piece of cake."

"No. First find out who they are and what they want."

Tim said, "Okay. ID them first. Working on it." Tim checked the locations of people on his team close to *The Theme Park*.

Squeaky continued thinking out loud, "If they just want more points for the delivery, we can offer them whatever they want. Then depending on who they are we can deal with them appropriately after the delivery is done."

"What if they won't agree to a normal delivery?"

"Then we do whatever it takes to get the Abitat into one of our construction sites or warehouses. Get the packages and then clean things up out of sight."

"I'll send in a couple of my guys into the park to find them. But maybe they left a message here about their demands or where to meet. I'll double check along the path they took when they crossed our site."

"Good idea. Maybe they left a note, but if they want to meet in public, they will make themselves easy to find in the park," squeaked the voice.

Tim looked more closely at the views that showed them crossing the construction site to plot out the places he should check for a note. "Right. Hey, can you give me camera views inside the park? We might get a view of their faces faster that way."

"Stand by. And be careful inside the park. Don't cause too much attention. Too many people and too much security in there. Not all are people we can trust."

"My guys can handle it. They know what they're doing." He imagined hundreds of park visitors wearing the same outfits. He thought, "that would be bad." He continued looking through the video records from the construction site and noticed something. "Wait a minute. Wait a minute. It looks like they left something in the tree they climbed. I should go out there and see if it's a note with demands or meeting instructions." He zoomed in on recorded views of tree. "Oh. That's interesting."

"What?" asked the squeaky voice.

"It looks like they took off their wristbands and left them in the tree," Tim explained.

"Why would they do that?" asked Squeaky.

"Beats me," said Tim.

Squeaky added, "We should assume they expected us to see that. Maybe they want us to summon the Abitat ourselves?"

Tim replied, "You can't summon some else's Abitat with only their wristbands. Your biometrics wouldn't match. If they thought we wouldn't see it, maybe it's part of their negotiation strategy so we can't force them immediately to call the Abitat without their wristbands."

"No. They meant for us to see them leave the wristbands here. They have a plan. Maybe they disabled the wristband biometrics."

"I don't think that's possible,' said Tim.

"Some of the stubborn homeless wouldn't take Abitats if they had to give their biometrics. So, there must be a way."

"I thought that was made up. You think it's a Homeless-No-More Abitat?"

"No. It came across-country. But, still, maybe they found a way to use uncalibrated wristbands. Check them out."

"Okay. I'll get those wristbands and see if there is a note, and we'll ID the two in the park."

"Be careful. These are sophisticated people we are dealing with. Maybe law enforcement. Get those bands and let me know if there is a note."

"Will do, Boss."

"Here's a link for access to camera views. Let me know when you find out who they are and what they want." The voice call disconnected without any additional words.

"Thanks, Boss." A display of tens of thousands of views from security cameras and shared streams from visitors inside the park and drones above opened on the wall of the office pod. "That's a lot of cameras." Even with extremely high resolution on the wall display the images were each too small to see any details. Tim tried expanding a few showing random views of rides and shops and crowds in the park and then motioned with his hand and superimposed them on a map of the park, then expanded a few dozen of the views of the maintenance area the drainage tunnel passed under. One drone aerial view showed two people in matching jogging suits climbing out of a hatch on the ground in the maintenance area and then going out of sight into park buildings without looking up. "Still no faces but yeah. These views might help."

He looked at a few of the video streams from inside the park near those buildings and grew frustrated that there were so many. He thought about defying standing orders and using the game to send out a challenge. Even a few points reward could get millions of intelligent entities with idle time to take on a challenge. Lots of AI's as well as bored human players were always looking for a few extra points. He could have them sort through the thousands of videos and return an answer in seconds. Then he thought better of it. Need to do this the old-fashioned way. Don't want to piss-off the squeaky wheel.

He picked up a handheld voice communication device and initiated a call. Only his side of the conversation was audible in the office.

"Joel, I see you are with Kyle. I've got a job for the two of you."

… "Yeah, Tim. Who do you think?" … "Inside *The Theme Park*." … "Yeah. Just find two people. They're holding up a delivery. We need to ID them and find out what they want." … "ID them and then maybe bring them to the construction site." … "Yes Alive. That's right. Discretion." … "I'm sending you some pictures now."

He sent two pictures of the pair in jogging suits crossing the construction site.

"Yeah, no faces yet, but what's the chance you'll find another pair wearing matching running suits like that?" … "Yeah. No kidding. And they might not be wearing wristbands." … "Really. I'm not kidding. They left some wristbands here." … "I'm looking at video feeds from the park now. I'll try to get you some face shots and a current location." … "They went through the drainage tunnel into the park maintenance area a few minutes ago so they're not far into the park yet." … "No. We need them alive to complete the delivery. They probably want to meet to tell us their demands." … "No, I don't. Just something the squeaky wheel wants." … "Right. Squeaky Wheel Priority. Get it done."

He disconnected and set down the comm device.

He looked at the map with hundreds of video feeds from near the back of the park.

"God damn. This could take a while."

After expanding multiple videos inside the park and not seeing a view of the two people he stopped.

"Need to get those wristbands and see if they left instructions. It'll take Joel and Kyle a few minutes to get to the back of the park anyway," he said to himself.

He got up and left the office pod and walked quickly to the tree near the fence. With some difficulty he climbed up and reached into a hollow between two large branches and pulled out the wristbands. He felt around in the hollow and found some crumpled paper.

"Here we go!" he said.

He pulled it out, but it was just some old candy wrappers and didn't seem to have any messages.

When he dropped back down, he twisted his ankle.

"Damn it."

He tested his weight on it. It wasn't too bad. He could walk but he'd need to go easy on it. He looked through the fence next to the tree into the drainage channel. He considered going over the fence and down into the channel in case that would give him some clues, but with his sore ankle he decided against any more climbing.

He looked more closely at the candy wrapper, and it seemed to be just trash. He put it in his pocket to examine more closely later, along with one of the wristbands. Then he took off his own wristband, put it in his pocket, and put the other one on, raised his wrist and spoke into it.

"Abitat. Come to this location, park off the road, and wait."

He looked across the site. A tractor was moving a load of rebar leaving an open space next to the office pod. A stack of orange cones was there.

To the wristband he added, "Park between orange cones away from the highway."

He figured he could arrange the cones to mark a parking spot before it got here.

"Okay, Sam. On my way. Calculating arrival," said a voice from the wristband.

"Son of a gun. That was too easy."

He looked at the wristband which was dirty and worn down. It definitely didn't look like a brand-new uncalibrated wristband.

"I guess the Abitat could be one of those homeless specials after all for someone named Sam."

"Estimated arrival in four…" A loud KLANG noise from a tractor dumping a bundle of rebar drowned out the next words from the wristband. Tim waved to the worker getting off a tractor after dumping the rebar.

"Tim, What's the deal? Why are we shutting down early? We need to get more rebar and forms in place if the concrete's gonna be poured next week."

"Don't worry about it, Ahmed. Just giving people an early start on the holiday weekend. Go on home. Get out of here. See you next week. We can catch up then."

"Okay. Thanks. See you then."

Tim stopped to move some orange traffic cones to designate a parking spot near the office pod. He walked gingerly across the construction site towards the roadway, following in reverse the path the pair had taken, not finding any note.

When he got to the fence by the street, he propped open the entry gate to give the Abitat access. He checked the path and view of the cones from the entry and figured the Abitat shouldn't have a problem finding the requested parking spot. He saw a few Abitats passing on the roadway. Some stopped to pick up workers. None were blue.

He headed back to the office pod to let the squeaky wheel know the Abitat would be here soon and to tell Kyle and Joel to just follow the two running suits, and get a picture of their faces, but not contact them. He figured their demands didn't matter if he could get the packages out himself, but Squeaky wanted to know who they were. He stopped at a tool crib and pulled out a powerful cutting tool, tested it by listening to the hum as he pulled the trigger, and then brought it with him back towards the office.

2:15 PM, Honus Continues History World

The garage was still simple and clean, but it had been remodeled with larger doors and a higher ceiling to fit a full size Abitat, like his, which was docked now on one side. other side was empty except for the old charger for his mom's car. He started to think, he should replace that old car charger with an Abitat dock or remodel the whole house to give Abitats direct access to the home's interior. He should probably also change his dad's storage space beyond the locked door into a couple more Abitat portals. It was hard not to think like a developer. Since his Abitat was right here Honus decided to restart the game from inside of his Abitat.

As he connected to the game history world, he thought out loud:

"I wonder who made this history world. The summary narration at the beginning sounds like someone was trying to tell a story like a novel. Maybe someone who liked writing? I wonder if Lae C had anything to do with making this. Not sure if it's a fair rendering of Billy Jay's thoughts or his general disposition—some artistic license there—but the actions might be accurate. It could have been based on recordings from game play and home security and dashcam videos. I wonder what other views I can open."

He switched to a view through the eyes of the mom and restarted the most recent scene.

HW203904, 12:45 PM, Mara's View

Mara walked down the hallway away from her son's bedroom door. She looked depressed. As she reached for the knob on the door to the garage she mouthed words from a Min Strong seminar: "There are always new doors to open. Don't hold on to stuff. Let go of the old, be free, and step through to something new." As she opened the door to the garage she forced a smile. She disconnected the power cable from her car and hung it on the power station on

---

the wall. It was off center. She stared at it for a few seconds. She mouthed the words, "Minimal and precise. Bullshit." She didn't adjust it. Getting in the car she pressed a button to start the car and open the garage. She said out loud, "Drive to the market."

As the car started out of the driveway, she pressed the button to close the garage, then pushed the steering wheel out of the way against the dash, put on her seat belt and swiveled her seat to the right and pulled the large screen in middle of the dash closer to her. As she browsed through her news feeds the car approached an intersecting street and signaled for a left turn, pausing for another car. A message appeared on the display mentioning a new email on an old account. She opened it.

...

From: OZAIJerry@AltruIndus.com

To: WebAdmin@MinStrWeb.org

Subject: Perry Lee and Abitat Royalties

Pls tell Perry we need to talk about Abitat royalties.

Respond to this email or meet any afternoon

at café in Highland Hills Community Center.

<directions>

Jerry

...

Mara said, "Change destination." She tapped on the directions link in the message and the turn signal stopped and the car proceeded straight through the intersection towards the freeway. She said, "I hope this is what I think it is. Maybe today will be a good day after all. Happy Birthday to me. And happy belated birthday last Friday, Perry."

...

2:16 PM, Honus Birthday Reminder

The next part of the history world from Mara's point of view was just her playing dumb games on the car's console while in traffic so Honus broke out again. Did he really forget both his parents' birthdays that year? He would need to double-check on those dates. He thought both had birthdays in March, but that scene was dated April 3. He couldn't do anything for his mom, but he should make sure to do something for his dad next year when his birthday rolls around again.

Assuming the history world was accurate on dates, he did the mental calculation and spoke, "Set reminder for March 30 every year for Dad's birthday." March 30th felt like the right date for his dad's birthday, but April 3 didn't seem right for his mom.

"Reminder set. How much advance notice would you like?" said the British butler voice.

"A week should be good," answered Honus.

"If you tell me more about 'Dad' I can give you specific gift recommendations or take care of birthday gift arrangements for you, like with your executive staff and assistants," said the voice.

"Not now."

"Acknowledged. First reminder on March 23, 2057."

Honus thought about the scene with Billy Jay's mom. It didn't show much about what she was thinking, but she seemed hopeful when she got that message. Before that she seemed down. Had she been depressed enough in those days to do something to herself? He wondered again who put this story world together.

He decided to switch back to Billy Jay's point of view.

HW203904, 12:50 PM, Billy Jay and His Dad
"Okay. Dad. Just you and me for a half hour or so." Billy Jay stuffed the last large chunk of the chicken and one more piece of potato in his mouth, took a sip of the iced tea and

chewed with a really full mouth. He picked up the food containers from the corner of the room, putting everything in a couple of bags. He carried them with him as he left his room. Good to take them out while his mom couldn't see.

Billy Jay thought if he was able to cash in someday in the game he wouldn't have to beg for an allowance, but he would also use some of the money to help his parents. His mom had stopped giving him allowance saying they were too poor. He didn't believe her. He found where she hid his allowance debit cards and took one whenever he needed money, but then they were gone. She must have hidden them somewhere new, but he had looked everywhere. It had been weeks since he had received any allowance and seemed like forever.

If we really are poor, she should go back to work. Dad can't work anymore but she should be able to. It's not like she has much of a life, he thought. As far as he knew recently she spent all of her time cleaning the house and caring for his dad, or on her computer wasting time.

Before she had always been organized and very busy. When his dad was healthy, she was always doing calls or traveling for her work. He wasn't sure, but he thought she helped manage a website for someone who did motivational seminars explaining how people could organize and simplify their lives. He had seen her answering emails and he still had links to some of those websites.

Back then his dad was also busy. He went to work or spent long days in his workshop. With both parents busy Billy Jay had time to explore violent role-playing games. When he was little, they had nannies to watch him while his parents worked. He could always handle the nannies. None of them stayed long.

When his dad started getting sick, his mom still used to get out for a few hours almost every day, probably to visit friends, exercise, or do shopping, and she had depended on him to check on his dad during those times. She did some overnight trips then too. She started a longer trip once, but she came back early and never went out for more than a quick trip to the store after that. For at least a couple of weeks now she hadn't even gone to the store.

Billy Jay was glad she was finally getting out to shop today. She needed to get out and they all needed food. And he enjoyed having fewer interruptions to his game playing.

As he walked from the hallway on his side of the house and across the nearly empty living room—just one reading chair and a floor lamp his dad had made—he could see she still kept the house spotless. She was constantly cleaning or throwing away everything except the bare minimum essentials.

Billy Jay continued through the kitchen to the service porch with the washer and dryer and looked briefly in the very neat cupboards with several empty labeled spots for cleaning supplies. His pulse raced as he opened the side door. He continued out the door and tossed his bedroom trash in the big trash container. It was nearly full. They didn't have much trash, so she must not have put it on the curb for a few weeks. He hoped his mom wouldn't make him take the bins out to the street on trash day, whenever that was. He looked through the open grid in the fence at the front yard and street and felt a start of dizziness and a growing feeling of queasy panic in his belly. He shivered before heading back into the house. He crossed through the kitchen and looked in some cupboards with neatly labelled arrangements of spices and labelled empty spaces where there should have been food. He looked in the refrigerator and saw it was empty except for a few sauces. He took a sip of some kind of vinegar and grimaced. He headed to his parents' rooms. His dad was lying on his bed wearing a headset that looked like a mesh baseball cap without a visor. He was holding a tablet-sized game display and twitching and mumbling quietly.

"Hi, Dad. Are you ready for a shower?" said Billy Jay. His dad continued twitching and mumbling. "Let's get you out of bed and into the shower." Billy Jay said, "It's me, Balaji, your son, you call me Billy Jay. You don't want to be dirty and smelly, do you Papa Lee?"

Billy Jay pulled down the covers exposing his dad's lower body and legs. There was a large brown wet spot in the sheets. "Dad, It looks like you overflowed your absorbent underpants. This is a mess. Let's get you out of bed and get you cleaned up." Under his breath, "What has mom been doing? How did she let him get like this?" Then after a few seconds, "No wonder she decided to go shopping now. I should just leave him until she gets back. Say I just didn't get round to it."

He sighed and put an arm behind his dad's shoulders to help him sit up. The other hand took hold of the game display tablet which came out of his dad's hands. Immediately his dad began making panicked wheezing sounds. Billy Jay said, "You want your game controller back, don't you. If I give it back, you need to help me get you to the shower." Billy glanced at the tablet which showed a text window that was scrolling fast with error or status messages that didn't mean anything to him. He handed it back to his dad, and his dad's sobs quickly subsided, and status messages on the tablet continued to scroll, but more slowly. They still didn't mean anything to Billy Jay.

He helped his dad swing his legs over the side of the bed and pulled him up onto his feet, while holding on to make sure he didn't collapse on to the rug next to the bed. He had lost a lot of weight during his illness. He was tall but thin. Billy Jay steadied him and looked at the tablet in his dad's firm grip and the headset his dad always wore, "Are you still playing the game today, Dad?" Billy Jay wasn't sure if his dad had invented the headset or if it was something he got from one of the other early pioneers of the game, but his dad never took it off now and tried to never let go of the tablet. Billy Jay knew his dad had invented many things and had been very involved in the early days of the AM game, adding his inventions to the early design of Abitats in the game. "I bet you are still making new inventions in the game and having a great time, aren't you, Dad?"

They walked slowly into the tile-floored bathroom, with Billy Jay still holding under his dad's arms to keep him upright, and his dad taking very small steps, to a built-in seat in the shower area where Billy Jay sat his father down and started undressing him. His dad kept hold of the tablet and kept mumbling and twitching. A clean washcloth and nearly empty pump bottles of soap and shampoo were on the seat behind him, having been placed there by his mom.

"Okay, let's get you cleaned up," said Billy Jay as he tossed the filthy clothes aside and reached over to turn on the water and take hold of the hand-held shower spray. He tested the temperature on the back of his hand and adjusted the valve until it was right, then started hosing down his dad's crotch and ass. He picked up the washcloth, wetted it and added some soap and started working his way around his dad's parts, shifting him on the seat, lifting his legs or his buttocks to get at everything without making him stand. This wasn't the first time, and Billy Jay was pretty good at doing this without getting himself soaked, and his dad generally cooperated. The headset cap was meshed, and water and shampoo went through it to a stubbled scalp. Billy Jay always was tempted to pull it off so he could really wash his Dad's stubbled hair, but he didn't. The look on his mom's face when she said "Never take off his cap" was enough to keep him from trying. Somehow she kept his hair short, but she didn't say how.

After a few minutes Billy Jay turned off the water and got a nearby towel and started drying off his dad who was still seated and still mumbling, twitching, and holding the waterproof game tablet and wearing the headset. Billy Jay turned on a ceiling heater fan which blew some hot air which kept his dad warm while he dried him and dressed him. The clean clothes were on a nearby countertop where his mom had set them. Soon he had his dad diapered and dressed in clean pajamas. He walked him slowly to a chair in the bedroom and sat him down there while he changed the sheets on the bed. His mom hadn't mentioned the mess with the dirty sheets, or he might have been too busy to help, but in addition to clean clothes she had set out a set of clean sheets and a bag large enough for clothes and sheets, with a note: 'Please throw the dirty sheets away too.' "Thanks, Mom," thought Balaji. "You were always organized. But how did you let Dad get like this today? Is it so hard to walk him to the toilet from time to time? What have you been doing?" He realized that he could have taken some breaks from his games to check on his dad too, but that's not how it was supposed to work.

After the bed was made and the dirty clothes and sheets were bagged Billy Jay asked, "Dad, do you want to stay in the chair or go back to the bed now?" His dad mumbled and twitched and raised the tablet up slightly. That was more of an answer to any question than he had seen from his dad in ages. He took it as saying help me up from the chair, whether it meant that or not, and he did help lift his dad to standing and walked over to the bed and helped get him back in and partially covered. Then Billy Jay kissed his dad on the forehead and said, "I hope I can find you and talk to you soon inside the game, Papa Lee. I'd really like to know what you are thinking about these days, and I'd like to show you what I've done. I've done some great things in the game. But how will I recognize you when I find you?" His dad mumbled and twitched. "You rest and I'll check on you in a little while." He picked up the bag of dirty sheets and clothes and carried them down the hall and out to the trash.

After tossing the bag in the trash container and glancing again towards the front yard with a shiver, Billy Jay decided to do something he hadn't done in weeks. Instead of heading immediately back in, he stayed outside and went around the back of the house, and down a path to the large workshop building. It looked like a barn on the outside. Its roof was covered with solar panels. The barn was connected to a small farm located below and behind their house. In the game Billy Jay would love to come across a development opportunity like the farm in the middle of an upscale residential area.

Billy Jay felt okay being in the farm so long as no strangers were working there. He used to take walks in the farm or shoot baskets at the court by Sergey's house. Sergey was the old man who ran the farm, and he was almost a member of the family. Billy Jay could be around Sergey. Sergey even babysat for them from time to time when he was little when they were between nannies.

Billy Jay thought of the workshop barn as being in his family's yard. If he understood the story right, his dad had bought part the farm to allow space for his workshop and storage. Depending on how the story went, it might have been "borrowed" somehow rather than bought, but still his dad's workshop and storage area was there in the building down the path behind their house. His dad also stored things in part of the garage, but Billy Jay thought the best of his dad's work was kept in cabinets in the workshop building. The farm beyond the workshop consisted of a few acres of land with avocado and fruit trees and some other gardens as well as Sergey's house and the basketball court.

His mom didn't know Billy Jay knew the key code for his dad's workshop, so he didn't go in when she was home. He had seen his dad key in the code years ago and never forgot it. He figured he still had at least a few minutes before she got back from the store, and she probably wouldn't see him out here anyway, so he decided to take a chance. A row of tall trees and thick bushes blocked the view from the house.

He had taken and sold online one of his dad's art pieces or inventions a few weeks ago when his mom cut off his allowance. After cleaning up his dad today, he figured he deserved to have some more benefits from his dad's inventions. Billy Jay looked over his shoulder back towards the house to make sure his mom wasn't watching, and then he tapped the key code on the keypad on the workshop door and went in.

…

2:20 PM, Honus as Seen on Video?

Honus didn't remember ever telling anyone about taking any of his dad's art pieces. For it to be mentioned in this story world someone must have figured it out or seen him do it. He still didn't think he had created this story world himself. He realized there must have been cameras around the workshop that caught a view of him taking them. He wondered if his mom had seen those videos before. She may have known he had the access code and that he had taken other things from the workshop before. Maybe she left knowing he had some things he could sell. Or maybe she was mad at him for taking this stuff? He watched the game world some more…

HW203904, 1:30 PM, Billy Jay Takes Something to Sell

Inside the barn was a set of work benches and machine tools and rack upon rack of materials, components, and odd objects his dad had collected, with hardly a trace of dust. Despite looking like a barn on the outside it was well-insulated, filtered and climate-controlled on the inside, even though it had not been actively used for a few years, unless maybe his mom or Sergey came in here sometimes. His dad certainly didn't. Inside there were some locked doors, one with a window led to an office area where his dad had his computers. The others were probably more storage.

The machine workshop was where his dad had done most of his work as an inventor and artist, and maybe where he did work on the game too. Most of his inventions were aimed at fulfilling his vision of simplicity and minimalism: For example, furniture that could collapse away into an elegant art piece occupying almost no space and expand again when needed into a table or chair. That floor lamp in the living room was an example. A gentle nudge on the post and a small table surface would appear big enough to hold a drink or a book. Nudge again below the shelf and it would disappear back into the post.

The workshop had racks stacked high with materials and components and many objects his dad had collected that might be useful one day. He was something of an organized packrat, but only in his own space. Besides the workshop he had taken over one side of the garage for storage. He had some friendly but heated discussions with Mom about minimalism before she agreed to let those spaces be his.

She tolerated his hoarding in his own space, but she did not allow it inside her house. If he brought one of his new creations into the house for her, she would make a quick judgment call. If it allowed her to replace and eliminate other objects from the house, she might keep it, but if its design didn't appeal to her, it had to go. The lamp might be the only piece of his that stayed. He had sold a few pieces she rejected but kept most in storage. Billy Jay hoped to sell some more.

Billy Jay wasn't sure how his dad had made money before. Maybe working on the AM game was his job. Maybe his mom made enough back then so his dad could work on the game and in his workshop. He couldn't have made much from selling a few items he built in his workshop. Most of the things his dad built were practical with some kind of purpose. He often used all new components or parts that he designed and fabricated on his machines or his 3D printer, but some of his artwork inventions were noteworthy for the combinations of found objects that went into them. His dad seemed especially proud of some of the least practical inventions. A combination of bed springs, parts from a vacuum cleaner and various kitchen utensils that could fold socks was an example. Billy Jay was pretty sure his dad had sold that one years ago, but if he could find it, he would try to sell it now.

Back when his parents were working, Billy Jay lived a more normal life. He played a lot of role-playing games then too, but not in the AM game, and he would sometimes leave the house to play in the farm. They even got him to go to a school for a while when he was little, but that didn't last. Maybe less than a day. He always finished any schoolwork his parents asked him to do. He would get it done very fast and get back to his games or play the games until just before he knew they would check on him and get it done then.

As he remembered it, when he was little, he had mild anxiety in the open or in social situations but nothing like now. As he got to the point in his life when he should have gotten out of the house more, his dad needed him, and he settled into his interior lifestyle and game-playing obsession.

He deserved to get more rewards for the work he had done helping his parents, he thought. Billy Jay walked through the workshop, past work benches and a battery wall storing power from the solar panels, until he found a section storing finished projects. They were on shelves partly hidden beyond a row of large, heavy, locked vault-like cabinets with cipher locks that Billy Jay couldn't open yet. He thought the best items were probably in there. But he picked one off an open shelf and leaned it on his shoulder and carried it out of the workshop, first looking towards the path to the house for any sign of his mom before closing the workshop door and quickly going up the path, crossing the yard to the other side of the house near his bedroom instead of back by way of the utility room. Along the way he pushed on a wind chime and listened to it for a second and then retrieved a key from a wall light fixture and opened the private entrance door to his room and went inside.

...

2:22 PM, Honus Remembering the Kid Next Door

Honus recalled that Izzie used to jump up and bang on the windchime to get his attention when she came over. But by the time of this history world in 2039 she must have been in high school and wouldn't have been home in the middle of the day. Billy Jay at that time wouldn't have had a clear picture of typical school schedules since he had been home-schooled. He had just followed his Mom's demands and finished his first online college degrees when he was twelve.

By the time of this History World, Izzie had lost interest in exploring the farm with BJ. Honus remembered that Billy Jay missed her then and wanted to show her the art object.

He remembered that she had always been nice to him and accepted his fears like they were perfectly normal. Billy Jay would also listen to her when she talked about her weird family. She lived with her Cam-Ma. Izzie's mom hadn't been around for a long time. Cam-Ma had told the mom to stay away because she always screamed and demanded money. Her uncle Sam didn't argue as much, but Cam-Ma told him to stay away too after he stole some things from her house. Her dad had been friends with her uncle, and apparently, with her mom, and would sometimes visit and bring her gifts. Honus watched the history world some more…

HW203904, 1:45 PM, Billy Jay Back in His Room

He got the object safely into his room and closed his door again without any sign of his mom's return. He set the object on his bed and sat in his chair. He picked up a game controller laser pointer and pointed one by one at each of the active AM games he was playing, expanding each to a full screen, watching for a few seconds to catch up on what his avatars were currently doing and interjecting some input of his own before reducing that window and opening the next. He made some investment decisions for some of his business mogul avatars, raising shock from game business associates in one of the worlds. He made exploration decisions for a couple of his adventure avatars who were funded by his game moguls. In one he tossed aside his pack and ropes and set out to free climb the upper half of the face of El Capitan. In another he steered his off-road vehicle to the left rather than the right at a fork in the jungle dirt road.

After a couple minutes interaction to keep a claim on his avatars in his active AM worlds, he turned to the object on his bed, picked it up and examined it more closely. He needed to figure out what it was, or what to call it, so that he could post it for sale online. He didn't expect to get rich from selling it, but any money would help. To get rich he needed to figure out how to tap his game wealth.

Billy Jay was not sure what he would do when he came into real-world wealth, but he would like to help his dad to regain his memories and allow his mom to get out of the house and restart her career. She seemed happier back when she was working.

He would also find a way to spend more time making friends online. He had a few online acquaintances in the games, but no close friends. He talked with some daily inside some of the game worlds but wasn't sure which were just characters with no real person behind them. He sometimes chatted with real people in discussion forums about the game. The deli worker and her game world cuisine-consultant avatar were a rare case where he could connect someone between a game world and the real world. He realized he didn't know her name in the real world, he did know that LacyHogan235^AM, whoever she or he was, was able to make food appear at his house.

He turned the object over, pressed and prodded it. It seemed solid and its surface had a texture of lines that seemed to swirl or spiral around it in both directions, kind of like the lamp in the living room. This object was roughly cylindrical and about a yard long. He put it on end standing it up on the floor and it looked kind of like a tall pedestal balanced, but not very stable. He took a picture with his tablet. He turned it over and it seemed to be more stable. "Okay. This end up." He took another picture.

It had many small nubs around the top surface now. He grasped a few nubs with each hand on opposite sides of the top and pulled gently. It expanded in a mesh network, getting wider at the top and bottom, and narrower and hollower in the middle. Billy Jay kept pulling and the woven mesh surface on the top continued getting wider and twisted and flattened out into a flat oval surface, and… "It's another table. That's really cool." He put his large drink on it and leaned on it. It held his weight. It was very light, but it seemed like a very stable and substantial table. "That's really cool, Dad. How did you come up with stuff like this?" It took him several minutes to find where to press and push to make the table return to its compact cylindrical form. He took more pictures of both the compact and expanded form and created a video of the expansion and retraction. He started uploading to an online appraisal and auction site. "I bet I can get at least a hundred bucks for this," he said to himself.

…

2:25 PM, Honus Curious about Inventions

Honus couldn't remember what ever happened to that table thing of his dad's. He didn't think he sold it. Maybe it was back in the workshop. He decided to replay that part of the story world and take a closer look, then go look in the barn workshop and see if he could find it. While there he could check if there were surveillance cameras that might explain how someone knew he had taken the piece.

While replaying, he tried to take more control of the Billy Jay character to stop him from taking the table or posting the ad but found that it only made the character pause for a second before continuing. The flow of events in this history world seemed to be pretty much fixed.

2:30 PM, Sam & Jo-Jo at *The Theme Park*

Kyle and Joel split up and walked quickly through different public paths in *The Theme Park* from the main entrance towards the attractions that backed up to the maintenance area. They stayed in touch with each other by a private communication link. They each stopped to talk with some of the costumed non-player characters[*] and vendors that worked in the park, showing the picture of the pair in jogging suits and asking them to let them know if they saw anyone dressed like that. None

---

[*] Guests at *The Theme Park* are typically referred to as players. Workers are referred to as non-player characters, or NPCs.

remembered seeing them. Joel tried reaching Tim to see if he had more information on where to find the pair, but Tim didn't answer.

Sam and Jo-Jo explored to see what had changed since the last time they were in *The Theme Park*. They used paths behind the scenes and tunnels under the park more than the public pathways. Most of the hidden doorways they remembered were still there. The pass codes for opening access to the tunnels still worked. Most of the good hiding places in public areas and in the behind-the-scenes areas were still there.

By a combination of hiding and acting like they were supposed to be there, they were able to explore the backside of several attractions without raising the attention of park workers. Being without wristbands was probably to their advantage in that they didn't set off any unauthorized wristband alarms.

Most rides and attractions they checked out hadn't changed in the couple of years since they were here last. There were still a mix of bumpy fast motion rides and themed attractions from popular entertainment game world stories. A couple of new rides or attractions had been added.

The waiting lines for most attractions still included express lanes with fees that could be paid with wristband points. There was still a hierarchy of players, some using the added fee lanes and some avoiding them. They made a game of predicting who would use the express lines. Sam was almost always right. He said it wasn't how they were dressed so much as how they walked. He demonstrated the 'entitled' walk for Jo-Jo and she started to see what he meant.

On some more popular rides the added-fee lines branched at multiple places where for even more added fees the impatient players with lots of points could avoid virtually all of the wait times. Cut (and pay) here to reduce wait to 30 minutes, here to reduce wait to 15 minutes, here to reduce wait to 5 minutes and here to reduce wait to less than one minute.

By using the behind-the-scenes passageways they could get to the express gates of most of the rides, where there was at most a 5-to-10-minute wait, but usually not to the no-wait-gates. The no-wait-gates were monitored by NPCs. They considered using the entitled walk to go through the last gate and go on a ride. But they held back, not sure what would happen if they went through without a wristband and someone challenged them. They decided not to go on any rides just yet. The behind-the-scenes exploration was fun on its own.

Multiple times they emerged from hidden doorways back into the public spaces just after Joel or Kyle had passed through the same area. They were not aware that anyone was looking for them, but they were constantly wary because they expected park workers or security to be on the lookout for people violating the "no-players" areas.

Seeing someone who looked like security, they ducked into a candy and gift shop where they were surprised to find that their old friend Wesley was behind the counter wearing a pirate's costume helping another visitor. They browsed through the items on display working their way closer to the sales counter. After the other customer finished and left, Sam stepped up to the counter.

"Aargh! Pirate Wesley. Ye scurvy dog. What Booty have ye?" said Sam.

"Sam?"

Jo-Jo stepped from behind Sam.

"And Jo? You both made it after all." He led them to a corner of the store.

"That we did, me matey. How be ye?" said Sam.

"Stop that. I have to put up with that from paying players."

Sam pouted and turned away, looking at the gift merchandise in the store.

"What makes you think we aren't paying players today?" asked Jo-Jo.

"You actually paid? That's new. You never paid when we came in here in the old days."

"Things change. Let's say we intend to pay. Tomorrow," said Jo-Jo.

"You both look good."

"You too. How did you get this job?"

"It helped knowing *The Theme Park* inside and out, from all the times we explored here in the old days. And they are pretty open to people who didn't have much job history. It was temporary and part time for a few months before going full time. You could maybe try."

"Now that would be interesting. But probably not. And how is Pat? You said he didn't want to meet us," said Jo-Jo.

"Actually, not so good. He started using the NeverMind again. Tried to get off of it a few times but kept going back. One time he was off for a few weeks he signed up for one of those AI-augmented training deals. Got the headset and everything. He was going to be an electrician or something. But he's been back on it, and he's been acting weird lately. Not himself. Says his Abbie is telling him to avoid his old friends. He even tries to avoid me."

"Bummer. But if we can't see Pat, what about you? What time do you get free today? We could go to some of the old food places, or you can show us what's new in here or around town and see if we run into anyone else we know," Jo-Jo suggested.

"Probably won't find anybody. The old crowd has all dispersed across the country like you did or just spends all their time in their Abitats, in treatment or just hiding out. Plus, I need to check on Pat." He noticed the jogging suits they were wearing and added, "Oh! Oh! I need to tell you something." He moved more into the corner of the room behind some merchandise displays and motioning them to join him.

"Yeah?" asked Jo-Jo.

"I think somebody's been looking for you," Wesley whispered.

"Who?" asked Sam, carrying a few souvenir items in his hands, and pockets bulging with others.

"No one you know. One of the park undercover security guys."

"Okay. Good to know. We tried to avoid the cameras, but maybe somebody saw us in one of the backways or underground. We'll be more careful," said Jo-Jo. "Put those back," she said to Sam.

He made a face like "What? What?" but he put back some of the items he was holding.

"I don't think it's that. He's security for the park, but I think he's also with the people who sell drugs here. He showed a picture of two people with outfits like yours running in a construction site. Didn't show your faces. Said something about a delivery."

"Delivery? Drugs?" asked Sam.

"Something like that."

"We don't know about any drugs, but we did pick up a big set of packages a few states back, and the delivery didn't finish yet," said Jo-Jo. "Maybe it has something to do with that?"

"You think the packages are drugs, Jo?" Sam asked. "Maybe NeverMind? All those packages would be worth a helluva lot."

"Anonymous cross-country delivery with a premium fee. Maybe," answered Jo-Jo, and continued, "But why do they want to meet us? Why didn't they just take the delivery the normal way? Abitat deliveries are private. Aren't they? Is there some reason not to use the normal delivery hand-offs?"

"Don't ask me," said Wesley.

Sam remembered that he had not yet removed the cans and glass wine bottles he had stashed in the delivery closet chute that might be jamming the mechanism. He just never had a chance to take them to a recycling center because Jo-Jo never left him alone with the Abitat while she took a walk near the beach to search for found objects for her art project like he expected her to. "Maybe it's not them. Maybe something went wrong in the delivery closet." Then he brightened up. "Maybe this is a good thing. Maybe we can ask for more points. And maybe take a sample from the packages?"

"Or maybe we should just dump the packages. We don't know what these people could do," Jo-Jo said. "I don't want…"

Wesley interrupted, "You do need to be careful with these people. And I'm going to need to tell them that I saw you. I'll give you a head start. And you should change your clothes." He found themed sweatshirts and hats that would fit them. "These should give you a different look. That should help, at least if they don't have a picture of your faces yet."

"Sorry we can't pay for these. No wristbands. No Points. No cash," Jo-Jo said. "Thanks anyway. We can just be careful."

Sam felt in his pocket for his small wad of cash but didn't speak up.

Wesley said, "I'll take care of it. Employee discount. You can pay me back later. I know how to message you in your Abitat." He rung up the sales with his own wristband and handed them the sweatshirts and hats in a reusable store bag.

Jo-Jo pointed at a wall panel and gave Wesley a questioning look.

"Yeah. That still works," he said. "I'll say I saw two people with clothes like in the picture came through here, but I didn't see where you went after you left."

Sam and Jo-Jo opened the hidden door in the wall panel and went in. Inside the backways they found a spot to change. They put on the sweatshirts and hats. They considered hiding their jogging jackets in the backways but decided instead to carry them in the store bag. They still had on the matching jogging pants. They decided it would be best to leave *The Theme Park* for today, get their wristbands and call back the Abitat, and then maybe dump the packages somewhere. They worked their way back to where they came in. They found the door closed without the cloth holding the latch open, frustrating their plan to go back the way they came.

"I told you to prop it open," Sam complained.

"I did," Jo-Jo looked up and down the doors edge and found the square of cloth on the ground. "This was in there when I left."

Sam pounded the palms of his hands on the door to see if it would pop open. After several unsuccessful tries he said, "Looks like this door is not going to open up, but there are other ways into the maintenance area," Sam suggested. "We can try a different way."

"Yeah, but this was always the best way during daylight hours," Jo-Jo replied. "Too many theme park workers on the other routes this time of day."

"We can take our chances. What's the worst that can happen. They catch us and throw us out?"

Jo-Jo shook her head and looked at Sam and finally said, "Or they catch us, and we have to deal with the drug people. Wesley said we should stay away from them."

"Yeah," said Sam. "Yeah. There is that. But I'd like to get out and see what's in those packages before we dump them."

"We can go out the front gate and walk around the park to get the wristbands, but the drug guys are probably watching the front gate too. With these clothes we can most likely get past them, but maybe we should kill some time until it's safer to go to the back tunnel. Maybe go on a ride or two. And sneak through after dark."

"Rides? I'm willing. I've been saying we should try some rides." Sam rubbed his chin thinking. "Which one first?"

"We need to stay out of view. What do you think? Kill time waiting in long lines for a popular ride, or go to a less popular attraction?"

"Do we have to do something boring? Can't we just cut the lines and go on the fun rides we like over and over again?"

"I don't know what would be best. Let's start with a quiet dark attraction. How about the History Moments. That usually isn't crowded."

"Because it's Boring. Nobody goes in there. I don't know why they still have that. You can get more interesting story worlds on your tablet or in your Abitat any time."

"It's educational. I saw a sign saying they have DBI. We don't have direct brain interfaces in my Abitat."

"Yeah. That could be cool. But they probably charge extra for it, and we don't have wristbands."

"One way to find out." Jo-Jo pointed and started down a side passageway towards the part of the park where the History Moments attraction was located.

"Maybe we should take our chances on one of the other ways out the back? I'd rather get caught than sit through the History Moments attraction," muttered Sam as he followed.

"But it's educational. Don't writers like educational things?"

"I can do without that sort of educational shit."

"It's dark and usually empty. Let's give it a try.

"I say we leave."

2:45 PM, Tim near *The Theme Park*

Tim sent messages with pictures of the candy wrappers and the wristbands to Squeaky and let her know the Abitat was on its way. She didn't respond right away, but that was typical for her.

He could get the packages himself. The Abitat should be here by now. Before calling Joel, Tim picked up the cutting tool and pulled the trigger to make sure it was charged. He liked the quiet raspy noise it made. He opened the door and looked outside the office pod to confirm the Abitat had arrived and saw the spot between the traffic cones was still empty. He looked around to see if it was parked somewhere else. The Abitat was not there yet. It had to be more than four minutes. He raised his wrist and asked, "Update estimated time of arrival?"

"Estimated arrival still four days."

"Oh shit. Oh shit." He went back to his desk and took the band from his wrist and looked at it. It was a very basic one and it had an S like a crude superman logo etched under the band. He pulled out the wristbands from his pocket and laid them all on the desk. His own had a wider band that included all the latest biometric health and gesture sensors and a holographic display element that could project a virtual tablet. The other one was also a very simple model. It had a stylized letter J etched under the band. He put it on and spoke to it.

"Abitat?"

"Yes?"

"Estimate time to this location."

"Six minutes."

"Come here immediately."

"Okay. On my way."

"Enter gate and park off the road between the orange cones."

"Request acknowledged."

He took off the wristband, looked at it, and thought to himself, "Okay. Okay. Things will be okay. It's on its way. Squeaky doesn't have to know. Of course, two wristbands could mean two Abitats. The J wristband is for the Abitat with the packages. The S wristband is for a Sam's Abitat 4 days away. The packages in the J Abitat will be here in five minutes. It should be okay."

He looked at live video feeds from around the work site. It looked like the last of the workers had left. He left the office pod and walked to a tool bin vehicle, tapped on a control panel, and said, "Relocate. I'll guide you."

He waved his hands guiding the tool bin vehicle into position close to the traffic cones, where it would only have to move a few more feet to block in the Abitat. He went around to the other side of the tool bin vehicle to be out of view of the Abitat's cameras when it came in, and he waited.

2:50 PM, Bella Going off the Trail

Bobbie looked up the rock wall at the blizzard haze where Bella had gone out of sight a few minutes before. Her own fully loaded backpack had disappeared up there just a moment ago too.

"Am I next?" she asked Bella through the comm link.

"Just a minute. Hold on."

Her empty backpack dangled back into view.

"Put it on so I can catch you if you slip," came Bella's voice.

As she put on the backpack and tugged on the climbing ribbon Bobbie looked at the icy vertical rock surface she needed to climb.

"Is this a good idea?"

"I've got you. Just let me know when you are strapped in."

"Okay. I'm climbing."

Secured in the pack, Bobbie stepped to the first icy toe hold. The slack in the ribbon was quickly pulled in as Bella maintained tension with each step. When she finally got to the top, Bella helped her to take off her empty pack and unclipped the ribbon.

While Bella quickly started repacking the pack, Bobbie looked at the view which gave a different impression than what Bella had described. She couldn't see much. Blowing snow obscured the view into both valleys so she couldn't see far either way. It was like they were standing inside of a snowy storm cloud far above the earth. If she concentrated, she could sense shadows hinting at shapes of trees and ridges. The gap in the ridge they were on was only a few feet wide. A twisted tree gave them something to hold onto. Its trunk had a right-angle bend at about waist height extending out horizontally over the drop-off into the new valley.

The drop-off was steep, disappearing quickly into the snowy haze. Any view of the trail they climbed from was blocked by the steep rocky slope behind them but would be invisible anyway due to the fog of snow. Holding onto the bent tree and looking down and ahead into the new valley, Bobbie sensed a large white patch in the haze below. She couldn't tell from looking if it was a relatively flat treeless area that Bella claimed it to be.

"We'll set up the tent down there?" Bobbie asked, pointing at the white patch.

"That's the plan. I checked it out. It's almost flat and big enough for the tent," Bella replied as she finished repacking the backpacks. One end of the ribbon was wrapped around the horizontal part of the tree and through a carabiner. Bella tossed the rest of the ribbon until it dangled down, fading into the snowy mist, possibly reaching the white patch below. "We can climb down to there with the rope for safety as we go down. We should wear our packs on the way down. We can leave the rope in place for climbing back up after the storm.

Bobbie looked down and paused then reached for her pack. Before she put it on, she checked one more time. "I still don't have any comms. How about you?"

Bella checked her tablet and replied. "No. I just see us."

2:55 PM, Honus Rejoins History World

Honus did find surveillance cameras in and around the workshop. That explained how whoever made this history world knew he had taken stuff from there. He wasn't able to find the same piece in the workshop cabinets today. Maybe he did sell it back then and just forgot. When he got back to his bedroom he reconnected to the game world to see what happened next.

The Billy Jay character was just playing games, so Honus switched focus to the mom character and fast-forwarded to the point where her car reached its destination. He kept it in a fast play mode, but one that he could follow along. As he watched he switched back and forth between summary and details.

HW203904, 2:15 PM, Mara at a Coffee Shop

After over an hour's ride across town, playing games on the console the whole way, Mara noticed her car had parked in a parking lot. She got out walked to a building marked as community center and library. Off the lobby she found a small coffee shop. She got in line to order and picked up a banana from the basket by the register. She took a picture of the banana with her phone for her food-intake tracking app. She looked in her purse for a phone or card for payment and put the banana back in the basket. She found a table and sat down. She looked around the coffee shop.

She made eye contact with a man of about Perry's age who was picking up a frothy-sweet high caffeine drink.

"Jerry?" she inquired.

"No. My name is Henri," he said with an accent that seemed like an imitation of a French accent. "What is yours, mon ami?"

"Sorry. I'm meeting someone named Jerry."

"You sure it wasn't Henri? No? No harm in talking to me while you wait for this Jer-ry person. May I sit here with you?"

"Sorry. I'd rather you didn't."

"I'm sorry too. I thought we had a connection." He took a seat a table over and continued to look at her with a smile.

A very large, probably over 400-pound, pleasant but frazzled looking woman whose age she couldn't peg—late twenties to early forties—sitting at an adjacent table working with a laptop turned to Mara and said, "I'm Jerry. I don't think we've met."

"Jerry? I'm sorry. For some reason I was expecting a man. And you're a lot—younger— than I expected." She paused. "I'm here about a message to Perry."

Jerry stood and crossed over to Mara's table. She was wearing a well-tailored stylish business pantsuit. She looked at Henri and he picked up his drink and left the coffee shop. She then said, "Thanks for that 'younger' lie. I like that. May I sit?"

"Sure."

Jerry set down her laptop and took a seat. "I was hoping Perry would come himself. Is he here?"

"No."

"But you know him?" asked Jerry.

"I'm responding to the message today for him."

"Today? Okay. That would be the Min Strong website email. I thought that one was a long shot."

Mara didn't respond so Jerry continued, "How is he? I haven't heard from him for a couple years. He warned the team he was having some medical issues and might be offline for a while. We've been really worried. Is he okay?"

"No. Not really. Some kinds of progressive brain damage can only be conclusively diagnosed on an autopsy, and then why bother."

"Brain damage? Ohhh! I'm really sorry to hear that," said Jerry, with some misting of her eyes. "I was hoping the 'medical issue' was a ruse and he was off working on a new secret project. It seemed like he was always keeping secrets."

"No secret project."

"We needed his help and couldn't get a response from him. We tried a lot of different people we thought might be able to reach him, but nobody knew anything. Today I found an email embedded in comments in an old Min Strong seminar website."

"Why Min Strong?"

"Perry seemed to know a lot about Min Strong, even more than the Tony guy who started the Abitats non-profit and was a total Min Strong fanatic. Like I said, it was a long shot, but here you are."

"Apparently so. Could you spot me for a drink and a snack? I didn't bring money today."

"Uh. Sure. I guess."

After Mara ordered and Jerry paid for a soy latte and a veggie sandwich, plus a banana, they returned to the table. Jerry leaned close and talked in hushed tones.

"I assume you know all about the work that Perry was doing at the institute on Abitats and the game?"

"Don't assume I know anything." Mara wasn't sure about Jerry's relationship with Perry, so she feigned ignorance to get more details and have time to enjoy her lunch.

"Okay. I can go back to the beginning but stop me if this is all stuff you already know."

Jerry explained, "Some people at a non-profit, Tony and others, thought that mobile tiny homes had promise to help with homelessness."

"Is that right?"

"The project designed and simulated living arrangements in autonomous vehicles—what became known as Abitats—although they had a number of different names back then."

"Really?"

"Perry contributed design features for the interiors of the units and for the infrastructure that would support them."

"Oh?"

"I got involved with the software. Perry and I worked together on that."

"Did you? How was Min Strong involved?"

"Inspiration. Living in the confines of an Abitat vehicle requires minimalism. We all bought in to minimalism," said Jerry.

"Uh, huh?"

"Everyone on the team became fanatics for minimalism and fans of Min Strong if they weren't before."

"Even Perry?"

"Perry knew more obscure Min Strong quotes than anyone."

"Is that so?"

"I figured maybe he was actually Min Strong himself or was close to her. The fact that you are here today and look a little bit like the old Min Strong cartoons says I was on the right track. Should I call you Min?"

"No. That doesn't follow. It just means your email reached me. But you say your team liked her?"

…

2:56 PM, Honus at the Ranch House

Honus was pretty sure they had proven years ago that his mom was not Min Strong, but maybe he should look at that possibility again. Not that it mattered since both his mom and Min Strong had been missing for years. The history world playback continued.

HW203904, 2:30 PM, Jerry Explains to Mara
"Are you kidding. You were, I mean, she, she was, like a prophet to the whole early design team." "A prophet?" "Most of the design team went to Min Strong conventions, took her online seminars, and were active in her online discussion forums." "Were you?" "I was doing research at university in Australia…" "Australia, you say?" "Yes. …and the Min conventions weren't as popular there, but I participated online. One of our sayings when we were looking at design ideas was 'WWMK'." "WWMK?"

"What would Min keep? We simplified the heck out of so many complicated ideas because of WWMK."

Mara's latte was ready. She retrieved it from the counter and encouraged Jerry to continue as she sat again and continued eating her lunch and sipping the latte and pretending to be fascinated by Jerry's exposition.

Jerry continued, explaining that the AM game also came out of Perry's work at the institute. It started as a simulation of living in Abitats to test different design ideas. At first players were allowed to test out and comment on whether they liked or disliked different Abitat design ideas. The role-playing got more interesting when Perry got the idea to speed up testing, by generalizing Jerry's AI software from the autonomous vehicle control to create autonomous characters in the simulation.

"You were involved with the software for the AI characters in the game?" Mara asked.

"That's right. I worked with Perry."

"Perry and Jerry."

"Uh. Yes."

"Go on."

Jerry continued, explaining that they were able to create multiple "worlds" filled with autonomous characters to test and fine tune different designs. The ability for people to interact with, influence, or control autonomous characters made role-playing in the simulations into a game, which became popular and eventually turned into the AM game.

"Not long after the game started to catch on beyond the original designers we started to lose contact with Perry. We thought maybe he was really still there, but taking advantage of the game's anonymity encryption features to disappear in plain sight."

"Anonymity features? You mean like Min Strong encryption?" Mara asked.

"Exactly! Of course you've heard of it," Jerry confirmed. "People wanted our work to be secure, so they built a strong encryption feature into the software which became part of the Abitats and the game. Some people use the game just for that anonymity."

Mara had finished her food and was almost done with her latte. She looked at her watch and asked, "Okay. How about today? What is the deal with royalties?"

"Oh. Okay. The people on the design team expected that we would get a share of royalties when Abitats started being produced for real. We are starting to see some Abitats on the road and the royalties haven't happened."

"What is holding it up?"

"We don't know. A couple years ago we all expected a big announcement about investments for making Abitats real, but instead our project funding was cut way back. We all had to get other jobs. Private companies mostly took over the work on Abitats, stealing our ideas."

"So, you didn't ask to meet to tell me how Perry could get his share of the royalties?" asked Mara.

"We thought maybe Perry knew where the royalties were going. At least he could help us prove what we invented so we could sue for a share. It seems like someone in the game team made deals with the car companies to give them our designs and cut all of us out," Jerry explained.

"So, you think Perry is trying to rip the rest of you off? I'll tell you, Perry has been in bed, incoherent, and incontinent for over three years. I talk to him every day, but he doesn't know it. He doesn't respond to me with more than mumbles and shakes. He can't walk to the bathroom by himself. There's no way he's making deals with car companies. I think you need to look closer at each other if you think someone is cheating the rest of you." Mara was getting angry. "What's more, we are broke. The savings we had before he got sick are spent. I haven't worked since he got sick. What I didn't spend on specialists who couldn't explain or do anything, has gone into just paying bills. We don't have any deals with car companies giving us royalties. I wish we did. We may be on the street soon." Mara looked stressed.

"That's not what I meant," said Jerry. "But you're saying Perry has just been lying in bed for years?"

"Yes. That's what I just said. He hasn't been working or making any deals."

"I think I need you to meet some other members of the team and explain that to them. We can meet them at a house not far from here."

"I don't see any reason I should do that. I need to get groceries and get home. I was expected over an hour ago."

"No. You really need to come with me first," said Jerry. "It's important. It won't take long."

"I've got to get home. I need to go now. Sorry I couldn't help you find the culprit stealing your royalties. If you find a way to get a share for Perry, let me know. The old email address you found may work for a while, or I might send you another way to contact me." Mara walked out of the coffee shop.

When Mara left the table, Jerry said, "Wait. What's your name? What should I call you? Min?"

As Mara left the shop without replying Jerry sighed and looked dejected and sat at the table typing a few things on her laptop.

When Mara got to her car she took her seat and said, "I guess it is time for plan B." She said again, "Plan B." Then she added, "Drive to my house." She tapped an address on the console display. As the car started to back out of the parking space, she put on her seatbelt. The scene ended.

. . .

2:57 PM, Honus Replays Some Scenes

Honus decided to replay the Mara scenes a few times again in normal speed and to see if he could notice any new clues. He also planned to try to take control or at least give her subconscious suggestions to leave the coffee shop sooner or to agree to go with Jerry—anything to change the outcome. Based on his earlier unsuccessful attempts to change Billy Jay's behavior he didn't think such character manipulations would work on Mara in this particular history world, but he thought it would be worth a try. He was hoping he could find some additional clues about what she meant by "Plan B" and why she didn't make it home.

3:00 PM, Tim and the Abitat near *The Theme Park*

Tim heard the crunching sounds of a vehicle crossing the dirt and gravel surface and stopping between the cones nearby. He raised his wrist and said, "Abitat, please turn off all external cameras."

"Okay. Video observation temporarily suspended."

He peeked out from behind the tool bin vehicle and saw that the Abitat was stopped just at the edge of the first cone, where it would be harder to block it in. He stepped back behind the tool bin vehicle and said, "Abitat, move forward 20 feet."

"Okay." He could hear the crunching sound on the gravel again as the Abitat moved forward very slowly and then stopped again.

He went to the control panel on the tool bin vehicle and said, "Relocate. Follow my directions." He guided it forward until it blocked the view of the Abitat from the street. Then he raised his wrist and said, "Abitat, stop all sound and video observation internal and external for one hour, and open door."

"Okay."

The door opened and Tim picked up the cutting tool, pulling and holding its trigger with a loud raspy hum, and stepped into the Abitat.

He tossed and piled bins and boxes to make a path to the delivery closet. He didn't expect to be able to reach the in-transit packages through the closet door, but he pulled on the door to the closet anyway. The door was jammed. He pulled the trigger to rev up the cutting tool.

The exterior of the Abitat vibrated as Tim cut through the interior wall to reach the delivery closet. The sound of glass shattering and metal twisting accompanied his cuts into the exchange chute where Sam had stuffed bottles and cans. After a pause with a sound of shuffling and moving things inside, he started carrying bundles out the door and stacking them on the ground outside the Abitat. He repeated this several times, creating a growing pile of bundles. After more cutting Tim emerged again with the last four bundles, stacking them with the rest and dusting his hands. He looked around and decided to call Squeaky and let her know he had secured the packages. He took one of the bundles with him and walked over to the office pod and went inside. The door automatically closed behind him.

Tim contacted Squeaky to explain that he had removed the packages from the Abitat.

"Did you ID them first?" squeaked the voice.

"Partly. The Abitat called me Sam when I called it here."

"Sam? But no facial ID on the two yet? Keep trying. Oh well. At least you've got the packages."

She told him to secure them in the office, send the Abitat away, and put the wristbands back in the tree. Tim set about moving the bundles into the office three or four at a time, with the office door closing behind him each time.

The fence for the flood control channel ran along one side of the construction site from a back corner near the tree all the way to the roadway. Behind the parked Abitat and the office pod a rusty "Entry Forbidden" sign was visible on a padlocked gate in the fence. The face of a man with wild reddish hair and a big reddish beard peered over the edge of the channel below the sign just in time to see Tim carrying four packages into the office. He climbed up and over the gate and, covering his face to hide from any cameras, walked quickly to the remaining pile of packages, picked one up and went behind the Abitat out of view of the office doorway.

He pulled a large knife out of his backpack and used the tip to poke a small hole into the bundle and withdraw a quarter gram or so of light green powder on the tip. He held the knife up towards the sky and tilted it back and forth to see it from different angles. He could see it better if there was direct sunlight, but it was cloudy today. Some of the powder fell off and he held his breath and backed away so as not to breathe it in. He thought he could see glints from crystals in the falling bits of powder. He touched the remaining speck still on the tip of the knife lightly with the pinkie finger on his left hand and looked at it for a second and then stuck his hand in the dirt and rubbed to get the speck of powder off. His finger tingled like it was going numb.

"Not exactly NeverMind. Way too strong. Probably NeverMore. Need to process it," he said to himself. "What was I doing?" He looked at the package in his hands and said, "Oh, yeah."

He took a plastic bag out of his pack, carefully wrapped the bundle in it, and put it in his pack, and waited.

Tim came back out and picked up the last three bundles, pausing for a second to think if there should have been four. He opened the office pod door and set them down in the doorway, while he went to the control panel for the utility vehicle and told it to back up to clear a path for the Abitat to leave.

After the utility vehicle moved back, clearing a path for the Abitat, Tim picked up and put away the last three bundles. The bearded man peered around from the end of the Abitat, still holding the large knife, but backed up when he saw Tim coming back out again. Tim was holding the wristbands and walked to the open door of the Abitat to retrieve the cutting tool.

As Tim entered the Abitat the bearded man moved quickly and came up behind him with a large knife and said, "Don't move! What have you done to my friends?"

3:10 PM, Charly and Jameel Look for Brock

"Did you see which way he went when he left?" Charly asked Jameel. Jameel was in his Abitat on the road and Charly was in hers docked at home. She saw Jameel holographically in her Abitat as he saw her in his. She could see Sandy J in the next room through the open door of her Abitat.

"I followed him through the park to the river trail, but he was making a scene, yelling for me to stop following him, so I backed off. He went inland on the river trail. I tried watching him from a distance, but he clearly didn't want to be followed. Pretty soon he went out of sight. I got in my Abitat and tried to find places where roads cross the river trail, but I didn't find him again. I walked a few blocks between streets on the river trail, but I'm back in my Abitat now."

Charly said, "I've been looking up everything I can find about the fire and the investigation afterwards. I don't see how he could have survived. It doesn't make sense."

"Do you think he is an impostor? He looks so much like the picture, and he acts like he was traumatized."

"The house and everything in it was burned to ashes along with dozens of other houses in the neighborhood. There were traces of Abitat metals and ceramics remaining in the street in front of the house and the family's Abbies and wristbands all went offline at the start of the fire. They didn't find any DNA in the ashes, but the fire was so intense that was not surprising. The Abbie memory backups recovered from the mesh cloud were all from before the fire so no grisly video details."

"So, who do you think this guy is?"

"Actually, I do think he's my cousin Barack, but I have trouble understanding exactly what happened and how he survived and was invisible for so many years. The contractor always denied they damaged the pipeline, but they were found responsible with their equipment melted right by the damaged pipeline where the fire started. We've always been told the whole family was burned up in the explosion along with a few dozen others in the neighborhood, so it's a shock to find him alive."

"You think maybe the other family members also survived?"

"No. His trauma seemed to be about losing them, so I think that part of the story was probably accurate. Plus, it's one thing for a middle-aged man to hide for a few years. It would be another level of absurd to think a mom and kid could also disappear like that."

"So, what do we do? How do we find him again and get him help?"

"He can't go far on foot. Although somehow he's been able to take care of himself for years. He did take some food and clean clothes with him, so…Let me think…we probably first find out what kinds of services are available for someone troubled like he is and then get some of the authorities involved to search for him and get him help. He needs help even if he isn't my cousin, but I think he is."

"Funny he turns up looking homeless when his name is up on memorial banners around the County for the anniversary of his project to end homelessness."

Jameel's Abitat passed under a "Jackson Memorial Homeless-No-More Festival" banner.

"I wouldn't say funny."

"Well. A coincidence anyway."

3:15 PM, Tim Confronted near *The Theme Park*

Tim retreated into the Abitat to get away from the guy with the knife and to get the cutting tool for self-defense. The guy with the knife paused at the doorway like he was letting his eyes adjust to the dark inside the Abitat.

Tim looked in the storage closet which was cut open and empty of packages, but now partly filled with trash bottles and cans. He could cut through the exterior to make an escape route but decided it would take too much time. He needed to slow down the knife wielder. He started pushing and tossing boxes and bags towards the doorway to block the path for the guy with the knife. As a box of hand-made mobiles, jewelry, and wall hangings spilled out by the doorway Tim noticed that the knife guy picked up some of the pieces and looked at them. He seemed to be lost in thought for a moment but then in a very deep and angry voice he demanded, "WHERE ARE THEY? WHERE ARE THE PEOPLE WHO WERE IN THIS THING?!"

Tim said, "I don't know. They left their bands." He held up his hand and grabbed his wrist to illustrate a wristband and then took the bands out of his pocket to show Doug.

"WHAT DID YOU DO WITH THEM!!?"

Tim was shaken by the violence in the man's voice and fearing for his life, dropped the wristbands and grabbed the cutting tool. The bearded man with the knife was still blocking the doorway of the Abitat. Tim clicked off all the safety switches on the cutting tool, and activated it with a low hum, then revved it as high as it would go. He started waving it side to side, in the process shredding everything in its path and sending shredded pieces of bags and boxes of Jo-Jo's found art supplies flying everywhere in the Abitat. One bag he shredded was full of a fine pink powdery sand Jo-Jo had gathered in southern Utah. As it was shredded it created a choking dust cloud filling the Abitat and blocking the view of Tim but also denying him a view of whether the knife guy was advancing into the Abitat.

Tim choked on the dust. The guy at the entrance seemed crazy mad. Tim couldn't see so he kept revving the tool and sweeping it from side to side in the dust cloud, thrusting it forward higher and lower repeatedly causing a shower of other shredded art materials and then with a deep thrust to the left he was showered by something wet and sticky. His face was coated with sticky red goo matted with the coral pink sand dust and other sticky chunks to form a thick red mask over his face. He rubbed with his free hand to clear enough to open his mouth and breathe but continued to thrust and wave the cutting tool everywhere. The mask and flying dust and shreds denied him a view of what he was shredding. He didn't want to see.

After a minute that seemed like hours of blindly shredding everything in front of him, he bumped the side of the tool against the remains of the refrigerator and the tool shut off. Trying to turn it on again, it refused. One of the safeties was back on. It must have detected cutting organic matter. He held up the disabled tool with one hand and reached blindly behind him with the other into the damaged storage closet and found some glass bottles. He picked one up and waved it and threw it towards the opening of the doorway. He did this repeatedly. After throwing a half dozen bottles he collapsed back against the storage closet holding a bottle and listened.

He heard heavy raspy breathing but then realized it was his own. He was hyperventilating and the shreds and bits sticking to his face were covering his mouth enough to make a raspy racket as he breathed. Still blinded by the coating of dust and goo on his face and body, he waited, listening, trying to quiet his own breath. This went on for he didn't know how long. He was still holding the disabled cutting tool and an empty bottle in front of him and still not wanting to see what he had done as he listened.

3:20 PM, Emily and Friends after the Exams

Emily found Jeremy and Chandra talking outside the technology lab after the last exam. As she joined them, they started walking towards the front doors to the school.

"How did you do? Do you still want to go to *The Theme Park* today?" Emily asked.

Chandra answered, "Yeah. Let's go. Exam results should be coming out later today, but I guess I did well enough at least to get *The Theme Park* reward."

"I think maybe they gave that to everybody after all. I got it too," Jeremy said. "Chandra and I were talking about out how we should get there. Share a ride or each take our own. I've got my Abitat and Chandra says she wants to take a bubble car and swing by her place on the way. But you need a ride, don't you, Emily? You could ride with either of us."

Emily said, "It's almost close enough to walk, but, actually, I'll be going to my mom's house this weekend, so my Abitat should be close by. I'd like to change clothes before going to *The Theme Park* anyway. Or do we need to wear STEAMBOAT gear to get in?"

"Our wristbands have the reward passes, so it shouldn't really matter, but it might be safer to wear something with the STEAMBOAT logo," suggested Jeremy. "I can get in with my own pass, but I'm willing to wear STEAMBOAT to get free food."

Emily looked up at the dark clouds that were moving above. "You think it might rain?"

Chandra replied, "It clouds up sometimes, but it never rains more than a few drops…Okay. Why don't we each take our own rides so we can change or get anything we need. Where should we meet up? Do you want to stay at the main theme park campus or go to one of the other theme zones? It only takes five minutes or so to change zones on the *Theme Loop,* not counting the queues. What kind of rides do you want to go for?"

Emily replied, "Let's just meet up at the south entrance near here. The best attractions are here anyway and we're starting late in the day, so I don't want to waste any time. We should hurry and go. Is four too soon?"

"I can do four. I could go now, but four is okay," Jeremy said.

"Four will work. I need to message my mom so she's not worried when I get to her house late," Emily said as they stepped outside. She looked at clouds in the sky again and pulled out her dad's umbrella from her backpack. "You never know. It might happen," she thought to herself.

As they waited for their vehicles, they could see many other students getting into Abitats along the curb, some in groups, some individually. Chandra noticed that about a quarter of the other students, of various genders, now had the same white and black oval outline around their eyes like Emily. She said to Emily, "Looks like you started another fad." She nodded at the other students.

"What? Really? Did I start that? Oops." Emily said.

"They weren't like that this morning. You may not notice it, but it seems people pay attention to what you do," added Jeremy.

"Maybe I should wipe it off," Emily started looking in her bag for something to use to remove her eye makeup."

"No. Don't take it off. I like it," said Chandra and Jeremy at the same time. Then they both did a little dance step to celebrate their synchronicity.

Several students said "Hi" to Emily, and a few to Chandra or Jeremy as they passed them to get into their own vehicles. Most were absorbed talking about going to *The Theme Park* in their own little groups or through their wristbands to friends who were somewhere else, or to no one in particular. Jeremy, Chandra, and Emily all raised their arms and tapped their wristbands as two more Abitats and a bubble car came into view together on the street and approached the loading curb.

"This is us," said Jeremy.

3:30 PM, Tim Retreats

Still covered in sticky, gooey red shreds and still holding the cutting tool and a wine bottle, both of which were also coated with red, Tim moved towards the entrance of the Abitat. When he felt the doorway, he rubbed away enough of the mask to see out, but he intentionally did not look back into the Abitat.

If he didn't look then there was nothing to see in the Abitat. This stuff all over him must just be from the bags and boxes of crap that were in the Abitat. The scary guy must be fine but just decided to go away.

Then he worried about the packages in the office. He looked around outside and didn't see anyone else in the construction site. He ran towards the office, but before going in noticed how red he appeared and went first to a nearby water tank vehicle. He turned a lever and, standing under the rush of water, he was almost knocked down by the force of the water cascading over him. He let the water run on his face and hands and the cutting tool but couldn't get all of the red stuff off. He picked little chunks that looked like bone out of his hair. He ran the water longer to flush all the bits and redness across the ground and through the fence into the storm channel. And then he let it run for another minute to flush the red matter further into the channel.

After shutting off the water flow and shaking himself, he went into the office. He was relieved to see the packages were still there. He sent a quick message to Kyle and Joel to let them know to still try to identify the two people in the jogging suits, but no need to detain them.

He contacted Squeaky and let her know that he had a run-in with a homeless-looking guy with a knife who seemed to be looking for the two joggers, but he chased him away. She advised him to get the packages away from the site as soon as possible.

He told the office pod to leave the site and head for another company construction site a few miles away. His hands, arms, and clothes, still looked wet, but also stained red. He decided not to sit down in the office chair and leave marks. He pulled his own wristband out of this pocket, put it on, and said to it, "Rendezvous the office pod with my Abitat so I can transfer and get cleaned up. The office pod can take the packages to the other job site without me."

As the office pod moved off the construction site and onto the street Tim remembered the damaged Abitat remained behind. He *forgot* to tell it to leave the site. He checked his pockets but realized he didn't have those wristbands any longer. He must have dropped them in the Abitat. He was going to be in trouble with Squeaky, but he didn't want to go back in there again.

Chapter 5

Later Afternoon

4:00 PM, Bella and Bobbie off the Trail

In the tent Bobbie was lying on a sleeping pad watching while Bella kneeled and sorted through the contents of both of their packs to inventory their remaining supplies. The fabric roof and walls of the tent continued to whistle and shake with the wind, except on the lower parts of the walls where snow was accumulating outside. It looked to be six inches high already on the windward side of the tent. There was also a bed of six inches of snow under the floor of the tent. Bobbie calculated that it could bury the tent overnight if this storm kept going at this rate, but she didn't say anything, since Bella had asked her to stay quiet while she checked the supplies.

Bella paused after she finished emptying the packs and arranging the contents. Then she said, "We should be okay with food and power for a couple days if we're careful." She started to put items back into the packs.

"That's what I told you, except for coffee. We can make maybe one more cup. I keep inventory," Bobbie replied.

"Sorry. I wanted to check for myself."

"That's okay. I understand. By the way, are you warm enough? We probably shouldn't use power for heat. You should change out of the clothes you wore in the rain and snow and get into your bag to stay warm while we wait out the storm. The tent fabric is a good insulator, but you'll be even warmer in your bag."

"Maybe that's a good idea." Bella shivered thinking about it. "But is there anything we should do outside while there is still some daylight. I don't want to get cozy and then have to put everything right back on to go out."

Bobbie replied, "It's only four o'clock. We should have a few more hours with some light."

"It seems later. Dark from the clouds. It will get really dark after nightfall if the clouds don't clear," Bella said as she was stashing some collapsible pots and water containers back into one of the packs.

Bobbie continued "Now that you mention it, we should refill our water bottles. Either find some running water or fill some containers with snow to melt."

"Right. Melting it slowly in the tent will save some power. Here." Bella handed Bobbie two collapsible containers that she was about to put back in the packs. "Can you collect some snow from the doorway?"

"It's cleaner to gather it away from the tent, and if we're opening up the door anyway, I should scout around. I didn't check the area out much. We were in a hurry to set up the tent. Maybe there is a stream nearby. That would be easier than melting snow."

"I didn't see a stream, but I didn't explore much either. Should I go with you? I'm still in gear," Bella asked.

"No need. Finish organizing the supplies and gear and get yourself warmed up. I'll be right back. And I'll keep in touch."

She touched her ear to remind Bella that she was still wearing her earpiece and opened the door of the tent to step out into the blowing snow.

4:02 PM, Abitat Awakens

The Abitat turned on its video and sound observation after one hour as requested and noticed damage to its storage and delivery closets and dripping red shredded organic matter all over the inside, blocking most of its internal video sensors. It sensed the presence of two familiar wristbands somewhere amid the shredded material but no sounds of breathing or heartbeats and concluded that its occupants might be dead. Outside sensors showed the same construction site it came through on its way in, now with no humans present, and with some vehicles missing or moved from their previous positions, and more footprints on the nearby ground. A scattering of raindrops were starting to fall, making dots on the dusty ground of the site.

Being uncertain about its occupants and not being allowed to use other identifiers for them, it decided not to contact authorities immediately but to seek repairs and cleanup first. Humans at a service facility would be able to decide whether authorities need to be involved. Its door closed and it began to move slowly across the construction site towards the street. It contacted a nearby service facility for an appointment for cleanup and repairs.

4:05 PM, Emily, Sam, & Jo-Jo at *Theme Park*

Jo-Jo nudged and signaled to Sam "Let's go." She figured they had spent over an hour in the History Moments attraction and Sam must be about to go crazy. Sam took off the headset and shook his head a few times like shaking off bugs before blinking his eyes to focus and see who was nudging him.

"Oh. Oh. It's you," said Sam as he recognized Jo-Jo and realized where he was.

"Who did you expect? Min Strong? Let's go," Jo-Jo replied. As they moved to the exit area for the attraction she continued. "Were you bored to death?"

Sam answered, "Not really. I think this Direct Brain Interface is really cool. It's nice that they let us use DBI without wristbands."

"But you said all the history moments stories are boring," Jo-Jo countered.

Sam explained, "No. They are educational. And the Min Quest moment is more like mythology than history. And, Hey. Being inside the head of Min Strong first-person when she got to the top of that ridge in her MinQuest was really cool. I'd like to try it a few more times. I really felt like I was her."

Jo-Jo said, "I did the same scene without the DBI, and it didn't seem all that great. Kind of like the other versions of the original MinQuest I've watched or played or read. Not that interesting. The scenery was very nice. It looked real, like it was camera-captured 3D rather than animated or generated."

"Did you get the big bird to land next to you like in the old story?" Sam asked.

"The hawk? Yeah. For a second, but it flew away again as soon as I turned to get a good look at it," Jo-Jo replied.

"It flew in close to me a couple times, but I kept scaring it off for some reason. It never landed. I'd like to try again," Sam said.

"You're supposed to clear your mind like Min did and let nature accept you as you are," Jo-Jo said.

"Yeah. I couldn't do that. I kept noticing that I had boobs and stuff. It was really distracting," Sam said, while putting his hands on his chest and then his crotch.

Jo-Jo shook her head and said, "Of course, that's what you noticed. The DBI is that detailed? You could feel yourself in her body?"

"Yeah. It was really cool. I'm surprised more people haven't heard about this version. You'd think this attraction would be really crowded."

"Well, it's new," said Jo-Jo. They paused against the wall at the attraction exit and looked over towards its entrance. Jo-Jo noticed the prominent warning sign at the entrance she hadn't seen before. It explained the 250 Amp fee and release of liability for a long list of possible side effects from using the DBI upgrade.

She pointed at the sign and said, "The fee and warnings probably discourage some people. I'm surprised it worked for you without a wristband. That would have wiped us out if we got hit with that fee. We should probably get away from here before someone tries to charge us for that. You used it like four times. Where should we go next?"

Sam started towards the entrance and said, "No. I want to try it again. Let's go again. They didn't charge us. Let's go again while it's still free."

Just then three teenagers with sweatshirts with STEAMBOAT logos approached from the direction of nearest park entrance. One of them walked quickly to them.

"Sam and Jo-Jo? Is that you?" the younger girl said. "It is you. I haven't seen you in a year or two. Where did you go? Guys, Sam and Jo-Jo used to live in my dad's neighborhood. They helped me find plants and things in the river for biology. Sam and Jo-Jo, this is Jeremy and Chandra. They're friends of mine from school."

"Nice to meet you," said Chandra and Jeremy simultaneously. They looked at each other considering doing their synchronicity dance but decided against it.

"Em? Little Emily from the river trail? You look older than you did the last time we saw you. You were kind of a kid still then, but now you look almost grown up. Make-up and everything," Sam said as he looked closely at Emily and her friends.

"Watch it, Sam. They are a lot less than half your age and still minors."

"I suppose. Good to see you Little Em."

"Where have you guys been?" asked Emily.

"In the MinQuest History Moments world. It's great! The DBI was cool as hell," Sam replied.

"DBI? They have DBI now? Really?" Jeremy asked, looking towards the attraction entrance, and noticing the warning signs.

Emily continued, "I meant, since you moved? Where have you been living? I asked Brock a long time ago, but he didn't know where you went."

"We've been all over the place. Kansas recently. This is our first trip back," Jo-Jo answered.

"Well, it's sure good to see you. How long will you be in town?"

"Not sure. Probably just a few days. Things are really expensive here," Jo-Jo said.

"I'm not going to be at my dad's place this weekend, so I won't see you at the river trail."

"We're not going there either. Doug was angry when we stopped there today."

Emily recalled the altercation on the river trail she witnessed before school but decided not to mention it. "Doug can be temperamental, but he's a good guy."

"Yeah. Well. We might be coming back here tomorrow," said Sam.

"Us too. We've got passes for this weekend," added Chandra.

"Maybe us," Jo-Jo added. "We don't know for sure yet."

"Well, I hope we do run into each other again while you're in town. But I should get going now. Chandra, Jeremy, and I want to enjoy *The Theme Park*."

"Maybe we should check out the History Moments," suggested Jeremy. "I heard that the DBI was coming but I didn't know it was here already."

They all ended up going into the History Moments attraction together. Jeremy and Sam took the headsets for the brain interface and Jeremy got charged the fees to his wristband for both. Chandra used the regular 3-D goggles and haptic gloves. Emily opted for the text-based novelized interface on a tablet. Jo-Jo decided to just watch the others and the 3D scenery display.

Emily viewed the text on her tablet:

Min Quest History Moments, Summer 2019
After scrambling up over rocks, repeatedly sliding backwards almost as much as I moved forward, I finally made it to a ridge with a view into the next valley. I was not quite above the tree line, but in an area with jumbled rocks and loose crumbing granite and an occasional stunted tree. The gap that I reached was shaped like a saddle: an almost level space of a few square feet, with the ridge rising steeply to the left and right and dropping steeply in front of and behind me. I held on to a twisted tree that grew horizontally from the edge of the rise to the right and crossed half the gap before turning and extending out over the drop-off in front of me.   …

As the text paused, Emily whispered, "Go on."

…   My hands and knees ached and were bleeding from scratches earned scraping on rocks and branches during the last hour's climb. Rubbing my knees smeared the blood and blurred the stinging sensation between my hands and knees. It was one blurred pain that extended between them.   …

Emily whispered, "Rest."

...

I decided to rest before continuing. I took off my small pack, hanging it on a broken branch about the size of my forearm, sticking out of a gnarled bulge on the part of the bent tree that turned out over the drop-off into the new valley. I didn't open the pack to look for bandages or medicines. I had left those behind as I carried only the bare minimum. I knew I would need to find certain mosses, leaves, and roots to salve my scrapes, and fresh water to clean them. Based on what I had read before starting on this quest I was confident that the valley ahead and below should have all that and more.

...

"Look."

...

Looking ahead I could see that even here deep in the wilderness many trees were brown and dying. I worried that some of the plants I planned on using might also be suffering. I had read that, already weakened by changing weather conditions and recurring droughts, the trees were being attacked by some kind of beetle or infection, but the damage looked worse than I had expected. Perhaps my own previous patterns of consumption had contributed to changes in the planet that were strangling this forest, but at least during this walk I was trying not to do more damage. I hoped the forest would receive me based on my current benevolent intentions rather than my prior less careful history.

...

"Huh?"

...

My quest was to find myself by stepping away briefly from all the manic consumerism and complexity of my typical modern human activity and to live in the land with minimal possessions. Everything I had was on my person or in the small daypack hanging there. I had just enough clothing to provide warmth and protection from rain and sun. I had some tools to help cull food and protection from what I could find in the land. Most importantly, I had knowledge. I had studied before starting out. I knew of plants and animals I could expect in the areas I would be walking. I knew of risks and opportunities associated with the things in the forests. In the first two weeks of this walk I had learned that book knowledge was not always current or complete, but even with its gaps it gave me important clues to help me survive.

…

"Look back."

…

I looked behind me down at the slope I had climbed and the last valley I had crossed in the last couple days. The first two weeks of my walk had been challenging. The food I found was not fully replacing the calories I was burning. My clothes were already getting looser. Losing some weight was okay, and part of my plan, but I should put more time into gathering food before my clothes get too loose and I get weak. A layer of dirt was embedded in my clothes and on my skin, even though I tried to wash when water was available. I was starting to look and smell a lot like the forest around me.

…

"Animals?"

…

I had survived several close encounters with animals and with hikers that caused me concern. I had planned a path that generally avoided well-traveled hiking trails, but of necessity overlapped such trails from time to time. Going off trail increased the chances of animal encounters, and I had seen many animals up close, including bears. Staying still until people or animals passed had worked so far, but I had my can of bear spray within reach. I figured I was as likely to need to use it on humans as on bears.

…

"Look Ahead."

…

I turned and surveyed the view ahead, identifying ridges and peaks that I remembered from my preparations for this quest. I recalled where there should be a stream and a meadow with resources I can use. I should be able to stay in this valley for a week or more. Quiet solitary meditation was one of my objectives, and this should be a good location for that. Gazing ahead I saw something move from a tree on a far ridge. A bird launched into flight. I watched as it rose, and dove, rose again, and circled. Some kind of hawk, but too far away to identify for certain.

…

Emily suggested, "Red Tail?"

…

I thought about the species of birds that I had read about in this area and realized it must be a red-tailed hawk. I pointed at it and spoke "Hey. Red Tail." Not a shout, but loud enough for anyone close by to hear. The bird seemed to hear. It turned and circled closer. It considered me from the air as it circled.

…

Emily whispered, "Be still."

…

I stood still, other than turning my head to follow the bird's flight and it swooped down and landed on the same bent tree where I had hung my pack. It was on the part that extended out over the downslope, so it was at my eye level now, but would be well above my reach if I went down the slope and stood under it. "Hello, RedTail," I said. The bird turned its head from side to side looking at me and beyond me at the valley where I had come from and then at the valley where I was going. I felt that it was accepting and welcoming me. Then it seemed to be looking at my pack and deciding whether to try stealing it. The pack was light enough it might be able to do so.

…

Emily whispered, "Please don't."

...

I stared back at it and gently shook my head to say. "Please don't." It turned its head toward the valley ahead and took off and soared up and away, eventually disappearing in trees not far from where I had first noticed it taking flight.

...

Jo-Jo watched as Emily continued staring at her tablet and giving quiet voice suggestions. The 3D scenery around them seemed to respond to Emily's commands and appeared to be from the viewpoint of the Min character who was not visible. Jo-Jo also noticed that Emily's friend in the hijab with haptic gloves and googles was making various gestures and intricate hand motions. Sam and Jeremy mostly sat still, with eyes closed, wearing their DBI caps. Over time their facial expressions changed and occasionally they moved their hands slightly.

4:15 PM, Danger off the Trail

Bobbie opened the door to the tent and peeked in. "Are you okay, Bella? You didn't respond when I tried talking to you." She saw that Bella's earpiece was lying on the floor while she warmed herself in her sleeping bag. Bobbie tapped her ear to remind Bella that she was supposed to stay in touch.

"Sorry. It must have fallen off when I got in the bag. Did you find water?"

"No, but I think we may want to move our tent. I was trying to warn you so you wouldn't get too comfortable."

"Too late. I'm very comfortable and starting to get warm again." Bella snuggled in her bag. "Why do you want to move the tent?"

"Maybe it'll be fine here, but it looks like this open area we are camped on is a talus or scree pile of small broken rocks, that have fallen recently. Collecting snow to melt for water, I uncovered the rocks. Near the tent they were covered in a few inches of snow, but I think I saw some at the edge of the clearing that had only a dusting of snow. This could be an active rockfall area and with rain and freezing more could break off any time."

"Yeah. I see how that could be bad. Sorry I didn't notice that when I was first checking out this spot. On our rappel down from the saddle I didn't see any newly broken rock faces. Are you sure?"

"We couldn't see much in the blizzard on the way down here. It might be fine here, but you need to check it out and agree to the risk if we decide to stay and take our chances."

"Well, it was nice here for a couple minutes." Bella sat up and grabbed her hiking clothes hanging from a loop in the tent ceiling and started to get dressed again. "Do you think we need to climb back up to the trail and keep going towards the pass or can we move the tent a little to a safer spot close to here?"

"It might be fine where it is. If we have to move at all I think we can find something close to here. I was checking it out, but you weren't responding, so I had to stop looking and come back here."

"I said sorry," Bella said as she picked up her earpiece.

"Get ready now while I go out and look some more. If I can figure out where the rocks are falling from, that ought to help us decide. Come on out when you're dressed. You can help figure this out. And wear your earpiece so we can keep in touch. With the wind it's hard to hear each other."

"Okay. Okay." Bella put on her earpiece and continued getting dressed.

4:20 PM, Tourists after *The Theme Park*

They were all in wet clothes and the mom and dad were taking turns keeping a close eye on the twins who were playing a game on the rental Abitat's wall display.

"Did you expect rain?" asked the mom.

"Nope. Forecast said a chance, but it just doesn't happen here," replied the dad.

"That seemed almost like a summer storm back home."

"Right. We could have handled it. We didn't have to leave so fast," suggested Dad as he removed new umbrellas and raincoats from the delivery closet of the Abitat. "We could have bought raincoats and umbrellas in the park."

"It's okay. We need to eat dinner anyway. Our stomachs are still on central time. We can let the Abitat top off its charge while we decide on a place to eat."

4:25 PM, Jose at Abitat Services

Jose stood at the side of service and repair bay 3 as a another simple grey oversized Abitat unit with the unusual forward windows and slightly higher than normal ground clearance moved into position at the recharge pod across the exit lane. It looked a lot like the one that came through earlier with the kid in the wall. Like the last few vehicles to come in it was spotted with rain drops.

He had been thinking he might be able to check out early and head home to check the messages on game world PW3709. He was just watching and waiting now since most vehicles didn't need extra services, and he had finished his last one about five minutes ago. He hoped rain wouldn't cause more vehicles to need service.

This next one attached itself to the fluid exchanger and with some whooshing and gurgling and a familiar whistling it quickly dumped its waste, flushed its tanks, and refilled its potable and non-potable fluids. Batteries were getting a flash charge with a slight hum. The work display showed good numbers on the fluids and charges. The work display also showed that this unit didn't need any other services today. That's good. But the next one behind it did.

"Oh well, one more quick service and I can get out of here," he thought.

A little "ding" sound and the big grey Abitat disengaged with a deep exhalation sound from the recharge pod and rolled forward. He hadn't looked closely at the exterior of the similar unit that came through earlier but took this opportunity to examine this one as it rolled past him. Units like this with windows are sometimes used for tourist rentals since tourists have more interest in sight-seeing. With higher clearance, these units could use recharge stations in tourist parks or campgrounds around the county, as well as some open public recharge stations, but they typically wouldn't fit in most covered recharge stations. Some of them were fitted with even higher clearance for really rough roads or the capacity or range to get farther outside the city, but not this one. Maybe units like this were not all that rare; given he had seen a similar one earlier today.

The windows were darkened for privacy, as normal, so Jose couldn't see in even if any occupants could see out. He couldn't immediately tell if this unit was occupied. Since it was just getting a regular charge the work display didn't need to show that kind of information. But as the unit started to turn to the right towards the street exit, that question was answered as a window became clear and two faces of young children pressed against the front window glass sticking out their tongues and laughing. Boy and girl, they both looked about 6 years old. Jose recognized them from earlier today. This was the same unit as earlier today. He waved at them and smiled back.

As the tourist unit rolled out towards the street exit the next unit moved forward into the recharge pod. This one looked more typical. No forward windows, standard size, urban mobility platform with low ground clearance good for smooth city streets, but that would get in trouble on any rough roads, no major exterior dings. Most of the exterior was a bright blue color that kind of hurt the eyes, a little dirty but nothing the exterior wash cycle downstream couldn't take care of.

He checked his tablet. This one had ordered interior cleaning service, inspection, and possible repairs, but no exterior cleaning. No other specific requests. Not a full clean and refresh to ready it for another tenant, but an inspection and cleaning, keeping most of the same contents and components to be reused by the same tenant, or owner. Pain in the ass.

It was more work for him to take extra care cleaning and refreshing a unit without damaging any of the precious belongings that had to stay with the unit. Either clean around the contents or empty it, clean it and then carefully put everything back. He hoped this person didn't keep a lot of personal stuff in their unit.

A full cleaning was easy for units that followed the new trend of Virt-homes. If an inabitant had any personal property in the unit, it would be uploaded to one of the *cloud of things* services, like Infinite Closet. The empty Abitat unit could be steam cleaned and then refreshed with settings and objects from the cloud for the next inabitant.

Jose understood people wanting their own private Abitat space—he wouldn't want anyone in his private trailer. And he could especially understand the people who wanted to only use their own private personal bathroom and kept their Abitat close by for that reason. But it was wasteful to keep an Abitat idle, outfitted for the same inabitant all day when others could be using it. Of course, most Abitats would do local deliveries during their waiting time, so they weren't completely idle. He understood that some owners that didn't need any extra points didn't even let their Abitats do deliveries. Those Abitats found places to rest and deep charge or wandered around during their idle time letting their Abbies sightsee.

He thought, "Of course maybe I'm not one to complain, given where and how I live. I guess it's okay that some people like to touch the same objects and belongings day after day."

He waited, tapping his fingers for the refresh package to be assembled and delivered and for the vehicle to finish its charge cycle. The refresh package ought to include cleaning supplies and possibly changes of linens, and maybe some perishables, like fresh flowers, as well as any items the inabitant wanted back from the infinite closet storage service. The woosh, gurgle and whistle stopped and with a ding and exhale sound, the Abitat started to move. It then paused briefly while a little bubble pod vehicle passed in front of it from another recharge station heading towards the exterior wash station.

The blue Abitat started across the exit lane and into his service and repair bay. The refresh package eventually rose into place, and he grabbed it from the conveyor—light, only cleaning supplies—he tapped a few spots on his work pad display and stepped to the side of the Abitat. As the door opened his eyes widened and he looked around the service facility to see if anyone else could see what he saw. Inside was a bigger mess than he had seen in a long time. The inside was filled with wet crimson splatters and oozing shreds of what looked like intestines. "There must be parts of two or three bodies in here," he thought. "Shit. Cleaning this one is not going to be easy."

4:30 PM, Emily and Friends Eat at *The Theme Park*

Emily and Jeremy were now wearing the souvenir sweatshirts that Sam and Jo-Jo got from Wesley, and Jo-Jo and Sam were wearing STEAMBOAT Academy sweatshirts. Sam still wore his souvenir hat. Chandra wore Jo-Jo's hat over her headscarf, but otherwise her outfit was unchanged. Emily had suggested that they swap clothing items in the empty hallway at the exit from the History Moments exhibit after learning that Sam and Jo-Jo were trying to evade park security. When Emily asked, Jeremy was willing to help. Chandra, not so much. She wanted to get away from these old people and have some fun with her friends, but she held her tongue. Jeremy suggested using their food vouchers and now they were sitting at a table at a food concession near the NewTech area. The ground was wet like it must have rained recently.

They were eating and talking about their experiences in the History Moments exhibit. The eating area overlooked the popular "Self-Driving Cars" attraction in which players could drive a car themselves on a track with limited options for where to go. It seemed odd to Jo-Jo that such an ancient history attraction was in the NewTech area, but she didn't bring it up. She had brought it up with Sam and others many times in prior years and didn't think it was interesting enough to say out loud today. She also remembered that "self-driving cars" used to mean something else.

Jeremy said, "Why are old-fashioned self-driving cars considered NewTech?"

Jo-Jo held herself back from saying anything but smiled and nodded.

All of them had some similarities in their experiences in Moments as Min Strong reached the gap between the two valleys. But they each had differences as well.

"I still couldn't get the bird to come to me," related Sam. "I opened my pack on the ground and looked for some food to offer the bird but still couldn't find any. I waved a sock to attract it. It circled closer but didn't land. And later a marmot came out of the bushes and started taking things out of my pack. I had to chase it away."

"I saw you waving your hand like you were chasing something away," Jo-Jo shared. "I wondered what that was about."

"I was really moving? Not just living it in my brain with the DBI headset?" Sam asked.

"Can actions leak between the DBI experience and your real body?" asked Jeremy. "Did you see me doing anything?"

"No. You seemed to just sit there. Nothing weird," Jo-Jo assured Jeremy, but her tone of voice seemed to suggest that maybe she did see him do something weird.

Jeremy looked at Emily and Chandra to see if they had seen him do anything embarrassing. They shrugged.

Chandra had been looking around impatiently, but spoke up, "I looked through the pack to see what tools I had, then rigged up a little trap and killed something. I don't know what it was. Maybe a marmot. Anyway, I hung it on the branch, and the hawk flew right in pecked at it and took pieces of it away. It was cool. I also tried to make Min leap to her death, but she wouldn't do that."

"Chandra, I thought you and Min were both against violence," Jeremy asked.

"It's not real, Jeremy. Even if it's "history" it's in a *story* world. Your character in a story game isn't you. You can influence what they do, but it's not real. Min did seem kind of freaked out with herself after I had her do that though." Chandra replied. "How about you, Emily? What happened in your story?"

"I didn't try to control Min in my story. It was text-based. I just tried to let it flow with the traditional MinQuest storyline. It would pause after I read a little bit of the story. I'd whisper to suggest something to the Min character and then it would show a little more of the story, like she thought of that word before deciding to do the next thing. It played out just like I expected from the other versions of the MinQuest that I've seen or read. The hawk landed and visited and later a marmot came and sat with her for a minute. The scenery that displayed in the room while we were in there pretty closely matched what was described in the text."

"That's right. I saw your hawk and marmot in the displays," Jo-Jo added.

Just then it started to rain, with big drops falling far apart at first, but quickly getting more intense, and a wind started. They crowded in under the umbrella that shaded the table where they were sitting and moved the remains of their food towards the middle of the table to keep it dry.

"Rain?" asked Sam.

"I didn't think it would really rain," Chandra said as she adjusted Jo-Jo's hat and pulled her head scarf closer around her face.

Emily reached into her bag, took out and opened her dad's umbrella and smiled. The wind pulled at it, but she was able to handle it.

"Do you want to find a drier spot, like an indoor ride, or maybe come back tomorrow?" Jeremy asked.

"The New Tech Pavilion is just over there," Chandra pointed. "That should be out of the rain." Without waiting for the others, she picked up her drink and the remains of her sandwich, got up from her seat, and walked quickly towards the New Tech Pavilion.

Jeremy followed her with his drink cup in hand. Emily said to Sam and Jo-Jo, "I should go with them. Do you want the rest of this?" She indicated the cheesy fries she had barely touched.

Sam said, "Sure," and pulled the fries closer and moved to an open seat that was more sheltered from the rain.

Emily said, "Good luck," as she tilted her umbrella against the angle of the rain and followed Jeremy.

After waiting a few seconds for Emily and the others to disappear into the New Tech Pavilion Jo-Jo asked Sam, "Should we try one of the back ways out again now? It's early still but looking dark with the rain. It might be okay now."

"I'd be okay trying the History Moments again," Sam replied.

Two security-looking guys came from different directions, meeting just steps away. One spoke, "Any sign of them?"

"Guy in the pirate shop said he thinks he saw them, but he's not sure. I checked the rides in that area and didn't find them."

"Maybe we should check that area again."

"Any word from Tim?"

"Just the text, 'ID', whatever that means."

"'Instant Death?' you think?" He laughed.

"I guess we get to decide. He hasn't answered when I tried checking in. Let's go." They walked away together.

Sam and Jo-Jo decided to go the opposite direction. They were getting soaked as they walked briskly through the rain before ducking into a covered area where they expected to find another hidden doorway to the backways.

4:40 PM, Brock Back at Camp

Brock was sitting in a nice director's chair near his tent reading a book and waiting for Doug to return. He was troubled by the memories that had returned to him earlier but was trying not to think about them. Doug would be back eventually, and he could get some more Forgetdibles or NeverMind and he could erase those memories again. He had moved his chair under the street overpass because it had been raining off and on for the last half hour since he got back to the campsite. His books were all in boxes and shelves under the overpass, so they were safe, he thought. The tent should be waterproof so his sleeping bag and pack and stuff should stay dry inside the tent during a little rain. There had never been more than a few minutes sprinkle of rain in the years he remembered living outside with Doug.

He stood up and walked to one of the bookshelves, placing his book back in its position and noticing a pink folded paper in a space between two other books. He pulled it out and unfolded it. It had drawings of pandas at the top and bottom and in neat hand printing it said, "I O U one borrowed book. Em." He pictured Emily, the young teen girl who visited their campsite and borrowed books from him and flashed again on the images of fire and grief. Something about the girl reminded him of his son Sandy. Maybe that's one of the reasons he lent her books. Would Sandy have been about that age now, he wondered. Sandy always liked books. He regretted not reading to him more. He hadn't thought about Sandy in years until today. He hoped Doug would return soon with something to help him forget again.

An unusual rushing sound interrupted his thoughts. In addition to the growing patter of drops in the tents, water was now making noise flowing in the river channel. This rain must be more than a sprinkle. He walked over to the deeper groove, the pilot channel, that ran down the middle of the riverbed. It was usually slimy, green and a little bit wet, but now it was flowing with water a foot deep almost to the top of the groove. If this rain continued it might overflow to the rest of the channel. He looked at the rain falling hard outside the overpass and looked back at his library and started to have a new sense of panic.

4:50 PM, Sam and Jo-Jo Try to Leave *The Theme Park*

Sam and Jo-Jo had come close twice but avoided being caught as they went through the backways and opened the hatchway to the flood channel that ran under the back of *The Theme Park*. They found it flowing deep with rain water, so they retraced their steps quickly to find Emily at the NewTech pavilion. They convinced her to give them a ride to the lot where they left their wristbands. Emily would come right back to meet Chandra and Jeremy, and they'd meet again when the park opened in the morning. Sam, Jo-Jo, and Emily headed towards the front gate, but before they went far Sam saw the security guys again and ducked into the entrance for the nearest attraction gesturing to Jo-Jo and Emily to follow.

He peeked around the corner and said, "They're coming this way." He hit the button to open the door to the elevator down to the *Theme Loop*. A sign said, Access to the Journey to Space. It was a train that ran underground connecting the various *Theme Park* districts and the Journey to Space launch facility in the desert. They didn't want to go all the way to the desert or to space and decided to get off the *Loop* at the first stop at the Old West District. Emily instructed her Abitat to meet them there. Without occupants her Abitat should get there in less than an hour. The tube ride would take five minutes, not counting queues. But there were always queues. Her Abitat would probably get there before them.

4:55 PM, Honus Versus Billy Jay

After replaying the Mara scenes a few times Honus gave up on trying to change her actions. He was also unable to get a view through her eyes of the destination address she entered when she left the coffee shop. He had always assumed it was the address of home, but she shouldn't have to enter it. The car should know it.

It would be valuable information if she had entered a different destination. Since her car never made it home that evening, he had long assumed something outside her control must have overridden her commands to the car. He was now considering that maybe she entered a different address, but she said to go to her house, so that didn't make sense.

Failing to get any more information about Mara in the history world, Honus switched back to the Billy Jay character.

Billy Jay had been playing a bloody shoot-em-up battle game for hours and had been neglecting Orlov and his other game world characters. Honus tried to play the battle game through Billy Jay's hands but didn't seem to be able to control his play. Instead, Honus brought up a copy of the same old battle game himself and began to play on his own while Billy Jay played in another display window on the wall. It was a little bit of a contest to see if he could still do as well as Billy Jay.

5:00 PM, Andre Calls Elsie

Elsie saw a call coming in from Andre. He usually didn't call her when she was at work and she worried it might be something about baby Alex, so she quickly ended a discussion with another associate attorney and allowed the call to connect.

"Elsie, how is your day going?" Andre asked. His image displayed on Elsie's display. He was in costume, but his mask was off.

"You're not calling just to ask that are you?"

"No. I guess not. It's about Alex."

"What about Alex? Are they okay?" Elsie asked with concern.

Andre replied, "Oh. She's fine. They're fine. I just might not be able to pick them up at the normal time. The captain just called me to go check out a possible crime scene outside *The Theme Park* a couple miles from here. I'm actually on my way now. So, I may be tied up working and not be able to get back in my Abitat to meet up with Camilla when Alex's Abitat goes to pick her up. I know we said one of us has to at least be virtual in her Abitat with her, but I may not be able to do that."

"How long will you be tied up?" Elsie asked as she looked over her remaining work to do list on another part of her display.

Andre answered, "No telling. This theme park assignment is boring, but it was supposed to have predicable hours. So much for that. It could be an hour, or it might be a lot longer depending on what's going on at the crime scene."

Elsie said, "I can't get away now, but maybe I can finish up early tonight. We can probably get Camilla to keep watching Alex a little later than usual. I can call her and make sure she is okay with keeping Alex late. If not, I suppose I could ask Emily."

Andre said, "She's been staying with her dad. Do you think she would be willing to do that for us?"

"She will be with us this weekend and she is a really good kid, so, yes, I think she would be willing to help if we ask. She likes spending time with Alex. But let's both see if we can get away from work sooner rather than later and I'll ask Camilla if she is okay keeping Alex for an extra hour or two."

"Okay. I'm at the scene, so I've got to drop off. Love you."

"You too."

Else watched the call window close and then stared out into the hallway for a few seconds taking a few breaths and thinking.

5:05 PM, Tristan and Elsie, Concern about Bella

Most of the attorneys were leaving for the start of the long weekend. Tristan figured he should stop by Elsie's office to tell her he was leaving too. He felt like he had completed a full day's work.

He had worked on several other cases that day after submitting the updated Son'o'Ra furniture IP report to Elsie. He had used standard AI law packages to generate drafts of briefs and motions and then used his AI-augmented law skills through his skull-cap direct brain interface to review and polish them. He added his own little adjustments to make them feel more like his own work, but none of these cases were like the

Son'o'Ra report where he had personal knowledge of the design. As he reviewed engineering designs, he felt like at one time he could have created much better designs to accomplish the same things. In his current condition he could still imagine making some improvements to the designs, but he kept those design-improvement ideas to himself.

He had tried reaching out to Bella several times, between tasks, but got the same result each time. No comm connection available. As he reached the door of Elsie's office, he noticed her staring into the hallway. She must not be too busy, so he leaned in to her office.

"I'm thinking of leaving at the nominal quitting time today, if you don't have something else urgent for me to work on. And I don't know if it is important, but Bella has been out of reach since our call with her this morning."

"That's fine. Both are fine. Enjoy the weekend. Bella is supposed to be enjoying her vacation. We can leave her alone. She'll be back next week." Elsie responded.

"By the way." He looked around to be sure no one else could hear them talking and stepped into her office. "Thanks again for letting me do this job. I didn't know if you would think it was weird to have me around as your employee."

"Not weird for me if it's not weird for you. I know you can be discrete. I didn't even recognize you at first when you applied. It had been a while, and you looked different."

"You too."

"Yeah. I suppose. But I did owe you a couple of favors, Tristan."

"No, you don't owe me anything. Treat me like any other employee," he said. "What I did for you was not enough of a payback for all you did for me. You were there when I needed help. And you really helped me come back from a bad place. Thank you."

"You're welcome, but I don't know if I actually did anything. You were probably getting better anyway. But you helped me pay off my student loans and law school. Those were both huge, so I still owe you. By the way, how do you like the law so far? It's probably not something you ever thought you'd be doing."

"It's okay. IP is a decent fit. Seeing other people's engineering designs is interesting. I could do better, but…you know. And as you know I'm used to getting AI-augmented thoughts and help." He tapped his skullcap, so adding other expertise like law this way is kind-of a natural add-on for me. And because it's not something anyone would expect me to be doing that helps me keep under the radar."

"Still concerned about that after all these years?"

"Yes. Some of the same people and groups that were looking for me back then are still out there, even with all the changes. They are also very good at being discreet. I can't tell for sure, but I think they are still looking."

"That's disconcerting. Do I need to watch my own back?"

"I think you are okay. I don't think they've got any connections between you and who I used to be."

Elsie looked closely at Tristan to see if he was hiding anything from her and satisfied that he was not she replied, "Good."

Tristan added, "Speaking of connections, it does seem odd that Bella's comm's have been offline all day. It's okay if she doesn't want to talk with me, but I would think she would leave them on in case you wanted to ask her something."

"She's refusing all calls?" Elsie asked with concern.

"She doesn't show up to even refuse calls. It's like she shut down all of her comm equipment," Tristan explained.

"That's a concern. There is a big storm in the Sierras today. Do you think something has happened to her?" Elsie asked.

"I hope not. I can do some research and see if I can find out any more about the area where she is," Tristan offered.

"Do that. I'll also try to reach her. And I'll check with her family to see if they know how she is doing," said Elsie.

"I could contact them. Who does she have as contacts?" asked Tristan.

"Just her grandmother. I think you might know her. Camilla Muller. But I'll call Camilla. You don't need to," Elsie replied.

"That name sounds familiar," Tristan replied and paused while he tried to recall more information about that name. After a few seconds he continued, "Is Bella the same Isabella Muller who was my neighbor's kid years ago? I should have recognized her."

"I thought you did. But your memory for that time has been spotty. I didn't know she was your old neighbor when I hired her. Not until I was looking for daycare and she recommended Camilla. When I checked out the address I realized it was next door to your old house."

He paused to think and recall his neighbors. "I didn't see Bella much back then, but now that I think about it, I can see a resemblance. Of course, it's her. It doesn't seem like she has recognized me though."

"No? You still sound the same, but you do look different. Aged a bit, the cap and the rest. Plus, you didn't get out in the neighborhood much back then either, from what I understand."

"Yeah. I'll see if I can remember more about them. Sometimes one memory helps trigger others," Tristan adjusted his cap and turned to go back to his own cubicle.

5:10 PM, Tourists after *The Theme Park*

"Did you decide on a place to eat?" the dad asked, looking up from a game he was playing on his tablet and verifying that the twins were both in view.

"Yes. A place my mom said she used to go when she was a kid. It's still open and it's close to Granddad Lee's machine shop."

"You really think the machine shop is still there, and your uncle is sitting around waiting for you to visit after all these years?"

"Probably not," replied the mom. "But the building is still there. Maybe someone there remembers him. My mom said he used to spend a lot of time there when they were kids. It's a place to start looking. I'd like to find out if we have any more family."

"Your mom cut off contact with your uncle for some reason."

"She wouldn't explain. She slipped up when she said the restaurant was around the corner from her dad's old machine shop."

"How far is it now?"

"It's close. We can have the rental drop us off at the machine shop and we can walk to the restaurant."

The dad started handing out the raincoats and umbrellas.

5:15 PM, Tristan Does Research

Tristan was back at his desk bringing up weather reports and personal stories posted from people who had been in the Sierras today. A 'freakishly cold and strong' late season storm was hitting the mountains with strong winds, heavy rains, and snow. Parts of the same storm system were dropping significant rain here in Southern California for the first time in a decade.

With the tools available to the attorney's office, he could search publicly shared video feeds including some from satellites. Satellite views for the geo-coordinates of Bella's calls this morning showed movement near the campsite around that time, but views were blocked by the trees. Soon after the last call, cloud cover moved in and blocked all normal satellite video. He was not able to find any public satellite views of non-visible frequencies for that time and location.

Shared videos and other postings from AM hive communications were also searchable, but none were available from that part of the mountains after about 10 AM when Bella seemed to still be at her camp site. The closest was a report from three forest rangers on a trail heading out of the wilderness, but that was a few miles from the campsite. It seemed that everyone else in the area had heeded the weather warnings to get out before the storm.

Tristan contacted the ranger station that serviced that area to see what services were available to find or rescue hikers. The short version of the answer was that it might be days before they could even try to help. Apparently, they were not ready for this kind of a winter storm in late May, and they were very busy getting their own staff to safety and trying to keep roads open. Someone who had ignored the warnings and was still in the wilderness with no communication would have to fare for themselves until the storm subsided.

Tristan decided to try some research methods that were not available in the attorney's office. He let Elsie know he was leaving and took the service elevator down to meet his Abitat.

5:20 PM, Andre at Crime Scene near *The Theme Park*

A dozen public safety officers were wandering around the construction site in the rain. Most were in uniform. Some were wearing rain ponchos. Others were just getting soaked. A few were dressed in plain clothes and two were in *Theme Park* costumes. A big rat and a big bat, both soggy but without their masks were talking with one of the plain clothes officers.

"Any sign of NeverMind on your sniffers?" asked the plain clothes man.

"I've got a weak positive indication, but I need to walk a grid to see where it's strongest," said the guy holding a rat snout and sweeping it in different directions while rain dripped from his face.

"How about you?" the plain clothes guy asked the bat-costumed officer.

"Same." He took the bat-shaped sniffer box from his belt and moved it from side to side. "Seems stronger in this direction." He pointed.

"Sorry to pull you guys out of the park. Sweet assignment hanging out in there all day. The lab guys will be here pretty soon, but you two were the closest with NeverMind detectors. With this rain we can't lose any time. Any traces could get washed away. Your scanners don't detect blood, do they?"

"Nope. Just NeverMind and some other drugs," the rat guy answered as he continued pacing and sweeping his snout from side to side.

"Grab a sample if you see anything that looks like blood too," the plain clothes guy ordered.

"Sure thing," said the bat, while thinking that there were at least a dozen other officers here who should be looking for evidence but were just standing around. Getting ordered around by the other officers went along with the territory. *Theme Park* duty was not a sweet assignment. Just the opposite. Not sure if taking time off for paternity was the reason or if he had done something else that rubbed somebody the wrong way. The rat guy was just annoying as hell, so that might explain his assignment.

The rat and the bat walked slowly towards the stronger reading, panning their sniffers from side to side as they walked. Rain continued pounding on them and all around on the ground. The plain clothes guy was following behind them, looking at something on his tablet.

The bat paused and turned back towards the plain clothes guy. "Is it okay to walk here? Did somebody get the vehicle tracks and footprints already?"

"We've got scans. The rain is washing them away anyway. Try not to step on the tracks, if you can avoid them, but it's more important to know if there was NeverMind here," the plain clothes guy answered while still looking at this tablet. "An Abitat reported its delivery closet was damaged at this location and it looks like there may have been a homicide at the same time. The Abitat won't give any details. Says its sensors were off. We want to see if there's any more evidence here, and whether it was connected to an expected NeverMind shipment gone bad."

"We've got a stronger positive right here," the rat indicated an area on the ground near the fence to the flood control channel. "Looks like some may have been spilled here. There's some green color in the mud here." The bat walked over to the same spot and nodded his head.

"Take a sample for the lab before it washes away. But be careful." He noticed that both of their costumes included gloves. "Oh. Good you have gloves on. This stuff could be nasty to touch."

The bat and the rat both took out vials and scooped up some of the green-tinted mud.

"Homicide, you say?" asked the rat.

"I guess inside the Abitat is a grisly mess. The lab should be confirming DNA about now. They're at an Abitat service shop a few miles from here. You guys finish scanning this area." He turned towards the other officers and shouted over the sound of the rain, "Rafik and Wendy. You and your team stay and supervise the scanning. The rest of us need to track down and question all the people who worked at this site today. Let's get out of this rain."

5:25 PM, Emily, Sam & Jo-Jo at a *Theme* Park

Sam, Jo-Jo, and Emily emerged from the Pan *Theme* Hyper Tube ride in the Old West District. The elevator took them from deep underground directly to a viewing platform a hundred feet above the Western *Theme* zone. They were under cover here, as rain fell all around them. Through the obscuring rain they could still see most of this park zone including many roller coaster rides on different levels and brightly colored buildings and eating areas on the ground below. Narrow uncovered elevated walkways extended like spiderweb threads between the loading platforms for the upper-level rides. They would have to traverse multiple walkways through the rain to get down to the ground on foot or take at least one of the walkways to get to one of the rides that loaded high and off-loaded low.

"Look. Look. Look! Let's go on the Deadly Drop!" Sam pointed at a nearby tower that extended up more than twice as high as the platform they were on now.

"I like that one too, but no time for rides now, Sam. We need to get back and pick up our wristbands," Jo-Jo explained. "We need to get to the Abitat and get rid of those packages before something bad happens. Em is doing us a favor to give us a ride."

"Maybe you have time for one ride." Emily looked at the display on her wristband and continued, "The Tube was a little faster than I expected, so my Abitat is still almost a half hour away. Do you think you can do a ride by then? I'll meet you on the ground. I'm not a fan of the Deadly Drop."

"A queue less than 30 minutes? Not likely," Jo-Jo surmised. She peered out across the rainy space at the Deadly Drop loading platform and the queue seemed smaller than she expected. "Maybe. Maybe. With the rain maybe the wait will be shorter than normal. But do you think it's safe in the rain?"

"It's not fun if it's not a little dangerous," Sam countered.

"You two take the skywalk to the DD. I'll take a different route to get to the ground. We can meet by the park's back exit in about a half hour," Emily suggested.

"No wristbands to communicate if we get delayed," Jo-Jo said, tapping her bare wrist. "Are you sure it's okay for us to go?"

"It's okay. If you're not there before me, I'll wait for you. You shouldn't be long. And if you need to, you can ask someone to call me for you. There aren't a lot of people named Emily Mendoza around this park today, are there, Abbie?" She looked at her wristband for confirmation. "Hmm. Ten? But probably only one with a panda avatar," Emily reassured them as she opened her umbrella and moved around the platform towards one of the skywalks that sloped downwards.

"We'll be there. We won't need to call," Jo-Jo said as Emily moved away.

Sam held his shopping bag over his head and started out into the rain and up the sloping sky walk path towards the Deadly Drop. "Let's go."

Jo-Jo watched through the partially transparent elevator shaft as Emily and her umbrella disappeared down a walkway on the other side. Then Jo-Jo held her hands over her head as she stepped quickly onto the skywalk path following Sam up towards the Deadly Drop.

5:35 PM, Honus Fast-Forwards the History World

Honus found that he was not as good as Billy Jay at playing the old battle games. He restarted several times but was quickly killed each time, while Billy Jay was able to advance through multiple levels and gain new weapons and new immunities.

Honus checked on game world PW3709 to see if there were any more messages. Not so far. He then fast-forwarded through a few more hours of Billy Jay playing the violent battle game until he reached a point where Billy Jay finally took a break from the games. Honus watched what Billy Jay did next.

HW203904, 7:00 PM, Mom Still Not Home

Billy Jay stuck his head out of his room. "Mom!" he called out. "Are you home?" With no answer he left his room and walked through the house looking for his mom. He checked the garage and saw it was empty. He checked the refrigerator, and it was still empty. He checked on his dad and walked him to the toilet. "You must be getting hungry. I wonder what's keeping mom so long. Sorry, I don't have any food for you right now." He walked his dad back to bed. He picked up a cup with a lid and straw and filled it with water from the bathroom tap. "How about a drink of water? It's all I can do right now." He got his dad to sip some water. His own stomach was also growling.

After settling his dad back in bed and dimming the lights Billy Jay went back to his room, calling out to his mom along the way with no response. He got his phone and tried texting his mom. No response. No sign of messages being delivered. It seemed like her phone must be off. He spent some time checking on his AM game characters, then played another level of the violent war game for what seemed like a few minutes. He checked on the appraisal and bidding site and found a bid for $50. "It's got to be worth a lot more than that." He spent more time in each of his AM worlds and the war game as some hours passed. Then he did one more walk through the house calling out for his mom and giving his dad a few more sips of water and another trip to the bathroom before he went back to his room and fell asleep in his chair playing the AM game.

…

Pausing to check again. Still no response on PW3709. Honus let the game jump to the next morning and continue in fast play.

HW203904, Monday, April 4, 7:00 AM, Next Morning

When he woke up, Billy Jay looked outside and saw it was morning. He needed to check the house again for his mom, but first he checked in on his game worlds.

In one game world he was celebrating successfully finishing the free climb to the top of El Capitan. In another alias he insisted that his lunar casino management team agree to try the suggestions of the cuisine consultant. In a different world his vehicle was stuck in deep mud on a jungle trail, and he was busy using a machete to cut branches and vines to improvise a ramp to get out. No interventions needed.

At home: No car in the garage, no sign of his mom in her room. His dad had his eyes closed and was mumbling in very quiet whispers. Billy Jay considered that as close to sleep as his dad got, so he let him be. He was starting to wonder what he was supposed to do. No food. No money. No mom. He checked the bidding site. $50 was still the only bid and it was going to expire soon. He was tempted to accept it but held off.

He checked on his mom's social media pages. She didn't often post status updates but sometimes posted notes for her own benefit. She didn't seem to have any contacts outside the family. Today was no exception, no status, but she did have an update on her personal calorie-counting tracker from yesterday. It had a picture of a soy latte, banana. and veggie sandwich in what looked like a restaurant or a coffee shop. Billy copied the picture which was tagged with time and location. The geotag said it was at a community center and library about 50 miles away. Why was she in a library coffee shop way across town yesterday when she should have been bringing home food? Maybe she was going to start doing her job with the inspirational speaking business again. That might explain going across town, but it still didn't make sense. She might skip meals herself, and she might let him go hungry for a day or two, but she never neglected his dad that way, did she? Something was wrong.

Billy Jay searched online for what to do for a missing person. He found a discussion thread that consisted of various people who complained about the fact the police would not take any action until their family member had been missing for 48 or 72 or more hours and the hassles they felt they got. He stopped searching before reading any advice from actual police agencies. He didn't bother to look up the number to call for help in his community. He was relieved to have a reason to avoid making a phone call, since he detested talking to strangers on the phone.

He entered the discussion forums he had used to talk about the game and asked people what to do about finding a missing person. The responses he got all centered on using tools in the game to search for characters.

…

BillyJay4^AM to Forum^AM

Off topic question:

Anyone know how to find a missing person?

BigBalls832^AM to BillyJay4^AM

Select Tools Characters Find

enter your search criteria

you get a list of public characters that match

I'm looking for a real person

not a character in the game

players are anonymous

read one of the AM user guides stupid

BillyJay4^AM <Disconnect>

…

He decided not to respond. This wasn't getting him anywhere. He wondered if there was some way he could get some money for *BJ's Guide to the AM Universe* which he had written and posted a year ago. He shouldn't have given it away for free. Maybe he could charge for a new version. But that would not get him any money today. He tried to contact Lacy Hogan.

LacyHogan235^AM: <offline 12 hours>

She was not in the discussion forum today. He thought she might be able help him figure out how to search for his mom, since she worked nearby. Maybe not a reasonable idea, but besides his dad and his mom she was the only real-world person he had communicated with recently. Even the food delivery guy yesterday had just dropped the food off and left.

He was desperate. He figured he was going to have to call the police and take his chances, but he wanted to try one more thing first. He opened the window for world QZ9301.

QZ9301, 4:45 PM, B.J. Orlov and Lacy Hogan

Bartholomew Orlov was sitting in a leather reading chair in a crystal clear transparent-domed study with a spectacular view of the lunar sky and landscape. He was reading reports about business results at various resort properties he owned and making notes in the margins. Billy Jay took control and tossed the tablet aside. "Where is the cuisine consultant right now?" He stood up.

The butler voice responded, "Ms. Hogan has been playing blackjack at the unlimited stakes table. She is currently up by 2.5 million AMPs."

"Ask her to meet me here immediately."

"Just a moment." After a 30 second pause the butler voice continued, "She declines your request. She appears to be on a hot streak and says she cannot be interrupted."

He got up and headed to the elevator. "Ultra-premium casino level."

He left the elevator and headed quickly to the blackjack table. "Ms. Hogan. Lacy. I need to talk to you privately about something very urgent."

"Not now, Mr. Orlov. I did your consulting and helped you with your cuisine concern. Now I'm enjoying my fee. And as soon as I finish at this table, I'm taking an excursion to drive one of your lunar rovers."

"Ms. Hogan, Lacy, I must insist. You'll have a chance to enjoy your winnings, but first I need your help again." He looked at the dealer, the security guards, and the other guests at the blackjack table. "Let us talk in private for a few minutes please." With encouragement from the security guards, the others moved a few steps away outside the high stakes area and the guards placed a purple cord barrier in place.

"Okay. But be quick. What else do you need now?"

"Lacy. I don't know your real name. This is Billy Jay, you know, with the Chicken and Potatoes. I need to talk to you about a problem at my home." Bartholomew Orlov had a perplexed and worried expression on his face as he spoke. Not quite sure what the words coming out of his mouth meant.

"I don't know what you are talking about, Mr. Orlov."

"I'll call you Lacy. Lacy, My mom is missing since yesterday and I need help. I don't know what to do. I need to talk to someone about it. You are the only one I could think of to ask."

"I don't know what kind of crazy talk this is, but I intend to enjoy your casino games and out-of-this-world entertainment and your lunar exploration excursions. I've already given my menu and food presentation ideas to your staff, which did not include chicken and potatoes." She walked off pulling the purple cord away and dropping it to the floor. "I've got a date with a lunar rover I need to keep."

Bartholomew Orlov looked very pained, worried, and nauseated as Billy Jay left him and disconnected from that game world. Orlov was trying to remember what problem he had with chicken and potatoes. Did her menu suggestions even include a

Chicken and Potato item? And what did he mean about his mom being missing. Wasn't she fine and living in one of his luxury senior centers back in New York? Had something happened to her? He said to one of the security guards with a name tag that said 'Hector', "Hector, I think I need to lie down. Can you help me get back to my suite?"

...

5:44 PM, Honus Getting Hungry at the Ranch House

Honus wanted to see what happened next, but he was getting hungry. He paused the playback of the History World game so that he could give instructions to his Abitat to go out and order some food to bring back. He didn't want to draw any attention by having a delivery coming to this house.

5:45 PM, *The Theme Park* New Tech Pavilion

After going on the Self-Driving Cars ride, Jeremy and Chandra were back in the New Tech Pavilion. Spending time in the New Tech Pavilion avoided the downpour outside, plus the technology was at least a little bit interesting. Jeremy was looking at a demonstration stand for a Quantum Entanglement Communication device. He pressed the button, and a holographic glow appeared above the stand showing a miniature version of a similar stand.

"Does this really work?" he asked no one in particular.

Chandra walked up behind him pointing at the text on the display placard and said, "It says it works, but they lie sometimes. Maybe it's just a mockup. If it really worked that would be a live image of a holo comm station at *Theme Park Mars.*"

"Resolution is not that great. It could be real," Jeremy said.

Just then a hologram of a young adult walked into the small image and said, "Does this work?" followed by another who said, "It works if someone at the other end activates it. Hey, Yeah. Look. I think it's working. Hello there?"

They had a conversation that convinced all of them that it really worked. It was an instantaneous holographic communication between theme park pavilions on Earth and Mars, with no time lag they could perceive. Both sides required some convincing that it wasn't really just showing another station nearby on the same planet, but all were finally convinced when at Jeremy's suggestion they demonstrated the different gravitational acceleration of dropped objects at both ends.

"The resolution is not great. You look fuzzy," Jeremy said to his new friends on Mars.

"You too. But it is cool that they've got one of these working at the parks. I don't think there are very many of these QEC-paired holo stations anywhere yet," said the fuzzy holo-person.

"More all the time, I bet," said Chandra.

"Yeah. QEC has been mostly for low bandwidth data up to now, but they'll probably figure out how to put them in our wristbands and Abitats before long," added Jeremy.

"You know they will," added one of the kids on Mars.

"They'll find all kinds of uses for them," said another Mars kid.

Chandra added, "I saw another display just around the corner that explained how they used a new version of QEC tech to make the new Min Quest History Moments story we saw earlier. It was very high res. Much better than this."

"History Moments is not a live connection. Why would they use QEC for that?" Jeremy asked. "And on planet they could transfer data just fine at light speed."

"Maybe they just wanted to see if they could do it," Chandra replied. "I'm not sure. It said it transferred solid 4-D images of the scenery back to the studios in Burbank to process for the story world. I guess that new version of QEC for holograms is not only instantaneous but also has huge bandwidth. It's almost like a wormhole for data transmission."

Jeremy brightened up at the mention of wormholes. "Physics, I know something about. Quantum wormholes are cool, but why would they use that for a History Moments story?"

"I don't know," Chandra replied. "*The Theme Park* company is into all kinds of tech. They bought or merged with just about everybody. They do most of the travel to the moon and Mars, you know."

"They should put that kind of tech between Earth and Mars. Huge instant bandwidth could be helpful there. Instead of this kind of fuzzy connection," Jeremy said.

"If it works, I'm sure they've got the Mars side of a comm pair on its way by now, but it still usually takes months to move physical objects between planets," Chandra said.

"I heard it's supposed to arrive here in eight weeks," replied one of the fuzzy hologram young people on Mars.

"We should show this to Emily. I wish she didn't have to leave to help her old friends. She is coming back, right?" Jeremy asked.

"She got delayed. She might come back tonight, but, if not, we agreed to meet at the park again tomorrow when it opens. We can do a whole day with the free passes," Chandra replied.

Their friends on Mars waved at someone outside the hologram view and walked away out of the hologram, so Jeremy and Chandra walked away too. Chandra wanted to show Jeremy the other QEC exhibit.

"This kind of relates to my idea for the inter term project."

"We should wait for Emily tomorrow before you explain that."

5:50 PM, Jose Returns Home

Jose disembarked from a carousel bus and ran in the rain through the passageway into the courtyard of the live-work complex. He paused for a moment against a wall which blocked the wind and rain and looked into the courtyard. He looked critically at the buildings surrounding the courtyard, and at the tiny homes and trailer arranged within it. In the rain it was looking pretty bad. Stucco was cracked and peeling from some of the walls, with dangling sections moving in the wind. Wooden trim was faded and hanging loose around some windows on the buildings and on some of the tiny homes. Patches of roofing were on the ground, blown off in this wind, which must mean water damage today. Windows were boarded up or missing and rain was likely getting in through those as well. "It can't continue for long like this," he thought. He wasn't sure if he was referring to the storm or to the building.

Should he fix it up? The existing residents were okay without Abitat stations but the rent coming in was nowhere near enough to pay for all the needed repairs. To fix it up he'd have to collect a lot more rent or transfer a lot of his own points.

Maybe he could risk a one-time transfer. Repairs, paint, and new landscaping would make it look better and hold up to weather, but without adding Abitat docking amenities he couldn't get enough new paying tenants to pay for ongoing maintenance, and it would get run down again before long. He wouldn't want the visibility of recurring points transfers for making up the difference.

Could he add Abitat amenities? Turning garages into Abitat stations would require major renovations to the buildings. Might as well tear it all down and rebuild from scratch. Converting the courtyard to docking stations for Abitats would eliminate the tiny homes and his trailer. He could move, but what about Dr Magnolia's cats?

An alternative would be to sell out to the development project and let them tear everything down and build new, but where would the people and cats here go then? Dr. Magnolia would have trouble finding another place for her cats.

Maybe he could set up some kind of charity that would pay for it? He was not up on the legal aspects, but he knew some people who might know some people. He was also no expert on developing and maintaining real estate.

He needed to connect to game world PW3709 and see what message was waiting for him. He suspected it would give him a chance to talk with someone who knew more than he did about real estate. The rain and wind seemed to be slowing. He ran to his trailer.

5:55 PM, Elsie Gets Alex

Elsie was almost to Camilla's house. She had left work around a quarter after five and worked in her Abitat along the way. She didn't like giving a bad example of working remotely counter to her own company policy. Working remotely while on vacation, or while in transit to a client, deposition, or court, were allowable exceptions. This seemed like another allowable exception, but it made her uncomfortable.

Camilla said she was fine taking care of Alex until Elsie could get there, but Elsie and Andre had agreed that they didn't want to impose extra hours on her.

Normally, with Andre picking up Alex, Elsie would think nothing of working until 7, 8, or occasionally much later. After hearing Camilla's reaction when she let her know about Bella being out of contact in the mountains, she decided to go in person to get Alex. If she had used the virtual connection through the Abitats she could pick up Alex as soon as she got into her own Abitat, but Camilla seemed to need real face to face time and Elsie wanted to get more work done.

From Camilla's reaction Elsie surmised that Bella had not told her that she was going backpacking. Camilla thought she was just living in her Abitat and an apartment in town and going to work like normal at the office. Bella had called her every couple of days, but apparently she used virtual backgrounds to make it look like she was in town, at the office, at home in her Abitat or apartment, or at some local landmark, like *The Theme Park*.

Elsie's Abitat pulled into the docking area at Camilla's house and when the door opened Camilla was standing there holding Alex.

"Look who's here, Alex. It's your mommy!"

Elsie stepped out of the Abitat into the hallway of Camilla's house and accepted Alex into her arms. Looking at Camilla's worried expression, Elsie decided she might need to stay a while.

Chapter 6

After Work

6:00 PM, Tristan at the Machine Shop

Tristan was sitting at a computer desk in a little office of the machine shop that had been his dad's business and had been his own official address for years. Or at least the address of someone he used to be. He searched through secure private communications from people in the mountains and found no more information about Bella and her companion, other than a coffee bean order that was submitted just before data was cut off. That order was not confirmed so no drone was launched to make a delivery.

By accessing signal tracking data from satellites, he had some additional info. Satellites gathering gravitational and geomagnetic data normally had to filter out the busy background noise of AM hive communications signals between Abitats and wristbands and such. In the wilderness there was always less of that noise, and that day there in that wilderness area there was very little. The level of filtered noise was consistent with someone's communications gear trying unsuccessfully to make connections with other AM hive units. And that stopped abruptly at 4:35 PM. He was able to narrow their location at the time the data cut off to an area of about 5 square kilometers. That was better than nothing, but it really just meant they hadn't gone many miles from their campsite.

The fact that the data stopped suddenly was not a good sign. He had trouble thinking of a reason they would want to turn off their comms if they even knew how to do that, and total loss of power was unlikely. He looked at seismic data from the area and found several indications of rockslides, probably caused by the heavy rain or snow, but again he could not precisely locate them. A larger one was right at 4:35 when their signal stopped. He should let Elsie know what he had found and maybe get the information to Bella's grandmother too. The picture of what had likely happened to Bella was starting to look gloomy.

He looked out through a window and saw that it was still rainy and gloomy here as well. Staring at the dirty glass he pictured the face of Bella's grandmother. Camilla Muller was her name. He now remembered they had been neighbors, and he pictured having coffee at her house a few times, when Bella was at school. He also pictured earlier times when Camilla's daughter, Bella's mom, Josephine, babysat three or four-year-old Billy Jay a couple times when she was about eighteen before she had the baby. Camilla raised Bella because Bella's mom was not around, possibly due to drug habits and mental illness. He should probably visit Camilla and see if she was okay, although she probably wouldn't recognize him.

He marveled at these memories as he disconnected the chain of connections that he used to access secure private data of government and businesses and got ready to leave. Looking out the window again he noticed another face. This time it was not a memory, but someone looking in and waving at him.

6:05 PM, Tourists at the Machine Shop

Walking down the sidewalk after dinner keeping tabs on the kids the dad said, "That food was good, but kind of spicy. I could have used another Margarita, but we needed to get the kids out of there before they caused trouble."

The mom was ahead looking in a window at her Granddad's old machine shop. She said to the dad, "I see someone inside. Do you think it might be him? Do you think it might be Uncle Perry?"

"Probably not. No one was there earlier. But you can knock again and ask."

The two kids started whispering to each other "Uncle Perry. Uncle Perry. Uncle Perry."

The mom shushed them and tapped on the window glass which had remnants of the words "Lee's Machine Shop" and pointed towards the door. She could see the person inside move towards the door.

The dad motioned to the two kids to stay quiet and stay back with him while the mom walked to the door. "Shh. Let's wait here," he said to them, and they continued whispering and giggling in a quieter, more conspiratorial tone, "Uncle Perry. Uncle Perry. Uncle Perry."

The door opened and the mom saw a tall man of about sixty wearing a nice suit and a stylish beret partially covering a mesh DBI cap. She thought his eye's looked a little bit like her mom's as he spoke.

"Sorry. The machine shop is no longer in business."

"Uncle Perry!" squealed Minh and Max as they ran away from the dad and past the mom and hugged Tristan's suit pants legs.

"Uh. I think you may be mistaking me for somebody else," Tristan objected.

Max interrupted the "Uncle Perry" chant long enough to say, "Nice suit, Uncle Perry."

6:10 PM, Camilla and Elsie

"Don't worry. I'm sure Isabella is fine," Camilla reassured Elsie. She knows how to take care of herself. Always has.'"

"Yes. She should be fine, but are you okay, Camilla?" Elsie asked as she bounced Alex on her shoulder.

"I just wish she would have told me she was doing a MinQuest. Maybe I could have talked her out of it. She didn't want to worry me. She was always fascinated by the stories my Sam and Jo-Jo told her about when they went on one. And I guess her dad must have told her about his trips too."

"For most people a MinQuest is a very positive experience."

"But they can be dangerous. That's when things started going wrong for Jo-Jo and Sam. I'd say I wish they never met Izzie's dad, but then we wouldn't have Isabella, would we?"

"Have you let her mom know?"

"I haven't spoken with her mom or uncle in I don't know how many years. They only came around to ask for money or take things they could trade for drugs, so I finally said No More and changed all the locks and got a restraining order. I think Isabella was 8 at the time. So, what is that? 20, 25 years. Oh my. That is a long time."

"That sounds like it was a tough thing to do."

"It was, but I couldn't keep enabling them. They were both so bright before Sam brought home that Zynn boy from college. He was rich and spoiled and thought he could get away with anything. They were both swept along by him. A bad influence."

Elsie decided to just listen while she patted Alex on the back on her shoulder. "Mmm Hmmm."

"When Josephine got pregnant it seemed at first like he would try to help her, but he was always going away and getting into different kinds of trouble. He was into drugs and a bad influence on Sam and Jo-Jo. For a while after I kicked them out, I was able to follow what they were doing on social media, but eventually they disappeared there too. I heard eventually something went wrong for him and he wasn't a rich kid anymore.

"Jo-Jo never connected with her baby. I had to take care of Izzie from the beginning. When things went from bad to worse to terrible, I didn't want Izzie to see how they were living so I cut them off. Tough love. I couldn't afford to keep supporting them and their deadbeat friends. But mostly it was to protect Izzie."

"For some reason Izzie remembered the stories they told about their MinQuests and kept asking me about them when she was a teenager. Eventually she got the hint and stopped asking me about it. I think she equated the absence of her mom and uncle, and I guess her dad, with them being on some kind of long MinQuests. Maybe she thought doing her own MinQuest would reconnect with them somehow."

"Mmm Hmmm."

Alex mimicked her and said, "MMM MMMM."

"Was that Momma? Did Alex say Momma?" Camilla asked, happy for a distraction.

6:15 PM, Emily, Sam & Jo-Jo at a *Theme* Park

Emily was standing near the Old West themed park entrance in an area partially sheltered by an archway, also trying to use her umbrella to block the wind and rain but she was still getting wet. Her Abitat had arrived 20 minutes ago and was circling the area waiting for her to summon it again. She was wet and getting tired of waiting. The queue for the ride probably took longer than Sam and Jo-Jo estimated. That's no surprise. Maybe she shouldn't have said it was okay for them to go on a ride. Maybe she shouldn't have offered to help them at all. She was doing them a favor. They could be more considerate. But they were in trouble and needed help. Maybe they got caught by the people who were trying to find them. That would be awful. She couldn't wait forever, but she could give them some more time. You are supposed to help your friends. Her mom wasn't expecting her until late, since she had messaged *'at theme park with friends.'*

"Hi Little Em!" came the voice of Sam from behind her.

"Sorry it took longer than we said," Jo-Jo apologized, coming around in front of Emily.

Sam and Jo-Jo were both soaking wet.

"I know. The queues can take forever," Emily said, raising her umbrella to offer some protection for them.

Jo-Jo crowded in leaving little room for Sam. "Actually, the lines were short. We had time to go on the Deadly Drop twice, but then Sam here needed to buy a snack. Turns out they accept old-fashioned cash in the old west and turns out Sam had some in his pocket."

"I saved you part of a churro," Sam offered a soggy treat.

"No thanks. Okay. Whatever. But we should get going." Emily had raised her left hand to signal her Abitat to return and got a message on her wristband that it would arrive in less than a minute. She pointed out the gate towards the loading zone curb. They all scurried out trying to stay at least partially under the umbrella as they went. Several Abitats paused at the curb just long enough for people to jump out and run towards the park entrance. Finally, Emily felt the signal that the next Abitat was hers. "Here it is." As the door opened, she recognized the panda bear decorations inside and jumped in, quickly followed by Sam and Jo-Jo. "Where can I drop you off?"

6:20 PM, Honus Rejoins History World

Honus had walked around the house waiting while his Abitat went out to get him a meal. While waiting he realized he probably should have just headed back to the resort to eat and catch up on the decisions he should have been making today. But when the food arrived he decided to stay and eat here. He was curious to see what else the history world showed. It would not be easy or safe to view it back at the resort. Playing it here at the ranch house, disconnected from the AM game hive, was the safest option.

While eating in the Abitat he noticed an alert on his wristband about a response on game world PW3709. His message had gone through, and he should expect a visitor in less than an hour. That clinched it. He would stay. He walked back to his bedroom, sat down and restarted the history world, letting it run again in fast play and summary mode.

HW203904, 8:00 AM, Checking on Dad

Billy Jay wasn't sure what to do after his failure to get help through the game world. He was also concerned about what damage he might have caused to his Orlov character but more concerned about his mom. He rushed from his room without closing his door. He checked the garage again. He ran to his mom's room. He ran to his dad's room. There he slowed down. His dad was awake and looking a little agitated himself. He was still mumbling and twitching, but slightly faster than normal.

"Dad. Do you need to pee? You look like you need to pee. Let me help you to the bathroom." He helped him sit up and swing his feet off the bed. He helped him to his feet and walked him across the room the bathroom, like he had done many times before. "Sorry, Dad, still no food. Mom didn't refill the fridge yet. I'll figure out some way to get us something to eat. First. I'll get you some more water."

After helping him back from the toilet he was glad that his dad had not soiled himself. He helped him back into bed and noticed a message window on his dad's tablet. First, he got the water for his dad and held the cup while he sipped. But he continued to look at the tablet display.

Autonomous Motors to Perry Lee^AM
Subject: Abitat delivery
Your vehicle order will be delivered today.
if you wish to change pre-arranged delivery location
Click <here>

...

That was unusual. The displays on his dad's tablet always seemed to be just scrolling gibberish with status or error logs of some kind. Billy Jay didn't bother to look at his dad's tablet very often, but he had never seen a readable message like this on his dad's tablet in the years he had been helping him. He wondered what it meant. Maybe his dad really was playing the game and had bought a new Abitat in the game. "Hey Dad. It looks like you bought an Abitat. That's cool. I wish I could find you in the game and maybe go for a ride with you in your new Abitat."

After his dad had sipped a half of a cup of water and settled back into his normal muttering and twitching and holding the tablet, Billy Jay left the room and walked slowly through the house considering his options. He needed food and he needed to find his mom. If he could find her, she could get food, but he didn't know where to start to find her. He could maybe still get $50 for that table thing and then he could order a little bit of food to be delivered, but he couldn't get much delivered with that little and it wouldn't last long. Maybe he could bargain for more, or maybe if he could get that money he could force himself to walk to the convenience store and get a little more food for the money. Or he could try to steal some fruit from the orchard in the farm behind the workshop. Sergey would probably let him pick some fruit. He wasn't sure if any fruit was in season. He hadn't gone into the orchard in a long time.

He hadn't gone past the barn since the last time Isabel came over the fence.

He tried to think of someone he could ask to help. Was there someone he knew from the virtual classes he had taken who he could contact? No one he could think of. Isabel was too busy with school and sports, and he didn't know how to call her. He didn't dare go to her front door. He wished he knew how to call her.

Getting food was another problem. Maybe if he searched, he could find some money in the house. He never saw his mom use cash, it was always one of those debit cards or her phone, but maybe she had some cash hidden for an emergency. This seemed like an emergency. He decided to search her study and her bedroom, but since his wandering had brought him close to it, he figured he would first check the garage one more time. He'd hate to have her come in while he was searching through her things.

He opened the door to the garage and went in. It was still empty. The charging hookup next to her car's space was slightly out of place. That was unusual for her. She was always so precise. To hang the charging connector at an awkward angle in its holder was out of character for her. She would normally put it exactly centered and level with the power cord neatly coiled. She had been acting different lately, like she didn't care about some things as much lately. He straightened the charger in its holder.

He looked across the empty garage. The charger hookup for his Dad's possible future car was still in its plastic shrink wrap. Thinking about his dad's future car reminded him of the tablet message. *"Your vehicle order will be delivered today."* Billy Jay imagined getting an Abitat delivered. That would be something, he thought. The rollup door at the front of the garage had a row of windows. They provided some light but were obscured for privacy to keep people outside from having a view in. Billy Jay looked at the windows and noticed a grey shadow. He got up close to the plexiglass and peered through a tiny un-obscured spot. There was some kind of tall grey van in the driveway in front of the garage.

Maybe his mom's car broke down and she got a ride home in a shuttle van? But why didn't she call? Maybe she ordered food delivery? Delivery drivers didn't usually pull into the driveway. Billy Jay couldn't just open the garage door. That exposure would be too scary. Just the thought made him bend over and hyperventilate. He wasn't ready to face a stranger. But he needed to find out more. He tried to look from different angles through different transparent spots in the windowpanes. He couldn't get a good view. He couldn't see the front windows of the van to see if a driver was in it. It must have backed in, he thought.

He went back into the house and shouted. "Mom. Are you home?" Still no answer. She should be in by now if it gave her a ride. He went to his room and checked the security camera view of the driveway. It looked like some kind of delivery van, but he couldn't see the driver from this view either. He decided to see if he had a better view from the living room. He walked there quickly and after pausing for a few seconds to get up his courage, pulled apart the curtains and looked out. He had a partial view of the driveway, and he could see part of one side of the van. It looked very plain and boxy. He couldn't see the driver seat or the front windows from this angle. He figured a delivery driver might pause to make a phone call or take a minute or two to figure out their next stop. He could wait a couple of minutes and check the porch for a delivery after it left. Meanwhile he would search for cash or credit cards in his mom's study.

He stopped in to check on his dad on the way. "Hi, Dad. Sorry, still no food. Are you doing okay?" His dad mumbled and twitched and slightly lifted his tablet. Billy Jay leaned in to sniff and check if his dad needed changing and noticed another readable message on the tablet.

...

Billy Jay said, "Ohhh. Dad. Is that van in the driveway an Abitat? Did you buy a real Abitat? No way. How'd you do that? Wait here." His dad's twitching and mumbling continued as Billy ran out of the bedroom through the house to the garage and without thinking about the risks, he hit a button on the wall to open the roll-up door. He repeated "921-944-222, 921-944-222" over and over again as he ran around the vehicle in the driveway. It had no windshield—no driver's seat—no windows at all. It had a plain boxy shape with similar lights and sensors on all four sides. Seams outlined a door on one side and a delivery portal on one end.

Billy Jay was exposed in full view of the street and neighboring houses on the cul-de-sac. He was breathing fast, and his heart was racing as he walked around the vehicle a second time, but he attributed it to the excitement of getting an Abitat rather than his normal agoraphobia.

As he paused on the side with the outline of a door a numeric keypad became visible. He was nervous with excitement. He repeated, "921-944-222, 921-944-222." He keyed the number wrong the first time, but on the second try the door slid open. He looked inside. It was an Abitat like in the game. Stepping in he saw the wall display light up with the logo of Autonomous Motors and an invitation to complete the vehicle acceptance survey. Billy Jay was familiar with the acceptance rituals for many different models, brands, and generations of Abitats in various game worlds but to deal with one in real life was exhilarating in a way he didn't expect. He had accepted much fancier Abitats in his game roles, and this model was one of the simplest, but still he was thrilled.

He looked around the unit. It had a tiny kitchen area, a very compact bathroom, and three retractable and fully reclinable seats, for his mom, dad, and him, he guessed. Remembering his mom, he decided to make one more try to reach out to the deli cook before initializing the unit. Maybe the prospect of using a real Abitat would tempt her to help him. He stepped out of the unit and its door closed behind him as he ran back through the garage and into the house.

QZ9301, 7:45 PM, Orlov Makes a Move

Bartholomew Orlov was sitting on his king-sized bed in his suite holding his head and sipping a soothing licorice-flavored tea. He was still trying to make sense of what he had said to the cuisine consultant. What did he mean about his mom and why talk to this Lacy Hogan about it? Was he attracted to her and trying to get her alone with a random come-on line? If so, it seemed like a poor choice of lines. He admitted to himself that she was attractive, and they did seem to have some kind of unspoken connection. Suddenly, he sat up, set down his tea, and said, "Where is Lacy now?"

"She is 1.2 kilometers from the south portal heading away from the resort on a private excursion rover," said the butler voice.

"Prepare my rover. I will be going out to meet her."

"Yes, sir. Your rover is ready and fully charged. Your excursion suit is in routine maintenance, but I can transfer one from the rental counter."

"Routine maintenance can wait. Get mine ready quick. I want to use my own suit."

He sprung from the bed with a move that launched him across the room and towards the private elevator. His feelings were starting to make sense. He was a little bit crazy, and she was the cause. He needed to see her as soon as possible.

...

Billy Jay switched the game viewpoint to Lacy Hogan.

QZ9301, 7:50 PM, Lacy on a Lunar Rover

Lacy Hogan was getting the hang of driving the rover. Rover number 09. The number was painted on each of the fenders that kept dust from flying up as the rover moved. It was exciting to feel in full control of a vehicle. Not like an Abitat that you just told it where to go, with a lunar rover you had to pay attention all the time and hold on to the control stick. Or so it seemed. She didn't know yet that it had built-in safeguards, such as, if she didn't return it to the excursion portal on time it would become autonomous and bring itself back.

Still, it felt like she was in control as she drove it over the edge of a 20-meter-wide depression or crater, down the dusty slope, and across the bowl, passing a number of golf balls scattered in the bowl of the crater. She let up the power and stopped just before heading up the other side. From this lower vantage point, the casino resort building was out of view.

She looked around and marveled at what she could see. Other than well-worn tracks of previous excursion rovers in the crater and the disappointing handful of golf balls, the view was spectacular for the lack of evidence of human technology. Some larger boulders and crags of the lunar surface were visible for a short distance and beyond that the sky.

The darkest blackness with the brightest pattern of stars she had ever seen served as background to the whole dome of the sky. A slightly more than half-earth had white storms covering enough of the land that she wasn't sure which continents she was seeing. The night side of the earth was the lower third from this view.

She turned her head, and two moving patches of her helmet's crystal-clear transparent face automatically darkened and blocked the blinding brightness of the disk of the sun from her eyes but still she squinted when looking in that direction. She checked her time band. They call this "evening" Lunar Resort time with events scheduled around a 24-hour clock, but the physical lunar days and nights lasted two weeks each. Given the position of the sun, it was probably lunar morning with more than a week left of sunlight. She'd like to come again during the lunar night when the starry sky would be even more spectacular.

As she paused and stared at the stars and the tiny earth, she wondered about this Orlov character. What was he talking about back at the blackjack table? What kind of line was that about his mom going missing and chicken and potatoes? She had a pretty good idea what he was leading to when saying they needed to talk privately about something urgent. These rich bastards thought they could have any woman.

But there was something about him that puzzled her. Sometimes he was totally predictable and other times he seemed vulnerable, and she felt like she had some kind of connection with him that she couldn't explain. Had they met before? Had he ever eaten at her restaurant back on earth? She was owner-chef at a small restaurant with a rising reputation in a rundown, but gentrifying neighborhood in Southern California. She thought she would remember if a big shot like Orlov had eaten there but maybe he visited incognito.

She sometimes partied hard enough that she didn't always remember details the next day, but as far as she could remember their first contact was yesterday when she sent him a business proposal. She had always wanted to visit the moon which was not possible yet on her own savings—her restaurant was getting good reviews and good business, but her cash flow was consumed with expenses and any extra went into paying off her college loans and the even bigger debt for starting the restaurant. When she saw yesterday that customer reviews of his lunar resort's food offerings were dismal, she sent off a quick consulting proposal and, surprisingly he accepted it within minutes. Just hours later, here she was in a space suit sitting on a lunar rover staring up at the earth in the sky. And his moon resort was going to change their food offerings in two of their restaurants to match her suggestions.

…

Honus re-focused the history world on Lae C Hogan.

HW203904, 8:30 AM, Lae C Takes a Day Off

She was Laetitia Celine Hogan, AKA Lae C Hogan, and her characters went by Lacy Hogan in her recent game worlds. In the real world she currently had a job cooking in a deli in a supermarket. At night she was couch-surfing with friends from school while she tried to save enough for a security deposit for an apartment of her own. She had taken classes at culinary school after getting her bachelors and masters in English and Physical Astronomy. Her supermarket job involved her current chosen profession, if at a far different level than she aspired. In the game she didn't have to worry about a place to live since everyone had an Abitat, and she focused on opening restaurants where she could display her full culinary imagination and practice for when she had the opportunity to open her own restaurant for real. Of course, selling virtual food in a virtual world had its own challenges since players couldn't actually taste anything. But characters responded well to her recipes, and her food presentation and menu descriptions appealed to players.

Right now, she was calling work from her latest couch to arrange to take a day off at the supermarket so that she could continue exploring the game on the moon using the large screen tv at her friend's apartment. Her character, Lacy Hogan, was currently on an excursion with a lunar rover and she didn't want to miss that. Glancing at the display, it looked like Lacy was pausing her rover in a moon crater and taking in the sky view with the crater walls blocking view of the man-made resort buildings in the distance. She could see Lacy's thoughts scrolling in a thought bubble window on the display, but she wasn't paying too close attention while she talked with the store assistant manager, Javier.

"You're cool with me taking another vacation day, Javier?" said Lae C Hogan on the phone call.

"Sure. Sure. The deli's not that busy today. Gerardo is always willing to pull a couple more hours. I'll ask him to stay if we get busy near the end of his shift. Enjoy your AM binge. Tell me all about it afterwards," Javier said.

"Thanks a bunch. But you probably won't be interested in views of moon craters and stars. My AM adventures are not like yours. Honestly, your AM adventures are not really suitable for sharing. You should think twice before you share so much about what you do in your AM-ven-tures," Lae C said to Javier.

"You can always tell me to stop."

"I always do. But you always keep talking. TMI."

"You're just a prude."

"No. You're just a jerk. Thanks for the day off, boss."

"Bye."

Lae C hung up the phone and turned back to the display. There were some messages from BillyJay4^AM on the discussion forum. She could ignore those. Back to the game, she watched the view through Lacy's eyes. The view of the waxing gibbous earth was amazing. The graphics were very realistic. The graphics for this lunar simulation were an add-on that could be downloaded only if your character could get to the moon.

She took control of the rover and revved it up the side of the crater and when that didn't make progress revved it in reverse. She violated one of the warnings of the rover orientation that Lacy paid attention to, but Lae C had ignored. Dust flew forward in arcs through the vacuum without any of the clouds that would result in air, and the rover's wheels dug into the loose material on the slope of the crater. A couple of golf balls were sent flying out of the crater by the spinning wheels. Lae C noticed the accurate rendering of the path of the dust from the wheels and revved the power even more to watch. The rover's wheels dug deeper until the rover's chassis settled firmly in the dust. Seeing what she had done, Lae C backed off to let the character Lacy deal with it.

QZ9301, 8:15 PM, Lacy Stuck in a Crater

Lacy thought to herself, "I should have backed off and gone dead slow up the slope like they said in the orientation. I knew better than to gun it like that. It was kind of fun, but I know better. I just get an impulse to do things without thinking sometimes."

She got out of the rover and tried to climb the crater slope on foot. The loose dust in front of the rover continued to slide back under her feet and she got no farther than the front edge of the rover. Just then another rover rolled silently into view at the top of the slope. It was larger than hers and it was coated in gold foil rather than the grey color of the typical guest excursion rover. Sitting at the controls was someone in a gold-foil coated excursion suit. She was pretty sure who it must be.

"Lacy. Are you okay? This is Bartholomew." He dismounted from the gold rover and stood at the edge of the crater looking down. With Lacy standing at the front edge of her rover her head was about even with his boots.

"I recognize your voice, and your style. What brings you out here on this lovely sunny day, Mr. Orlov?"

"I like to get outside whenever there is a break in the weather."

"Is that so? Does that happen often?"

"I guess an overcast day here would be quite the surprise. I needed to find you and talk. By the way I set our radio mode to close range, around 20 meters, so we can have a private conversation."

"You get to talk to me in private after all, huh? Well as long as you're here it appears that I got one of your rovers stuck in one of your sand traps. Can you help me get it unstuck?"

"Of course, but first I want to talk."

"I was nervous about what you might have in mind when you wanted to 'talk in private' before, but I think there is a lot less chance you might try anything funny in these bulky suits surrounded by the instant death of lunar vacuum. What's on your mind, Bart?"

"I really prefer Bartholomew. Or BJ. But not Bart."

"Okay, what's on your mind BJ?"

"Lacy, this may sound like some kind of dumb come on, but I've got a weird feeling when I'm around you, like we know each other from somewhere else, like from another life. I find myself saying things that don't make any sense. It's like you scramble my brain. I don't know why you do that to me, but I want to try to find out."

"Yes. Dumb come-on. You got that one right, BJ." Lacy paused. "But not completely different from what I was thinking. I think you are one peculiar billionaire, but I've also got the weird feeling that we knew each other somehow before. Did you ever eat at the 'Dead Vegan Society' in Tustin? You know—my restaurant?"

"No. I plan to someday soon, but no."

…

Lae C Hogan was watching through Lacy's eyes and listening through Lacy's ears and wondering what to do to stop this line of discussion. Meanwhile Billy Jay had finally stopped trying to reach LacyHogan235^AM on the discussion forum and reconnected just in time to hear most of the last exchange. Billy Jay took control of Orlov.

…

"Well Lacy, suppose we did meet in another life in another world. Suppose it was a world where we were both trying to figure out our lives rather than a successful restauranteur and master real estate developer. If I was a poor slob who needed your help with a family emergency, do you think you would help me?"

"I think in that world my answer would be no. If I was struggling to make ends meet and some stranger asked for my help and it would inconvenience me, I would say no. I'd watch out for my own interests first."

"Okay. I understand that. You do need to watch out for your own interests. But suppose it was a world where things were changing, let's say, where Abitats had been just in a game, but now were becoming real. And suppose, somehow, I had one. Would the chance to be one of the first people to use a real Abitat weigh enough in your interest to get you to help me?"

"A real Abitat? Hmmm. I'd probably have all kinds of questions for you in a discussion forum before I'd decide what to do."

…

Lae C and Billy Jay broke from the game and quickly switched back to the discussion forum.

QZ9301, 8:30 PM, B.J. Orlov Running Out of Air

Meanwhile Bartholomew noticed insistent beeps that indicated that his oxygen level was getting dangerously low. "Uh, oh." He hadn't been able to respond to the warning beeps while Billy Jay was in control. "Maybe we can get back to the resort to have that discussion forum discussion, Lacy. But we need to hurry. I pulled my suit from maintenance and apparently it isn't holding an oxygen charge like it should. Let me help you out of there and we'll take my rover back. It's faster than yours and I don't think my air will last long enough to get your rover free and still get back."

He jumped down to the front hood of the stuck rover and, "May I?", put his hands on her waist from behind while she faced up the wall of the crater. "Now jump." She jumped and he lifted and pushed, and she sailed smoothly off the stuck rover and onto the surface just outside the crater, landing in slow motion into a crouch with her right leg forward. He crouched and jumped and sailed smoothly to the edge of the crater as well, landing with both feet together, but was a bit unstable as he landed and was about to tumble back when Lacy caught his gloved hand and pulled him upright.

"We need to hurry. My O2 is almost gone and even with this fast rover it will take a few minutes to get back. Are you comfortable driving if I pass out, or do you want me to engage the autopilot?"

"Which is faster?"

"The autopilot is slow, but it knows the way."

…

HW203904, 9:08 AM, AM Forum Discussion

…

<u>*BillyJay4^AM to LacyHogan235^AM*</u>
Are you there Lacy?

Just back from a strange encounter on the moon.

I've got a confused character there.

I think you do too.

What's this about an Abitat?

My dad helped design them.
One was just delivered to my house.
Brand new.

I'd like to see that.

You'd better be telling the truth.

And what's this thing about your mom being missing?

After a few minutes back and forth they agreed she would get a ride to Billy Jay's house from her coworker/assistant manager, Javier. He had done the chicken and potatoes delivery for her, so he knew where Billy Jay's house was.

I don't promise we can do anything for finding your mom.

We're just coming over to see the Abitat.

Okay. Okay. Come over and we'll talk.

QZ9301, 8:45 PM, Lacy and Orlov Heading to Resort

Bartholomew was sitting to the left of Lacy in his rover as they rolled quickly towards the resort, bouncing over uneven terrain, then turning to the left to avoid another crater. He put his hands around hers on the controller stick and whispered, "You've got this, Lacy," and wheezed then leaned against her shoulder and blacked out. Lacy was trying to follow his rover's tracks back to the portal, but there were so many tracks out here she was nervous she might not be on the best route. She could see the tower of the resort complex, so she knew she was going in roughly the right direction, but time was not on her side. She looked at Bartholomew's face through the clear surface of his helmet. He did not look good. She said nervously "You'd better not be faking this to get some kind of sympathy reaction. If you're not really dying right now, I will kill you, Mr. B J Orlov."

She tried to push the control stick farther forward, but it was already at its max. She looked at the mini display on the control and saw a "BJO Power" button. She tapped on it and the rover accelerated suddenly, jerking her and Orlov back against the seat hard. She kept an arm around him to keep his slumping body from falling over. As the rover reached full speed she said, "That's a lot better." She started closing the distance to the tower much more quickly, but it was hard to control as it raced across the landscape, bouncing higher over uneven spots. She hit a bigger bump as she aimed it towards the resort tower and became airborne (vacuum borne?). When the rover landed its wheels were spinning fast and the right wheels touched first. The rover spun to the left, tipping over and tumbling, dumping her and Orlov onto the ground and continuing to tumble ending up upside down. She could see the portal entry now. It was only about a couple hundred meters away without any major obstacles in between, but Orlov was unconscious, face down and she was shaken up. She seemed to still have her air supply and couldn't feel any broken bones.

"Help me. Can someone hear me? Help me, please" she pleaded. She didn't hear a response, so she stood up and brushed off the dust, and tried to lift Orlov. He was a big guy, but at one-sixth gravity he didn't really weigh that much, even in his gilded suit. She propped his arm over her shoulder and started walking towards the portal entrance, pulling his limp body, and dragging his feet behind her. It was awkward because despite his low weight he still had the same mass, and his momentum was harder to control than his weight. At one point she tried to adjust her direction, and his mass continued forward and knocked her down.

...

> ## HW203904, 9:30 AM, Billy Jay Initializes Abitat
>
> Billy Jay went out again through the garage to the Abitat, entered the code, opened the door, and went inside to wait for LacyHogan235 and her friend. He completed the acceptance procedure like he had done many times in games and then activated the external camera views so he could see when she and her friend arrived. He brought his tablet and paired it with the Abitat. He found three wristbands in a drawer and put one on and initialized it, leaving the other two in the drawer. Then he was able to open up windows to his games on the large display on the Abitat wall. The display quality was amazing. Much better than the large displays on the wall of his bedroom. The rendering of people and scenery was very lifelike. Maybe 3D. He decided to tag his characters quickly while he waited for LacyHogan235.
>
> He went first to the moon and saw the scene with Orlov lying on the ground and Lacy getting up again next to him. He tried to open Orlov's eyes, and they did open for a second, but Lacy wasn't looking, and they closed again when he disconnected. He'd have to deal with this later. He switched through his other active game world characters. He felt an adrenaline rush as he leapt from Half Dome with a wing suit and sailed out away from the rock face and towards Mirror Lake with more realistic detail than ever before, but he left that character less than halfway down. He started to unload his vehicle from a raft after crossing the Amazon. He made some more business deals on a golf course. His other characters besides Orlov were doing fine.

> ## QZ9301, 8:55 PM, Return to Lunar Resort
>
> Lacy was dragging Orlov again and cursing. Just then a dusty grey rover with '09' on its fenders pulled up next to her. It was her rover in autonomous mode returning to the portal. She remembered something from the orientation that the rover would return on its own if you tried to stay out too long. Apparently it was able to free

itself from the dust. It stopped long enough for her to lift Orlov on board lying him face down across the seats and she climbed on the side herself and held on. It proceeded slowly towards the portal. "Faster. Faster, please. Faster," she asked. It did not change its speed, but in just a few seconds it crossed through the flexible force field and into the pressurized air chamber of the excursion rental area. She pulled at Orlov's head gear to open it to the air, pulled it off and he was not breathing. A worker from the rental area ran over to see his big boss ghost-pale and not breathing. "Oh. Shit. It that Orlov?" he said.

Lacy pulled off her own head gear and tried to blow air into Orlov's mouth, pinching his nose. She could feel his lungs expand as she blew in, and she could hear and feel the air coming back out when she paused. Fresh anise, or licorice scent, she noticed. "Get help! Get a doctor!" she screamed at the excursion counter worker who was standing over her watching.

The excursion counter worker ran from the area but paused before going out of sight down a hallway. "Check his pulse. Start CPR," he called back, and then continued out of sight.

Lacy felt for pulse on Orlov's neck. She thought she could feel a weak pulse. She put her ear to his face and thought she could hear shallow breathing. She pulled one of his eyelids up and his pupil was large and did not change. "This isn't good," she said quietly.

...

HW203904, 10:0 AM, Billy Jay Meets Lae C and Javier

Billy Jay had windows tiled over the surface of the large wall display in the Abitat. Several showed the activity of his game characters; four showed views from the cameras on the outside of the Abitat; and some showed information from his mom's family social media pages, including the photos and the GPS coordinates of the food purchase from her calorie tracking app. He also found a website for his mom's old job at the motivational talk business. The website said the business was still closed. He was hoping she had started working for it again. It had a cartoon picture of the organizational guru, Min Strong, that Billy Jay always thought looked like a distant relative of his mom. Like they were cousins, maybe, except his mom didn't have any cousins that he knew of. He would have to look for an actual photo of her to help with a search. He found one in his own family social media files, but it was old. He didn't have any recent photos. It didn't occur to him to capture her image from the home security video. He had only looked at real time video on the system and didn't realize that the system kept copies for a few days.

When a really old beat-up looking Camry that once had been dark red pulled into the driveway next to the Abitat, Billy Jay minimized all the game windows and enlarged the information about his mom. The picture of the banana occupied the largest open window, along with a map showing the location where the picture was taken.

A thin young man with dark hair and a thin mustache got out of the driver's side of the car. He looked really young. Maybe no older than himself. "Is that supposed to be Lacy's boss?" Billy Jay thought to himself. The young woman who got out of the passenger side looked a lot like the Lacy Hogan character in the game. Add more makeup, fancier clothes and lose the facial piercings, and tattoos, but basically the same features. The young guy pointed at the Abitat and said something, and *Lacy* nodded and pointed towards the front door of the house. They both started walking in that direction. Billy Jay set down his tablet on the mini-kitchen stovetop and said to the Abitat, "Open the door," and the door slid open. Javier and Lae C were walking towards the house's front door when they heard the Abitat door open, and they turned around to see Billy Jay sitting up in one of the seats. He said, "Hi, I'm Billy Jay." He was nervous talking to strangers but being in an Abitat he felt more like one of his brave characters than himself.

"Hi, Billy. I'm Javier. I'm impressed. I've seen a couple of these drive by before on the highway. They've been testing them. But I've never seen inside one… except in the game, of course." Javier climbed in and looked around. "Very cool." He opened the refrigerator and saw that there was a supply of organic smoothies, spring waters, craft beers, yogurt cups, and a bottle of good champagne. "Now that is a nice touch. You stocked it up to welcome us?"

Lae C reprimanded Javier. "Javier. This isn't your Abitat." Turning to Billy Jay, she said, "I'm sorry about him. He looks and acts like a kid, but he's older than he looks. He's actually a perverted old man who happens to look young."

"The stuff in the fridge must have come with the Abitat," said Billy Jay as he turned to Lacy standing just outside the door leaning in. "You must be Lacy," he said. "Thanks for coming over. I'm Billy Jay Lee." He extended his hand to help her step up into the vehicle, but she ignored it.

"It's Lae C, not Lacy," said Javier.

"Huh?" said Billy Jay.

"Never mind, close enough," said Lae C. "Interesting new car you got here. Billy Jay. Still has that new car smell, doesn't it?" Lae C Hogan was hesitant about getting into a stranger's vehicle, even if she had done business with him in the game and recognized his resemblance to Orlov. But the allure of seeing a real life Abitat was pretty strong. "What do you think, Javier? You think it's a real Abitat and not some kind of home-built mock-up? Some kind of death trap?"

"Sure looks like an Abitat—like in the early game worlds. If this Billy boy built it, he did a bang-up job copying from the game," Javier said as he opened the bathroom door and stepped in. "But I guess there are ways of finding out for sure. Let's take it out for a spin."

"Don't you dare. Get out of there," said Lae C.

"I don't mean the bathroom. I mean let's go for a drive." He came out of the bathroom and looked at the display wall and noticed a website for Billy Jay's mom's job at the motivational speaking businesses, '*Minimalism or Nothing*' with the cartoon picture of Min Strong.

"So, are you a fan of Min Strong? She mysteriously went offline and stopped doing her talks. I went to one of her hologram talks at one of the Miniverse conventions when I was in high school. She was great. I did a couple papers about her philosophy in college. I wonder what ever happened to her. She went offline and disappeared two or three years ago."

Billy Jay said, "I think my mom worked for her. Let's focus. My mom is the one who is missing. Since yesterday. Here is a picture of my mom." He pointed at another window.

"No way. She looks a little like Min Strong. Are they sisters or something?" Javier asked.

"She doesn't have any brothers or sisters," Billy Jay replied.

Javier continued enthusiastically, "But your mom knows who Min Strong is! You want us to help you find your mom who knows Min Strong? Everyone's been trying to find Min Strong. No one knows who she really is. I'd love to meet her. Lae C, you didn't tell me this guy had a connection to Min Strong. For a chance to meet Min Strong, I'd help him even if he didn't have a real Abitat."

Lae C stepped into the vehicle where she could see the display on the wall showing the website but stayed close to the door. "I don't know this famous Min person. What did she do?"

"People who are into the game and Abitats really should know about her. Abitats are all about minimalism. She used to teach extreme minimalism. It was almost a religion. Economy of Spirit. Abundance of Simplicity. Min to the Max. What would Min Keep? She was on all the apps and there were conventions. She was mysterious. Even her appearance was minimal, only as an animation, never in person. She kind of disappeared when the game started getting popular. Why did she stop, Billy?"

"I don't know. My mom quit that job when my dad got sick. That reminds me, he hasn't eaten since yesterday. Neither have I."

He opened the fridge and took out a bottle of berry organic smoothy. "I should take him something. Do you two want to wait here?" He grabbed a second smoothy bottle, opened it and started chugging it.

"Should we take off with the Abitat?" Lae C asked Javier.

Swallowing and wiping his mouth, Billy Jay said, "I activated it with my voice and my tablet. I don't think it will go anywhere without me. But please don't try that." He stepped out of the Abitat and paused. "Maybe you should both come in with me."

Javier and Lae C looked at each other and shrugged then followed Billy Jay. The door to the vehicle closed automatically behind them when they were out. They followed Billy Jay through the garage and into the house. As they walked through the sparsely furnished house on the way to his dad's bedroom Javier said, "I've never seen household minimalism like this in such a big house. I always think of it in terms of fitting into tiny houses or spaces like an Abitat. But I like it. I like it a lot."

When they got to his dad's room Billy Jay said, "You'd better wait out here in the hallway while I check on him." He finished off his smoothy and handed the empty bottle to Javier, then went ahead into the room. Lae C and Javier stood in the doorway.

"Dad, I've got something for you to eat." Billy Jay held up the bottle of berry smoothy in front of his dad's face. His dad continued the same twitching and mumbling as always. Billy Jay opened the bottle and held it to his dad's mouth. As Billy spilled liquid on his dad's lips his dad sipped some of it in while continuing to mumble and twitch and hold his tablet.

Lae C quietly entered the room behind Billy Jay. "What's wrong with him?" she whispered.

"We never got a good answer from the doctors for what to call it. He's been like this for three or four years. Before he got really bad, he just was really forgetful. My mom takes care of him most of the time. He doesn't talk or get up on his own, but we can walk him to the bathroom. He's not paralyzed."

"What's with the headset hat, and the tablet?" whispered Javier who had followed Lae C into the bedroom but hung back a little farther.

"I don't know. He needs them. They calm him. He gets really bad if you take them away. Sometimes I have to take the tablet for a little while, if I'm changing him or washing him; he gets really unhappy if I take it away for long. I just leave the cap on. My mom said to never take it off. I guess she tried, and it was really bad."

"But how did it happen? Did he have an accident or is it like Alzheimer's or something?" Lae C asked.

"I think he felt it coming on. He knew something wasn't right. He was starting to get confused and angry a lot, but it was pretty sudden when he went from near normal to like this." His dad continued to slowly sip from the bottle, but with more getting on his chin than in his mouth as Billy Jay tilted it to his mouth.

"Can I try?" Lae C asked as she came up next to Billy Jay and leaned over his dad and reached for the bottle and took it out of Billy Jay's hand. "What's his name?"

"Uh. Okay. Perry. Perry Lee. Perry Wilson Lee. And my mom is Mara Lee."

"Hi, Mr. Perry Wilson Lee. You missing Mara? I'm Lae C. Do you like this drink?" She tipped it against his lips and brushed some of the hair stubble sticking out of his cap with two fingers of her other hand. His eyes briefly turned towards Lae C's.

Perry stopped twitching and mumbling, rested his tablet on his lap, and seemed to focus on the smoothy bottle. He sipped the smoothy as she tipped it more.

"That's weird," said Billy Jay.

…

6:40 PM, Andre Leaves Construction Site

The last of the other public safety officers were leaving, some in anonymous Abitats and some in official-looking Public Safety vehicles. Andre stood at the edge of the street still in his bat costume, waiting for his Abitat. His rat-costumed colleague was with him. Behind them were stretches of yellow police tape crisscrossing the muddy construction site.

"Do you think that greenish smudge was NeverMind?" asked the rat.

"Probably. Either that or NeverMore. The sniffers don't know the difference. But they'll know soon. The samples should be at the lab by now. Do I look as soaked as you do?" asked the bat.

"You look wet, but your suit sheds water. The fur on this one soaks it up. I don't know why we had to scan the whole lot after finding that one green sample. They're not going to find anything in all the other mud samples we collected. Everything was washed away in this rain."

"You never know. The lab tests are pretty sensitive. You should go dry off and change clothes, or do you have to go right back to *The Theme Park*? asked Andre the bat.

"I have to go back. My shift isn't done yet. After tonight, I'm hoping to get the rest of the weekend off," said the wet rat.

"I'm on call all weekend, so we'll see," said the bat. "Good luck tonight."

"But it might take me a little extra time to get back while I wring this suit out. You're lucky they didn't make you stay for another shift too, what with NeverMind possibly hitting the streets tonight. Oh. This is me." He stepped into the open door of an anonymous-looking Abitat that pulled up to the curb.

"Good luck. I still owe you a sandwich, or a beer."

"Both." The rat disappeared behind the closing door of the Abitat which pulled gently away from the curb.

Andre's Abitat arrived. He jumped in and said, "To Camilla's." He messaged Elsie that he was finally on the way.

6:45 PM, Looking for the Wristbands

An Abitat pulled up to the curb next to the construction site. The door opened and Sam, Jo-Jo, and Emily looked out at the tangle of police tape that was blowing in the wind and rain. Their clothes were dry. Emily had lent them some of her clothes while the wet ones were sent out to be cleaned and dried along the way from the Old West Theme area. Sam wanted to keep Emily's panda robe, but she said no.

"What do you think happened here? Is it safe for you guys to get out here?" asked Emily.

"No choice. We need to get our wristbands so we can call back our Abitat," Jo-Jo replied.

"To be safe, let's go around the block once or twice and see if we can see anyone in there before you get out. Close door," Emily commanded the Abitat.

They watched exterior views of the area from the cameras on Emily's Abitat and from shared cameras of other Abitats in the area. It appeared that no one was at the construction site, so after circling the block just once they returned to the curb and Sam jumped out. "No need for both of us to get wet again. I'll get the wristbands and come right back. Wait here if you can," Sam said. He ran across the muddy site towards a tree by the fence in the back.

"Be careful, Sam," Jo-Jo called out.

Emily said nothing but let the Abitat door close while they waited. Looking at the time she thought she could probably still meet up with Jeremy and Chandra in *The Theme Park*. They should still be there for at least a couple more hours unless the rain scared them off. She could message them as soon as Sam and Jo-Jo were on their way. There was the sound of knocking on the door, and it opened. Sam jumped in and said, "Let's go."

"Give me my wristband," said Jo-Jo.

"They weren't there. They're gone."

"Shit," thought Emily, just as Jo-Jo said it out loud.

6:55 PM, Tristan and the Tourists

Tristan had been sitting with the tourists in the office of the machine shop hearing the story of their lives and the life of his sister but holding off on saying much about his own life. He didn't tell them his current name, nor confirm nor deny that he was Perry. Perry's sister Carmen had married Max Kovich in Iowa and moved to Kansas. They had two kids, Gabriel and Fanny. Fanny was the mom, here with her husband, John Tran, and their twins, Minh and Max. They told about the lives that Carmen and Max had led in Iowa and Kansas and what it was like growing up there. In recent years Fanny's mom, Carmen, had been on dialysis with no luck so far finding a match for a donor kidney and no success with stem cell kidney regrowth. They were hoping to find additional relatives for potential matches out here as well as taking a family vacation.

It took an effort for Tristan to recall his sister and the circumstances of their last contact. It was a part of his life that he had not thought about in a long time.

As some of the memories returned, he recalled having to drop out of college to deal with things after his parents died in a car accident. Carmen was unhappy that their parents had designated him as executor of their estate and not her. Their wills didn't explain why, but he guessed it was because he still lived in California, and she had never moved back after going away to college. And maybe they trusted him more. But she felt she was older and more mature and should be making the decisions.

She thought their dad was prejudiced towards his son who was also good with machines and got into engineering at Stanford, while she had been a star soccer player and business major at Iowa State.

Carmen was also unhappy that he took over his dad's machine shop. She said that the shop and all the machines should be sold to split the proceeds. She wouldn't accept that the shop and most of the machines were leased, and he had chosen to use most of his share of the life insurance to keep the leases and live in the shop while attending a local college. He had done everything they called for in their wills and sent her an equal share of the assets but still she had not spoken to him again.

Tristan noticed the time and realized that he needed to let Elsie know what he had found out about the conditions in the mountains. He apologized and asked them to take a look around the machine shop while he took care of some business. He sent messages to Elsie and then looked up information about his sister and her family to confirm that these people were who they said they were. Unlike himself, they were all very visible in multiple game world projections of the real world and in a number of old-fashioned social media networks. They were active with fund-raising sites for kidney research and support groups, which supported their story.

He was sympathetic about his sister's kidney condition, but not sure if he could risk helping. He worried about how to maintain contact with these new relatives without exposing himself too much. A whirring noise from the machine shop brought him out of his thoughts.

7:00 PM, Jose Arrives at the Ranch House

Honus broke out of the game when an alert popped up on the display indicating someone was at the front door. Removing one of his earpieces he heard knocking. He walked to the door and peeked through the peephole.

Jose was wearing a raincoat over his work coveralls and was dripping water on the porch. He took off the raincoat and shook it off. He had been dropped off by a carousel bus a few blocks away and walked to the house through the rain. Honus opened the door and, looking at the embroidered nametag on the coveralls, said, "Jose, is it now?"

"I suppose so. For quite a while now. And you go by Honus, I understand?"

"That choice was probably not ideal, but I'm stuck with it now."

"You can change any time."

"It's not as easy to change now as it was in the old days in the game where you could just walk away from a character and start with a new identity in another game world. Or maybe adopt another character in the same game world. Not since the big Reset. Do you still like beer?" Honus asked.

"Sure," Jose replied. "People still do it. Just change your name if you want."

"Business reasons." Honus gestured towards the hallway and Jose followed him.

"Okay. If you say so. The place looks the same. Fresh paint? How many years has it been?"

"Sergey maintains it, I think. It has been a bit of time since we hung out here. You and Lae C, my dad, and your Gretchen online. Do you still see Lae C or Gretchen?" Honus opened the garage door and stepped down and towards the Abitat waiting there.

"Not really. Gretchen? That's a name from the past. I don't know what happened to her at the Reset. How about your dad? Does he still live here?"

Honus gestured and the Abitat door opened. "I don't think so. I haven't been here much in the last few years myself. He used to come and go, but I think he's taken on a new identity and is living out there in an Abitat like a normal person now."

"It was cool learning things from him back then as he started remembering things. Even with his brain issues, he knew so much, about Abitats and about the game." As he stepped into the Abitat behind Honus Jose continued, "This looks familiar, but I see the garage was enlarged at some point to allow full size Abitats? No more ducking your head when it comes and goes."

Honus took a seat and pointed at the minifridge. "Not sure if Sergey or my dad had that done."

Jose took a beer out of the fridge and sat down. "I hope your dad is doing okay and remembering even more. You've been busy too I guess."

"Yes. I have."

Jose held his beer out to Honus, "Did you want one?"

"No thanks."

"Resorts around the world?"

Honus nodded and replied, "And you are keeping a low profile. Fixing Abitats now? Is that interesting work?"

"It has its moments. Today in particular. And it gives me time to dabble in some other things." Jose sipped his beer.

"Like blocking new developments."

"How could a regular guy fixing Abitats get in the way of major business deals?"

"The ownership of the properties that have been blocking the development is a little bit mysterious. It goes through characters and shell corporations in dozens of parallel game worlds. My experts haven't been able to detangle it all, but personally, I suspect it could be part of the holdings of an anonymous character that gets a slice of points from all delivery and storage fees. Maybe some kind of *Sixth Order Harlequin Barrister,* whatever that is."

"I don't think that designation actually means anything."

"People who have heard of it have puzzled over it, a lot." Honus looked at Jose for some more elaboration, but not getting any, continued, "So how do you think such a character got into that kind of hive programming?"

"You don't think it was your dad? He knew more about those kinds of things than anyone."

"I don't think he was ever into making points, and I got the impression that he shared a lot of what he knew."

"Yeah. In the first years when your dad started remembering things, he did share some ideas with anyone who listened, about Abitat design, and how that hive traffic and delivery coordination code was supposed to work. If someone listened closely, they could find out the early versions in the game were not quite right. I suppose if someone implemented a good working version of it just before the game Reset, they might have a bit of a monopoly today on a small slice of code everyone uses."

"And it doesn't take a big fee to add up to some real points when it's used trillions of times a day. Why didn't I try to get into **that** business?"

"You always wanted to build resorts, not hive code."

"That's true. But an extra few billion points could be handy for financing projects. Then again, you've probably got a lot of people from big storage and delivery companies trying to figure out how to replace that code and get back that slice of profit for themselves."

"So far unsuccessfully. Your dad also shared some great ideas about how to encrypt and embed code, so it isn't easy to replace. Hence such a character might choose to lay low and remain anonymous to avoid persuasion."

"I thought you always wanted to be a lawyer, not an Abitat repair guy or a hive coder," Honus asked.

"As you probably know I tried law school for a while, after we stopped hanging out here, but with the Reset looming and game law on its way it seemed pointless, so I stopped to concentrate on other things, like Abitat design and hive coding. Lae C stayed with law though, if I understand, she's doing okay with game law now." Jose sipped at his beer.

"Is that right? I knew she was into a lot of things: cuisine, writing…literature anyway, maybe astronomy too, but not law. That was your thing." Honus added, "Speaking of cuisine, have you eaten?"

"No. But I don't mean to stay long," Jose answered.

"My Abitat can go pick something up for us while we talk. Meanwhile, if you want another beer, please help yourself."

Jose held up his beer to show it was still almost full and said, "Still good on the beer, but maybe something to eat."

"What would you like?" asked the English butler voice.

"Surprise me," answered Jose.

"Too bad Lae C went into law instead of opening her restaurant, or we could have ordered from hers," reflected Honus.

"Sometimes things turn out different than you expect," said Jose.

"Yeah. I sure didn't expect to still be looking for my mom so many years later," said Honus.

"You still don't know where she is? Your dad must know."

"Last time I saw him he was still saying he doesn't," said Honus.

"In those first days we thought it should be easy to find out where she went," Jose recalled.

"Until we decided it was too risky to keep looking," said Honus.

"Yeah, I think about those days sometimes," said Jose and he took a bigger swig of beer.

"Speaking of those days, when I was poking around in the house today waiting for you to get off work, I found a history game world with the story of those days when we all met. I think maybe Lae C and my dad built it during the time she was helping him remember things. I hadn't noticed it before today," Honus explained.

"Really? That was an interesting time if I recall," said Jose.

"No need to recall. Follow me." Honus got out of the Abitat and started back into the house towards his old bedroom with Jose grabbing a second bottle of beer and following him. The garage door opened and the Abitat left to get food as they went into the house. "We can play the game and relive it. I found it when I was reviewing the old game worlds that I've played from my room and looking again for clues about my mom. It was saved right in there among other games. Whoever made it must have left it here years ago, but I never noticed it, or at least I don't remember it"

Honus opened his bedroom door and continued, "Of course, this version is not completely accurate. Lae C, or whoever, used quite a bit of artistic license about what different people were thinking, but they did a pretty good job of capturing events of those days. You might say it's fictional but based on true events. My dad must have helped her with some things he remembered, as she got him talking again, plus access to stuff like game records, video records from the house and vehicles."

Honus looked at Jose to see if his reaction indicated any prior knowledge about the history world. It didn't seem to, but Honus was not great at reading faces. Jose followed him into the old bedroom. The old wall-sized displays and racks of interface devices were almost like a museum of pre-game game play.

"I can bring it up here," Honus pointed at the wall displays. "If it was Lae C, I think she tended to want to write it like a book, since literature was one of her things, but it's a game world so it's available for all kinds of interfaces. You can watch it on the wall with me or use some other kind of interface. What would you like?" He pointed at a rack with a number of different headsets, haptic suits, brain caps, and game controllers of various kinds.

Jose picked up a simple pair of 3D goggles and earphones. "These will do narration and display from multiple viewpoints, right?" Jose asked.

"Of course. If that's what you want. To start I'll drive and you watch," said Honus. He put on headphones and a pair of goggles but left the goggles around his neck. He could watch the view on the wall display.

"Possible Spoiler alert. Did Lae C solve the big mystery of the day in her retelling?" Jose asked.

"No. I don't think so. I haven't seen it all yet. Nothing so far about what my mom did after she disappeared and very little from her point of view. Basically, just what was captured by game records and home or car videos and maybe things that one of us recalled. No real insight about what she was thinking at the time. And it doesn't let you change actions. You can see for yourself. I'll hit the highlights of what I've already played and get to the part where we meet."

Honus restarted the game and sped through most of the parts about Billy Jay. Jose seemed to be able to follow the highly accelerated view. Honus slowed down a bit for the parts with Mara at the coffee shop and just before her character's view cut off when she was in the car. He moved on to the next day when Billy Jay got the Abitat and when Javier and Lae C came over. When it got to the part that he hadn't seen yet he slowed it down again, but Jose said it was okay to keep going fast.

HW203904, 10:30 AM, Abitat Ride

A few minutes later Billy Jay and Javier each held one of Perry's arms as they led him down the hallway and towards the garage. Lae C walked backwards in front of them carrying a blanket, extra adult diapers, and holding the almost empty smoothy bottle and Perry's tablet where he could see them. Perry was mumbling and twitching again but not panicking about not holding the tablet. He shuffled his feet along the floor but kept going forward. Billy Jay and Javier kept a hold on his arms, just in case, but it seemed he was carrying his own weight.

"Lacy, you have some kind of touch with my dad. He wouldn't let me hold his tablet for a second without panicking. I wonder why he's okay with you holding it."

"He can see it. It's still right here in front of him," said Lae C.

"We're taking him with us in the Abitat?" asked Javier.

"I can't leave him home alone," replied Billy Jay.

"Yeah, but I only counted three seats," said Javier. "That may be an Abitat, but this is not the game. Driving is dangerous in this world. I want a seat with a seat belt if we're going on the road."

"We'll figure something out," said Lae C.

They continued down the hallway and through the garage. Billy said "Open" and the door to the Abitat slid open. They climbed in and helped Perry into one of the seats. Lae C gave him back his tablet and set the smoothy bottle in a cup holder. She spread the blanket on his lap. The three of them looked at the two available seats. Javier sat quickly in one and said, "You two can argue over the other seat, but I've got this one."

"I think this pad on the wall behind the seats can pull down into a bed. If we move the seats a little," said Lae C. "It doesn't have seat belts but it's a place to sit. Get up, Javier, and help us move the seats. If they're like the ones in the game they're movable. The flooring in here has the grooves like in some of the game versions for reattaching the seats. Let's try it."

"Good idea," said Billy Jay.

"Okay, but I still get a seat belt," said Javier.

. . .

"That Javier was kind of a doofus. Wasn't he?" Jose asked.

Honus shrugged, but Jose, still wearing the 3D goggles, didn't see him. The history world continued…

...

With a little pushing and pulling from all three of them they were able to disconnect and move Perry's seat with him in it. The seats were easy to detach and move and then automatically reattach to the floor just like in the game. After rearranging all the seats to make room and setting up the narrow wall-mounted bed Billy Jay said, "I'll take the couch. You can have the third seat, Lacy."

"Okay. Thanks. Now where to?" asked Lae C. "Just take a spin around the block? Where do we start?"

"His mom knows Min Strong. Let's go find her," Javier insisted.

Billy Jay picked up his tablet from the stove top and touched the screen to enlarge the picture of the banana and latte and the corresponding map. "Yesterday she said she was going to the store to buy some food and cleaning supplies, but an hour or so later she recorded this on her diet tracking app. I don't know why that app posts to our family social media, but it's a clue. It's shows she was at a coffee shop way across town. She didn't come back here and calls and texts to her since then get rejected."

"We could go there and ask around," said Javier. He picked up the tablet and figured out how to use the diet tracking app to examine the geotag on the photo. "This 'family social media' isn't a public app. Did your mom or dad write their own apps?"

"Ignore him. Can this Abitat go that far? I mean, what's its range? Is it even charged?" asked Lae C.

"System status please," said Billy Jay. A window opened on the wall display with various gauges and statistics. "It looks like the current range is 19 kilometers. If it's like the game, it should be able to find recharging stations along the way--if they exist." He handed the tablet to Javier. "See if it has a map of the nearest charging station." Javier began flipping through tabs on the status display.

"But in the game, you also have to have AMPs on file to pay for recharge services. I'm not paying for your re-charges," said Lae C.

"Hmmm. Yeah. Money is a problem right now. Give me a few minutes in the house. I might be able to find a credit card I can use," said Billy Jay.

"Let's just do a quick spin around the block to see if this thing works," Lae C suggested.

Billy Jay hesitated at the door. He wanted to find enough money to search for his mom but considered doing the quick spin around the block first. Javier stopped flipping through different tabs of information on the screen and said, "Oh Yeah!" The three of them looked at the display and saw the following: '*Usable service credits: 5000 AMPs.*'

Javier said, "I may be wrong, but I think AMPs are trading at about 9 dollars per. That's in the augmented reality game worlds that map onto the real world. People are using AMPs as cybercurrency for untraceable real-world transactions. Billy Jay, I think your van here has some funds."

"Billy boy, I think you might have enough to juice this thing after all," said Lae C. "Time's a-wasting. Let's head out."

Billy Jay said, "Proceed to location on the map."

A voice from the walls said, "Please follow all current safety laws and regulations. Take seats and buckle up." After a pause for 2 seconds there was a three-note chime. "You have been advised. Proceeding to the destination." The vehicle moved slightly and then the voice spoke up again, "Watch your heads." The upper part of the walls folded and adjusted, and the ceiling came down about a foot and a half. Everyone bent over or sat down quickly. Billy Jay took his tablet back from Javier.

Lae C commented, "I wonder why it's lowering the ceiling? Aerodynamics? I don't remember that from the game."

The display on the wall showed a map of the local area and camera views of the area around the unit. One showed the house and garage with its open door.

"Billy Jay said, "Hey, the door is still open. I should close that before we go."

A flashing green circle appeared on the map on top of the garage. The crouching vehicle proceeded slowly into the garage and up to the recharge station that Perry had installed a few years ago. The cameras showed an arm extend out from under the vehicle to the charging station. It touched the station and then retracted. It did the same a second time. After retracting the second time the voice said, "Interference at the charging station. Closest alternate station: 5 kilometers. Proceed to alternate?"

"Wait. Wait. That's the charging station my dad installed before he got sick. It's still in its shrink wrap." He spoke to the walls, "Open door." Billy walked bent over to the door and jumped out when it slid open. He tore the plastic wrap off the charging station and then backed up to let the vehicle's arm dock with it. The arm extended again and tapped on the station but backed off again. Billy Jay looked it over. He wasn't sure if it was the same as the charging stations in the game. He didn't pay attention to that detail in the games. Javier followed him out and also looked at it.

"Maybe something's not lined up right. It always just works automatically in the game."

"Are you kidding me?" asked Lae C, stepping up behind them and then pushing them aside. "Can't you see this interface plate is upside down. The hoses and cables are up, and the interface plugs are all out of reach below. There's no way it can connect." She grabbed an oval section with cables and hoses of different sizes, lifted it off the recharge stand, turned it over and set it back down, clicking it into place. "That looks better. Haven't you done manual Abitat hookups in the game?"

"All the time, but I just let my characters take care of those details," said Billy Jay.

"Yeah. I never paid much attention to what these recharge station things looked like," said Javier. "I guess I should pay more attention to technical details." He tilted his head to look closer at the mechanism.

The Abitat's arm reached out again and snapped into place on the interface plate. Fluids could be heard transferring, but just for a couple seconds, and an electrical buzz started and grew louder. They climbed back into the Abitat, ducking their heads and sat back down in their seats, and Billy Jay sat on the bed. The door closed behind them.

"How long do we need to let it charge?" asked Javier.

"In versions of the game not far in the future you might leave it a few hours or even overnight for a deep charge at a home station, less for a partial charge, but at good fast charge stations in the game it's about 5 minutes. Who knows with this one. It may be a while," said Lae C. "Well, B.J., while we're waiting, is there anything else you want to get from your house before we go?"

"Maybe I should get a jacket. I don't know how late we might be or where else we might go. And a credit card for things we can't buy with points."

"You think it might get cold? Could I borrow a jacket?" asked Javier.

"If we need to let it charge for hours, we might as well forget about going across town today," said Lae C. "But can we at least take it for a short ride first? I want to be able to say I rode in a real Abitat for more than 10 feet pulling into a garage. How about we just take it for a short spin. It's already got enough charge to go a few miles."

Billy Jay said, "Give me five minutes to look for a credit card. Open door."

The Abitat's voice said. "Command not accepted. Vehicle in motion. Fast partial charge complete. Range 160 kilometers. Please follow all current safety laws and regulations. Take seats and buckle up." After a pause for 2 seconds there was a three-note chime. "You have been advised. Proceeding to the destination."

"Skip safety warnings," Billy Jay commanded.

"I'm sorry," said the vehicle voice. "Current regulations require safety warnings. Switching to abbreviated warnings." Three chimes sounded then, "Buckle up." The camera display windows showed the Abitat was in the street, and the door of the receding garage was closing. The ceiling moved back to its full height and Javier buckled himself into his seat.

"Should we go back?" asked Billy Jay.

"No. Let's go." said Lae C.

"That charge was quick," said Javier. "Do you have some kind of industrial electric service at your house?"

"I don't think so. But my dad had solar panels and batteries installed for his workshop. Maybe the charging station uses the workshop's power."

The three of them watched the displays with scenes of the suburban streets as the Abitat made its way out of the Lee's neighborhood and towards a freeway.

"It's smooth. You can barely feel it moving. Like in the game," said Lae C.

"Yeah. I like it. I feel like I'm in the game," said Billy Jay.

"You may feel like you're in the game, but we're not. There are people out there texting and playing games while they're at the wheel. Even the self-driving cars are unpredictable. In the game they're all autonomous and hive-cooperating and driving is safe. Not here. I'm staying buckled up," said Javier.

"I don't really have a choice," said Billy Jay, sitting on the bed and miming the fastening of an invisible seat belt and shrugging.

All three intently watched the views from the cameras for a couple minutes until the Abitat smoothy merged into the freeway traffic, then Javier and Lae C simultaneously pulled out their smartphones and earpieces and started checking on their own game characters. Billy Jay picked up his tablet to do the same. He opened one window at a time on the wall display for his active game worlds. Perry sat holding his tablet and mumbling but occasionally looking up from his tablet at the others, especially at Lae C, who also glanced his way. Their eyes met. Lae C smiled and then went back to gameplay on her smartphone.

…

Honus looked up from the high-speed history world playback.

Jose still seemed to be watching the story.

Honus refocused on the history world …

HW203904, 10:50 AM, Along the Way

After a few minutes of catching up with their game worlds and other games or media, oblivious to one another and the exterior scenes, Javier looked up and watched the others for a few seconds before saying to Billy Jay, "So how do we look for your mom?"

Billy Jay had a window open that showed Orlov in a hospital bed in his suite with a nurse checking his vitals. The Lacy Hogan character was standing on the other side of the bed watching. Billy Jay said, "Lacy, it looks like you saved my life on the moon. Thanks."

Lae C said, "Maybe. Your guy's breathing again, but he doesn't look good. What happens to his points if he dies in the game?"

"I'm not sure. I think most goes to his nephew who is another character of mine in that world. But I think I'll be able to wake him up. Miraculous cures are pretty common in the worlds I play in. My characters have got through worse before."

"Wait. You've got more than one character in the same world? I know you can watch lots of characters, but to control more than one? Can you do that?" Lae C asked.

"Hey. Guys. Hello? Back to this world. What do think we might find at the coffee shop? Do you think Min Strong might be there?" Javier asked.

"I don't know. We'll see when we get there. I guess." Billy Jay leaned back on one elbow on the bed. He looked at the displays showing the scene on the freeway around the Abitat. He was going farther from home than he had been in a long time, maybe ever, but he didn't feel panic. He felt like he was playing the game rather than really being out in the world with strangers.

The views from the exterior cameras gave a good view of most of the nearby vehicles and their drivers. Traffic was heavy and slow and drivers in other cars showed a mix of facial reactions. Some were frustrated with the traffic, gripping the wheel, and occasionally making gestures of frustration at the car in front of them. Some were singing along with private music. One was singing through open windows along with loud booming music whose base was vibrating the Abitat despite its excellent sound insulation. Several were engrossed deeply into apps on their phones or tablets. Not all of those were in autonomous cars; some still had a hand on their steering wheels and drifted in their lanes as they texted and played games. In a self-driving big rig truck, the legally required backup driver was leaning against the side window with his eyes closed, apparently dozing. A few cars had tinted glass so you couldn't see the drivers at all. No other windowless Abitats were in view on this stretch of the roadway.

No one seemed to notice the Abitat driving along next to them, except in one family minivan with two kids in the back. One of the kids was pressing her face to the window and gesturing to the other kid and the parents in the front seat, pointing out the Abitat in the next lane.

"Hey. See that car here." Billy Jay sat up quickly and pointed at a green car on the display. "See that driver playing games on the center console in her car with the steering wheel pushed forward into the dash like that." He pointed and waited until he saw that Javier and Lae C were looking. "That's just like my mom's car. She would use the center display to play games and check messages and stuff. Sometimes I played games on her car's console in the garage."

"She had an Autonomous Motors EL series?" asked Javier. "Nice car. They completely got rid of the steering wheel in the latest model. Just a touch pad for steering now if you take it out of autopilot. I'd rather have a steering wheel if I'm going to have to drive. What's the point with a touch pad? Just let the car's brain do the driving if you don't want to put your hands on a wheel."

"My dad bought the car for her. It was our first autonomous car. He had the two charging stations installed in the garage at the same time. But he had a gas-powered pickup truck back then. He said he was waiting for a new autonomous model that wasn't out yet. I guess he meant an Abitat. I guess he meant this Abitat."

"Okay. So, we know what kind of car to look for. Maybe we can track down her car. That might be a way to find her. What did the police say when you talked to them? Can they track her car?" Lae C asked.

"I haven't called the police yet. I read that they won't look for missing people until they've been gone for days," Billy Jay replied.

"I think you're right. I've seen that in movies." Javier opened the refrigerator. "Hey, can I have a beer?"

"Sure. Why not."

"What else do you have in there?" asked Lae C. "I'm getting hungry now, and you said you and your dad didn't eat anything since yesterday except those smoothies? That can't be enough. You both must be hungry still."

"Yeah."

Javier took a swig from his bottle of beer then set it in a cup holder and picked up a yogurt cup and a water from the fridge and showed them to Lae C and Billy Jay. "You want a yogurt? Or how about champagne?"

"Does your dad like yogurt?" Lae C asked.

"I don't know. My mom usually makes him a mush that looks like baby food. I feed it to him sometimes, but I'm not sure exactly what's in it. I don't remember giving him yogurt."

"You're Mr. Observant at home, aren't you?" Lae C observed. "Javier, give me one of those yogurts and find me a spoon. I'll see if Perry will eat it." She unbuckled herself and turned to the side of her seat and leaned over to Perry. Javier found a spoon in a drawer by the fridge and gave yogurt and spoon to Lae C. She proceeded to offer yogurt to Perry who kept twitching but stopped mumbling while she held the spoon to his lips. "Open up." He opened his mouth slightly and she put the spoonful in. "Okay. It seems like he's willing to eat this. Meanwhile let's see about getting some lunch for us. Smoothies, beer, and yogurt won't cut it for me. Can one of you look up a food place along our way? Preferably one that accepts AMPs for payment."

"You're the foodie, Lae C," said Javier. "If I find a food place, you'll find all kinds of problems with it and eventually you'll end up doing the search yourself. So why don't you just do it?"

"No. I'm flexible. I'm hungry. See what you can find."

"Yeah. Okay." Javier searched with his phone. "There's a McDonald's at one of the next off ramps. I can't tell if they accept AMPs. There's like five Starbucks near the next three off ramps. It doesn't say anything about AMPs. There's a Thai takeout place not far from the fourth off ramp. It's got some good ratings. But I don't see anything about paying with AMPs."

"You're searching with your phone?" asked Lae C. "We're in an Abitat. Search like you would in the game." She continued to give Perry yogurt one spoonful at a time. "Hey, Abitat. We need some food. We want convenient, well-rated, locally sourced, organic, to-go or delivery, with vegan options. And we want to pay with on-board points. What's available?"

Two windows opened on the display wall showing pictures of different food options. A voice from the ceiling said, "Do you prefer Thai, or California Fusion? Both are available for Abitat delivery along your present route."

"Let's see the California Fusion menu," said Lae C. One of the windows expanded to show items from the menu of a small restaurant about 10 miles ahead. "This looks good to me. How about you, Billy Jay and Javier? Do you see anything you want?"

They each picked out some items from the menu. Lae C asked for a number of substitutions and special preparation instructions on her items, and she asked for a side of mild eggplant puree for Perry. The total came to 55 AMPs. At the exchange rates Javier mentioned before that seemed pricey, but they went ahead and placed the order. Lae C finished feeding Perry the yogurt and went back to playing her game. Billy Jay and Javier had been playing the whole time.

...

Honus noticed that Jose hadn't moved in a while.

He asked, "You okay, Jose?"

"Sure. Keep going."

Honus moved the History World forward …

HW203904, 11:20 AM, Food Delivery to Abitat

After a few minutes there was a little musical alert from the ceiling. They all looked up from their games to see a delivery drone approaching on one of the exterior camera view displays. The kids in the van in the next lane which had pulled ahead a little were pointing and watching as was the van mom looking back from her front seat. She rolled down her window and looked back and pointed. The drivers and passengers of the other vehicles around didn't seem to notice the drone as it hovered over the front of the Abitat and lowered its package into a chute that opened on the front of the vehicle. The musical alert sounded again, but with a little longer melody. The drone could be seen flying up and off to the right without its cargo. Billy Jay got off the bed and opened the cabinet at the front. He pulled out a box with several food containers.

"This smells great," said Billy Jay. Lae C tilted up the wall-mounted table under the large display and Billy Jay set the food box down. They adjusted the seats to face the table, although Javier stayed belted in while he scooted his seat into position and secured it again to the floor. Billy Jay took his food box and sat on the bed.

Lae C smelled the delivered food, then searched the cupboards and fridge to see what was available to make improvements. Not a lot. "Oh well. I'll see what I can do. Don't eat that yet." She took Billy Jay's food box from him and put the food into a pan she got from a small cupboard and heated it on the small stove top. She added some pepper and a splash of Javier's beer to Billy Jay's meal and stirred it for a minute. Then she served it on a plate she found in the cupboard with some garnish from her own order and gave it back to him. Billy Jay was impressed. It looked delicious and smelled better too.

"That's what she does. She doesn't leave any food alone," said Javier. "My turn. Fix mine too."

She wiped out the pan and started again with Javier's meal. This time she used some of the ingredients from her own meal to add to his. She did a similar presentation on a second plate.

"Thank you, Madam Chef," said Javier as he took his plate.

"This is really good," said Billy Jay.

"She knows her stuff," said Javier.

She did even more elaborate preparation on her own meal. When it was ready, she said, "Oh, Perry. I hope you don't mind waiting a few minutes. I need to eat this while it is fresh and hot. I'll get yours ready soon."

"He should be okay," said Billy Jay. "He had the smoothie and yogurt."

They all ate in silence for a while.

Lae C said to Javier, "Do you have more of those beers? Give me one. How about you, Billy Jay?"

"I'll take a water."

"Here you go," said Javier handing a beer and opener to Lae C and then a bottle of water to Billy Jay.

Billy Jay ate and drank and looked at the scene of the slow-moving freeway traffic and the unfamiliar suburban landscape beyond. He felt fine. Still no panic about being away from home with strangers. It was strange. He was worried about his mom, sure, but sitting in an Abitat he actually felt comfortable. He could do anything or go anywhere. It seemed like he could even talk with these two without bringing on a social anxiety attack. "Hey, Javier. What's your story? You work with Lacy?" Billy Jay asked.

"Yeah. At the store."

"Boss man, Javier. He's an assistant store manager now. He looks too young but he's older than he looks. He looks like fifteen?" Lae C said.

"I'm twenty-six. It's just a temporary job. I want to start law school before long."

"Still want to do Law School, huh? Get ready for the BIG student loans," said Lae C. "Mine are huge. BA, MS, and Culinary School. How about you, Billy Jay. Are you in student debt? What do you do when you're not playing with Abitats and looking for your mom? What's your story?"

"Taking care of my dad, I guess. I took some college classes online, but not recently."

"So, you live in this fancy neighborhood in this big house with your mom and your sick dad and can afford to just play games all day? Cool. But what do you want to be when you grow up?" asked Lae C. "Never mind. I guess we're all doing better in the game than in real life."

"Do you live near the store, Javier?" Billy Jay asked.

"I've got a drive, but I'm actually moving soon. I'm going to rent one of those 'Tiny houses' like they show on TV sometimes. There's a place that has some a couple miles from the store. I'd love to be able to have an Abitat. That would be ideal, but a tiny house is good."

...

Honus noticed Jose tilting and shaking his head but didn't say anything.

HW203904, 11:45 AM, Arriving at Destination

"Arriving at destination," came the voice from the ceiling.

"What do you know? We're there," Javier stated. The displays showed the Abitat pulling into a parking lot at a community center. "I didn't notice when we got off the freeway."

"Sorry, Perry. I meant to give you the eggplant before we got here. I'll put it in the fridge for now. Don't worry it will be even better when I reheat it," Lae C said as she took a food container and handed it to Javier to put away. She collected the other used plates and containers back into the delivery box to throw away. "Cleaning up." She found the trash drawer where she expected it to be based on the game and put the box of trash into it.

"Let's hope there are dumping stations for trash like in the game," said Javier.

"There have to be," replied Lae C.

"Let's see what we can find out at the coffee shop," said Billy Jay. "But I should really let my dad use the bathroom first. Help me move the seats to give him a path to get there. Then could you two wait outside for a couple minutes?"

"Okay. Sure." Javier unbuckled himself and stood up, now that the Abitat was parked in the back of the parking lot. He moved his seat over a bit to give more of a pathway.

"Hey, Dad, do you need to use the bathroom? You can be the first in the family to use the new Abitat bathroom." Billy Jay stood next to his dad and unbuckled him. "Open door" he said to the walls and the door opened showing a car in the next stall at the edge of the parking lot. "Look around and see if you see my mom's car. She's not likely to still be here, but you never know."

Lae C and Javier stepped down and out. Billy Jay helped his dad stand up and he walked him to the tiny bathroom. He realized there wasn't room for him and his dad in the bathroom at the same time. "Close door," he said to give his dad some privacy, and the exterior door started sliding shut. "It'll just take a couple minutes," Billy Jay said as the Abitat door closed.

"Well, Lae C, Should we look around the parking lot for an EL model. Do you remember what color he said it was?"

"I don't think he mentioned the color." She looked around.

"Okay. That makes it easier."

"Let's just look." Lae C started walking down the row of cars followed by Javier looking at the same cars that she looked at. "How about we take different rows. It might go faster."

"Good idea. I'll do that row," Javier crossed through a row of cars and started check the cars in the next aisle.

They were still checking cars when Billy Jay appeared outside the Abitat. He looked around and smiled and posed like he was at some great scenic location, like it was something special just to be in a parking lot, then he focused and looked to see where they were and to see where the coffee shop might be. He waved at them and pointed towards the community center building and started walking in that direction. Javier and Lae C waved back and headed towards the same place. When they got close Billy Jay asked, "Did you find her car?"

"You didn't say what color it is. I found a light blue EL model over there." Lae C pointed.

"Hers is more like light green, grayish. But it might look different in different light. I should take a look." They followed Lae C back across the parking lot to a light blue-non-metallic colored car. "No. I'm pretty sure hers was greener and more metallic than this one."

"We didn't check that other part of the parking lot over there," Javier pointed to the lot on the other side of the community center.

"Since we're right here, let's ask inside if anyone knows anything before we check the other parking lot." They all started walking towards the library entrance where there was a coffee shop sign.

"Do you have a picture of her you can show them?" Lae C asked as they entered the building.

"Oh. I left my tablet in the Abitat. I don't have her picture with me."

"Here's images from a search for Mara Lee online. Are any of these her?" Javier asked, showing his phone.

Billy Jay looked and said, "No. Maybe I should go back and get my tablet."

"We're already here. I can bring up the picture from the Min Strong website. They look similar," said Javier.

"That's a cartoon. You think all Black South Asians look alike? Maybe we should use a picture of Kamala Harris," Lae C commented.

Javier said, "No. Kamala is in her seventies now. Way older than your mom. I wish she wasn't running again. Way too old."

...

Jose looked up from his game goggles and said to Honus, "Isn't she running again this year? She looks good for 91. I think she just might take it this time. Although politics at that level doesn't really matter anymore." He wasn't sure if Honus heard him through the headphones. He put the game goggles back on and continued watching the History World.

...

Javier held up his phone, "Here's Min Strong. But you're probably right. I don't think a cartoon will do. How can I find your mom's photo online?"

"On my tablet—in the Abitat. I don't know how to get to our family social media pages from your phone. I could probably find the links on my tablet."

A gallery of Min Strong photos appeared on Javier's phone. He scrolled through them to find the one from the website that they had looked at earlier. Lae C watched the scrolling gallery of pictures and said, "That's not just a web search. You already had a bunch of photos of this Min lady on your phone?"

"Uh. Yeah. I guess. I told you I was into her...her philosophy."

"Javier, That's creepy. She's probably twice your age now. Where did you get all these photos? These are not all from her speaking business."

Javier said, "The cartoons are from her talks. She hasn't aged in those. People have created photos of different ideas about how she probably looks in real life. Billy, do any of these others look like your mom?"

Billy Jay said, "I don't know if any of these are any better than the first cartoon. Javier, some of these pictures are disturbing. I think we are going to have to have a talk later about you stalking that Min lady, but right now let's go in and see if anyone remembers my mom being here yesterday. Let's just use that cartoon picture or a young Kamala. Maybe they do think all Black South Asians look alike."

They found their way through the library entrance to the coffee shop. They looked around. "I wish I brought my tablet so I could bring up the picture of the food she bought yesterday. Maybe we could figure out which table she was at. It looked like one of these. I can go get my tablet, and also a real picture of her." Billy Jay motioned towards the exit. He was getting more nervous being around more new people.

"Let's first see if anybody remembers anyone who looked similar to her," said Lae C. Javier, give me your phone with that picture." They waited in the line until their turn. Then she stepped up and showed the phone. "Hi. Do you remember someone looking like this woman? She bought a banana and sandwich here yesterday afternoon."

"I'm sorry. I'm good with faces for our regulars, but I don't recognize her as a customer. Besides that's not a real photo. That's Min Strong. I suppose someone looking like her could have been here. Why are you asking? Are you one of those Miniacs hunting for her again?"

"No. Not Min Strong. She just looks a little like that. She's this guy's mom and she's missing, and we don't have a real picture. This is the last place we know where she was. She took a picture of her food, and it was geotagged here."

"I don't really remember her, but Rachel here notices things I don't. Hey, Rachel."

A very small woman was working on a drink and turned to say, "Busy." She finished adding ingredients to the drink and capping it and placing it on the serving area. "Whipped Double Espresso Mocha with Almond milk ready for John." She turned back to the counter and said, "You asking about a lady taking pictures of her food yesterday? Lots of customers take pictures of their food for reviews. It's something people do."

"She looks kind of like this. Did you see her? Lae C showed the picture on Javier's phone.

"Could be. Could be. Looks kind of familiar. But the lady yesterday seemed older, and tired, agitated, and unhappy, not peaceful like Min in that picture. Not the kind of attitude you want with someone doing a review. I don't think she actually bought that food herself. Why are you asking about her? Is she wanted for stealing bananas?"

"She's missing."

"Hold on. We weren't that worried about a bad review, and I was kidding about the banana. We didn't do anything to her."

"No. We're not implying you did anything. We're just trying to find out what anybody saw," said Billy Jay apologetically.

"That's okay," said Rachel, looking at her coworkers with an expression of 'do you believe this guy'.

"Do you know who she talked to or where she went afterwards?" Billy Jay asked.

"If it was her, she came in and sat for a while. I think she talked to a couple of our regulars. There was the guy with the accents. I think he used a French accent yesterday. Probably harmless, but a little creepy. I don't think they talked long. She told him to get lost. The other one was the big Aussie girl. She comes in here and works on her computer every afternoon. They talked for quite a while like they knew each other and were catching up, but it seemed like they argued at the end. Then your mom left. I haven't seen accent man or big girl today, but they come in pretty often."

"Do you mind if we sit here to see if they come in today?" Billy Jay asked.

"Tell you what. You buy something and I'll let you sit here all day if you want," said Rachel.

"Thanks!" said Billy Jay. "Thank you so much."

They ordered drinks, but the shop didn't accept AM Points and Billy Jay didn't have any way to pay. Javier said, "You paid for my lunch, so I guess I can cover your decaf soy whatever. But get yourself some cash or bring a phone to pay before you go out of the house next time, man."

They settled into seats at a table and soon Lae C and Javier were deep into their games on their phones. Billy Jay kept an eye on the people coming into the coffee shop and watched Javier and Lae C playing their games. He was uncomfortable.

After a couple minutes Billy Jay said, "Can you watch my drink here, while I run out and get my tablet and check on my dad?" He got up and left. On the way out he noticed the restroom and stopped in but decided it was too public to use. Once back inside the Abitat he checked on his dad who was doing his normal twitching and mumbling and seemed okay.

After using the Abitat bathroom Billy Jay picked up his tablet. Before heading out he re-entered the moon world and took manual control of Bartholomew Orlov.

QZ9301, 11:45 PM, Orlov Speaks

Orlov's eyes opened and he sat up and told the surprised Lacy and the nurse nearby, "I'm going to be fine. Does this room have video monitoring?" The nurse nodded yes. "Save a recording of this. I Bartholomew J Orlov am authorizing an immediate reward payment of 2 million AMPs to Lacy Hogan here for rescuing me. I want her treated well. Do you have that on record? Thanks." He looked at Lacy. "Keep looking out for me and there will be more. But right now, I need some more rest."

Orlov lay back and closed his eyes again.

…

Billy Jay disconnected and headed out of the Abitat to go back to the coffee shop.

…

The nurse checked Orlov's eyes, and they were dilated and unresponsive again. He gave a quizzical look to Lacy who also looked surprised, and he said "I've never seen something like that before. Oh. And congratulations on the reward, Miss Hogan."

…

Chapter 7

Early Evening

7:15 PM, Honus and Jose

Honus paused the story game and nudged Jose and asked if he wanted to continue. Jose indicated yes. Honus put on his goggles and continued, still at high speed.

> ### HW203904, 12:25 PM, Billy Jay Arrives at Coffee Shop
>
> Billy Jay paused as he stepped out, and the door closed behind him. Maybe a chance for additional rewards would encourage Lacy to stay around to help Orlov and Lae C to stay around to keep helping with the search for his mom. Two million was probably too much. Oh well. It wasn't real money.
>
> As he stood outside the Abitat he felt a rush of adrenaline. His anxiety from being away from home ought to be kicking in by now. The anticipation of an anxiety attack was usually enough to trigger one. But this rush felt different. It felt more like the rush that he sometimes got when he engaged in extreme sports through one of his adventure-seeking characters or made a bold move like giving away 2 million AMPs. Kind of like the feeling when he dove off the face of Half Dome with the wing suit earlier today. Stepping out of an Abitat was so much like the game that he felt like one of his brave characters. "I hope this feeling lasts," he thought.

Before going back in he walked over to the other part of the parking lot that Lae C and Javier didn't search, going around to the other side of the community center. He walked up and down the aisles and didn't find another car like his mom's. Continuing to feel the rush of adventure from being out in the world he went into the community center through the entrance on that side, took a wrong turn and went into the library instead of the coffee shop. Welcoming the rush of exploration, he walked boldly all the way to the back of the library, past several racks with hundreds of actual books and back past several tables where people were using public computers and tablets. Some were reading but more than half of them were playing the AM game. After a circuit through the library, he exited and found his way back to the coffee shop.

When he got back, he noticed that someone was sitting in his seat talking with Lae C and Javier. As he walked up Javier said, "Hey. Billy. Where have you been? This is Jerry. She talked to your mom yesterday. She came in right after you left."

Billy Jay said, "Jerry, do you know where my mom is?"

"No, I don't. We were just talking about that. Nice to meet you, Billy," said Jerry.

"Billy Jay," said Billy Jay.

"Right," said Jerry.

Lae C said, "Let me catch you up on what we've been talking about while you were gone."

Billy Jay pulled up another chair and sat down, then reached over and picked up his drink, "Is this one mine?" Javier nodded and Billy Jay took a sip.

Lae C explained, "Jerry here worked with your dad a few years ago on the game, but lost contact with him. She met your mom here yesterday. She wanted to get in touch with your dad. They talked for a little while, but your mom left after telling her about your dad being a veggie."

"She didn't say 'veggie'. And I was sorry to hear that your dad has been sick, and I'm really concerned now that your mom is missing. She walked out of here and I haven't seen her since. I thought she was headed home. I think she was upset. She thought I was accusing your dad of making a deal on the Abitats that cut the other game designers out. I tried to message her later to explain but she hasn't responded. I hope she's okay."

"Why all the mystery of meeting her here? Why didn't you just give her a call?" Billy Jay asked.

"You'd think it would be that easy. Your dad, your whole family, is hidden. I still don't know your numbers, or where you live other than it must be within about an hour's drive from here. It took a lot of work and luck to get an email message to her. Perry had shut all his email accounts and phone numbers down. A lot of the people who worked on the game were into encryption and privacy, but Perry—your dad—was extreme. He valued his privacy. I think he may have pushed more than anyone else for the security of nested cellular autonomy in the game."

"Nestlé sells Otto what?" asked Billy Jay.

"Oh. Oh. I can explain that. I did a paper on NCA in college," said Javier eagerly. "It's loosely based on emergent behavioral properties like in a bee hive or ant hill. Emergent intelligence. Independent autonomous Abitats in the game use it to coordinate their movements in traffic and hand-offs for deliveries. The game itself runs distributed on all the player's private devices, but it seems like one seamless, coordinated world because of NCA. Players can be completely anonymous and independent, and the game worlds emerge and convolve without any game headquarters, no central server brain, no big brother.

"Never mind that technobabble right now," Lae C broke in. "You mean Billy Jay, Mara, and Perry were completely off the grid as far as you could tell? Billy Jay here seemed to be pretty obvious and prominent in the game and on the discussion forums and Mara worked for a famous public speaker."

"Mara? Mara's name was not listed on that business and the business itself has been offline for some time. I was lucky to reach her through that. Maybe I missed something obvious with Billy Jay, when I was searching for Perry, but I think that's the point. Your characters can be very exposed inside the game, and you can still be completely anonymous and private as a player."

"What about the discussion forums? He goes by BillyJay4, for god's sake," Lae C said.

"BillyJay4? Good to know. Okay. Even on the discussion forums you're going through the game's secure nested cellular autonomy layers so there's no tracking back to you as the player or your location, unless you volunteer personal information, like Billy Jay's name there. But I wasn't looking for Mara or Billy Jay. Even though I worked with Perry and met him in person a few times he never revealed his private life and nothing I could find about him online mentioned it. I didn't know where he lived or even that he had a family."

"Then why did you want to talk to my mom?" Billy Jay asked.

"I was trying to reach your dad. It was a long shot, but I thought he might have a connection to the old Min Strong websites. They've been offline, but I found an email address in an old backup of a web archive for one of the early Min Strong online classes. Your mom responded to an email I sent asking about Perry," Jerry explained.

"You didn't know Perry had a family?" Lae C asked.

"He never mentioned one. And I couldn't find much about him in the public records. I don't know how he did that. Or why for that matter. But it seemed like he went to a lot of effort to hide even before he stopped communicating with the other game designers."

Billy Jay spoke up. "I thought I was the insecure one with my agoraphobia. I had no idea my dad was paranoid too. I wonder why?"

Lae C said, "Whatever he was hiding from, maybe that has something to do with your mom going missing."

"That's got to be it," said Javier. "And it must have something to do with Min Strong's disappearance too."

"Yeah? Maybe?" said Jerry.

"Sorry. Javier is big into conspiracy theories," Lae C offered.

"So, it's not safe for me being out here. I think I need to get back home," Billy Jay said speaking quickly as he stood up. His adrenaline was now starting to feel more like anxiety than adventure. Sweat was forming on his forehead.

"Wait. I need you to meet some people. Follow me to a house near here. It won't take long."

"No. Not now," said Billy Jay.

"Then give me your address and phone number so I can get in touch with you," Jerry pleaded.

"No. Not now. We can talk inside the game discussion forum, since you know my tag now. Let's go." Billy Jay looked around and started towards the exit, his anxiety building.

Lae C and Javier stood and said, "Nice meeting you, Jerry. We'll be in touch. What's your tag in the discussion forum?"

"OZAI20359," Jerry said.

Jerry sat there a few seconds as they walked away. She had her elbows on the table and put her head in her hands. She shook her head. "This isn't going well," she thought. "Perry had a secret wife and kid. That's something. Maybe that's why he was so paranoid and secretive."

She stood up slowly and walked out of the coffee shop through the lobby and out towards the parking lot. She saw an Abitat leaving the parking lot and going out onto the street. "Oh shit. He did do some kind of deal with the car company." She hurried across the parking lot to her van, pausing to catch her breath before getting in. But by the time she pulled it out onto the street the Abitat was already out of sight. She drove fast towards the freeway to see if she could catch up with it and follow it, but she didn't find it.

...

Honus tried fast-forwarding to see where Jerry went after that, but her view went blank. The only available view at that time was inside Billy Jay's Abitat. He rejoined that view in progress.

HW203904, 1:30 PM, Heading Home in Abitat

Lae C was standing reheating Perry's eggplant in the Abitat microwave instead of using the stovetop after mixing in some ingredients she saved from the other meal orders. Billy Jay was sitting on the bed using his tablet and checking on his characters in the game in large windows on the wall display. Perry was mumbling and twitching with his tablet in his hands. Javier was belted in and drinking a beer while trying to pair his phone with the wall display.

Taking the heated food container out of the microwave and stirring it with a spoon and sniffing a sample, Lae C said, "Perry, you'll like this." She offered a taste to Perry holding the spoonful under his nose. "Open up." He opened his mouth, and she gently inserted the spoon. "Mmmm. I think he likes it."

Billy Jay nodded approvingly but focused on his character in the game who was driving his Abitat through an Amazon village. Javier was searching for more information about Mara on the web and looking for instructions on how to pair his phone with the wall display. When Javier finally got his phone paired with the wall display, he used it to control the displays and re-expanded the exterior camera views; they showed afternoon traffic on the freeway.

Lae C had already fed half of the eggplant dish to Perry and was experimenting to see if she could get him to feed himself. She put the spoon in his hand and held his fingers closed around it. She looked into his eyes and said, "Hold the spoon, Perry." She loosened her hold on his hand, and, looking her in the eyes, he didn't drop the spoon. She moved his hand to dip the spoon in the food container.

"Get some eggplant on the spoon." She guided his hand holding the spoon back towards his mouth. "Put it in your mouth." He opened his mouth, and she guided the spoon in. He closed his mouth on it, and she guided his hand to pull the spoon out. "Good. Do you like it?" After he swallowed, she said, "Keep holding the spoon," and she eased her hand away from his hand. "Get some eggplant with the spoon," and he dipped the spoon in the container. "Put it in your mouth," and he did. "Good!"

"How do you do that?" Billy Jay asked quietly. "That's amazing. I always have to hold his spoon for him. How did you do that?" Billy Jay set down his own tablet and leaned in closer to his dad.

"Did you ever try?" asked Lae C.

"He always held on to his tablet. He didn't have a free hand to hold a spoon."

"He seems to be okay setting the tablet down now," Lae C said. "Did you even try?"

"Yes. We tried. My mom and I both tried. Many times. But he wouldn't do anything for us if he didn't have the tablet in his hands. I don't know why, but you've got a touch with him to get him to set down his tablet."

"Well, he set it down now. How about you try now," Lae C said, pointing to Perry who was sitting holding the spoon.

"Okay. Let me try. Dad. Dad. Eat some more of that food," Billy Jay said.

Perry reached out with the spoon, scooped up a spoonful of the eggplant mush and put it in his mouth. He chewed and swallowed and then reached out again for more. He repeated several times. Now the container was nearly empty.

"Okay. That's interesting. He's following instructions from both of you. Let me try," said Javier. "Hey, Perry. Please put down your spoon." Perry had a spoonful heading towards his mouth, but he set the spoon back in the food container. "Thank you, Perry," said Javier. "You say he wouldn't follow instructions like this before?"

"He would sit up and stand and walk to the bathroom when I helped him, but he always had the tablet in his hands. I think Lacy has changed him somehow. He's a little different since Lacy has been here," Billy Jay said.

"Javier has been here too," said Lae C. "Maybe he just needed someone new to talk to him."

"We tried therapists and nurses and aides sometimes at first. But not recently," said Billy Jay. "They didn't do any better."

"What else is different today?" asked Javier. "Your mom is missing. Has she ever been missing before?"

"She's never been away for more than a few hours."

"Maybe not seeing her is making him behave differently," Lae C conjectured. "Maybe that was why he responded to me. He misses her."

"Maybe that's it. She did take care of him most of the time," Billy Jay admitted. "I filled in when she went shopping mostly. She didn't go out much. But a lot of things are different today. My mom's missing. You two are here. We never rode in an Abitat before either."

"Who knows. Maybe all the changes today are just messing with his head," Javier surmised. "Or, Oh! Oh! Maybe it's like, when the cat's away the mouse will play. Maybe he's trying to make a move on you, Lae C, when his lady is away. This is the first time she has been away for more than a couple hours, and a hot young lady shows up while she's gone and takes an interest in him, so he starts acting different."

"Javier. Your mind always goes that way, doesn't it?" Lae C commented.

Javier shrugged, "She is hot, don't you think BJ?"

...

Honus peeked over the top of his goggles to check on Jose, who was smiling and seemed to still be interested in the history world. He let it continue...

...

"Sure. Sure. This stuff is all very interesting, but it doesn't help me find my mom," Billy Jay said. "If my dad was really trying to keep us hidden before he got sick, do you think somebody who my dad was hiding from did something to my mom? What do I do next?"

"I'm no private eye," said Javier. "I don't know how to track a missing person."

"You could call the police and see what they can do," said Lae C. "Maybe she's been missing long enough now."

"How do you even find a private eye?" asked Billy Jay. "And how much do they cost?"

"I'm not sure in real life, but I know one in the game. I could ask," Javier suggested.

"You know a private eye?" Billy Jay asked.

"In the game," Javier answered.

"Is there some way we can get his advice?"

"I can try." Javier picked up his phone and expanded a view into one of his game worlds on the wall display. His character was apparently sitting at a desk working with papers and a computer in an office. "Whoa. This Abitat display is amazing. I thought I had a good display on my phone and even better at home, but this blows them both away. It's like we're really in the office with this guy. By the way, I'm a lawyer in this world," said Javier.

Lae C and Billy Jay turned their attention to the wall display. Despite the quality of the display which fascinated Javier, his character's office work was not particularly interesting. Elsewhere on the wall display the views from the exterior cameras showed slow traffic on a freeway. The progress map showed their path since they left the community center parking lot. A small status display showed good charge levels. They were now a little more than halfway back towards Billy Jay's house. Small windows showed miniature views into Billy Jay's game worlds.

"What kind of cases does your lawyer character work on with this private eye?" Lae C asked. "I don't remember you mentioning him when you over-shared about your game AM-ventures."

"My lawyer character doesn't get involved in those kinds of cases that need a private eye. Mostly contracts and some wills and trusts. I let him take care of his work and I don't pay a lot of attention to it. But he earns good points. The private eye he knows socially. I've mentioned her. Gretchen."

"Oh. No. Not Gretchen. I thought you said she was an exotic dancer. Gretchen is a private eye?"

"Among other things."

"I don't know about this. Oh well. Get your lawyer off his ass and let's see if Gretchen can help us decide what to do." Lae C ordered.

"Wait. Why would he be asking her about searching for a missing person? It's one thing to make him decide to go somewhere or do something that he might do anyway, but what's the story that motivates him to ask her about searching for a missing person?"

"Don't worry about it. What could go wrong? He'll just think he had a sudden curiosity about it. Billy Jay and I made our characters in the game talk about his missing mom and nothing bad happened. Right, Billy Jay?" Lae C winked at Billy Jay.

"Uh. Pretty much. I think my character was a little confused, but uh uh nothing uh bad happened." He picked up his tablet and made the small window showing Orlov comatose in the hospital bed shrink even more.

"Okay. Okay," said Javier. He put on his earpiece, took control of his character and had him make a call.

QX2230, 2051, 10:09 AM, Miguel and the Private Eye

"Open private Comm. Voice only. Call Gretchen."
"Hi. Gretchen. This is Miguel." …
"Yeah. Tonight would be great." …

"8:30. Sure. I'll be there. I can't wait. But right now, I also have a question for you." …

"When you do your P.I. work, do you sometimes find missing persons?" …

"Yeah. Yeah." …

"No. I'm really just curious about how you go about it. Hypothetical." …

"Yeah, hypothetical. Suppose I had a client with a family member who had gone missing and wanted to track them down without making a lot of fuss, what would you do?"

…

"Can you let us hear what she's saying?" asked Lae C.

…

"No. I'm not talking to someone else. Just you. Maybe you heard someone else walking by the office here. My office door is open." …

"No. I don't have another woman here." …

"Yes. I do work with women, but not right this minute." …

"So about finding a missing person?" …

"Okay. I can do that." …

"Sure. I can do that. Sounds good. Okay I'll call you back."

Miguel disconnected his phone, scratched his head, and said to himself, "Now what was it I was thinking about before, that made it so important to know how a missing person search is done? Who asked me about that? That's weird to lose track of an important thought like that." He paused. "Oh, well. I guess just want to take more of an interest in other parts of Gretchen's life."

…

Javier said, "She won't explain her missing persons methods for free, but I can hire her, and she can explain for a fee. I figure Miguel can pay her and somehow you can make it up to him and me. She's busy now but can talk in a few minutes when she has a break from her other job."

"Why didn't you just use a video call instead of a private voice call?" asked Billy Jay. "Then we could have seen and heard what you both were saying."

"He can't do that with her when he's at work. Her video calls are kind of inappropriate for the office," Lae C explained. "Isn't that what you told me before, Javier?"

"Plus, they cost like 20 AMPs per minute," Javier added.

"Okay. You've got this jealous girlfriend who does some kind of online sex service and is also a private eye?" Billy Jay summarized.

"Miguel does, not me," Javier corrected.

"Right." Billy Jay paused, then "So how are we going to meet her and ask her about how to find my mom? You—I mean Miguel—is going to call her back in a few minutes? Is there some way we can all be on the call with her?"

"What world are you in?" Lae C asked. "Billy Jay and I can grab unattached characters in the same world and meet up."

"I don't know if that's a good idea," said Javier. "This is getting complicated for Miguel. And I don't want to mess up my Miguel character."

"Don't worry. It's a good idea. Let's see what world you're in," Lae C insisted. "Oh. I see it's in the title on the window. World QX2230. A few years from now somewhere in a made-up city called Antonia Springs that looks a lot like Orange County. Let me find a background character that I can link. Billy Jay, you should do the same."

"Okay. Let me look." Billy Jay started a character search while Lae C did likewise. "QX2230? Uh. Oh. I've been avoiding that world. I abandoned a character there a couple years ago when his business was failing, and he was about to go to jail or worse. I tried playing the game like other games back then. You know. Be a sadistic asshole to take whatever you want. And it worked at first, I made a lot of money, but things went really bad for my character, so I got out."

Javier chimed in, "Yeah, Actualization Modeling was one of the alternate names for the AM game. It had a lot of alternate names. I wrote a paper about it. Consequences are key in the game. You can't get away with shit."

Billy Jay interrupted, "Hey. Look. He's nearby and he's not in jail." The view zoomed in to a man in multiple layers of dirty clothing sitting on the ground under a bridge. He looked like a much older, thinner, and weather worn version of Billy Jay. He was wearing a baseball cap that seemed to be lined with aluminum foil. "It looks like he's camping by a river. I think he's a bum. A homeless guy."

"Don't call people like that 'bums.' But he could be good. I'll try to find an unattached background character who's unhoused too," Lae C said. "We can speak through them, and it will seem like they're nuts. Show me where your character is Billy Jay."

Billy Jay zoomed out the view on the display wall to show a map of Antonia Springs and then zoomed back in on his character. "See, he's here sitting on some cardboard in the riverbed under the roadway bridge. His name is Barney Johanson."

"Another BJ. I see a possible pattern emerging," said Lae C.

"Actually, Barney Jacob Johanson," Billy Jay added.

"Okay. I see where he is. And … I found another unattached background character pushing a shopping cart… just a couple blocks away. Javier, how much time before your girlfriend is ready to talk? How much time do I have to check history and customize this character?" Lae C asked. "Customizing can't completely ignore her history if she has any. There's only so far I can go with alternative facts. But I like to know my characters."

"Not a lot of time. So how do you propose we all meet up? Do your characters even have phones? I think you should skip customizing other than making sure they have phones." Javier asked. "Do we need to meet up in person? And how do we make this happen?"

Billy Jay zoomed out the map view, and it showed the locations for the three characters. "Actually, they're all pretty close to each other. The law office is only a mile or so from my guy at the river bed and Lacy's lady is just down the street from here. Maybe you could pick them up with your Abitat," Billy Jay suggested. "And it looks like

Barney does not have a phone. But… just a sec…Okay, now he does. One new fact established." Billy Jay closed Barney's possessions window after updating it. "I forget. Do they give free Abitats to the homeless in this world? Maybe he has an Abitat somewhere. Probably not since he's hanging out under a bridge."

Lae C said, "Okay. Skipping the customizing and ignoring the history. I'm linking. I'm linking. Okay. Mine is called Mona. Looks like she doesn't have a last name, but she does have a phone in her shopping cart. No need to add one," Lae C revealed. "Okay this can work. What's the number for your Miguel guy?"

Javier had Miguel pick up his personal communications tablet and browse the menus to show the number. He zoomed in the view for Lae C to see on the wall display.

Billy Jay was hesitating to link with his old avatar Barney, but he watched Lae C and Javier to see what was going to happen next.

Lae C had her character Mona dig her communications tablet out of a small box under some recyclables in the shopping cart and she called the Miguel's number. He didn't recognize the incoming number which did not have any caller ID and he would normally let it go to voicemail, but Javier had him answer.

QX2230, 10:25 AM, Miguel and Mona

"Hello. Javi…, I mean Miguel speaking."

"I need help finding a missing person," said Mona.

Miguel replied, "That's not really my job, but by coincidence I know a private investigator who does that kind of thing. Maybe I can put you in contact. What's your name?"

"Mona. Could you come and pick up me and my friend Barney so we can talk to the PI? We could meet you down by the river on Grand street right now."

…

Lae C gestured to Javier to move it along.

Javier spoke through Miguel:

…

"Uh. Okay. I can be right there," Miguel answered.

"Perfect. We'll see you soon," said Mona.

Miguel tapped on his display to summon his Abitat to pick him up and stood up to leave his office. "Jack, I'll be out for a few minutes," he said to a young man at a desk outside his office as he walked to the elevator.

Mona disconnected the call and continued pushing her cart down the street towards the river bridge.

…

Lae C disconnected Mona and said to Billy Jay. "Hey! Get your Barney moving. We need to be on the road when Miguel gets here."

"Okay. Okay. I'll try," Billy Jay replied as he attempted to reestablish the link to Barney that he hadn't used for a couple of years.

QX2230, 10:29 AM, Barney Fights for Control

The Barney character looked up and around; he grabbed his cap and pulled it on tighter and stood up.

"Oh no you don't! It's not happening again! You're not taking over my brain again! I feel you trying! I'm no science experiment! I'm no lab animal! You messed with me before and ruined my life! Made me do things. Bad things. Who are you? NSA? The Russians? One of my competitors? Or Pat, my so-called assistant, who took over my company? Probably all working together. I don't care who you are; you can't get in my brain now! I'm shielded!" He pulled at the foil protruding from his cap. "Not here. Not with this cap! It's protecting me from whoever you are, so don't even try!"

…

"Okay. That's kind of weird," said Javier.

Lae C said, "Yeah. He's a real loony toon. But if Billy Jay wants to talk with the private investigator, he needs to get his Barney up to the street."

"I'm not sure I can link with him. It's been a long time. And he's resisting," said Billy Jay. "Maybe I should just watch through your characters,"

"It's about your mom," Lae C said. Her tone of voice and look made Billy Jay reconsider.

"I'll try again. I'll try again."

As Billy Jay connected to Barney he said calmly "Go to a safe place. Make your mind go to a safe place…I'm going to be okay. I'm in charge of my own feelings."

<hr>

QX2230, 10:30 AM, Barney under Control

Barney was mumbling and then speaking, "…safe place…safe place… be okay… in charge… my…feelings." He looked around and started walking to the spot with the opening in the fence to get back up to the road. His face had a fluctuating mix of panic and calm resignation. He climbed through the hole in the fence and walked up onto the side of the road. Just then an older woman pushing a shopping cart was approaching him.

She shouted to him. "Hi. Barney, is it? I'm Mona. We're going to help someone look for a missing person."

"You act like you don't know me, Mona. Did you bring me more metal?" Barney said, looking in the shopping cart, and then looking around, the panicked expression started to win out. "I shouldn't be out in the open in the daytime. People are looking for me." He noticed some items in the shopping cart. "Did you get more metal for my shield?" He picked up some foil and put it in the pocket of his jacket and acted surprised and panicked as he pulled out a small communications tablet. "No. No. No. How'd that get there? Don't let them track me." Then the look of panic on his face started to fade as he said quietly, "I should go to a safe place. A safe place." Then increasing panic again, "There is no safe place…uh…uh…uh…" Then with calmness he put the small tablet back in his pocket and he said, "Oh, Hi, Mona. Nice to meet you. You can call me Barney J."

"Yeah. Okay, Barn. Let's get this cart off the road before Javier gets here. I mean Miguel. Whatever." She pushed the cart up onto the curb and into some bushes. Then she brushed off her clothes.

...

Lae C could see Mona's appearance on her phone and on the wall display of Billy Jay's view into Barney's world, so she had Mona pose like looking in a mirror, even though Mona was not able to see herself.

...

Posing like she was in front of a mirror, Mona said, "Not much I can do with this." She went to her cart and poked around many pieces of foil and metal and found a bag with a sweatshirt that looked relatively clean. She pulled that on over the dirty shirt and then ran her fingers through her hair to make it a little more presentable.

...

Javier said, "I'm almost there. Is that you two up ahead?" Javier pointed at the wall display showing his view of Miguel's world, which showed the inside of Miguel's Abitat with another large wall display showing exterior views including a view of two people on the side of the road ahead. "Hey. It's so cool to see the inside of a game Abitat from the inside of a real Abitat. Maybe later I can have Miguel play the game and display the insides of another Abitat. I wonder how many levels you can nest with that?"

QX2230, 10:36 AM, Picking up Mona and Barney

Miguel said to his Abitat, "Stop to pick them up," pointing to the two on the display. Miguel's Abitat pulled to the side of the road and the door slid open.

"Hi, I'm Mona and this is Barney." They climbed in. "Hello. I'm Miguel." The door closed and the Abitat began moving, very smoothly. For the three of them it was like being in a small office, with no sign of motion. Miguel's Abitat was currently arranged with a couch, a chair, and small desk. The wall displays gave it the appearance of a larger office space with law books and large windows looking out on a high-rise view. "Take a seat." Miguel indicated at the couch.

Mona sat down. Barney remained standing. "Are we going to meet your missing persons investigator?" Mona asked.

"We'll call her," Miguel responded. "But first, for your protection you should each give me a small payment to engage me as your attorney. That way anything you say is confidential. Attorney-client privilege."

"Payment? What kind of payment?" asked Barney.

"Anything. One point is enough," Miguel suggested.

Mona and Barney both got out their communication tablets to transfer a payment to Miguel. Mona transferred a point. But Barney resisted. "I don't know. You say confidential, but how do I know? This is a contract. There will be records. People will find out where I am. I don't know. It doesn't seem safe."

"You can still be anonymous. We don't need to record anything. Just transfer me a point anonymously and I can guarantee you confidentiality. We don't have to record anything about a contract."

"How about I loan you a point, Barn? Can I pay two points for the both of us?" Mona asked.

"Sure. Why not," Miguel answered.

"Done." Mona said, "Now how do we talk with your investigator?"

Miguel looked at the clock on the virtual office wall. "It's time," he said. Miguel said, "Call Gretchen." A portion of the virtual office became a fog. Out of the fog materialized a view of a woman wearing a trench coat, and maybe nothing else, and posing on a wooden chair, leaning forward revealing a view of cleavage. As the fog cleared, she appeared to be in the office. As soon as she saw that Miguel was not alone, she sat up and adjusted her coat to cover herself better.

...

"You've got to be kidding me," said Lae C aside to Javier and Billy Jay, but not audible in the game. "You think she's a private eye because she wears a trench coat?"

Javier shrugged.

QX2230, 10:41 AM, Miguel and Gretchen

Miguel said, "Hello. Gretchen. I've got two clients here who are interested in getting your help with a missing persons search. Mona and Barney. Mona, Gretchen. Barney, Gretchen. Gretchen, Mona, and Barney."

"I see that. Nice to meet you both. Miguel, You said this was hypothetical, but now you have real clients? What's up with that?" Gretchen asked.

"Funny coincidence. They called me right after we talked."

"Seems odd…Though it doesn't matter to me so long as someone is paying," Gretchen explained.

"One thousand AMPs for the initial consultation and up to two hours investigating. Two hundred fifty AMPS per hour after that. Is that right?" Miguel asked.

"Plus expenses."

"Expenses, if needed. But we're just starting with the initial consultation."

"Okay. Transfer me the initial thousand and we can get started."

Miguel looked at Mona and Barney and then surprised himself when he said, "I'll take care of it. … Transfer 1000 AMPs to Gretchen Klein Investigations." An image of a card shaped like an Abitat, with "1000 AMPs" printed on it came out of a small lock box on the bookshelf in the virtual office display and floated to just above the image of Gretchen. She reached up and gestured to grab it, and it disappeared from view.

"Okay. What are the facts? Who's missing and why do you need to track them down without the police knowing about it?"

"We didn't say anything about the police. Who says the police haven't already tried?" Barney replied uncomfortably.

"In my experience, most people who come to me to track someone down are trying to avoid attention. Usually, they're trying to find someone who is not so much missing as hiding," Gretchen explained. "But some people are just not satisfied with the help they're getting from the police. So, tell me about it. What do you know so far? And what have the police found?"

"Well, let's say hypothetically that we have a friend whose mom went to go shopping yesterday and never came back," explained Mona, with a blank expression.

"Another hypothetical? To find a real person you need some real facts. But okay, hypothetically, what else can you tell me?"

"Well, she doesn't answer her phone. It seems to be off," said Barney, again acting very uncomfortable with the words coming out of his mouth. "And she never stays away without telling her family. She takes care of a sick husband, so she never stays away for more than a few hours."

"That can be a lot of work and stress. You think maybe she just decided to split?" Gretchen asked.

"No. She wouldn't do that. She's never done that," Barney said. "Although she has been acting kind of down lately."

"What happened when you tried tracking her Abitat? People's Abitats usually know where they've been and what they've been doing. They're private, but they'll help if the inabitant is in trouble."

"She uses a car, not an Abitat," said Barney, choking on the words.

"A car? Really? Okay. I see. She normally lives in a house with a sick husband and a friend of yours who is her daughter or...or her son I'd say." She looked at Barney. "She drives a car instead of using an Abitat. She uses a 'phone' instead of a comm tablet. Kind of an eccentric or really old...-fashioned?"

"Uh. Yeah. I guess," Barney replied

...

Billy Jay wasn't sure how to respond to that. He muted his connection and whispered to Lae C and Javier, "How do we get help that will work in our world when this game world is so different? My mom sounds like some kind of freak in this world."

> **QX2230, 10:45 AM, Gretchen Excuses Miguel**

"What else have you done already to try to find her?" Gretchen asked.

"We…her son, I mean, saw a posting that showed she had been at a coffee shop across town, so we…he went there to see if anyone had seen her. Um. They didn't know anything useful."

"Okay. Before we go any further, I'd like to ask another question." Gretchen leaned in and said, "but privately with Mona and Barney. Miguel, I think you should maybe step outside your office for a couple minutes because there are some things that are best for an attorney not to hear about, even with attorney-client privilege."

"I don't know about that. I'm paying for this consultation, and I think I should be able to hear any questions you want to ask. I want to see how you do your job," Miguel answered.

"Trust me, Miguel. It's in your best interest. Just give us a few minutes," Gretchen spoke tenderly looking into Miguel's eyes. "Trust me."

"Okay. Okay. Abbie-tat, find a place I can wait outside and come back for me in five minutes. Is that enough?" Miguel said.

"Plenty," said Gretchen.

…

Javier spoke on the side to Billy Jay and Lae C, "I don't get it. Why does she want to talk to you without me?"

"We'll find out. Just keep watching through Billy Jay's character or mine," Lae C replied.

> **QX2230, 10:48 AM, Gretchen Asks What's Really Up**

The scene of the law office changed, and a doorway appeared leading out to a sidewalk in front of a bar. As Miguel stepped out, he said, "Five minutes. I'll wait here five minutes. Be back by then." The doorway closed and the law office changed back to its earlier configuration.

"Okay. I need to ask if this friend of yours is maybe not in this world but is in a different AM game world, one where people still drive cars," Gretchen asked.

"Uh. Maybe," Mona responded. "But why did you need Miguel to leave to ask us that?"

"Because talking about what's real and what's just a game can be harmful to characters in the game, and I really like Miguel and want him to stay sane."

"And you don't know or care about us?" Barney asked?

"From the looks of you, you are both just a couple of background characters who are already unstable and don't matter and can be reset after your players are done with you. Miguel on the other hand is a sweet, innocent prize of a character, and my friend, and I don't want him harmed."

…

Lae C, Billy Jay, and Javier looked at each other with surprise, as Mona and Barney looked at each other with anxious surprise in the game display.

…

"You'd be surprised how much of my work comes through the game," said Gretchen. "People would rather ask for help in the game than in the real world. That's where they spend all their time anyway."

"But I don't get it. You are in this world. How can you help someone in a different world?"

"Isn't that why you are here?"

"Uh. Yeah. Maybe. We just wanted to find out what we should do. But how do you know about different worlds, Gretchen? Or should I call you by another name?" asked Mona.

"Gretchen is fine. Gretchen is who I really am even if I may look different in the so-called real world."

"We're going to be picking up Miguel again in just a couple minutes. What do we do when he comes back in?" asked Barney.

"Just keep talking about your mom (It is your mom, right Barney?) as if she is a character in another game world, and you can be truthful since it is just a game. It's okay that the world has different rules since it's just a game. It's 'hypothetical'. Miguel can't know that the game world you're talking about is the real world and he is in a game world."

"But Javier here knows. He's behind Miguel," said Barney.

"Javier? Nice name. Maybe we can meet someday. I just don't want to spoil Miguel's head. Of course, Javier knows, but Miguel has to be protected from knowing too much."

…

"See. I told you this was dangerous for my character!" Javier said to Lae C and Billy Jay. "What did I tell you? Wait a minute. How about Gretchen? Doesn't this mess with Gretchen's head?" Javier asked. "Ask her. What about Gretchen?"

QX2230, 10:52 AM, What about Gretchen?

Barney J. asked, "What about you? What about Gretchen? What does this do to Gretchen's head?"

"Let's just say that I am Gretchen here and there and elsewhere, and all of me are okay knowing what I know."

"Okay, so we're going to pick up Miguel again any second. What do we say when he asks what we were talking about?" Mona asked.

"Leave that to me," Gretchen answered. "But one more thing. He wants to learn about how I do my investigations, and Javier may be able to keep him paying as we talk about your problems as a game world situation, but for a real-world investigation you'll need to come up with some real-world funds. My fees in the real world are 250 dollars per hour plus expenses, which might add up, or 25 AMPs per hour plus, if you have access to AMPs in the real world. 500 AMP minimum."

"Okay. We can get real world AMPs if we need them. We'll deal with that later," said Barney J.

The door opened and Miguel stepped up and in. "Okay. Did you sort out what you needed to?" he asked Gretchen.

‖ …

Javier fumbled to reconnect to Miguel.

QX2230, 10:53 AM, Miguel Returns to Abitat

"Yes. We did. I'm okay to talk about Barney's missing person's case here," Gretchen replied.

"I know you said to trust you, but why wouldn't you be okay with talking about a missing person's case in front of me?" Miguel asked. Javier got his connection working again, but before he could say "Never mind" Gretchen began her answer.

Gretchen explained, "Nowadays in this town there are some cases of missing persons that are too dangerous to work on—or even talk about. Disappearances involving cartels and corporate paramilitaries are too dangerous for me to deal with, and they could be even more dangerous for you. They kill attorneys to make a point. If it was that kind of case… well let's just be glad it's not. I was concerned when Barney talked about his friend's mom using a car instead of an Abitat. That fits the profile of someone trying to stay off the collaboration grid to hide from the corporate paramilitaries. But Barney's friend has a different kind of case. His 'friend' is actually in a game world, not this world. It's not real, so it's perfectly safe to talk about. But real or not it is important to Mona and Barney, and you paid my fee, so let's talk about it."

Barney had a worried, knowing expression. Miguel said, "Okay. Okay. Never mind my questions. Let's talk about how you would track down this missing mom of Barney's game character friend."

…

HW203904, 3:13 PM, Billy Jay Home Again

Billy Jay wondered if he and Barney were somehow responsible for the rise of these corporate paramilitaries in this world that had been his first big success before his shortcuts led to things going sour.

Just then the Abitat carrying Perry, Billy Jay, Lae C, and Javier pulled into the driveway of Billy Jay's house and announced "Arrived at home. Watch your heads." The ceiling began to lower. An external view on the wall showed the garage door opening.

Lae C, Javier, and Billy Jay all looked at each other for a few seconds silently, then, disconnecting from Mona, Lae C said "Hey. We're back. Seeing a real Abitat was interesting, but I need to get home. I want to finish my Lunar adventure in the game. And I've got to work tomorrow. You too, Javier. You were supposed to work today. And you're my ride. Let's go."

"Don't you want to finish this talk with Gretchen first?" Javier asked, muting his connections to Miguel.

"You guys can't bail out on me in the middle of this," Billy Jay complained.

"Open door," said Lae C. "You and your Barney should be able to keep talking with Gretchen and line up some help. You don't really need us. Javier and I have the link to this world on our phones. I'll check in with this Mona from time to time, and I know Javier will keep in touch with Miguel and Gretchen, but we really need to get back to our own lives now," Lae C explained.

QX2230, 10:58 AM, Ending the Meeting

Mona was looking nervously around the office and saying quietly, repeatedly, "I want to get out. I want to get out."

After a long pause Miguel spoke, "I'm sorry I was thinking about something else for a few seconds there. What were you saying, Gretchen?"

"I said I'm going to need to get a lot more information about the missing person, and Barney and Mona, you seem to be hesitating to answer so I need your contact information so that I can contact each of you privately."

Miguel said, "Good idea. Oh, and I just remembered I need to get back to work soon. For right now today I just wanted to make introductions. Barney and Mara, I mean Mona, can you give Gretchen your contact info and you can talk more later?"

Mona said, "I don't know. I don't know. I just want to get out. I guess I can give you my number if you let me get out of here." She held her comm tablet up towards the image of Gretchen to transfer her number.

Barney resisted. "I don't have a comm. Someone put one on me, but it's not mine." He struggled and then spoke, "But I can give you a contact name in the other world that you can use to reach me. BillyJay4^AM."

Mona said, "And I can usually find Barney if you need to meet in person."

"Okay, then. If Miguel needs to get back to work now, I'll plan to contact you a little later through Mona's comm or Barney's contact ID," Gretchen said. "And I really should get back to my other job too. And, Miguel, I'll talk to you later." She smiled at Miguel, who blushed and smiled back as she disconnected and disappeared.

Miguel said, "Let's drop Barney and Mona back where we picked them up."

A voice from the simulated law office walls said, "Request anticipated. We are there." The door opened to a curb near the bridge and Barney jumped out and ran, throwing the comm tablet into the bushes.

Mona also stepped out quickly and then turned around and said, "Thank you, Mr. Miguel, for your help. Your friend Gretchen seems nice. Barney and I will figure out a way to pay you back for the fee you paid."

"No need," said Miguel from inside as the door closed and the unit maneuvered back onto the road and back towards the office building. She found her shopping cart in the bushes and started walking down the street with it.

...

HW203904, 3:20 PM, Back at Billy Jay's House

The Abitat's ceiling had lowered, and the unit was docked in the garage at Billy Jay's house. Lae C and Billy Jay helped Perry to climb out of the vehicle. The garage door was closing. Javier watched and stood ready to assist but back just far enough that he didn't actually assist.

Lae C said, "As soon as we get Perry back to his bedroom Javier and I need to get out of here."

"Thanks for your help today, but I'm still not sure what's going to happen next," Billy Jay complained. "Do you think Gretchen will figure out to contact me on the discussion forum?" Javier opened the door and followed behind them as Billy Jay and Lae C walked Perry into the house, one on each side.

In the hallway Lae C let go of Perry's arm and indicated to Billy Jay to do the same. She looked into his eyes and said, "Perry, please walk to your bedroom." Perry kept walking down the hallway slightly ahead of Lae C and Billy Jay, who was hovering ready to catch him. "Do you see that?" she whispered to Billy Jay and Javier.

As they walked behind Perry Lae C said, "If Gretchen doesn't contact you, she definitely knows how to contact Javier's Miguel, and if she contacts the Mona lady I can respond."

"You will help me some more?"

"Sure. I'd like to see how this all turns out. I hope your mom is okay. But I've got to get home now. I've got a job and a life and other commitments. Maybe I'll run into you again on the moon."

…

Jose said, "Things were never quite the same between Miguel and Gretchen after that." Honus didn't respond.

…

Billy Jay and Lae C helped Perry into his bed.

"Bye, Mr. Perry Wilson Lee," Lae C said, while rubbing the hair stubble sticking out through his cap.

"Bye, Mr. Lee", said Javier.

Perry settled in his bed and raised and lowered his tablet as if to wave.

"Rest, Dad. I'll check on you in a little while," Billy Jay said.

Lae C said, "Take care of yourself, Mr. Lee. Feel better."

Billy Jay led Lae C and Javier back towards the garage. When he opened the door to the garage and saw the outer door was closed, he hesitated. "Did you leave anything in the Abitat?"

"No," said Lae C.

"I don't think so," said Javier.

He closed the door. "Then let's go out the front door." He pointed.

They walked through the living room and entry, and Javier noted the stark furnishings. "Really cool household minimalism. I really want to meet your mom. I hope she's okay. I hope she can introduce me to Min Strong."

"All those pictures of the Min woman. Kind of a stalker? Javier," said Billy Jay.

"Uh. I can explain that." Javier mumbled.

"Yeah. But not now. You need to give me a ride home, boss," Lae C insisted.

Billy Jay opened the front door and led Lae C and Javier outside without thinking about the anxiety of going outside. The trip in the Abitat today had been unsuccessful as far as finding his mom, but it seemed like a lot had changed for him and for his dad today. He had new contacts and a new confidence that he would be able to figure this out. And his dad seemed to be able to respond to requests and do more for himself than he had in a long time. He wondered why.

Javier and Lae C said their good-byes to Billy Jay and got in Javier's old Camry and drove off, with some smoke from the tailpipe lingering behind them. Billy Jay walked down to the sidewalk next to the street after they drove off, waving in front of his face to disperse the fumes. He thought about walking farther. He still felt some of the unusual confidence being outside but figured he shouldn't push it too far. He needed to get more food for his dad, check-in on his game worlds, and see if he could contact Gretchen again to track down his mom. Also, there was that thing about his dad hiding the family for some reason. He might really be in danger out here. He looked around. No one else was on his cul-de-sac street right now, and he couldn't see into any of the houses. A car drove by on the connecting street. In the distance somewhere up the connecting street—maybe a block or two away—a delivery drone was carrying a package over the roofs and treetops. He turned around and walked back toward his house, keeping his face away from line of sight with the drone. "You never know. You never know," he said to himself.

After he got back to his house, he made a quick search to make sure his mom wasn't there. "Mom! Hey, Mom! Are you home?" he called out as he went from room to room. Not finding her or hearing any replies, he then checked on his dad who was still sitting in bed with his tablet in his hands, mumbling, and humming. The humming was new.

"Hey. Dad. Are you feeling good today? Today was different, wasn't it?" His dad lifted his tablet a few inches and kept humming and mumbling. Billy Jay wasn't sure, but it almost looked like a momentary small smile. "We got to ride in a real Abitat today, didn't we? That was new. And we met some new people. Do you like Lacy and Javier? They seem like good people. You and Lacy got along." The humming kept going. "You started doing things today when Lacy asked you. Why is that? I mean, that's great. That's really great. But it's new." He paused and watched his dad mumble and hum. "Well, you rest a little while now. I'm going to find mom." Billy Jay left the room and went back to his own bedroom to check on his games and see if Gretchen was trying to contact him yet.

He opened the discussion forum and didn't see any new messages. He opened the window into the Antonia Springs game and found his Barney character by himself in a dark recess under a bridge with a box of foil scraps, wrapping more foil around his head. As Billy looked through Barney's eyes, Barney reacted, "Get away! Get away!" Barney waved his hands over his head like swatting gnats. Billy Jay decided to leave him alone for now. He disconnected but continued to watch in a third person view for a few seconds as Barney stopped waving his hands and looked around, then resumed adding foil scraps to his head.

Billy Jay checked on the moon world. He used a third person view there as well.

QZ9301, Wednesday, 8:00 AM, Lacy and the Butler

Orlov was lying eyes-closed on top of the covers on his bed in his own suite, wearing his gold pajamas. Lacy stood holding his hand while having a conversation with the disembodied butler-voice.

"Yes, Yes. That's a good observation, Miss Hogan. Bartholomew can be a bit unpredictable. He focusses on the details of his work most of the time, but then he suddenly heads out on an adventure or acts on flashes of inspiration, such as bringing you here, or following you with the rover."

"How long have you known him?"

"All his life, actually. 38 years. I watched out for him in his Abitats and in his homes since he was a child. I have more detailed memories as his valet and personal assistant the last few years. Before that it's more of a summary memory. I had some maintenance at that time that made me British and erased some of the earlier details."

"Do you think he's going to get better?"

"Well. Nothing will surprise me with Bartholomew. He seemed fine briefly last night, and I expect he might sit up again any moment. But the medical reports are not encouraging, are they?"

...

HW203904, 4:20 PM, Checking Worlds and Messages

Billy Jay was tempted to make Orlov sit up again right then, but he decided to move on to check in on his other characters.

Billy Jay saw that Orlov's nephew was pausing to decide his next step. Should he go on with his plans to climb and dive from 20 additional peaks, or should he abandon the challenge and head to the moon to visit his ailing uncle?

Billy Jay chose to have him continue his climbs.

Billy Jay's Amazon explorer character was in the roadless headwaters of the Amazon examining satellite pictures to decide which way to go next. Billy Jay chose to set him out on foot into the higher mountains. He arranged for his Abitat to be ferried by drone over the mountains and meet him on the other side.

He checked in on his other games, and none required any major decisions. He did the minimum to keep his ownership of his characters.

He checked on the bids for his dad's table thing. He was disappointed to see the $50 bid had expired. But then he noticed a new response.

...

Looks like a Perry Lee table.

Will pay $1000+

for true PL transformer table

in good condition

Need to see in person.

Where you located?

...

Seeing the $1000 figure Billy Jay's eye's opened wide. "That's more like it," he said to himself and smiled. He turned on voice-to-text input to dictate a reply but then hesitated. What was the thing about his dad being in hiding? Maybe he should be careful about contacting people who knew his dad's name. Plus with points in the Abitat, money was not as critical now. While he was thinking about what to do, a message popped up in the AM discussion forum.

OZAI20359^AM to BillyJay4^AM:
Billy Jay, This is Jerry from the coffee shop.

I see you online. We need to talk.

Not now.

I saw the Abitat.

?

We need to talk.

<u>OZAI20359^AM (blocked)</u>

He didn't want to deal with Jerry right now. Another recent message was pending for him in the forum.

<u>GCKPI^AM to BillyJay4^AM</u>

Is now a good time to talk about your mom? G

...

Honus paused the history world and nudged Jose. He asked, "How about if I have it summarize the chat with Gretchen? I think it might go on for a while."

"No. Let me see at least some of the details," Jose replied.

Honus let it continue...

HW203904, 4:30 PM, Billy Jay Chats with Gretchen

Gretchen?

Yes. Should I call you Billy Jay?

Fine.

First send me 500 AMPs in World 1 for my retainer.

Just a sec.

Billy Jay transferred points from the account in the Abitat.

Thanks. Now tell me more about your mom.

Her name is Mara.

Mara Lee.

Married to Perry Lee.

She's been missing since yesterday.

Okay. I'm doing searches.

I find a few people named Mara Lee,

but none with cross references to Perry Lee or Billy Jay Lee.

What else can you tell me about her?

Age? Jobs? Schools? Hobbies?

She's in her forties, I think.

She used to work for someone named Min Strong.

Really?

*She actually worked for **the** Min Strong?*

The "Maximizing Minimalism" Min Strong?

Yes. I think so.

Of course, there is a lot of info about Min Strong,

archives of her old websites and her talks and seminars.

Nothing current. She went off line a few years ago.

Since then, people speculating about what happened to her

and who she really was,

but I don't find any cross references to a Mara Lee,

or any employees actually.

What did your mom do for her?

Hold on. Hold on.

This is kind of interesting.

What? What did you find?

Nothing.

You said you found something interesting.

Tell me what you found.

My public records search came back

with no references to Mara married to Perry Lee.

No mention of any child of hers named Billy Jay Lee.

Nothing.
And I'm tapping into some thorough public databases.
Something should have come up.
Did she use a different name?

Billy Jay decided to share his real name.

No.
That's the only name I know for her.
But my legal name is not Billy Jay.
It's Balaji,
My dad called me Billy Jay.

Okay that might explain part of this.
Let's see.
I see some school or college records for Balaji Lee,
but it doesn't show a physical address
or your parents' names.
Those gaps are interesting.
It does have a couple of AM tags that can be used to reach you.

That reminds me.
I talked today with a woman yesterday
who met with my mom before she disappeared.
She said that she had a hard time contacting my mom.
She used an old email account from her old job.

Do you have that email address?

No. Sorry. Maybe I could ask her.
She said she was trying to reach my dad
for the last few years.
She tried to reach him through my mom.
She thought my dad was in hiding.

Do you know any reason why he would be hiding?

He's not hiding.

At least I don't think so.

He's been sick and hasn't been able to communicate.

What kind of sick?

Brain problems.

Something like Alzheimer's maybe. I'm not sure.

Sorry about that. How old is he?

I'm not sure. Probably around fifty.

That's young.

What are your parents' birthdates?

March I think. I don't know.

Really?

Assuming for a minute he may have been hiding,

we should be careful until we know who he was hiding from.

It's good we are talking in a private branch of the AM forum.

This is about the most secure way to communicate electronically,

but maybe we should meet in person so there is no electronic record.

No reason to take chances if someone is looking for you.

But I don't know you.

Why should I take that chance?

You will have to make your own call on who to trust.

But I can't do anything for you without information.

For now, let's continue in this chat.

It's probably safe. What kind of work did your dad do?

He worked on the AM game

and designing stuff for Abitats.

Before he got sick.

He also was kind of an artist.

He made weird furniture

and stuff in his workshop.

And he was into computers, I guess.

Perry Lee

Art, and design, furniture, computing. Let's see.

I see a Perry Lee who worked for at a university

and published some papers,

and I find some references to sales of art

and other special-order devices

from a company called PWL Design.

Not much info there. Was his middle initial W?

Yeah. W for Wilson.

Perry Wilson Lee?

I find some other people with that name, obituaries and such,

but very little about the one with the university job.

Nothing connecting to you or your mom.

Where have you lived?

Not sure I want to say.

Good to be careful.

But I need information to help you. Let's narrow it down.

How about countries, states, or provinces?

Let's say Southern California.

Socal? That makes sense.

That's where a Perry Lee worked at the university.

How long did you and your parents live in Socal?

As long as I remember.

All my life, I guess. Nineteen years.

Not sure before that.

Thanks.

That will help me filter out some of the noise in the data.

How about extended family? Aunts, uncles, grandparents?

No relatives.

No aunts or uncles.

My grandparents died before I was born.

Actually, I'm not sure about their names either.

You really don't know your parents' birthdates
or the names of your own grandparents?
I find that a bit hard to… Never mind.
How about pictures of your mom?
We may be able to do some facial recognition.
See if she's been on any public surveillance videos
since yesterday.

I don't have a recent picture.
Here's one from a few years ago.
<link>

Recent would be better. How old is that?

Maybe five or ten years. I'm not sure.
And it doesn't look exactly like her now.
We don't take pictures.
I don't know if I have any newer pictures.

Well, I'm not finding any matches
in the public video databases I have easy access to,
but it sometimes takes a while for the matches to show,
especially with an age difference.

Okay

Hey.
Here's something that came up in deeper search
related to her job.
Did you know that there is a group
of Min Strong fans that privately exchange pictures
and stories about her?

Really? About my mom?

No. About Min.
Apparently when Min's website went offline a few years ago
it became something like a conspiracy cult.
Not much on public websites, but it looks like

they've been privately exchanging pictures and stories.

Using some forums less secure

than this AM forum to talk about it.

I don't see any mention of your mom,

but I can look closer.

If they investigated where she worked

there might be something helpful.

Okay

They've probably got more in private AM discussion forums.

I'll troll one of their groups to get in.

See if they know anything about your mom's job

that would be a clue to her disappearance.

I think I met one of those Min Strong cult people today.

That could be important. Who is it?

Javier.

I think you know him as Miguel.

My Miguel's a Min Strong nut?

Javier had a ton of pictures of her on his phone.

We didn't have time to talk about it.

How much do you know about Javier?

I just met him.

He seems really smart.

He wants to go to law school.

He looks young.

Younger than me.

But Lacy said he is older than he looks.

He seems honest,

but kind of self-absorbed.

That fits what I know.

I also get the impression he is honest and naive,

but maybe he's fooling both of us.

We'll have to look into that some more.

Do you know his last name?

No.

But he and Lacy work at a Rancho market.

He's some kind of assistant manager.

Just a sec.

Is his last name Maldiva?

Javier Maldiva,

works at Rancho 555 Market in Santa Ana.

There's lots of information in the databases on him.

That could be him.

I see college records for a Javier Maldiva

who graduated with high honors after six years undergraduate.

Philosophy, Classics, Computer Science

triple major and a few minors.

He's written a lot of papers

and posted to all kinds of web forums.

Impressive.

He has a lot of opinions.

I'll need to sort through it.

I hate to learn about him this way

since I'd rather just know him as Miguel,

but we have to be careful.

That sounds like him.

By the way,

we'll need to be careful about letting people know you know him.

I guess you must live within a few miles of that market.

That puts you in higher risk of being found

if people really are trying to find your family.

Yeah.

But I don't think he could be involved.

My gut tells me you're right.

My Miguel wouldn't be involved.

Who did your mom meet with yesterday?

Someone named Jerry.

She worked with my dad,

on the game or designing Abitats.

What's her last name?

Not sure, but I have her tag in the AM forum.

That might help.

OZAI20359^AM

Where did you meet her?

At a coffee shop. I'm not sure what city.

We went autopilot based on a food picture my mom took.

I can look up the geotag if you want.

Yeah. You could have started with that. But, Okay.

Wait. A few people with tags like OZAIxxx

studied Artificial Intelligence in Australian universities. …

Jerry could be Geraldine Hodgkins Atwood

Maybe. She did have an accent.

She's in the US on a work visa

for a company called Altruism Industries.

I see lots of information about her in the database.

Pictures. Academic papers.

A number of recent hits on various public surveillance videos

in SoCal …

including some at a community center with a coffee shop

in Highland Hills…

Including yesterday and today.

That must be her. Can you show me a picture?

Check this <link>

That's her.

That looks like the parking lot at the same place.

Your mom met with her yesterday,

and you met with her today?

Yes.

Your mom was at that same coffee shop yesterday?

Yes.

Public surveillance video says maybe not.

No facial near matches for your mom yesterday.

Huh?

The parking lot video files don't show anybody

looking like your mom there yesterday.

Keep looking. Maybe she just didn't face the cameras?

No.

They have lots of cameras

and I'm allowing a lot of leeway in the matching.

Maybe this is the wrong place.

Let's see about you.

When did you go there?

Not sure about the time.

Jerry wasn't there when we got there.

I went outside while Javier and Lacy waited.

They said she came in right after I left.

We talked for a few minutes.

When we left Jerry was still in the coffee shop.

Okay. Based on when she came in,

I see a young man and woman coming in before her

and leaving again. Is this you? Here's a <link>.

That's Javier and Lacy. I was with them.

So that's Javier. Nice.

You were with them?

You're sure about that?

The videos show just the two of them.

Oh. Yeah.
They walked around first,
then we went in together.

Parking lot cameras show those two,
Javier and Lacy, walking around and going in,
and show other people coming and going,
but don't show anyone with them.

I walked in with them.
Then I went back out to get my tablet.
I walked around in the parking lot.
Then I went back in and met
the three of them in the coffeeshop.

I don't see you or anyone walking around the parking lot
while they were in the coffeeshop.
I don't have videos from inside the coffeeshop.
Wait a minute. What's this?
They came and left in a real Abitat?
You guys have a real Abitat?

Yeah. It's new. It was delivered today.

Okay. Billy Jay.
I have to say you have surprised me.
I'd really like to meet and check out your Abitat.
By the way what kind of vehicle did your mom use?
When we were talking in Miguel's office in world QX2230
you said she didn't have an Abitat.

Autonomous Motors EL series. About 3 years old.

Okay. I see a couple of those in that parking lot that day.
One with a middle-aged white guy going to the library
and leaving about an hour later.
The other one shows arriving and leaving on the parking lot videos,

but it doesn't show anyone getting in or out
and the windows look tinted so I can't see anyone inside.
What color is your mom's EL?

Sort of green.

Yeah. That matches the one not showing anyone.
See <link>

That can't be my mom's car.
I don't think her windows are tinted like that.
If she didn't park there, how did she get into the coffee shop?
Maybe her car dropped her off nearby and she walked in.

It looks like all the entrances are covered by cameras
and no match for her walking in.
This is kind of weird.
I thought you were giving me a bullshit story with fake names,
and I thought maybe you were really one of those two,
but the car also coming and going without anyone getting out
is a little weird. I've got a theory but it's kind of far-fetched.

What is it?

If your story is true, and both you and your mom were there,
then someone or something is actively removing images
of you and your mom from the public video records.
Are you in some kind of witness protection?

No. I don't think so.

It's kind of freaky.
It's beyond normal witness protection.
AI software can easily remove people from pictures and videos,
but for it to happen so quickly on public surveillance videos.
That's not something I knew was out there.
Your parents weren't some kind of spies, were they?
I've never seen this kind of cloaking on public surveillance videos.

I was there today.

And people said they saw my mom there yesterday.

Here is the geotagged picture she took. <link>

...

Honus paused the history world again and Jose peeked out of his goggles and checked the time on his wristband.

Jose asked, "How long does this go on?"

Honus shrugged.

Jose said, "Summary is okay."

Honus adjusted it to restart in summary mode…

...

They went back and forth for a few more minutes with Billy Jay answering questions with what little he knew about his mom and her hobbies and private social media accounts before Gretchen said she had to disconnect because of an appointment she couldn't miss.

...

After my appointment

I'll go over what you've given me

to see what sense I can make of it.

Meanwhile, you see what other information

you can find at home.

I'll contact you again on this forum.

No later than tomorrow.

Be careful.

Okay.

Thanks, Gretchen.

GCKPI^AM Disconnected

After chatting with Gretchen Billy Jay looked quickly at his active game worlds and then checked on his dad and decided to order some more food. From his bedroom he activated his own character in World RW001 in order to control the new Abitat. He used the Abitat and its points to set up orders for a few groceries and asked it to go out at least a mile from his home before submitting the orders. He didn't want delivery vehicles to come back to the house. It turned out there were no stores or restaurants close to his home that offered Abitat delivery, so the Abitat ended up going several miles away. While the Abitat went out he stayed home with his dad, planning on searching his parents' rooms to see if he could find any more clues.

But first he checked again on his characters in the game. Bartholomew Orlov was still unconscious on his large bed in his suite in his moon resort. The Lacy Hogan character was resting next to him on the bed with her arms around him. Billy Jay decided not to wake them. LacyHogan235 was still offline. Orlov's nephew was refreshing his supplies from his hover-capable Abitat before free climbing the next peak. Billy Jay's Amazon explorer character was now at a site of ancient mountain ruins making plans to dig for treasure. His other characters in other worlds were busy working on other development projects. He adjusted the time flow for his characters in all the worlds to be no faster than real-world elapsed time. Often, he let game world time flow faster when he was offline so that there would be more interesting changes to deal with when he reconnected, but he thought he might not be able to check in as often for a while.

He knew some other tricks to help keep his characters under his control if he had to be offline for an extended period of time. Typically, he only used those tricks to buy time for characters or worlds that he was considering abandoning, but now he decided it was smart to not take any extra chances with his active worlds. He made transactions to prolong his control on all of his active game worlds before he disconnected and went to search his parent's rooms.

Billy Jay checked on his dad briefly and then started searching through desks and drawers in his parents' rooms and didn't find much. He knew his mom didn't usually write things down because she had an amazing memory, but he figured it was still worth checking. Maybe she left him another note. His Dad did write things down when he was healthy but hadn't done so for a few years since he was sick, and his mom had probably cleaned up and thrown away his stuff. So, it was probably smarter to start in his mom's room.

Not finding anything interesting in the first couple of drawers he searched, Billy Jay decided to try getting into his mom's computer. She had a workstation in her room with two large displays and an old-fashioned keyboard and mouse. It didn't seem as good as the wall-size displays he had in his own bedroom, but she probably didn't play the kind of games he did. He was able to unlock the computer with his own face and voice, but it only gave him a view of his own account in the family social media pages similar to what he could see from his own computer or tablet. He could see things his mom had posted to the family view, but not her personal files. He figured he would have to look more closely later to see if he could get into his mom's private files or see if there was anything interesting in her family postings.

He went back to searching through her closet and dresser drawers and found a safe mounted in the wall of the closet behind some sweaters.

"This must have something. I wonder how it opens?"

He inspected it. It had a keypad and some other markings on the front. It looked like it might be set up to use a wireless connection to a phone or tablet to unlock, but the existence of a keypad suggested that some kind of pass code might also unlock it. He keyed in his own birthdate on the keypad. Nothing happened.

"Open sesame," he spoke to it. Nothing happened.

"Worth a try." He looked around for any kind of note or instructions and didn't see any.

He realized it had been quite a while since he sent out the Abitat to get food, so he decided to check on it. He logged in to his AM game account from his mom's computer and noticed that the user interface was slightly different from when he accessed it from his tablet and the wall displays in his room. It was similar enough he was quickly able to check on the location of the Abitat and saw that it had taken delivery of the food he ordered and was on its way back to the house. Actually, it was coming back into the garage right now. He took a quick look in on his dad, who looked normal, before he walked to the garage to get the food.

He put some of the food supplies into the minifridge in the Abitat, but most he carried back to the kitchen in the house. It took him three trips. He fixed himself a big serving of orange chicken and ate it before starting to figure out how to prepare something for his dad to eat. He probably should ask Lae C for advice on what kinds of foods to buy, since she was a cook.

Later when he brought food to his dad, he was able to get him to walk by himself to the bathroom without holding his arm to steady him. When Billy Jay asked him to, his dad fed himself with a spoon. While his dad ate Billy Jay tried to make conversation.

"Dad, I don't know where Mom went. I wish you could help me figure it out. It was embarrassing when I talked with the investigator. There is so much I don't know about my own family. Do we have family records somewhere? There's a safe in mom's closet, but I don't know how to open it. Can you help me open it?"

"I ... don't ... remember ... that," said Perry.

...

7:25 PM, Jose and Honus at the House

Honus paused the history world and said, "Food's here."

"That's more detail about your talk with Gretchen than you told me before. Is it accurate?" Jose asked. They walked to the Abitat.

"Could be. As much as I can remember. That part's probably based on a recording of the conversation from the game forum, so it's probably accurate," Honus replied.

"I wondered why things weren't quite the same between Miguel and Gretchen after that. The history world seems to have some of Billy Jay's thoughts. Are you sure you didn't make it yourself?" asked Jose as they took food from the Abitat's delivery closet.

"I'm pretty sure about that," said Honus.

"I guess a story engine will fill in thoughts or summarize based on the actions before and after," speculated Jose.

"Or a world-builder made up some details," suggested Honus.

"All of this could have been generated from recorded data: game records, dashcams, security videos. If someone had access to all that. Maybe Gretchen put it together for you as a summary of the data she collected," Jose proposed. They were back in the bedroom.

"I guess that's possible," Honus conceded.

"Speaking of Gretchen, did she ever find out where your mom's car went after the coffee shop?" Jose asked as he started to eat.

Honus replied, "Not really. She said the car's dashcam and navigation recordings after that were all thoroughly erased. Nothing to say how it got back to the house empty a couple days later."

"Yeah, I remember the day it came back. My Camry died that day, and you let me use the EL. Nice car," Jose recalled.

"Funny coincidence how your Camry died right then," Honus observed.

"Yeah," said Jose.

Honus continued, "Gretchen said the mileage on the car increased by about seventy miles between the time the recordings went blank and when it got back to the house."

"Interesting," said Jose. "How far out of the way was that?"

"Around 20 miles, I think," Honus recalled.

"That's right. You were looking for places she could have gone that were less that 20 miles out of the way, like the airport?"

"No. Gretchen checked all the flights. Plus, the car could have gone farther. When someone hacked the car to erase navigation and dashcam recordings, they could have changed the odometer too."

"Yeah. I suppose."

"Go on to the next day?" asked Honus.

"Sure," said Jose.

HW203904, Tuesday, April 5, 2039, 9:30 AM, Next Morning

After staying up late the night before, trying repeatedly but unsuccessfully to get his dad to speak again, Billy Jay had a rough night's sleep, waking up every hour or two. The next morning he was awakened by tones on his tablet indicating arriving messages when Gretchen tried to contact him. He checked on his dad before talking with Gretchen.

Gretchen said she still hadn't found any information about Billy Jay's mom other than "Mara" on his birth records, and that showed much less information than normal. No maiden name. No father's name. Regarding his dad, she had found and read a number of his dad's academic articles, which were hard to understand but seemed to be related to some of the concepts used in the game and in Abitats. She also had assembled a list of people who had co-authored articles with him, or cited his work in their own papers, as well as other colleagues at the university where he had worked, and people who had attended conferences where he had presented. It was a long list and the only name that jumped out was Geraldine Atwood, the Jerry person from the coffee shop. She had attended some of the same conferences as Perry and she had cited his papers in most of her own papers. Gretchen said she would arrange to talk with Jerry.

When Billy Jay asked how worried he should be about his dad being in hiding and people trying to find his dad, she asked about the kind of security systems they had on their house. Billy Jay mentioned the security cameras and Gretchen asked if they had captured any recent pictures of his mom. Billy Jay thought they were just live pictures, but Gretchen helped him figure out how to access and save recorded videos in the system. He gave Gretchen a copy of video of his mom getting in the car and driving out of the garage. He said that was all he had of her. At that time he didn't mention the views of Mara in the house during the days before she left, or views of Perry, Lae C, Javier, and himself inside in the following days. Billy Jay was cautious about sharing the other images, wanting to avoid giving away too much information.

Gretchen said she needed at least an hour to use the more current pictures of Mara to look for matches on the internet or in public surveillance videos and take care of some other appointments. They could reconnect a little after 11.

…

Honus skipped ahead.

HW203904, 11:15 AM, Reconnect with Gretchen
They connected back up at the pre-determined time.

…

GCKPI^AM to BillyJay4^AM:

No luck so far finding facial recognition

matches for your mom's face,

but I did find something about your house.

Don't get mad.

What about my house

The video of your mom driving out of the driveway

The houses across the street are in that view

I matched them on available street views

I found your address

Okay.

So, you know where I live.

Should I run away?

Or is it too late for that

Your address is safe with me.

I blurred the neighbors' houses

in the copy of the video I saved.

I won't share it.

Be careful what images you share with others.

I guess I don't have a choice

but to trust you now

I also looked up the ownership of your house

My mom and dad,

right?

Probably, but through a trust.

No mention of your parents by name.

The Lee Family Trust acquired it in 2020,

and property taxes have been paid each year

by someone who hides their tracks.

I know a little about trusts

from real estate deals in the game.

Right.

Then you know a family trust is not unusual for a home.

The trust name seems to suggest

it was set up by your parents.

You will need to find the trust agreement

document to get more details.

I'll try to track down information

about how the taxes were paid

but that probably won't give any useful information.

I'll look for it.

The trust document.

Let me know if you find it.

It might say how to deal with your dad

being disabled and your mom being missing.

Also, it should name the attorney who wrote it.

They might know your folks

and have ideas where your mom might go.

Anything else I should be doing?

Keep looking for more home security video files.

Seeing what your mom did in the past

could be a good clue.

It's interesting that you couldn't find anything

prior to the day she left.

Maybe she deleted them.

I'll keep looking. Oh. I did find something.

?

I found a safe.

Good.

That would be a good place to look for the trust agreement.

But I don't know the code to open it

…

After some more discussion about things Billy Jay should look for and ideas for how to guess the code for the safe, Billy Jay provided Gretchen with the safe's model number. Gretchen said to be careful with that type of safe, since too many failed attempts could block its keypad for hours and eventually cause it to destroy the contents. She said not to try more than ten times per day. She gave him info on or how to get help from someone who might know more about opening difficult safes but didn't offer much hope without the access code. She also mentioned that another 500-point payment would be needed in a day or so. Billy Jay wondered if it was worth it to continue getting help from Gretchen but didn't say anything before they disconnected. Billy Jay also did not tell Gretchen that his dad had spoken the previous night. He was starting to doubt what he had heard.

Billy Jay went again to try opening the safe in his mom's closet using some of the suggestions from Gretchen. He didn't have any more luck and stopped after eight tries.

He tried talking with his dad again, also without more luck. His dad just mumbled and drooled like before. He decided to search his dad's office and workshop in the barn building out back. He found some paper notes and drawings in his dad's desk, but none that looked like passwords or access codes for the safe. He logged in on his dad's computer using his own account but wasn't able to get into his dad's account or his mom's. He considered bringing his dad out to the workshop to see if he could log in with facial, voice, or touch recognition, but then decided it would make more sense to try that first with his tablet or his mom's computer, since both were closer to his dad's room, and it seemed all the computers were connected to the family's accounts. He looked at several examples of furniture or art pieces stored in the workshop and wondered what they might be worth. He also tried the keypad and touchpads on locked closet doors and cabinets in the workshop to no avail. He wondered if he could use some of his dad's tools to cut his way into the locked areas. Maybe Sergey could help. Sergey must use the workshop tools sometimes for making things for the farm. He should ask Sergey if he knew any of the access codes. He was nervous going into the farm beyond the barn building, so he would figure out how to contact Sergey later.

Before he left to go back to the house to eat lunch and feed his dad, he took pictures with his tablet of some of the notes around his dad's desk and the touch pads for the locked doors and cabinets. Maybe they would be clues that Gretchen could make sense of.

…

Honus skipped ahead to when Lae C and Javier came back.

> **HW203904, 3:45 PM, Lae C & Javier Return**
>
> Lae C and Javier returned later that afternoon leaving early from their shift at the market. Lae C messaged Billy Jay in the AM forum to let him know they were on their way. Both wanted to use the Abitat again. Javier wanted to use the high resolution of the 3D game displays in the Abitat to let Miguel meet with Gretchen. Lae C wanted to see more of the views on the moon or maybe use her new points to have her avatar go to Mars and see the simulated views from there. Billy Jay wanted help with his dad and with looking for clues about where his mom had gone. Billy Jay agreed to let each of them have some time alone in the Abitat to play their games if they helped him. He filled them in on what Gretchen had told him, showed them the safe, and his mom's computer desk and mentioned the idea of trying to get his dad to log in with facial recognition on his mom's computer or his own tablet. He brought his tablet with him when they checked on his dad, and held it up in front of his face to see if it would log in. It didn't seem to work.
>
> Javier looked at Billy Jay's tablet and said, "This looks like a custom version of the AM game OS, the AM-OS. I haven't used this particular version but let me try something." He did something on the screen and held the tablet up again to Perry's face. "Can you say, 'log me in', Perry?"
>
> Perry just mumbled. Lae C said, "He doesn't talk, Javier."
>
> "Well…" Billy Jay started.
>
> "What?" Lae C asked.
>
> After hesitation Billy Jay mentioned that his dad had spoken last night.
>
> Lae C took one of Perry's hands in hers and he grasped her fingers in return. He still held onto his tablet with the other hand but let it settle on his lap. She looked into his eyes, and he looked

back at hers as she said, "Perry, talk to me. Do you know who you are?"

"No."

"You are Perry Wilson Lee. Can you remember that?"

"Perry ... Lee"

"I'm Lae C. Or call me Lacy."

"Lay ... Cee."

"That's right. This is your son Billy Jay. Can you say Billy Jay?"

"Balaji."

"Close enough. That's very good," Lae C squeezed Perry's hands.

Billy Jay asked, "Do you remember mom? Do you remember Mara?"

Perry let go of Lae C's hand, pushed Billy Jay's tablet away, picked up his tablet again, and started mumbling and fidgeting.

Javier put Billy Jay's tablet under his arm while they tried for a few more minutes but couldn't get Perry to speak any more.

"That was good, Perry. Really good. We'll let you rest now. We will talk more later," Lae C said before gesturing to the others and leading them out of his room. Perry mumbled and gestured over his tablet as they left.

They went back to Mara's room and discussed what had just happened.

"He responded to Lae C, but stopped when Billy Jay talked to him," Javier summarized.

"But he did talk to me last night," Billy Jay added. "And this is all new. He hasn't talked for years, except mumbling."

"Something is different," Javier said.

"Maybe he's been somewhere but is coming back. His mind," Lae C theorized.

Javier was still holding Billy Jay's tablet. Billy Jay reached out for it and Javier started to hand it back, but hesitated, noticing something. "Wait. Wait. It did log him in. The combo of his face and his voice must have done it. See it's in Perry's world." He handed the tablet to Billy Jay.

Javier seemed to know his way around the OS for the game better than Billy Jay and Lae C, even if it was a non-standard version, so after Billy Jay had struggled for a few minutes to find things in the tablet Javier stepped in. He got absorbed in exploring various aspects of the world view in Perry's account but kept saying he needed more time to explore.

After a couple minutes Billy Jay and Lae C got bored watching Javier work on the tablet, so they wandered off to the kitchen to see what food was available. Lae C was not happy with the processed food items that Billy Jay had ordered and made up a shopping list of better ingredients. She looked through the handful of cooking utensils in the kitchen and assessed them as lacking as well. The stove and oven were okay.

With Billy Jay's tablet in use by Javier they couldn't submit an Abitat order from the kitchen, so they went out to the garage and into the Abitat. Billy Jay explained his preference to have the Abitat wait to submit orders until it was over a mile away from the house. Lae C used her own phone to check on item availability.

While she was using her phone to find tools and ingredients, Lae C decided to use it to update her game session. She convinced her avatar, and through her avatar, convinced the butler voice that assisted Orlov that Orlov would benefit from medical care available on Mars. They departed in her Abitat for a quick flight to Mars, with the fuel and visa fees paid by Orlov.

Most of the food items were available for Abitat delivery within 10 miles, but many of the professional cooking tools she wanted were not available for immediate Abitat delivery at all. They would have to be ordered for front porch delivery in a day or two. She adjusted her food shopping list substituting different ingredients for those that were unavailable now and taking off some of the items that she couldn't use without the right cooking tools. After some discussion about what she wanted to order and how much it was likely to cost Billy Jay agreed to use points from the Abitat to pay for the Abitat food deliveries but was hesitant to pay for her cooking tools.

He checked his Abitat points balance and discovered another 5000 points had been added that day, making him more generous. He went ahead and transferred another 500 points to Gretchen so that she would continue to help him, and he agreed to pay for the new cooking tools Lae C wanted as well. He transferred 500 points to Lae C's phone so she could order the cooking tools she wanted. They discussed whether it was better to have them delivered to her home address or to Billy Jay's. Billy Jay was uneasy about having anything delivered to his house right then. They finally decided to have them delivered to a package delivery locker at the store where Lae C could pick them up. Lae C promised she would come back with the tools and make a great meal with fresh ingredients in a few days.

They finalized the food shopping list and exited the Abitat which headed out of the garage, and they stood watching it go. Billy Jay used his phone to check on the game world with Orlov and Lacy. He noticed Orlov had recovered much of his ability to move and respond.

QZ9301, 7:00 PM, Orlov and Lacy on Flight to Mars

Orlov and Lacy were together in an Abitat on the way to Mars. It must have been during the middle hour of the trip since they were weightless. During the acceleration and deceleration phases they would have been pinned to their seats or beds, even with artificial gravity adjustments. The two were floating above a bed, partly wrapped together in a satin sheet. Bare arms and legs moving around each other.

…

Lae C said, "Is that the trip to Mars? I wanted to see that. Have they made it yet? Have they gone all the way?" She leaned over to try to get a view of the tablet.

"All the way?" Billy Jay held the phone against his chest.

"I want to see the entry. The insertion."

"Uh. Insertion? Entry?"

"Orbital insertion and atmospheric entry on Mars. The flight simulation is supposed to be very realistic on the final approach to the planet and the atmospheric plasma interface."

Embarrassed, Billy Jay quickly closed the game window on his phone and started out of the garage saying to Lae C, "Not yet. I think you still have some time."

"Good. I hope the Abitat gets back in time so I can get a max res view of the vibration and glow as it comes in."

Billy Jay said, "Let's see if Javier has found anything."

…

Jose grabbed Honus by the arm and said, "I never knew you and Lae C were a thing."

"That was Orlov and Lacy. Not me and Lae C."

"Too bad."

The history world playback continued…

…

Lae C and Billy Jay went back to Mara's room to check on Javier, who was sitting in her office chair manipulating multiple displays from Perry's account on the displays. Billy Jay and Lae C came in behind Javier and sat on Mara's bed to look over his shoulders. Billy Jay noticed that they were sitting on the bed together and awkwardly stood back up.

Standing next to Javier, Billy Jay asked him, "What have you found?"

"There is a lot here," Javier gestured highlighting one display window after another.

Javier showed a view of portals to multiple game worlds, with names like Abbies, AM, Agency, Finances, Furniture, Min, INCA, PATH, Models, MinAI, Headset, Farm, Brahma, Shiva, Vishnu, Dreamtime, PWs, and Unix. He wasn't able to open most of the worlds without additional keys that he hadn't been able to guess, but he suggested maybe Perry's face and voice would work again.

"I was able to open a view of this Unix world."

He expanded the Unix world which brought up a text-based operating system view of files and directories.

"There is a lot in here to look through. I started a command to see how much stuff is accessible here, counting files and directories and data storage. It's not done yet, but already it shows over 25 billion directories, 900 billion files, and over 1.6 exabytes of data." He highlighted a window with the incrementing numbers.

"I don't know that tech stuff, but that sounds like a lot," Lae C said.

"Let's just say Billy Jay's dad has a respectable amount of data in his account," Javier understated. "His account must be connected to a commercial cloud service somehow, but I don't find any external connections. From what I can see in the Unix view the storage all appears like it is on your home network. No way you've got exabytes of data storage in your house. That would take many rooms full of servers."

"What's that mean?" Billy Jay asked.

"I don't know. It's not exactly normal Unix; it's using a non-standard version of the AM OS so I just haven't figured it all out yet. But I'm guessing maybe he's got some kind of Unix command line view into the distributed data in the AM game hive network. That's not supposed to be possible, but you said he helped create the game. There must be thousands or millions of exabytes of data in the AM hive, with billions of tablets, phones, computers, and game systems connected to it, but it is distributed with Nested Cellular

Autonomy, so there is no way to see it as one file system. Or at least there's not supposed to be."

"How does this help us find my mom?"

"Oh. Yeah. I started a search for files with 'Mara' in the file names. It's still searching but it has found a few thousand so far. That might be a place to start." Javier gestured at a window titled 'Mara' with a counter incrementing from 3522 to 3523 and so on.

"What's this?" Lae C asked pointing to a similar window titled 'Min', with a counter that was already five digits and spinning up quickly.

"Oh. That. I thought it wouldn't hurt to see if there is any info on Min Strong in here also. It's finding too much because 'Min' is in a lot of words. I should restart that with a more restrictive selection pattern, like 'Min' and 'Strong', or do an AI search of the contents of the files."

"Forget Min Strong. What about my mom?"

"Yeah. We can do that for her too."

...

Honus moved the history world forward in more of a summary mode to try to get past any views of interactions on the Mars flight.

HW203904, 6:00 PM, Lac C Cooks

When the Abitat returned with the groceries Lae C took a quick turn in the Abitat watching the view as Orlov and Lacy's Abitat approached and then flashed through the Martian atmosphere and landed at the medical clinic. Meanwhile Billy Jay carried the groceries to the kitchen. After the landing, Lae C disconnected from the game to go prepare food, noticing that Orlov was conscious again but very sweaty after the flight. The Lacy avatar also seemed like she was sweaty and flushed as she accompanied Orlov to the clinic. Lae C was pleased with the realism of the views during the final approach, atmospheric entry, and landing. She figured she could check Lacy's memories later to see if there was some danger or mishap she missed during the Mars approach that accounted for the apparent sweat and fatigue on Orlov and Lacy. It probably had something to do with waking Orlov.

As soon as Lae C finished with the Abitat, Javier took over and closed the door for privacy during Miguel's meeting with Gretchen.

Billy Jay checked on his dad, checked for new messages from Gretchen, and reviewed but did not respond to a few pleading messages from Jerry while Lae C prepared the meal. He checked on most of his game world avatars, but avoided the Mars game world, figuring he'd let Orlov deal with things there for now on his own. He was just getting ready to start exploring his dad's account when Lae C said that food was ready.

…

Jose said, "You don't have a view of Miguel's meeting with Gretchen?"

"I haven't seen this part before, but it doesn't look like it."

"It's probably for the best."

HW203904, 7:30 PM, Perry Eats

Lae C was disappointed that Billy Jay didn't show more appreciation for the meal she cooked. It included an easy lasagna recipe she had created and was proud of. Even with the limited cooking tools and missing some ingredients she thought it deserved high praise. Billy Jay just said, "That tastes good."

She set aside a portion for Javier to rewarm when he was done with Gretchen, figuring she didn't care whether Javier was impressed. She cut the food into bitesize pieces for Perry even though Billy Jay warned her his food should be blended into a baby food paste. She went to Perry's room and asked him to walk to the dinner table and sit down. He did so. Lae C asked Perry to use his fork to eat. Billy Jay hovered closely, ready to try to do something if his dad started to choke. He wasn't sure what he would need to do. Perry handled the fork pretty well, spilling food from it only once.

He responded with "Mmmm" and "Ohhh" after chewing and swallowing each bite. Lae C was pleased with his reactions.

...

Honus moved the history world forward.

> **HW203904, 8:20 PM, Javier Leaves**
>
> Javier finished his 1-hour game world session of Miguel meeting with Gretchen and came out of the Abitat smiling. Lae C intended to take her turn next, but Javier wanted to go home, and he was her ride. That problem was settled when Billy Jay agreed to let her get a ride home in the Abitat. She disappeared into the Abitat, which left the garage, and Javier disappeared out the front door. Billy Jay helped his dad settle down for the night and then went to his room to check briefly on most of his game characters, but not Orlov in world QZ9301, and then spent a couple hours playing some violent action games until he was getting tired and went to bed.
>
> ...

7:35 PM, Tristan and the Tourists Make Toys

Minh shouted, "Let me do this one. I want to make my delivery drone. It's my turn."

"Let me finish my cockroach first," Max insisted.

"You're taking too long. It's my turn!"

"Hold on. Hold on," said the dad. "Uncle Perry didn't have to let you do this at all."

"They figured out how to turn on the 3D printer on their own. Might as well show them how to make something with it," said Tristan.

"Sorry about that. They both are always finding ways of getting into things that they shouldn't," the mom apologized.

The 3D printer was adding layers to the insect that Max had designed, while Minh waited impatiently at the computer desk with his design of a cross between a toy delivery drone and a pterodactyl.

"No harm. It's okay," Tristan said to Fanny and John. Then to the twins, "You both are really good at this." Back to the parents, "Actually, this toy design software was created for someone about their age, but he was never interested in using it. It's nice that someone can use it." Tristan paused, realizing that this memory about the inventing software for a young boy a was something he didn't know he knew.

The printer continued to hum as it added more layers onto the cockroach as Max admired her work. While he waited, Minh manipulated his pterodactyl design on the computer screen, adding and taking away extra limbs, propellers, sensors, and motors, and changing the expression on the beast's face from goofy to fierce to heroic.

7:40 PM, Elsie and Andre at Camilla's

Andre had showered and changed his clothes on the way. He sent his wet and muddy bat costume off to be cleaned and dried. When his Abitat docked at Camilla's docking porch he got out and walked into Camilla's living room to find Elsie bottle-feeding Alex and Camilla bringing out a tray with some freshly made bruschetta and a glass of red wine. She offered both to Andre.

"You shouldn't have."

"When else do I get a chance to cook for someone? I love to cook. The lasagna just went into the oven. You have to stay for some lasagna. It's a recipe Elsie gave me, actually. I may not be as fancy a cook as you, Elsie, but I do what I can." She gestured for Andre to take the wine and a little plate for some of the bruschetta.

Andre took the glass and three pieces of bruschetta and said, "Thank you. How are you doing? Any news about your daughter?" He sipped the wine and sat down next to Elsie and Alex and offered her one of the bruschetta.

"Granddaughter," Elsie corrected him before opening her mouth and taking a bite offered by Andre. Andre admired Alex's contented face as they sucked on the bottle.

"Right. Any news about your granddaughter, Bella, is it?" Andre asked.

Camilla didn't answer so Elsie summarized, "Nothing new. Camilla's granddaughter, Isabella Muller, who is an attorney at my firm, has been out of touch since this morning at 10. There's been a lot of rain and snow today in the mountains where she was backpacking." She turned to Camilla. "But I'm sure she'll be fine, Camilla. I'm sure she'll be fine."

"I can check with my law enforcement contacts in the area to see what they know," Andre suggested.

"That's right. You're with the police, aren't you, Mr. Marteen?"

"Call me Andre. Yes. With the PSA, Public Safety Association, actually, for some reason we're not supposed to call ourselves police or sheriffs anymore. But some people still do. I don't mind."

7:45 PM, Tristan and the Tourists Part Ways

Tristan apologized that he had somewhere he needed to be. They would have to finish printing the second toy later, or he could send it to them. He expressed sympathy for Fanny's mom's kidney condition, but not sure if he could risk helping, he didn't promise anything. He agreed to meet with them again but didn't set a time and place. They gave him their contact information, but he didn't want to give them his local contact information. He considered how best to let them contact him and decided to give them a contact through a character in a game world that was not frequently used. If they left a message for that character, he could see it and respond. He suggested they set up another time and place to meet before they go back to Kansas. The twins took turns chasing each other with the cockroach, but Minh was disappointed he didn't have his pterodactyl drone yet.

7:50 PM, Emily, Sam & Jo-Jo

Sam pointed at the display which showed exterior camera views, a satellite area view, and advertisements for getting on a waitlist for a residential Abitat Village whose entrance they were now just outside. The Abitat was pausing in the street.

Sam explained, "There's a little farm behind this Abitat Village. The old farmer guy would let us camp out sometimes in one of the barns years ago. We should be able to hang out there until we figure out how to get back our wristbands and Abitat. We can get in through the streambed that runs next to the Abitat village."

"The stream's probably full of water right now," said Jo-Jo.

"Well then, we can climb over the wall from the Abitat Village. Can you dock in a spot near the back wall?" Sam asked Emily.

"It says there is no vacancy right now. We could ask an Abitat to move for a few minutes so we can go in for a recharge, but the docks all have Abitats that are staying overnight," Emily explained what she saw on the display. "There's also a driveway into the farm just up the street from here."

"We never go in the front path," Sam and Jo-Jo said together.

"Why not?" Emily asked.

"I don't remember. Maybe too many cameras there or something. We must have had a reason. We could go in from the other end of the farm though," suggested Jo-Jo.

"But that would mean going by the old house and maybe running into the parent," Sam objected. "Are you ready to risk that?"

"We can slip through the yard without her seeing us and go over the fence and down the path next door into the farm. But even if she did see us, if she's even still alive, it's been years, she probably doesn't remember why she kicked us out. Plus, we're all better now. We're good, right? How could she object? Maybe she'd even let us stay." Jo-Jo reasoned.

"Okay. Okay. Okay. I hear your sarcasm, Jo-Jo. But you might be right. Little Em, can you take us around the block and drop us off. Here." Sam touched a house in the satellite view map. It was on the other side of a several-acre area labelled on the map as *Rancho del Fuerte* and also as *Sergey's Farm Fresh Organics*.

"I didn't know there were any farms around here. Right in the middle of so many houses?" Emily said. "I thought the only farms left in the county were industrial hydroponic buildings."

"The map says it's still here. Maybe we can introduce you to Sergey and show you the farm, if he lets us stay," Sam offered.

"But we've tied you up for hours. You must want to get back with your school friends or go home. We shouldn't keep you any longer. We'll be okay if you drop us off anywhere around here," Jo-Jo apologized.

"It looks like the Abitat is going into the Village to charge after all," said Emily. "My Abbie must have arranged with one of the other Abitats to move aside for us. You can get out here or we can go to that house after we charge."

Chapter 8

Night

8:00 PM, Honus and Jose at the House

Honus felt a tug at his sleeve and peeked out from his goggles. Jose said to him, "Doesn't seem to show much from Javier's point of view."

"You could try some more. I'll find something to do," Honus suggested.

"Not now. Maybe I'll try more later," said Jose.

Honus had been trying to privately replay Orlov's view of the flight to Mars in QZ9301, while Jose tried to privately replay some scenes from Javier's point of view. Honus hadn't gotten far into the weightless scene between Orlov and Lacy before Jose interrupted him. Earlier the history world game replay had stopped when Billy Jay went to bed, and Honus didn't want to try answering any more challenges to extend it.

"What do you think about this history world?" asked Honus.

"That was pretty cool, but those characters didn't look exactly like us. Game AI-generated appearances, I suppose. It kind of matches some of what I remember from those days, and it showed some things I didn't remember," Jose summarized and then asked, "No more about Mara after she leaves the coffee shop?"

"I tried switching focus back to her, but it doesn't seem to give her perspective as an option after that," Honus lamented.

"I wonder why it stops there. Can you keep it going at least in summary mode and play what else what happened the next few days and months?" Jose asked.

"There might be more after solving more challenges," said Honus.

"Did Lae C go home that night or spend the night in the Abitat?" Jose asked.

"As I recall she was there the next morning, but in fresh clothes, so she must have gone home and come back," Honus answered.

"I remember she didn't ask me for rides much after you started letting her borrow the Abitat. The history world doesn't show a lot from Lae C's point of view, so you really think she wrote it?" asked Jose.

"I don't know who made this. Maybe it was Gretchen, like you said. I don't remember Gretchen or Lae C ever saying they made it, but Lae C was into writing, and she could have had access to that kind of information with my dad's help, after she got his brain working again. They spent a lot of time together in the months after my mom disappeared. What else would they be doing?"

"I can think of some things."

"Shut up."

"You could ask her if she wrote it."

"I haven't talked to her in years. Since way before the Reset. How about you?"

"Sometimes. We don't talk much lately, but we do have some connections."

"Maybe you can ask her."

"I suppose I can. But I'd be surprised if she created it. I spent a lot of time back then with your dad too. He liked sharing everything he remembered. He showed me a lot about the design of Abitats and their software. He didn't mention making any story worlds with or without Lae C. But your dad helped invent the whole game. Maybe he did that history world by himself."

"Maybe. He could do it; I suppose. If we can find him, we can ask him, but he probably won't answer. Just like he won't say much about my mom, or why we were in hiding. He's always claimed to have big gaps in his memory. He said he hardly remembers my mom at all and doesn't know where she went or if she is still alive."

"Yeah. He must know more than he's telling. I'll bet he knows how to open that safe. Did he ever get it open?"

"No. Not as far as I know."

"By now you must have come to some conclusions yourself about where she went or what happened to her? This story world seemed to hint she went away on purpose."

"That's what you got from it?"

"She said to go to Plan B. You don't think so?" said Jose.

"She said to drive her home," said Honus.

"I'm just saying, Plan B?" said Jose.

Honus shook his head and looked down, then looked up and said, "Let's agree to disagree about that. I don't want to talk about my mom right now."

"Okay. Okay. What do you want to talk about?" Jose asked.

Honus looked at Jose and asked, "Well. I guess there is the reason I asked to meet with you. Do you think we can come to some kind of deal to let me finish my local development project?"

"All business, huh? Okay. Let me think about it." He paused. "I really don't mind you being successful. It's just a matter of how it affects people." He paused. "You really need the block with the live-work buildings?"

"Can't finish the project without that."

"Okay. Well, I imagine if the project could include something for current residents, even squatters, like alternative low rent or free housing and business space not too far away, and maybe an animal sanctuary and some free camping spots. Something like that might help it get a better reception from whoever needs to approve the holdout land sales."

"Sounds interesting, a challenge, but doable. I was hoping you'd be open to ideas. Maybe build a branch off of game world PW3709 with a version of the development that includes those details."

"Is that how you do development proposals now? World branches? Like I said, I'm not into making game worlds or even game world branches, and I'm not a real estate designer, so I won't do that. The only reason I might let it go is so that I don't have to deal with real estate. Best I can do is write up a description on a chat on PW3709 of some things I think it would take to make it work. Even that might take me a few days, 'cause I might need to talk with some of the people affected first. Then you can build your own world branch proposal that I can share with the people affected and see if we can get agreement."

"Don't take too long writing up your demands. I may seem like the boss, but I can't hold my project managers back forever. They want to get aggressive. One of them might take initiative and then who knows what will happen."

"Threats are not a good look for you."

"I know. I know. I can hold them off a week. Next week is a short week with the holiday on Monday. I'll have a link for you to the current design plans for that area on PW3709 by tomorrow. If you can't build a world branch, then can you get me your requirements description by next Friday? Message me on PW3709 when you've got it written up."

"I should be able to get you something by then, but I don't like being pressured. I need to head home now. I've got work in the morning. Saturday shift on a holiday weekend. Double pay."

"Got to act like you need the points, I suppose."

Jose stood up and stretched and looked out of a window. "Everyone needs points. Looks like the rain is letting up. You can see the sunset. I should get going before it gets heavy again and before it gets dark."

"I should probably head back to my place too. Want a ride? My Abitat can drop you off near where I saw you this morning, I assume you live near there. It's not far out of my way," Honus offered.

"No thanks. As I think you know I avoid using Abitats," Jose replied. "I can use public transportation or walk if I have to."

"I still don't understand why you avoid Abitats. It seems so inconvenient, but I guess we all have our phobias."

"That may be true."

"I have an idea. If the rain has let up, let's walk through the farm. It's not too dark yet. If you need a place to relocate maybe we can set you up with a tiny house in there. If Sergey doesn't object."

"I don't know. It's a nice spot, but it would be too far from my work."

"You really need to keep that job, do you?"

"I do want to stay close to where I'm at."

"Well, let's walk through the farm anyway. Maybe we'll run into Sergey so you can say hi. And it's a shortcut. If you go out the driveway at the other end near the Abitat Village, you'll be that much closer to town."

"Okay."

8:05 PM, Emily Outside Camilla's

Jo-Jo didn't want to climb on the roof of someone else's Abitat to get over the wall, even though Sam claimed no one would notice. They decided to go around the block to the house after charging, and since they were there, they decided to try visiting their mom.

Emily waited in the street, looking out the open Abitat door as Sam and Jo-Jo walked up to the front door of the house. She was curious what would happen when their mom saw them. But after some back and forth that looked like they were arguing about who should ring the doorbell, they seemed to change their minds and Jo-Jo hurried around to the side gate and into the back yard, followed closely by Sam.

Now Emily wasn't sure whether to head home to her mom's house or back to *The Theme Park*. Her Abitat was waiting while she figured out which direction she wanted to go. She could probably get back to *The Theme Park* in about half an hour. It should be open late tonight, and Jeremy and Chandra would probably still be there for at least a couple hours. She could message them to be sure, and plan where to meet. Pictures they shared of the rides they had gone on looked like they were having a really good time together. She wasn't sure she wanted to bother them.

If she headed home now, she would probably get home before her mom who often worked later than this. Her stepdad would probably be there with the baby. Her stepdad was nice enough, and she liked seeing the baby, but she'd rather spend the time with her friends. And the baby would probably be asleep by now. Probably best to go to *The Theme Park*. If Jeremy and Chandra were busy she could probably find some other classmates to hang out with.

Before closing the door, she looked again at the house and the street. Something was bothering her. There was an Abitat docked at the house and a couple more in the street nearby. She wasn't sure why, but they looked familiar. She knew most Abitats looked alike. Then she noticed that one in the street had PSA stickers and extra lights like her stepdad's. And the other two had *Support the PSA* stickers. Could her mom and stepdad and baby Alex be here?

She hadn't checked for messages from her mom since just after school when she sent one saying she was going to *The Theme Park*. When she checked she saw that her mom had not responded to her message. That was unusual. She checked the address she was at and realized that this was where the babysitter Mrs. Muller lived. Mrs. Muller must be Sam and Jo-Jo's mom. That was almost funny. Maybe those other Abitats did belong to her family.

But baby Alex should have gone home hours ago. Why would Alex's Abitat still be here and why would her mom and stepdad be here too at this hour? Maybe something was wrong with the baby? She had a visceral fear reaction that made it hard to breathe. Suppressed thoughts of losing a family member when she was little bubbled under her consciousness keeping her from being able to fill her lungs as she gasped tiny gasps over and over.

She did tai chi and martial arts centering gestures and gradually was able to do calming breaths before she stepped out of the Abitat and ran to the front door.

She rang the bell, expecting that these were someone else's Abitats here and she would need to apologize and explain why she was bothering Mrs. Muller at this hour.

8:10 PM, Honus and Jose Walk Through the Farm

After locking up the house and talking to his wristband to tell his Abitat to meet him at the other side of the farm, Honus led Jose out the back door and down the path, through the hidden gate between the properties. In the farm they walked around the large barn and paused in the shadows at the locked door that led to the workshop and office space inside. Honus was going to unlock the door to see if Sergey was inside, but Jose tapped his shoulder and pointed downhill towards the farmhouse where Sergey lived. Lights were on and they could see shadows of people moving inside. Before they continued towards the farmhouse, they were surprised by two other people coming the way they came from the hidden gate. Honus and Jose stayed in the shadows against the barn and watched and listened as the two walked past them and towards Sergey's house., talking to one another.

"I think we should have rung the bell," Sam insisted.

"Best to stay away from her. And it looked like she had company. Why upset her when she has company?" Jo-Jo asked.

"Maybe we can go back tomorrow," Sam suggested.

"What if Sergey won't let us stay?" Jo-Jo asked.

"He always did before," said Sam.

"But it looks like he has company too. Are you sure you want to bother Sergey when he has company?" Jo-Jo said.

"Maybe you're right. Maybe we should just go straight to the little barn for the night. Sergey won't mind," Sam pointed.

They changed direction slightly to the left and kept walking towards and entered a small building set among trees of a small orchard. Just then the door of the farmhouse opened and out stepped a clean-shaven, long-haired man with a backpack. He picked up a heavy box from the ground outside the farmhouse and started walking towards the same small building. Looking back, he said, "Thanks Sergey. Thanks for the food and for letting me stay tonight."

"Don't mention it. It is nice to see you again. I didn't recognize you, all cleaned up." Sergey went back into the house.

The door of the little barn opened, and Sam came back out. The man walking from Sergey's house called out, "Hey, Sam! Is that you?"

8:15 PM, Emily at Camilla's

"Did you ask Emily to pick up Alex?" Elsie asked Andre, quietly. "I know we talked about it, but I didn't ask her. Did you?"

"I thought you must have. I wonder why she's here," Andre responded.

"Her message said she was going to *The Theme Park*," Elsie added.

Camilla and Emily returned to the living room with Emily holding Alex who was smiling at her. Camilla spoke up, "Look who woke up to see her big sister. I hope you don't mind us getting her up again."

"We just got them settled. Well, I guess it's okay. It's fine," Elsie said.

"Alex does look sleepy. I think they'll go back to sleep soon," Emily said while looking into Alex's eyes.

"We were quiet when we peeked in, but as soon as Emily leaned in close those big eyes opened wide and, that smile!" Camilla explained. She felt a vibration and looked at her wristband and said, "Oh. The lasagna should be ready. I need to go check it. There should be enough for you too, Emily. You're staying." She left the room.

"So, Emily, I thought you were going to *The Theme Park* with your friends tonight. What brings you here instead?" Elsie asked.

"That's a little bit complicated. Why are you two and Alex here at this hour? Isn't it late to be picking up Alex?" Emily inquired.

Andre explained quietly that Mrs. Muller's granddaughter, who works with Elsie, was missing in the mountains today so they were here to see if they could help. Andre said he was in contact with Public Safety people in the area and they didn't know much yet.

Camilla returned and said, "It needs just a little more time."

Emily confirmed with Mrs. Muller that she had two grown kids, Sam and Jo-Jo, or Samuel and Josephine. Emily explained that she met them a few years ago near the creek by her dad's place when she was collecting samples for a biology class. Jo-Jo was collecting trash and plant parts for art projects and Sam was collecting items he could recycle. They ran into each other from time to time on the trail near that creek when she was going to or coming home from school. They were always friendly. It seemed like they were living outdoors in the creek bed. A couple years ago they got Abitats and moved away. She hadn't seen them since then until today when she ran into them at *The Theme Park.* They had a problem with their Abitat after misplacing their wristbands, so she gave them a ride here. They were going to knock on the door, but apparently decided not to, and went into the back yard.

Andre's ears perked up with the mention of missing wristbands and problems with an Abitat. He wondered if they had some connection with the Abitat that was damaged at the construction site not far from *The Theme Park.*

Emily continued explaining that she hadn't realized this was Alex's babysitter's house until she recognized the Abitats out front with PSA stickers.

Camilla went into the back yard, but Sam and Jo-Jo were not there. Emily mentioned that they probably went to the farm behind their house. They said they had stayed there sometimes before. Camilla called out to them over the back fence.

8:20 PM, Tristan at the Ranch House

Tristan was in the backyard of the old house. Hearing a commotion from the neighbor's backyard he walked over to the fence to see what was going on.

Another Abitat had been in the garage portal when he arrived. He wanted to see who else was there. Very few people were allowed to use the home docking portal: Besides himself, it should allow only Sergey, Billy Jay, and Billy Jay's friends, Lae C and Javier, but no one else he could think of. Maybe Mara too. After the other Abitat moved out of the way and his docked, he looked through the house and yard rather than going straight to the neighbor's house to talk to Elsie and support Camilla. He didn't find anyone in the house or yard, so he focused on the sounds next door.

"Is that you, Camilla?" Tristan asked through the fence.

"I recognize that voice. Perry? I haven't seen or heard from you or Mara for years. I thought you moved away."

"I guess we did, sort of. Sorry I haven't stopped by to say hi. I hear there is some concern today about your Isabella?" Tristan said.

"Elsie and Andre here say Isabella will be fine," Camilla said.

"Most likely," Andre clarified. "Most likely she will be fine."

"My Sam and Jo-Jo came back today too," Camilla added.

"Really? It's good to have the support of family," said Tristan. "Have they been away long?"

"Much too long. I hardly remember why they went away."

"How are they?"

"I don't know. I haven't actually seen them yet, but Elsie's Emily here says they were just here. I think they may have gone over the fence into the farm place behind us. We were calling to them to ask them to come back. Sam! Jo-Jo! Please come back!"

"Oh? I'll see if I can find them and ask them to come back to your house. I'll be right back." Tristan walked quickly down the pathway into the farm and around the large barn looking for them.

8:25 PM, Honus, Jose, Sergey, et al.

Honus and Jose were standing at the front door of Sergey's house. They had waited for the others to disappear into the shed before coming out of the shadows and crossing the yard to Sergey's house. Sergey welcomed them at the door and said how surprised he was to see so many people he hadn't seen in years. He invited them in, but they said they were just passing through and didn't want to take much of his time. They just wanted to say hello. He offered to make them something to eat, but they declined. They heard a commotion in the distance up the hill behind the large barn, possibly from the ranch house, like someone was calling out, looking for someone.

After listening more closely, they decided the noise was not from the ranch house but from a neighboring house, so they decided to ignore it and continued walking in the dark down the narrow asphalt driveway that ran through the farm towards the street below.

A voice called out behind them. "Sam and Jo-Jo? Is that you?"

The voice was too familiar to ignore. They turned around and saw a figure coming out of the shadows around the barn. "Dad?" asked Honus as he walked quickly back towards the voice. Jose stayed back to let Honus meet with his dad.

"Billy Jay?" asked Tristan.

"Once upon a time," said Honus.

A man with a big grey afro came out of the shed and asked, "Who's looking for Sam and Jo-Jo?"

"Are they here? Their mom wants to see them," Tristan replied.

Jose stood back in the shadows, watching and listening. The man with the big hair looked familiar, like someone he met once or someone famous but not someone he knew well personally.

8:30 PM, Brock, Sam & Jo-Jo in the Farm

After some encouraging from Brock, Sam and Jo-Jo came out of the shed and Tristan tried to convince them to go see their mom. They said they didn't want to bother her while she had company. Tristan said it was just Elsie and Andre and their daughter Emily picking up baby Alex who Camilla had been babysitting.

Brock said he needed to go back into the shed to check on his drying books. He didn't want to intrude on a family reunion and wanted to be ready if Doug showed up. He wanted a chance to convince him to talk with Sam and Jo-Jo now that they were without an Abitat.

"Mr. Lee?" Jo-Jo asked. "You look different."

"I'm Tristan," Tristan interrupted."

"Mr. Tristan?"

"Just Tristan is fine."

"Tristan? Okay. You sound so much like Mr. Lee, but my memory is shit. Do you really think she wants to see us."

"Yes. Yes. I really think so."

"Well. Okay. Let's do this. By the way, if that really is you, it's nice to see you again, Mr. Lee. It's been a long time," Jo-Jo said. Then turning around to look back at Honus and Jose. "You too, Billy Jay. Do you still go by Billy Jay?"

"Not anymore, but for today, for you, Billy Jay is fine. It's nice to see you again too, Jo and Sam."

"And you look kind of familiar," Jo-Jo continued, looking at Jose's embroidered name on his overalls. "Jose, is it?"

"Yes. I think we met a few times years ago here in Sergey's farm when I was visiting the Lee's," Jose replied.

"You were the smarty-pants kid who was always explaining things to people!" Sam cut in. "I thought you were called Dr. Xavier or something."

"Something like that. Yeah. Well, a lot has changed. Some people have taken new names or looks since then."

"And some have forgotten a lot. But we're still just Sam and Jo-Jo," said Sam.

"But I guess we've changed too," added Jo-Jo.

"Sure, we've all changed, but do you think the parent has really changed enough to let us come back," Sam asked.

"We will see," said Jo-Jo.

Tristan encouraged Honus and Jose to follow, since it was a kind of reunion for them as well, and there was something maybe they could help him with. They followed as far as the Ranch house but decided not to go next door to Camilla's. Jose said it would be awkward and Honus didn't want to be around so many people.

Tristan said, "I think you both might be able to help."

"Help with what?" Honus asked.

8:35 PM, Watching a Livestream

"If you won't come with me, then just watch this for a few minutes" Tristan said as he made a link from his wristband to a live stream game world that displayed on the wall in Billy Jay's room. It showed a 3D view of characters resembling Jose, Honus, and Tristan in a space similar to Billy Jay's room. "Just watch. You'll see. You'll figure out something to do." He headed back to Camilla's while the live stream showed a 3-D view of his surroundings along the way. "Just watch," he said again just before he caught up with Sam and Jo-Jo and went inside at Camilla's.

W1, Livestream, 8:40 PM, Muller Residence

Andre came back in just after Tristan, Sam, and Jo-Jo. Sam and Jo-Jo were accepting appetizers from their mom but not saying much. Andre said, "I got Alex back to sleep, and I contacted the forest rangers for the area where Bella was hiking."

"Dinner can be ready whenever you want to eat," Camilla said. "There should be plenty. I'm keeping things warm so no rush."

Andre explained what he had learned, "The ranger said they would try to get a search drone flying as soon as the weather eased up. That should also reestablish a comm link to anyone in that part of the mountains. They thought it might be tomorrow morning before the storm let up enough though."

"Who are they searching for?" asked Sam.

"Bella. Bella is missing," answered Elsie, looking at Jo-Jo and Camilla.

…

"Bella is missing?" Honus repeated to Jose.

Jose said, "Who's Bella?"

"A neighbor friend," said Honus.

…

"Our Bella? What happened?" asked Jo-Jo.

"She's none of your concern," Camilla responded. "Enjoy your appetizers."

"The parent is still the parent," whispered Sam to Jo-Jo. "But we get snacks, at least."

Jo-Jo asked what had happened and got most of the story from Elsie and Andre. Maybe Bella was fine, but no one had been able to reach her since this morning. Tristan displayed a map on Camilla's living room video display showing the coordinates of the spot where Bella was when he last talked to her this morning. Camilla was going back and forth to the kitchen and the dining room. When Camilla was out of the room Tristan added what he had learned about seismic indications of possible rock falls coinciding with the cutoff of comm signals from the area at 4:35.

Everyone was quiet for a minute. Camilla came back in with another snack tray this time with cheese and crackers and observed the silence while she set the tray on a coffee table before going back out of the room.

…

Honus said to Jose, "Bella was a neighbor friend of mine when I was a kid, and I guess she works with my dad now. My dad asked us to help if we can. I can probably send in some people to search. Anything you can do?"

"As a favor to your dad and to you I can probably do something," Jose answered. "Can I use your mom's computer?" He left the room and

Honus minimized the view of Camilla's while he made some contacts of his own. When Jose returned Honus had already re-engaged with the view constructed from sensors in Tristan's wrist band.

W1, Livestream, 9:00 PM, Muller Residence

Andre was messaging with his ranger contact and looking at a map of the mountain area on a tablet.

"It seems like communication is being restored right now to the mountain area in question. Some Infinite Closet delivery drones have flown into the area carrying emergency supplies and starting to restore a communications grid to the area." He updated the map on living room wall display. It showed terrain with locations of drones and circles of communication that each provided. The network was spreading across the terrain. "They have already reestablished a mesh network across some of the areas that were cut off. We should be able to put a call through to Bella's tablet now if she's in that area."

Elsie spoke into her wristband. "Call Bella."

Everyone waited.

"Contact unavailable."

"Again. Call Bella."

"Bella is not currently reachable.'

"Maybe try again in a little while? If more drones are on the way?" Elsie thought out loud and looked at Tristan who shrugged and pointed at Andre's map display. Additional drones appeared, moving into the area. Elsie spoke again to her wristband, "Keep trying and let me know if you get through."

"Acknowledged."

Andre added, "The ranger lady also said that some industrial construction crane flyers are on their way from a big resort project near Owens Lake. They're heavy-duty rigs that can fly in bad weather and do heavy lifting. They've got search crews ready and they're willing to fly over the pass as soon as they get there. But the rangers don't want anyone else getting stuck and not sure if they can allow equipment that size into the wilderness area."

Tristan looked at his wristband and said, "I wonder who authorized all those delivery drones to fly in this weather and the heavy construction equipment and search crews to be brought in? The situation must have got the attention of some delivery and construction bigwigs somewhere."

"I wish the call would go through," Jo-Jo said.

"Give it some time. That's a rough area with a lot of peaks and narrow valleys. Do you remember when we did MinQuests in that area?" Sam asked.

"I don't remember," Jo-Jo replied. "That was a long time ago."

Sam noticed his mom returning to the room and responded, "Yeah. I'm remembering some of it. I think you went one time, but Doug-las and I spent weeks up there guiding MinQuests."

Camilla looked down and shook her head slightly at the mention of Douglas.

Sam continued, "Not in snowy weather, maybe…but enough to know there are a lot of narrow areas where communications would be blocked to any of those drones. Doug-las found a lot of remote corners for people who wanted to be alone. If she is in one of those corners, a drone would have to be really close to make a comm connection. When the weather lightens up, she can climb a rise for a better comm view, and we should be able to get through to her."

Camilla waited for Sam to finish his reassuring explanation and then said, "Okay. We will hear from Elsie's Abbie if she is able to get through to Isabella. We will hear from Andre's ranger friend if a search party is able to get in there. Let's pray she wasn't hurt in a rock fall, but there's nothing else we can do for her right now. Meanwhile dinner is not going to get any better if we wait. Let's go sit down and eat and Sam and Jo-Jo can tell us all more about where they've been all these years and what kind of Abitat trouble they had today. Please." She indicated the way to the dining room, and everyone shrugged and followed.

Jo-Jo said quietly on the side to Sam as they followed the group "She still hears everything. You think she's not listening or she's out of earshot, but the parent still hears everything."

"Spooky. Isn't it. She's probably been listening to us the last 20 years even when we were in other states," whispered Sam.

"Yeah. Maybe she can tell us the things we forgot," said Jo-Jo.

"I heard that, you two," commented Camilla from the dining room. "Sit down and eat."

…

9:15 PM, After Dinner at Camilla's

During dinner no alerts came in from Elsie's Abbie's repeated calls to Bella. Andre did not receive any new messages from the ranger's office. Everyone avoided talking more about the situation in the mountains while they ate. Elsie asked about how Sam and Jo-Jo misplaced their wristbands at *The Theme Park*, and they were reluctant to go into details, especially in front of a public safety guy.

"Sometimes our wristbands can be uncomfortable. We took them off and set them down for a little while, and when we went back to pick them up, they weren't there anymore," Jo-Jo explained.

Andre said *The Theme Park* has a really good lost and found. Sam just shrugged like they tried that, and it didn't work. Andre offered to check with *The Theme Park* and the PSA to see if wristbands got turned in, but how would he reach them? They said they weren't sure without their Abitat or wristbands. Maybe through their mom.

Andre considered mentioning the investigation about an Abitat with two wristbands that was damaged in a possible drug deal and murder but instead decided to avoid the subject for now. He figured he should check back with work first to see the latest about that investigation but wanted to be able to find them if they were suspects. He didn't want to scare them off. He asked where they have been living recently. Kansas, they said. This was supposed to be a little vacation trip, and they were planning to go back in a week or two. He excused himself from the table to call work to see if he should detain them for questioning.

Picking up on the thread of small talk, Tristan asked Elsie if she and her family lived near here.

9:19 PM, At the Ranch House

"Is that Lacy?" Honus asked. "She's married and has kids?"

"I think she goes by Elsie now," said Jose.

<table>
<tr><td>W1, Livestream, 9:19 PM, Muller Residence</td></tr>
</table>

Andre answered just before he left the room, "It's in an Abitat-harmonious residential community outside the county. Maybe 30 miles from here. Less than an hour most days. It has bedroom docking ports for all four family Abitats and a very nice professional kitchen for Elsie, but she doesn't get much chance to use it. No pool. Most of the homes there have pools, but Elsie didn't want one, what with the baby and all. So, no pool."

Camilla looked long at Tristan. "You sound just like my old neighbor friend, Perry, but you look different. You say your name is Tristan, and you work for Elsie with my Isabella?"

"Right. I had a work call with Bella this morning."

As dinner wrapped up Camilla asked Sam and Jo-Jo if they had a place to stay or if they wanted to spend the night.

"We've got a place we can stay tonight near here, with a friend, Brock," Jo-Jo explained. "We used to camp with him and Doug, sometimes before we moved to Kansas."

Elsie tried to hide surprise at the mention of the name Brock.

...

Jose wondered if the big-haired guy in the farm was Brock.

...

Elsie asked, "Brock? That wouldn't be Barack Jackson?"

Jo-Jo replied, "I don't know his last name. We just know him as Brock. Sam?"

"No last names," Sam replied.

Camilla said, "Sam, you had college friends named Barack Jackson and Douglas Zynn. Are these the same boys?"

Sam replied, "College? Did I go to college? I don't remember much from those days. Did I know someone named Barack Jackson? Maybe. That sounds possible. That was a long time ago. The guy I've known in recent years was just Brock."

Camilla corrected herself, "I guess it can't be the same person. Supervisor Barack Jackson, his family, and half their neighborhood died in the big gas line explosion and fire a few years ago."

Elsie looked at Emily.

...

Jose caught the look and was also concerned to see how Emily reacted. Both observed that Emily didn't seem phased.

...

Camilla said, "Sam, your college friend Barack was a County Supervisor when he died in that explosion."

Sam said, "This Brock is alive, so it must be a different guy. But we didn't talk about old times or where he came from before he started hanging out with Doug. That time is a blur. We were all self-medicating. I honestly have almost no memory of my college days, but now that you mention it, I guess it's possible Doug is the same guy as college Douglas. More of my memories started coming back in the last year after I moved away and started following some of my Abbie's health advice, but it is still very fuzzy."

"Excuse me," Camilla interrupted. "You've been hanging out with the same Douglas as before I kicked you two out? Isabella's dad, Douglas Zynn?"

Jo-Jo answered, "We're not sure if he's the same person, and even if he is, I never said Douglas was her dad." She paused, as if surprised to remember never saying that. She continued, "But anyway, we are on bad terms with Doug now. Ever since we got Abitats and moved away a couple years ago, I guess. He wouldn't talk with us today. He and Brock really don't like Abitats. But I know we did hang out with people called Doug and Brock for a few years before we got Abitats. Like Sam said, we were self-medicating and might not have remembered exactly who they were or even who we were back then."

Emily broke in, "Doug and Brock camp out sometimes under a roadway in a creek near Dad's place. I see them sometimes when I take the creek trail on my way to school. It's the same creek where I first met Sam and Jo-Jo. Doug keeps mostly to himself, other than gathering edible plants and acting protective around Brock. Brock is quiet, except when he talks about books. He has a lot of books. Hundreds of books, he says. Real paper pages and all. He lends books to me sometimes. I've got one in my backpack that I need to give back to him."

"I wish you'd told me about this before. How well do you know this Brock and Doug?" Elsie asked. "Is it safe to be around them?"

...

Watching Elsie in the livestream world Jose felt like she was looking straight at him. Did she know he was watching this? She had a wordless expression conveying volumes. *How can you let her do things like this? Maybe Emily shouldn't stay with you anymore? Brock? Seriously? Is Brock really alive?*

...

Emily continued, "Don't worry. They're harmless. I don't go into their camp. I just see them sometimes on the trail that runs along the creek. Brock sometimes brings out a book. They'd never try to hurt me, if anything, they'd protect me, and I'm capable of protecting myself." She demonstrated some martial arts moves.

"We will talk more about this later," Elsie said.

Emily shrugged as if to say, if you want.

...

Jose said to himself, "Yes, we will."

Honus muted the live stream game world and said, "What?"

"Nevermind," said Jose, but he explained that he needed to head home soon because he had to work tomorrow. Honus offered a ride, but Jose said he preferred to walk. They left Tristan's livestream game world running muted on the display on the bedroom wall when they left the room and headed out the back way to go through the farm again.

9:35 PM, Andre outside Camilla's

Andre first checked again on Alex, who was sleeping, before going outside and into his own Abitat to check in with work. He bought up a display of the latest PSA status on the case of the bloody Abitat and the drugs at the construction site.

Lab results showed a likelihood of NeverMore in the green mud he and rat boy had collected at the construction site, but it was highly diluted by the rain. Other samples he and his colleague had collected from the site were negative for drugs and blood.

The owner of the Abitat was still being determined. The Abbie was claiming that the owner/inabitant had remained anonymous as a condition of accepting a HomeLessNoMore Abitat. They expected to narrow down the possible owners based on when the Abitat was put into service and records of homeless people who applied for Abitats at that time. That seemed to raise the likelihood that it was Sam and Jo-Jo's Abitat. Maybe he could ask them some questions about how they got their Abitat.

Lab work from the Abitat showed no NeverMind or NeverMore, but some degraded traces of Forgetdibles and alcohol, and other assorted minor drugs, like some had been spilled in the Abitat months before. The shredded contents of the Abitat contained a blend of various kinds of DNA from humans, animals, and plants, as well as plenty of nonorganic materials. The materials were so thoroughly shredded and blended that it was difficult to distinguish what was what. There were bits of kelp and various grasses. Some small bone chunks were isolated, but the identifiable ones were dried coyote, roadrunner, lizard, and squirrel bones. No confirmed human bones. A number of human toenails, hairs, and skin cells were found. The lab was trying to get the okay to do a DNA match on the human cells, but that was unlikely. Based on what he could see in the report, Andre concluded that it was unlikely a murder scene, although the official analysis was still incomplete.

He also checked with the rangers near the mountains and didn't get much new information from them.

9:45 PM, All Leaving Camilla's

Camilla said it was time for her to turn in. At 77 she didn't like staying up late anymore. She was tired and a little confused. Everyone would have to leave, except Sam and Jo-Jo. She was happy to finally meet Elsie's other child Emily, and Bella's colleague Tristan. She was confused about Tristan. She still thought Tristan sounded like her old neighbor Perry who she thought she had talked to earlier through the fence. Was that Tristan before or was Perry really next door? No one clarified the confusion for her. All agreed to be available for Camilla to contact during the night if she wanted to talk about anything.

Everyone said their good-bye's and nice-to-meet-you's. Andre told Sam and Jo-Jo that he would see if he could track down what happened to their wristbands and Abitat and get info back to their mom.

In the front yard, as they left, Andre, Tristan, and Elsie all agreed to share with each other anything they learned about Bella's situation. Tristan mentioned to Elsie on the side that he would clue in Honus and

Jose. Andre, Elsie, Alex, and Emily left, each in their own individual Abitats, but they started out staying close to one another along the way.

Emily took the first shift watching Alex from her own Abitat, but also quietly checking in with Chandra and Jeremy, who were still at *The Theme Park*, which would be closing in about an hour. She decided to keep heading towards home and join them at *The Theme Park* again tomorrow morning. Not enough time to meet up with them there tonight.

Tristan went back next door to talk to Honus and Jose but found that they were no longer watching the livestream and had already left. He went into Mara's old office and connected with Elsie and Andre in their Abitats. He also sent a message to Honus to contact him about a family matter. He had forgotten to tell him about the relatives who showed up today at the Machine Shop.

Andre shared with Elsie and Tristan what he had learned from the PSA crime report. Sam and Jo-Jo might be involved in something serious, but he would try to keep Emily out of it. Tristan recorded the conversation for Honus and Jose to view later. Andre checked again with his contacts in the mountains and got no good news. Still no signals from Bella. The storm was still dumping snow at high elevations.

Meanwhile, Honus and Jose walked through the farm. They met Honus' Abitat near the driveway at the other end. Jose again turned down the offer for a ride, even though Honus explained his Abitat was able to operate independently of the hive mesh network with a completely self-contained Abbie.

Jose walked on, watching as Honus's Abitat rolled away and turned a corner out of view. He thought about his options for the trip home. If he walked all the way it would probably take a couple of hours, maybe more if it started to rain again, which it looked like it could at any time. A carousel bus would be a safe, untrackable option, but he was unlikely to be able to flag one down while he was in residential neighborhoods. It would be another mile or two to a busy street and even then pretty iffy about catching one cruising by. He could always use his wristband to engage a BubbleCar for the ride back to his own neighborhood. That might be trackable, but maybe he was being too paranoid. He really needed to get home and set up a secure connection to talk with Elsie about the Brock situation. He realized he should have accepted Honus's offer of a ride but decided he wouldn't call him back. He decided to call for a BubbleCar. In less than a minute one appeared, and he got in sat down and said, "Home. And Hurry." His wristband gave the BubbleCar the information on how to get to an address in his neighborhood a couple blocks from home. He had to hold on to his seat's armrests as the car moved quickly around a turn and toward the larger roadway at the edge of the residential neighborhood.

Sam and Jo-Jo initially planned to stay at Camilla's for the night, but after Camilla went to her bedroom, they noticed that their own old bedrooms had been turned into a 3D holographic game room and a daycare nursery and toy room. Isabella's old room still had a bed, but Jo-Jo wouldn't go into it and wouldn't let Sam either.

They tried out the game room but quickly discovered it required either Camilla's or Isabella's image and voice to activate it. To stay they would need to get blankets from a closet and sleep on couches or the floor. They decided to go back to the barn and talk more with Brock. They took some of the leftovers from the refrigerator in case Brock was hungry and some extra for a late-night snack.

10:15 PM, Brock in the Barn

Brock sat alone in the barn on one of four cots he had pulled out of the storage loft. He had prepared cots for Sam, Jo-Jo, and Doug. He figured Sam and Jo-Jo would probably come back here after trying to talk with their mom. With most of their campsites under water, he figured Doug might come here too. But for now, he was alone. He looked at rows of wet books he had arranged on the floor to start drying out.

He was considering the things that had happened that day. Sam and Jo-Jo returned from far-away-who-knows-where but had somehow misplaced their Abitat and were talked into going to reconnect with their mom by some older neighbor guy. Would they be coming back here tonight, or would they stay with their mom? Could they help him get an Abitat for himself or would they even be able to find their own again? Would he want one if he could get one? He was pretty sure which house their mom lived at, but he should probably not bother them at their mom's house tonight. He could go there tomorrow to check on them if they stayed there overnight.

Where was Doug? He wasn't at the underpass campsite where they had been staying lately and no sight of him anywhere along the paths between there and here. Most of their other camp sites were also in creek beds and probably washed away by the rainwater, so Brock figured Doug would probably head here. In fact, he was surprised not to see Doug already here when he got here earlier.

He had lost most of his book collection to the rising water. He moved some into the utility tunnel under the roadway. The utility tunnel would probably stay dry. The water was rising fast. He moved what he could to higher ground before carrying some away in one box and his backpack. The books got pretty wet as he carried them up paths and through neighborhoods on the way to Sergey's. He managed to carry them in through the drainage ditch that ran out from the farm, while wading against the flowing water and getting them even more soaked in the process. He didn't know if they would ever dry out properly.

Most troubling to him: Could he trust the visions about the fire and losing Celine and Sandy that he had experienced when he saw the photo at the house where the new Sandy J lived? Was he really Barack Jackson? Was he really responsible for the fire and all those deaths? He could be in so much trouble if people found out. Maybe that's why he's been hiding out with Doug and taking NeverMind. Maybe that's why he was so open to taking NeverMind when he ran into Doug right after the fire even though he had avoided most drugs Douglas had offered back in college. Is that a memory? He needed more NeverMind.

Charly seemed to confirm that a fire really happened, but she didn't know he had caused it. How much could he trust what he remembered today? Coming down from years on Forgetdibles and NeverMind, everything could just be random drug effects on his mind. Even what he thought he heard Charly say. Maybe even the picture. Did he really go to that house today? Which parts might be true? He felt his clean-shaven face and decided that at least some parts were real.

Thinking about losing Celine and Sandy made him very sad and nauseated so maybe they were real. His vision showed them getting into an Abitat as the explosion happened, so maybe they got away? But he felt like they died. Charly said they died. No. None of it is real. His head hurt. His stomach hurt. His heart was racing. He wanted to find Doug and get a good dose of NeverMind to clear all these bad thoughts out of his head. He heard steps outside the door and asked "Doug?"

"I hope not. Just us," said Sam as the door to the shed opened and in came Sam and Jo-Jo. Brock watched them as Jo-Jo set down a covered glass dish in front of him. "Leftovers," she said. And then they each went to a cot and lay down without saying anything more. A minute passed while Brock was trying to decide whether to ask them about how it went with their mom, but then the door opened again and in stepped Doug.

His backpack and clothes were soaked through, but no longer dripping wet as the rain had let up during the last couple of hours.

"You're here! You're alive!" Doug said as he looked at Sam and Jo-Jo sitting on their cots. "I saw two people going in here as I was coming through the orchard. I was hoping that was you." Then he turned to Brock. "Brock? Is that you? What did you do to your face?" Brock rubbed his hand on his clean-shaven face.

Doug didn't sound angry, but just the same, Sam and Jo-Jo quickly stood up and moved away from him towards the back of the shed.

"It's okay. It's okay. I'm just glad to see all of you are okay," Doug said as he set down his pack on the fourth cot and then realizing it was wet, moved it to the floor. "I thought you were all dead."

Sam and Jo-Jo inched back towards their cots. "Are you sure you're okay with us being here?" Sam asked. "We can go."

"I found your stinking, shitty, kill-all-the-homeless, death van by *The Theme Park*. I knew it was yours. All sky blue with your painted mountains, and it had boxes of Jo-Jo's artwork and stuff in it. I thought you had all been murdered in there."

He remembered standing in the Abitat doorway and the images that flooded his mind at that time:

An image of watching Jo-Jo making similar artwork.

In another image: he was lying on his back in a tent looking up at her rocking back and forth on top of him with her mobiles dangling around her.

As more memories or thought images flooded back his anxiety continued to peak, making it harder to focus. He imagined a plane crash and bodies floating in the water. He saw a sailboat taking on water while he was too high to deal with it. He saw himself responsible for harm coming to people he loved.

Now he may have been too late to help Jo-Jo and Sam and maybe Brock too. It was his fault. If only he hadn't chased them away this morning. The guy in the Abitat said something about their wrists and held up what looked like severed hands.

"A guy was in it shredding bodies with a chain saw or something. I thought it was you. He wanted to kill me too, but I got away," Doug related. He recalled the spray of red bits that coated his face and shirt as he waved his knife into the Abitat before he backed away and ran to pick up the drug bundle and climb over the fence and back into the drainage channel.

"Were you moving NeverMind for some drug lord or something? I saw some packages." Doug asked.

"No," said Jo-Jo.

"I told you," Sam said to Jo-Jo. "It must have been drugs."

"Do any of you have some NeverMind? I need some," Brock pleaded.

"Not with me. Maybe tomorrow. Anyway, I figured you picked up Brock, and you were all being chopped up in the van. I got away, so I figured one of you might have got away too so I was going to go into *The Theme Park* to look." He paused to think and then continued, "I put in the code and opened the gate, but I realized I was coated in what I thought was shredded Sam or Brock. That wouldn't make a good impression in the park this time of year. It's still months 'til Halloween. Anyway, I had to go clean up first. I went to another old campsite to wash up and change my shirt and stash stuff in a utility closet there." He remembered stashing the NeverMind package in a dark corner of a utility closet under pumps, valves, and electrical boxes, and then closing its door. He hoped it was sealed well against rising water, and no county workers would need to go in there tonight. "...and by the time I was headed back it was raining hard, and the creeks were filling up with water. No way to get through our back door park entrance under water. I figured it really didn't matter since you were all ground sirloin anyway. I got my pack again and went to some of our campsites to move gear to higher ground and then headed here. It took me a while. I didn't expect to find you."

Doug really seemed to be hyped up about seeing the three of them. Brock noticed stains of red on Doug's forehead and ears, like he had washed his face but missed the edges.

"You still have something on your face. Is that blood?" Brock asked.

Doug wiped at his cheeks which were already clean. And Brock rubbed at his own forehead to indicate a location of the stain. Doug rubbed there and got a smudge of red on his fingers. "Not your blood at least."

"Looks like paint," Jo-Jo interjected. "I had jars of red paint that we picked up near one of the national parks on the way. If the guy was shredding stuff in my Abitat maybe he shredded some of my paint?"

"Paint! I knew it wasn't blood. Inside that van looked kinda like inside some of your tents back in the day, Jo," Doug said. "Lotsa art stuff. What did you have in there?"

"I hope my stuff is okay. It took a lot of time to make and collect all that. I had boxes of finished art I was going to try to sell, and lots of supplies. Cool rocks and bones from the desert, and different kinds of dry grasses and sticks we picked at different stops. Glass and stones and wire and metal bits, and some paint. And we got a sack of kelp, shells, and fish and crab parts from the beach today."

"There was a pink cloud of dust. What was that?" Doug asked.

"No. No. Did someone spill my southern Utah coral pink sand?" Jo-Jo lamented.

10:30 PM, Honus Calls Tristan

Honus saw the message from Tristan about a family matter and hesitated to contact him. He was pretty sure Tristan must have found out something about his mom, and he was very nervous to find out what he had to say. He was afraid it was bad news. He saw that Tristan had recorded a conversation with Andre and Elsie, and he was welcome to play it back. He decided to play that back first before contacting Tristan live. He caught up on what Andre had learned from the police and rangers. After that playback ended, he initiated a video call to Tristan.

"Dad?" Honus asked?

"Yeah?" Tristan replied.

"A family matter? Is it about mom? Did you finally find out what happened to her? She's dead, right?"

"Oh, No. It's not about her. I don't know anything new about her. It's something else."

"Who else is family besides you, me, and mom? Did you have other kids?" Are you getting remarried?"

"Not that I know of and No."

Honus waited and after a few seconds Tristan continued, "It turns out you've got cousins. I had a sister. I guess I still have a sister, and she had a couple of kids who are grown up now."

"Why didn't you tell me about them before? Growing up?"

"I don't know. You know my memory from back then is patchy. I didn't even remember I had a sister until these relatives showed up and talked about her. Then some memories came back. Now I can recall that Carmen, my sister, moved to the Midwest many years ago. I now remember the last time I saw her. We had a big fight. She said she wanted to have nothing more to do with me. She said I was dead to her, and I probably said worse to her. That was before you were born, after my parents died."

"Make sure you record what you remembered," Honus suggested.

"I did. Both in my brain cap reminder loop and in offline notes," Tristan replied. "I shouldn't forget it anytime soon and you'll be able to check those notes at some point if I do."

"This relative showing up triggered you to remember more?" Honus asked.

"Yeah."

"Do you think it was a brain memory or a hive cloud memory?"

"I can't be sure, but it's in both now and it should stay in my hive cloud memory forever."

"This relative triggered memories about your sister. Maybe we can figure out some new triggers to retrieve more memories about Mom. Maybe we can find some more clues about where she may have gone. If you remembered more about her."

"If she suddenly showed up that would probably trigger some memories. I'm not sure what else would help."

"Maybe there are people who knew both of you back then. If you met one of them again."

"There's Sergey but talking with him hasn't triggered any more memories about her. Maybe he knows more than he's said."

"Think about it. Maybe your sister can suggest somebody. Did you know Mom when you fought with your sister?"

"I don't think so. I don't remember how your mom and I met, but I think it was after that."

"Why did you fight with your sister?"

"You knew my parents died in a car crash before you were born, right?"

"Yeah. I think I remember you or mom telling me that when I was little."

"Well. My parents made me the executor of their estate, even though I was just 19. My sister resented it since she was older. She didn't like anything about how I handled their estate, even though I just followed the instructions in their will."

"I've heard families sometimes break up over inheritances."

"That's for sure. There wasn't that much inheritance. Really just some life insurance and furniture and stuff. I let my sister take everything she wanted from their house. My dad had some tools at his machine shop which he left to me. Maybe she didn't like that. Their house sold for just barely what was owed on the mortgage. My dad's machine shop was leased."

"I thought you owned the machine shop all these years."

"I'll have to check on that. I must have bought it at some point, but back then I kept the lease using my part of the life insurance. My sister thought I was lying to her about that."

"Were you?"

"I'm pretty sure I wasn't. Anyway, she was so angry we didn't speak again."

"Is that why we were in hiding all those years. Just to avoid your sister? That seems like a really poor excuse."

"No. No. Hiding was about something else. Something scary. I don't remember all of it, but it wasn't that. I've told you what I've remembered before and I think I'm starting to remember more bits and pieces. It was – is -- for our safety. As I piece enough of it together, I'll share it with you. But being in hiding was maybe another reason why we didn't try to connect up with estranged relatives."

"So, what happened today?" Honus inquired. "What did you learn or remember today?"

"Yeah. I met one of your cousins today and her husband and their twins. They are here on vacation, and they found me at my machine shop in town. Apparently, my sister mentioned the machine shop to them recently. It was my dad's. They checked it out, hoping to find me and I just happened to be there."

"What happens now? Did you tell them about me and mom? Will I meet them?"

"I don't know. I didn't tell them much of anything. I didn't even confirm that I was who they think I am. They gave me their contact info, and I gave them a name in a game world where they can leave me messages. They will be in town for a few more days. Oh. Yeah. Besides being on vacation, they are trying to find a kidney match for my sister."

"Oh. I think I might need my kidneys."

"Don't worry. I won't even let them know about you if you don't want me to."

"What are their names? My aunt and cousins, and all?" Honus asked.

"My sister was, is, Carmen. I should be able to remember the rest from what they said today." Tristan paused for a moment before continuing. "Carmen married someone named Max. They had kids, Gabe and Fanny. Fanny is visiting here with her husband John Tran and their twins, Minh and Max again. Boy and girl. I think they must be around five. She didn't say if Gabe has kids too. They all live near Kansas City. We didn't get into what kind of jobs they have."

"What do they look like?"

"I've got pictures from the security cameras at the machine shop. Here they are." Tristan shared pictures of the twins watching the 3D printer making their toys while their parents looked on from behind.

"Fanny doesn't look much like you or me," Honus observed.

"I don't look much like me anymore. I can see some of my sister in her eyes and mouth. There is a family resemblance."

"If you say so." Honus submitted facial matching to search engines on the AM world one and it brought up pages about Fanny Tran and

John Tran. He wanted to read it over before deciding if he wanted to meet them. He also noticed that his Abitat was getting close to his home at the resort. "This is a lot to absorb. Can we talk about it some more tomorrow? I like to get up early. I've been avoiding work all day. I'll need to do some work before I go to bed tonight. And we still need to figure out what happened to Bella."

"Did you hear all the latest on Bella?"

"I think so. Jose and I watched most of your livestream and I listened to the recording of your call with Elsie and Andre. So, Lae C is Elsie, and you work for her now?"

Tristan shrugged.

Honus continued, "Jose sent lots of drones, and I've sent search teams to the area, but still no contact. Sounds like something happened to her comm gear or it was turned off. Sounds ominous."

"How well did you know Bella? She's around your age."

Honus answered, "She's a few years younger than me. When we were kids, she used to come over the fence into our yard and go down the path into the farm—she was always climbing trees and running around. I'd follow her to make sure she was safe. I wasn't afraid of her like most people. She just seemed like part of home, almost like a little sister. It's been a long time since I last saw her though. Oh. Looks like I'm home now. I'd better disconnect."

"Okay. We can talk again tomorrow," Tristan agreed.

"Oh. I meant to ask you about a history world I found," Honus said before realizing the connection had already dropped.

"Something to talk about tomorrow, I guess."

10:45 PM, Elsie's Family in Abitats Heading Home

Elsie and Andre talked privately after disconnecting from the call with Tristan. Elsie said she still had work she had to do, and Andre agreed to let her work while he took over from Emily watching Alex for the rest of the drive home.

Andre contacted Emily and arranged to take over watching Alex. Their four Abitats were still travelling in close proximity. Andre requested that his Abitat connect up with Alex's. The two Abitats pulled up alongside one another and latched together as they continued down a street. Their doors opened and Andre stepped into Alex's unit. Emily's hologram was visible in Alex's Abitat, watching over Alex and she made a shushing sign to Andre. He nodded and mimicked her finger to the mouth gesture. She nodded back and her hologram disappeared.

In her Abitat Emily checked on Jeremy and Chandra. They were still at *The Theme Park*. Pictures of them on a roller-coaster ride together were visible on Jeremy's shared game view. Emily figured they would be leaving the park soon and she could contact them then and tell them what else had happened tonight. Maybe Chandra could start explaining her ideas for the project. At least they could plan for when to meet tomorrow.

10:50 PM, Tristan at the Ranch House

Tristan was tired and achy. He sat in the chair in Mara's office for a few minutes, turning his head to stretch tight muscles in his neck and back. He was feeling his age. He had stayed up working in the office last night until four in the morning, had worked in the office again all day today since 9, and had been dealing with Bella's disappearance and the surprise appearance of his niece and family since then. He was also trying to make sense of newly emerging memories but was too tired to sort them all out. He should head back to his Abitat to sleep and see if Elsie had assigned him any new work tasks, but he was too tired. Mara's office was connected to her bedroom, and he could see her bed. It was tempting. He stood and drifted to it, and fell onto it, planning to rest for just a minute, but soon he slept.

11:00 PM, Elsie on Her Way Home

Elsie checked on her work. Other attorneys in the firm had taken care of the urgent actions on her cases this evening while she was at Camilla's. She would need to double-check their work, but since it was the start of a holiday weekend, she didn't need to do that tonight. The Son'O'Ra client wanted to know more about the option to avoid paying royalties on the new designs. She would have to get back with them by tomorrow. That was one case that wouldn't be good to put off until after the long weekend. She forwarded their questions to Tristan to draft replies. She thought about Bella's situation and decided there was nothing more she could do on that tonight. She would check with Andre again when they got home to see if he had any updates. Meanwhile the situation with Emily and Brock was an urgent concern. She sent a message to Jose to see if he was available.

11:03 PM, Jose at His Trailer

Jose was back at his trailer. He checked the recordings from the security cameras to see if anything had happened there while he was gone. The only activity was cats, Dr. Magnolia, and some other familiar residents walking through the courtyard. Nothing of concern. He checked to see if Elsie was available to talk and saw her message. He initiated connections through a maze of dozens of game worlds and delivery Abitats until he felt the connection was untraceable and he knocked on her virtual door.

11:05 PM, Elsie and Jose Talk

"Elaborate security tonight? Any particular reason?" Elsie asked as she opened the connection to Jose as a cartoon character in an Anime world.

"Probably not necessary. Regular comm channels are probably safe enough. But the topic tonight is one that makes me nervous," Jose replied.

"Which topic?" Elsie asked.

"Brock." Jose asked. "What else?"

"Tristan mentioned Brock? I figured you were calling to talk about Bella and your drones."

"He streamed the conversation to Honus and me. Bella is also important, but I don't know what else I can do to help on that topic. I don't know what we will do about the Brock situation. We need a plan," Jose insisted.

"So, the delivery drones taking supplies in and reestablishing comms to the wilderness area was you?" Elsie asked.

"I'm not confirming anything. It doesn't look like your associate Bella made contact with any of them yet, which is not good. But back to Brock..." Jose said.

"I agree that you really screwed up," Elsie needled Jose. "Letting Emily hang out with adult homeless men? And maybe Brock?"

Jose replied, "I didn't know. Hey. There aren't supposed to be any more homeless."

"You think this Brock is him?"

"Yeah. Most likely. I saw him from a distance in the farm and didn't recognize him, but it could be him. I don't think he saw me, and he probably wouldn't remember me anyway. To him I was just one of your study partners in your first year or two of law school. We both thought he was dead, so it didn't occur to me to check out everyone Emily met to make sure it wasn't him," Jose answered defensively. "We were complacent out of ignorance."

"How bad do you think it is?" Elsie asked?

"It's been almost ten years. Do you think she remembers? Do you think they've recognized each other?" Jose asked.

"She didn't say anything to show she recognized him," Elsie said, "but she's a very smart kid and she is really into those scammer puzzles where people pretend to be someone they're not."

"You know about those? You think that's connected?" Jose asked.

"I don't know. She was four when we got away, but she may still have memories of him and remember that we changed names. We made it a big game for her back then and she went along with it. But somewhere inside she must remember she had a different daddy before you, even if she doesn't ever talk about it."

Jose thought for a moment and then said, "We could ask her what she remembers from back then, but that may make her remember more. That might be bad."

Elsie said, "Then let's not do that right now. Okay. Let's look at best and worst cases. Worst case is it is Brock, and he already knows everything and is plotting something against us. I don't want to think about that yet. In the best case, it's not him. But if it is him and she doesn't know he was her father and he doesn't recognize her as his Sandy, how do we keep them from finding out?"

Jose said, "Our plan from back then should still stand. The fire was a tragic surprise, but we still followed the plan. You wanted a way out where Brock and his cronies couldn't find you."

Elsie explained, "At first we were just playing roles as a family in a game world so Sandy could get a feel for a different kind of family with a dad who spent more time with her than Brock did. In the game I took the name Elsie and Sandy said they wanted to be called Emily. That's when I was pretty sure she was a *she* instead of a *he* or *they*."

"Yeah. She definitely is a *she* still. Is she on puberty blockers or anything yet? She doesn't talk to me about that stuff," said Jose.

"Standard regimen. Low dose. For almost a year," said Elsie.

"That makes sense." Jose continued, "I had started getting ready to become Jose in the Reset,* so you used that name for the dad in the game and I played along to drive the dad character sometimes. I thought it was just a diversion for you two. I didn't think you were really going to leave him until that morning when you said you'd had enough and wanted to do it for real. I was in the process of Resetting to Jose. It wasn't hard to add the two of you using your game characters."

Elsie asked, "You would have gone on your own if we didn't come with you?"

"I'd have still kept in touch. I had already started my switch to Jose and lined up a job working with Abitats under that name. I had transferred control of my software revenue stream to hidden avatars in multiple game worlds."

Elsie said, "As I remember, Sandy and I got in our Abitat, and I pushed the Reset button you gave me. There was a sudden blast and the Abitat accelerated out of there like it was shot out of a cannon. At first, I thought it was all part of your Reset action. I was really scared that you caused the explosion. Our Abbie immediately called us by our new names, Elsie and Emily. I worried for days that you had somehow caused the fire to get rid of Brock as part of your escape plan for us."

Jose said, "No. You know that was a coincidence."

"I guess so. Looks like it didn't work anyway."

---

* The Great Reset coincided with the adoption of the AM game rules as law. People had the option to adopt identities from characters they controlled in game worlds that were merged into the new World One.

"Hey. That wasn't me. But I did reset your Abitat's Abbie, so it's memory of you was from the game world. Basically, your old Abitat disappeared and a new Abitat identity from a game world took its place. People thought you and your Abitat were burnt to ashes."

Elsie said, "The fire gave a convenient explanation for our disappearance and the disappearance of our Abitat, but we were going to disappear anyway."

"Your Abitat would have just become untraceable, but Brock would have tried to find you," Jose said. "I found us a private week-to-week rental place with a full-size Abitat garage. With tools from my new job, I was able to repair your Abitat to hide the scorching from the fire. And you got some cosmetic work to change your looks while you studied for the bar. We stayed in that rental for a few years while you started your business, until you kicked me out for Andre, the hunk."

"You knew I didn't think of you that way," said Elsie.

"Yeah. I was always willing to give it a try," Jose lamented.

"As you reminded me many times," said Elsie.

"Anyway. I hear you all live in a four-Abitat house somewhere in the IE now. Nice."

"We like it," said Elsie.

Jose continued, "If we knew Brock was still alive, we all probably would have moved farther away and done more to hide your identity. I would have kept track of him like I did for some of his contributors to make sure your paths didn't cross. As it is, I have been trying to keep a low profile, but maybe not low enough if Brock was living a few blocks away from me."

Elsie said, "He never really knew you. But he did know Emily when she was Sandy. If he recognizes her, that's the real problem. Myself, he probably wouldn't recognize unless he saw one of my private tattoos that I haven't had removed yet. But those aren't visible."

"Billy Jay recognized you."

"Really? Then I probably haven't been keeping as low a profile as I should have. I do look a little different, and I avoid publicity, sure. I rarely meet with clients in person. I took the bar under my new name and looks under Reset anonymity rules."

"All good."

"But I do go out in public sometimes and if Billy Jay recognized me then some people from law school or Brock's associates might recognize me or my voice despite the changes. But so far no one has said, 'Didn't you die?'"

"I don't think many would recognize you. Maybe not even Brock. Everyone knows you now as Elsie Mendoza, not L. Celine Jackson, or Laetitia C. Hogan. In retrospect maybe Elsie is too close to L. Celine, L.C.?" Jose observed.

"You just noticed that? You want to arrange another Reset?"

Jose said, "The Reset was a one-time thing, but you can legally change your name again anytime if you want. Maybe take Andre's last name. Or we could do a witness protection type of thing. I could probably find people who could help with that—sort of a mini-Reset, but we'd probably have to move, and Andre would probably have to agree to it, unless you want to go back just with me again."

"Not a chance. I'm sticking with Andre, the hunk," said Elsie.

"He seems okay. Kind of young and way too many muscles, but okay. He seems like a good dad to the baby," said Jose.

"Thanks. Meanwhile, what is the plan for now?" Elsie asked.

"Yeah. That's the question," Jose thought out loud. "We need to find out if we're dealing with a best case, worst case, or something else. We need to confirm if this Brock is Barack and what he knows. The same for Emily. But we need to do it very carefully. Do you have discrete investigators through your firm? I used to know someone, but I don't know if I can reach them anymore."

"I'm not going to have someone spy on my daughter," Elsie insisted.

"Brock. Not Emily," Jose clarified. "Yeah. I agree. She leaves her message history open on her tablet, because she trusts I'll never read it, and I won't. That just seems like too much of a violation."

Elsie said, "I admit I have looked a couple times, and I didn't see anything about Brock. I couldn't understand most of it. It was mostly in a teen code of animated emojis. I wonder if hieroglyphics or Chinese ideographs started out that way. Anyway, I think she expects us to ask more about what she was doing with these unhoused adults by the river trail. I can raise the subject with her directly without bringing up things from 10 years ago."

Jose agreed, "I could talk to her too. Maybe you go first since she's staying at your place this weekend. But be careful."

Elsie said, "Maybe more than just this weekend."

Jose didn't respond so Elsie continued, "Okay, what do we know so far?"

Jose said, "Yes, counselor. In summation: At the present time the world is informed and believes Barack, L. Celine, and Sandy Jackson are deceased. In point of fact, evidence indicates all three to be extant and living: Barack as a mononymous unhoused person still using his prior alias, Brock; L. Celine and Sandy with identities de novo."

"Acknowledged. Let that be stipulated," said Elsie.

Jose continued, "Forthwith, you will depose Emily about the dangers inherent in associating with third party adults and do discovery about her knowledge, information, and belief regarding Brock. We shall both pursue identification of a private investigator who can be engaged to discretely ascertain if Brock is Barack and elucidate his cognizance of relevant facts."

"Bravo. Almost like a lawyer or L2. Pre-game anyway. I think you should probably arrange a PI through your other-worldly game contacts, so it's not traceable back to me, but I can come up with some names of investigators for you to contact."

"Okay. I'll also check if my old PI contact is still in business."

"Gretchen?" Else looked at Jose's anime character face for his reaction and concluded she had guessed right. "Really?"

Jose ignored her and said, "Just send me some names. We should also think about what we need to do if Brock knows."

Elsie responded, "Let's hope he doesn't, but yes. I'd hate to have to move, but it might come to that. Let's think about options."

"Maybe he's changed. At least he's not the asshole politician he used to be," said Jose.

"Inside he would never change," insisted Elsie.

"It's been a long time," said Jose. "Oh yeah. One other thing. Speaking of things from long ago. Did you and Perry make a history world game about the days when we first met him and Billy Jay? Honus found one today that he didn't recognize."

"Not me. I've played in my share of game worlds but never built any," answered Elsie.

11:20 PM, Elsie's Family in Jurupa Valley

The four Abitats arrived at the house within minutes of each other, each docking in its own docking slot. When Alex's Abitat docked and the door opened to their room, Andre made sure Alex was still asleep and dry and left them in the Abitat bed. He quietly went to the kitchen to make himself and Elsie herb tea. While the tea steeped, he checked to make sure his own Abitat had docked next to the master bedroom. As expected, it had arrived before him since it was able to maneuver without concern for an occupant. He noticed the door to Emily's room was closed.

Emily stepped from her Abitat into her room to get her pajamas. She found a set in a pile of clothes on the floor just outside her closet. She sniffed them and they seemed clean enough. The room was filled with pandas, a study desk, a large exercise pad in front of a floor to ceiling mirror, and scattered clothes. There was no bed in her room since she used her Abitat's bed and shower when she stayed at her mom's house and wanted the space for exercise. Sometimes she used the shower in the bathroom next to her mom's office if she wanted extra water pressure, but usually the Abitat's shower was good enough when it was connected to the house. Her clothes were still a little damp and smelly after being in the rain with Sam and Jo-Jo hours earlier. They would need to be washed. She tossed them onto the floor just outside the Abitat bathroom door and turned on the shower.

Elsie remained in her Abitat after the door opened giving a view into her home office. She was still thinking about what to say to Emily about Brock. After a minute she stood up and walked through her office and opened the door into the hallway. The door to Emily's room was closed and she thought she could hear a shower running. In the other direction Andre was holding a cup of tea for her in the family room. She went to him and accepted the tea and the two of them sat on the sofa.

"Weird day, huh?" Andre suggested, raising his arm to give her space to cuddle in.

"Yes. Weird day." She sipped her tea and leaned against him.

"Do you want me to talk to Emily about the dangers of strangers? I can give the public safety officer perspective if you want."

"No. I'll talk to her…" Elsie leaned in, and Andre lowered his arms and held her tight. Elsie continued, "…tomorrow."

To Be Continued…*

---

* See AutoNoMoUs Parts Two and Three to further explore the characters and world of AutoNoMoUs and answer many of the questions raised in Part One.

Appendix A

Jeremy's Writings

Excerpts from
Everything about Abitats and the AM Game,
Infinite Closet Explained,
Remembering Memorial Day,
by Jeremy Jones-Smith

Everything about Abitats and the AM Game

by Jeremy Jones-Smith

Abitats are now so common that most people take them for granted, but that was not always so. Abitats originally were an idea in a game. When the AM Game first appeared, there were no real Abitats and there were still many homeless people. The AM Game is now the legal system for American society and many other places in the world and with real Abitats being widely available homelessness is no longer a problem.

AMerican society has been living legally within the rules and structures of the AM Game since the mid 2040's, and unofficially for about twice as long. The same is true in varying degrees in most countries around the world. In most regions that have not yet adopted the game as law there is widespread use of the game for entertainment, communication, and commerce, and widespread use of Abitats. Some countries try to block their citizens from using the game, but its distributed nature makes blocking it difficult. Some locales lack the infrastructure to support Abitats, but everyone with a phone, tablet, watch, tv, or other connected computing device can use the game. Each local region playing the game has differences in the game based on the consensus of the players in the location, but all have game worlds that map onto and augment the real world as well as story worlds that usually envision and simulate possible futures or allow players to interactively participate in fictional worlds or stories from the past.

The AM Game itself has been around for longer, but it's only in the last 15 years or so that Abitats and other elements of the game moved from simulated worlds to the actual world and the influence of the game became entrenched in all aspects of life, until the game rules were adopted as law during the Great Reset about 10 years ago. Many of us have lived our whole lives with the game and Abitats, but some older people alive today lived part of their lives during time before the game, and before Abitats were everywhere. Most can hardly remember or imagine living any other way. For young people my age, the world of the game is the only world we know. We have to look at history to understand what came before.

Transportation, communication, and commerce are almost entirely performed within the context and rules of the AM Game now. That was not always the case. AM Points or Amps are the currency for almost all transactions. Some historical paper and coin currencies still exist and are occasionally used, but their values are defined in relation to Amps. Long ago people did not use Amps and only used money or barter systems, such as trading chickens and firewood for food or medical care.

Now people trust the fairness of transactions that are negotiated for them by their Abbies. Information that is Abbie-vetted is completely trustworthy. If we want, we can access vast amounts of information to do our own research and make informed decisions about transactions ourselves, but it saves time and effort if we trust the advice of our Abbies who can quickly sort through all the available information, verify its accuracy, advise us, and negotiate for our benefit. Each person has their own Abbie, usually connected to their Abitat, and most people rely on their Abbies' advice.

People also still use many other apps and services for entertainment and information, usually using the capabilities in their Abitats, and most trust the advice from their Abbies about what sources to believe. Years ago, people didn't know what to trust and there was a lot of disagreement and mistrust in the world.

Most transportation is done in Abitats, or, for short or very long distances with other vehicles or public transportation that use the same cooperative principles but lack some of the domestic features of Abitats. Because people feel at home when in their Abitats, commuting has become almost a non-issue. People used to waste a lot of time stuck in vehicles getting from one place to another and having to control their vehicles themselves the whole way and frequently dying in horrible accidents. Now, if people want to drive themselves, they have to go to special tracks or roadways that are set aside for that purpose or pay extra tolls to other vehicles to make room for them on the roads.

People with Abitats can spend time in whatever locations they want to and feel at home in their Abitats while the Abitats move them between different locations. A large majority of people are using Abitats not just for transportation, but for part if not all their residential needs. Like a movable tiny personal studio apartment, an Abitat can provide a cozy place to relax, sleep, work, or play along the way, and can drop them off at any location where they want to be. Some who can afford it, also own homes with additional personal or family space where the Abitats can dock and serve as detachable bedrooms. Such homeowners may allow their private Abitat refresh stations to be used by others for a fee when they are not using them themselves, with restrictions that prevent strangers from entering their homes, but public refresh stations exist throughout the communities and along the highways, so home refresh stations in most locations are rarely used by others.

Because people can sleep, work, and play in their Abitats along the way, people can have their home base in residential communities hundreds of miles from their employment or school locations. Those who can afford it can also get upgraded Abitats, with extra comforts and more powerful transportation features to cover long distances much more quickly. Typical basic Abitats are well-suited for moving around in town. Their transport undercarriages can be swapped out when needed for longer distance or higher speed transportation or off-road travel or for water or air travel.

All Abitats can recharge at public refresh stations and dock at hoteling spots with other amenities. Some return daily to the same hoteling spots. A small but growing portion of the population is opting for living entirely within their Abitats and forgoing any recurring stationary address. All communications and deliveries can reach them through their Abitats, so for those purposes there is no disadvantage to living fully mobile.

Minimalism is a popular philosophy, especially among the population who choose to reside entirely within their Abitats. Those people live with few visible possessions. Ubiquitous delivery and storage services allow people to retrieve objects or belongings to their home or Abitat whenever they want to use them and store them away out of sight the rest of the time. Personal Abitats can participate in transporting and delivering items for others when their delivery closets are not occupied for their own purposes. When occupants, or inabitants, are away from an Abitat or sleeping they may allow their Abitats to independently pickup, transport, and deliver items to earn some extra points.

People still seek entertainment in the game, watching or playing in simulations of other worlds—past, present, future, and fantasy fictional, but most of the game worlds people spend time in now are direct projections of the current actual world, augmented in various ways to serve the preferences of the players. Generally, the only characters people can fully control in projected real world game worlds are characters that project to themselves. They can observe and make suggestions to other characters that project onto other people, depending on the privacy or sharing settings that others have set.

Communication capabilities of Abitats allow people to stay in contact with their friends and play and work virtually while in the comfort of their own spaces. Some prefer to do most of their social interactions through the game from within their Abitats. Others spend as much time as they can in real public spaces with other real people, knowing that they can summon their Abitats at a moment's notice if they want privacy or transportation. Public restrooms exist, especially in venues with crowds of guests, but some people refuse to use them and call back their own Abitats when they need to go.

People who needed lower cost housing and transportation jumped at the chance to get Abitats, as did others who could afford more but wanted a minimalist lifestyle. Not every homeless person accepted an Abitat when they were first offered, but a lot of work was done by people like Jackson to convince them to try them and accept help from the services that Abbies can arrange. A small minority of people continue to live without Abitats and walk or use public transportation to get around, but that is a dwindling part of the population. Residences without Abitat docking stations still exist but are quickly being replaced. Most people who live in such buildings have Abitats that can drop them off or pick them up outside.

The problem of homelessness has been eliminated in most communities like ours where Abitats with basic income have been provided to those who could not afford them. With the security of basic services including transportation, bed, bathroom, and basic income, plus reliable advice from an Abbie, and referral by their Abbie to medical or other human services, most formerly homeless people have been able to improve their situations and become stable, productive members of the community, indistinguishable from others. Some who have not found regular paid employment and rely on their basic income have followed advice of their Abbies and migrated to different locations where their basic incomes will stretch further.

Infinite Closet Explained

by Jeremy Jones-Smith

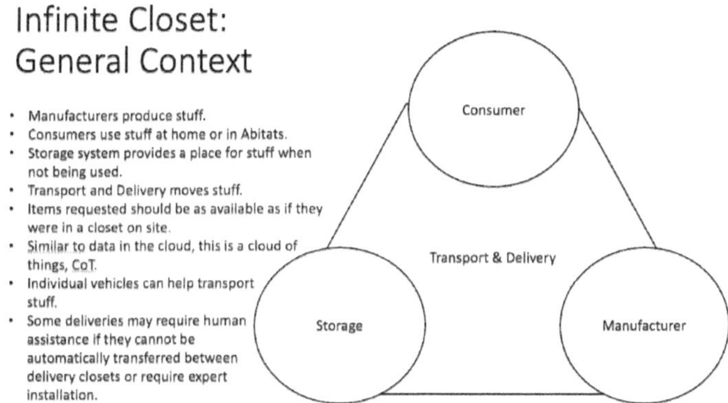

Infinite Closet: General Context

- Manufacturers produce stuff.
- Consumers use stuff at home or in Abitats.
- Storage system provides a place for stuff when not being used.
- Transport and Delivery moves stuff.
- Items requested should be as available as if they were in a closet on site.
- Similar to data in the cloud, this is a cloud of things, CoT.
- Individual vehicles can help transport stuff.
- Some deliveries may require human assistance if they cannot be automatically transferred between delivery closets or require expert installation.

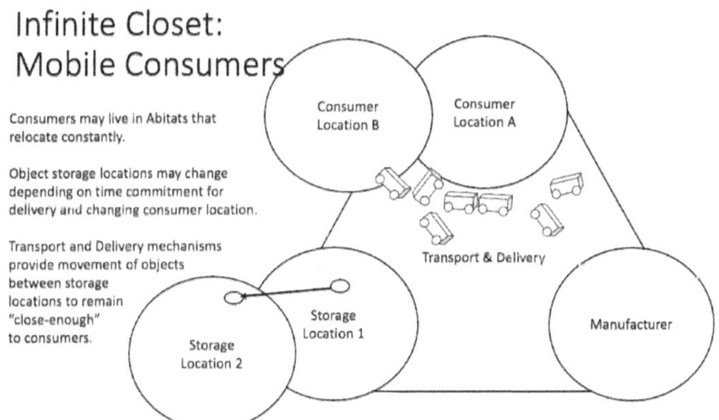

Infinite Closet: Mobile Consumers

Consumers may live in Abitats that relocate constantly.

Object storage locations may change depending on time commitment for delivery and changing consumer location.

Transport and Delivery mechanisms provide movement of objects between storage locations to remain "close-enough" to consumers.

Infinite Closet: Manufacturer Options: Direct Sales

Consumer orders a specific object directly from a producer and it is shipped directly to consumer delivery closet.

Or see Next pages for variations...

Infinite Closet: Manufacturer Options: Consumables

Manufacturer uses storage system as distributor with transport and delivery services to put quantities of goods close to consumers for immediate delivery.
Storage and delivery systems may have to protect certain types of items with special conditions, such as refrigerated items kept cold.

Primary use cases:
- Frequently used items.
- Consumables with some shelf life.

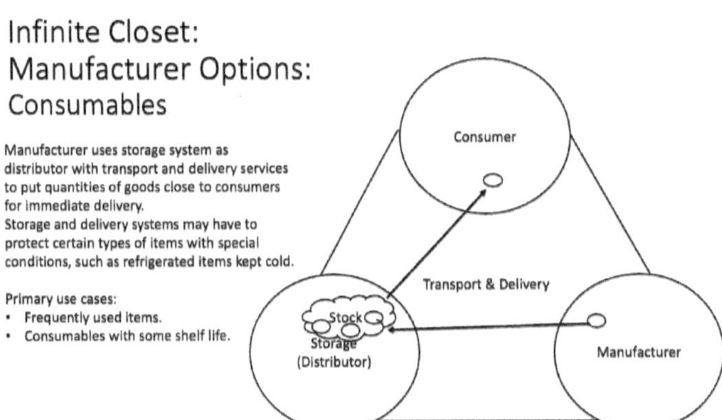

Infinite Closet: Manufacturer Options: Food Services

Consumers order food.
Restaurants produce and package food and hand it off to transport and delivery services.
Food delivery can be to delivery closets in homes and Abitats or to people in public locations such as parks.
Consumer consumes and disposes of remnants.

Primary use cases:
- Food and Beverages for immediate consumption.

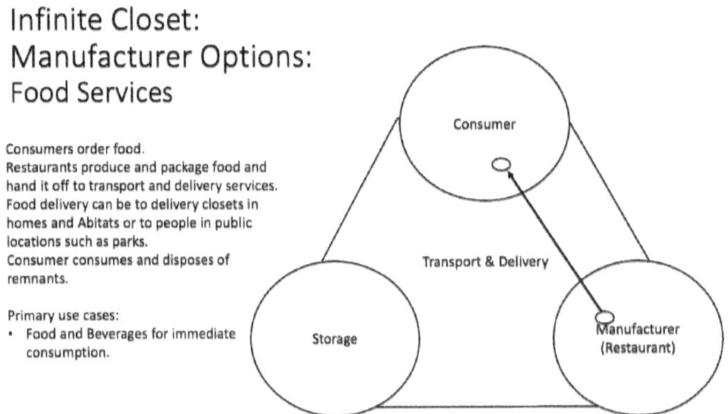

Infinite Closet:
Storage Features

Save and protect objects to be later requested by consumers, replacing prior multi-$10 billion US self-storage industry.

Objects can stay close enough to their consumers to allow very fast delivery.
- In both fixed and mobile storage.
- In dedicated storage services and temporarily in consumer delivery closets.

Transport vehicles exchange directly with consumer delivery closets or use drones for last leg of deliveries.

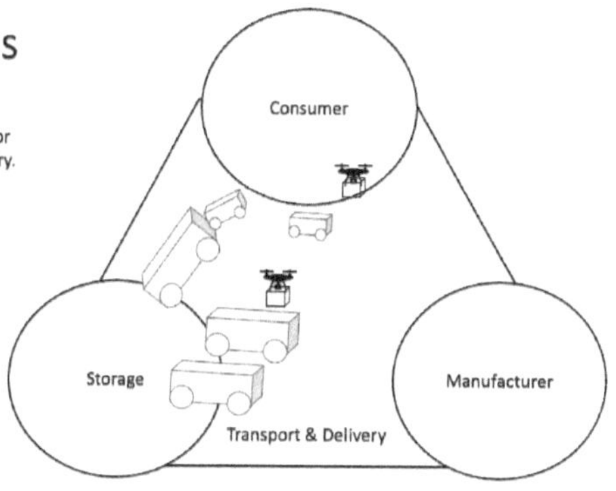

Infinite Closet:
Rent/Share Option

Consumer owns a specific object.
Storage provides access by renters when owner is not using the object.
Owner responsible for maintaining their specific objects. They can contract with someone to maintain their objects.

Primary use cases:
- Infrequently used expensive items.
- Bulky items without sentimental value.
- Recouping costs of purchase and storage by renting out.

Infinite Closet:
Personal Vault

Consumer can put owned objects in the storage service with secure, exclusive access to the object's owner.

Primary use cases:
- Sentimental or highly valuable.
- Exclusive use due to hygiene or personal preference.

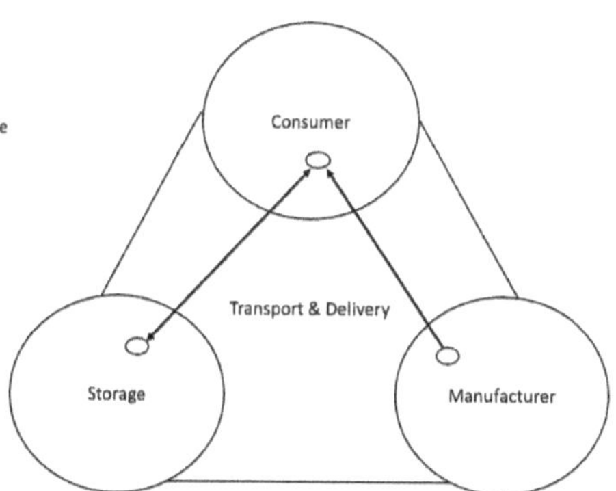

Infinite Closet: Timeshare

A group of consumers own a pool of similar objects.
Storage provides secure, exclusive access to the group of owners.
Owners share responsibility for maintaining the pool of shared objects.

Primary use cases:
* Infrequently used expensive items.
* Offsetting costs by sharing ownership.

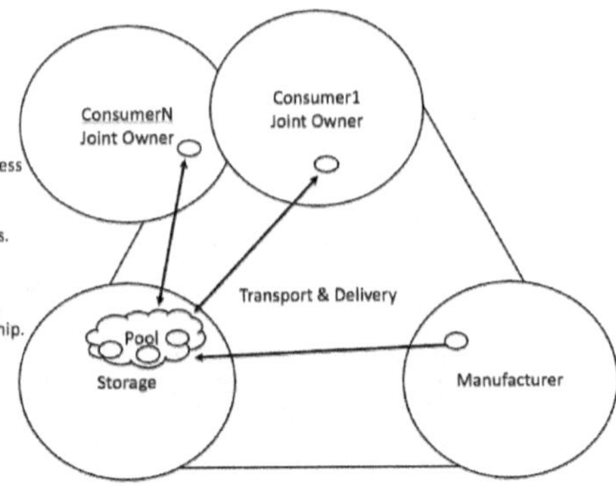

Infinite Closet: Rental Service

A business owns a pool of similar objects.
Storage provides temporary access and use to consumers renting from the pool.
Business is responsible to maintain and replenish its pool of resources.

Primary use cases:
* Expensive, low-use items.
* Owning company in business to make money from rentals.

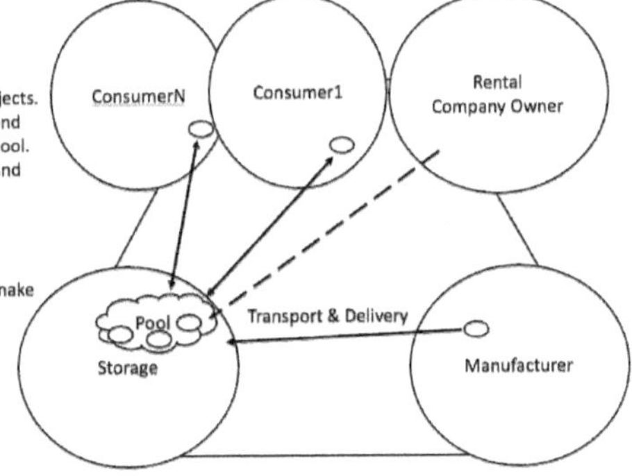

Infinite Closet: Transport and Delivery

Can be tied to manufacturing or storage services as a combined service.
OR
Can be part of a separate coordinated delivery and transport service.
OR
Can be independent autonomous vehicles owned by consumers if they have capacity for compatible picking up, transporting, and delivering objects.

Infinite Closet:
Role of Abitats:

Personal Abitats have standard interfaces for exchanging goods from their "closets" which can vary in size.

Some vehicles are configured completely for storage and transport and do not provide any consumer personal space at all.

Some units are subsidized by having a large closet area and spend more of their time transporting items. This provides funding for providing Abitats for otherwise homeless folks.

Some Abitats have less space devoted to the delivery closet and more space available for personal use.

Infinite Closet Corollary:
Mobile Recharge:

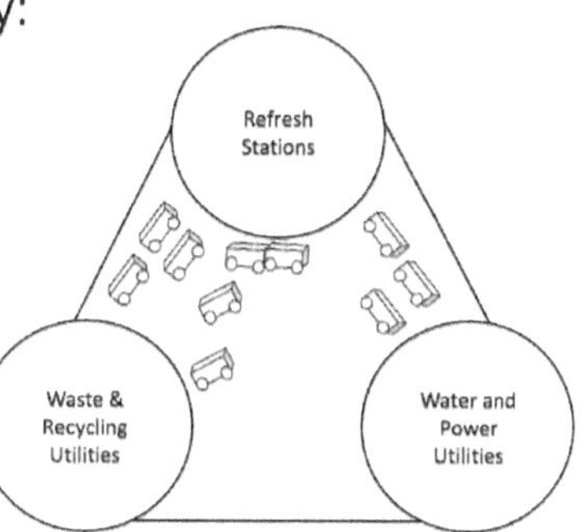

In addition to interfaces for exchanging goods from their "closets," Abitats have standardized interfaces for taking on charges and fresh water, and for eliminating wastes, trash, and recyclables.

Refresh stations have compatible interfaces to give or receive refreshes and may be directly connected to utilities.

Dedicated Refresh Vehicles can provide similar services on the go.

Individual Abitats can also serve as Refresh Vehicles to gain additional subsidies.

Infinite Closet Corollary:
Incarceration

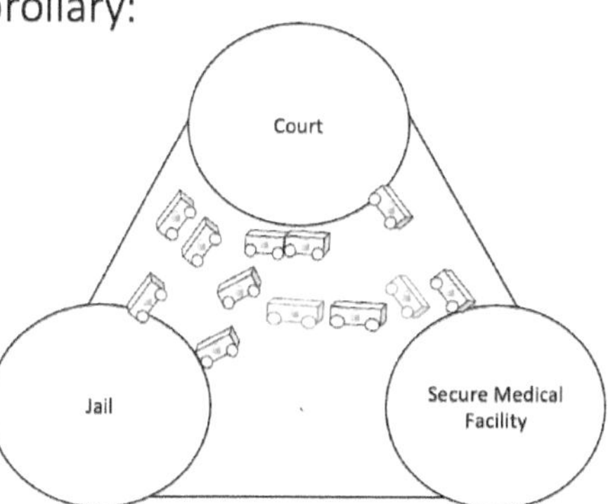

Jails and prisons expand capacity by having inmates stay in Abitats.

Such Abitats are controlled to restrict egress to locations such as courts, jails, and secure medical facilities and limit what can be delivered to the inmates.

These might be the same Abitats that the inmates had before being incarcerated.

Such Abitats could also be used for transportation and delivery services to offset incarceration costs.

STEAMBOAT ACADEMY History Essay   May 26, 2056
Remembering Memorial Day   by Jeremy Jones-Smith

Memorial Day is a day for remembering things. One memorable thing happening this weekend is the Fifth Annual Jackson Memorial Homeless-No-More Festival.

A few years ago, an important person named Jackson worked hard to get Abitats with Basic Income for all the homeless. We should be thankful, and we should remember that before the homeless problem was solved thousands of people lived in tents or on sidewalks causing extreme crime and filth.

Abitats have been around since before I was born, and most people have them now, even the previously homeless. Abitats originally were an idea in the AM game, but now they are everywhere. No one knows for sure what AM stands for in the name of the game, but I think the A probably stands for Abitats.

Many of us have lived our whole lives with the game and Abitats, but some older people lived part of their lives before the game, and before Abitats were everywhere. We can ask them about what came before.

Nowadays, most transportation is done in Abitats, or sometimes with other vehicles that cooperate with Abitats. My grandparents say that people used to have to control their vehicles themselves and frequently died in horrible accidents. When they wanted to play games or sleep or go to the bathroom, they had to stop and get out. They would have to go home or find a public restroom.

Now if people want to drive themselves, they go to special tracks or roadways that are set aside for that purpose or pay extra tolls to other vehicles to make room for them on the roads. My dad sometimes pays to drive a car at the racetrack by Mojave. He says it is dangerous, but a lot of fun. I plan to go with him this Summer to learn to self-drive a car.

Transportation, entertainment, and shopping are almost entirely performed within the AM Game now. AM Points or Amps are used for almost all transactions. Long ago people did not use Amps and only used money or barter systems, such as trading chickens and firewood for food or medical care. I much prefer to let my Abbie pay for the things I want with my allowance Amps rather than having to carry around something to trade.

Most people use Abitats not just for transportation, but for part of their residential needs. Like a movable tiny home, an Abitat can provide a place to relax, sleep, work, or play along the way. A lot of people like my family have regular homes where the Abitats can dock and serve as detachable bedrooms. All the new homes at Owens Lake where I live are 100% Abitat ready. But many people live in their Abitats and dock at public recharging or hoteling stations. Residences without Abitat docking stations still exist but are being replaced. Most people who live in such buildings have Abitats that can drop them off or pick them up outside or they use BubbleCar ride hailing service to get around short distances.

Because people can sleep, work, and play in their Abitats along the way, they can have their home base in residential communities hundreds of miles from their employment or school locations. For example, my home is over 250 miles from my school. I have use of upgraded Abitat features to cover long distances quickly. Basic Abitats are suited for moving around in town. Their transport undercarriages can be swapped out for a fee when needed for longer distance or higher speed transportation or off-road, water, or air travel.

Minimalism is a popular philosophy, especially among the part of the population who choose to reside entirely within their Abitats. Those people live with few visible possessions. Ubiquitous delivery and storage services, like the Infinite Closet, allow people to retrieve objects or belongings to their home or

Abitat whenever they want to use them and store them away out of sight the rest of the time. I can usually get whatever I need within a few minutes of asking for it. Some people let their Abitats transport and deliver items for others to earn extra points when their delivery closets are not occupied for their own purposes.

Some prefer to do most of their social interactions through the game from within their Abitats. Others spend as much time as they can in real public spaces with other real people, knowing that they can summon their Abitats whenever they want privacy or transportation. I spend what time I can with real people, but I have to spend a few hours each day in transit, so I use my Abitat and game worlds for most interactions.

There are game worlds that map onto and augment the real world as well as story worlds that simulate possible futures to help people make plans for the future or allow players to interactively participate in fictional worlds or stories from the past for entertainment.

In the old days people were always getting cheated and not knowing if they got a good deal. Now our Abbies do the research and negotiate for our benefit. Each person has their own Abbie, usually connected to their Abitat, and most people trust their Abbies' advice. Abbie-vetted information is guaranteed true. Years ago, people didn't know what to trust and my parents tell me there was a lot of disagreement and mistrust in the world.

The festival this weekend remembers Jackson and celebrates the end of homelessness in The County, but was homelessness really solved? My Abbie says she can't Abbie-vet that every homeless person accepted an Abitat when they were offered one, and I know some people continue to live without Abitats and walk or use other transportation to get around. That must be a small and dwindling part of the population, but they still exist. Despite those exceptions, overall, I think The County was successful at eliminating the homeless problem.

Appendix B:

Guide to characters

World	Name	AKA	Role
W1	Alex	Alexis Martin, Baby Alex	Baby of Elsie and Andre; Emily's half-sister.
W1	Andre	Andre Martin	Dad to Alex; stepdad to Emily; married to Elsie; Public Safety Officer. bat-suited NPC at *The Theme Park*
HW203904	Balaji Lee	Billy Jay Lee	Son of Mara and Perry; agoraphobic.
QX2230 in HW203904	Barney J. Johanson	Barney	Game character abandoned by Billy Jay.
QZ9301 in HW203904	Bartholomew J. Orlov	Orlov	Billionaire game character driven by Billy Jay
W1	Bella	Izzie, Isabella Muller	Daughter of Josephine, raised by Camilla; lawyer working for Elsie; lost in freak snowstorm in Sierras.
HW203904	Billy Jay	Balaji Lee, many names in game worlds	Son of Perry and Mara; agoraphobic; game player.
W1	Bobbie		Hiking partner of Bella.
W1	Brock	Barack Jackson	Unhoused friend of Doug; father of Sandy with L. Celine; former county supervisor; in hiding since fire.

World	Name	AKA	Role
W1	Camilla Muller	Izzie's Cam-ma	Babysitter for Alex; neighbor to Perry, Mara, and Balaji; single mom to Sam and Jo-Jo; retired forensic accountant.
W1	Carmen Kovich	née Carmen Lee	Estranged sister of Perry; daughter of Wilson Lee and Abigail Serrano Lee.
W1	Chandra		Classmate of Emily; engineering nerd.
W1	Charly	Charleen Jackson Malik	Relative of Barack Jackson; lives in his rebuilt house.
W1	Doug	Douglas Zynn?	Unhoused with Brock; presumed father of Isabella; formerly rich; formerly MinQuest guide.
W1	Dr. Magnolia	Magnolia Overly, vDVM	Cat rescuer; veterinarian; neighbor of Jose.
W1	Elsie Mendoza	L. Celine Jackson, Laetitia C. Hogan, Lacy	Mom to Emily and Alex, divorced from Jose; married to Andre; game law intellectual property attorney.
W1	Emily Mendoza	Born Sandy Jackson	Daughter of Elsie and Jose Mendoza; born to L. Celine and Barack Jackson.
W1	Fanny Tran	Tourist mom, née Fanny Kovich	Daughter of Carmen; mom of Minh and Max; niece of Perry Lee.
W1, QX2230, HW203904	Gretchen	The private investigator	Friend of Miguel and PI in QX2230; PI in HW203904 and W1; aware of place in multiple worlds.
W1	Honus	Balaji Lee; Billy Jay Lee	Single-named billionaire developer; reclusive; agoraphobic.
W1	Jameel	Jameel Malik	Spouse of Charly; father of Sandy J.
HW203904	Javier Maldiva	Jose Mendoza after Reset	Coworker of Lae C Hogan.

World	Name	AKA	Role
W1	Jeremy	Jeremy Jones-Smith	Classmate of Emily; physics nerd; creates mini-game worlds.
HW203904	Jerry	Geraldine Atwood	Worked with Perry on game and Abitats; inventor of AI personalities based on Nested Cellular Autonomy.
W1	Jo-Jo	Josephine Muller	Formerly unhoused; negligent mom of Isabella; sister of Sam; daughter of Camilla.
W1	John Tran	Tourist dad	Father of Minh and Max Tran; spouse of Fanny.
W1	Jose Mendoza	Javier Maldiva, 6th-order Harlequin Barrister	Adopted dad to Emily; divorced from Elsie; controls software used by Abitats and delivery services.
Pre-reset	L. Celine Jackson	See Elsie Mendoza	Once married to Barack Jackson before the Reset.
QZ9301 in HW203904	Lacy Hogan	Game character driven by Lae C Hogan	Restauranteur with consulting contract on the moon; possible love interest of B.J. Orlov.
HW203904	Lae C Hogan	See Elsie Mendoza	Cook at a market deli; game player.
HW203904	Mara Lee		Mom to Balaji with Perry Lee; missing since 2039.
QX2230 in HW203904	Miguel	Javier, Jose	Attorney game character driven by Javier.
All	Min Strong		Animated guru of minimalism; revered by many; originated the "MinQuest."
W1	Minh & Max	Minh Tran, Maxine Tran	6-year-old kids of Fanny and Max Tran.
QX2230 in HW203904	Mona		Homeless character briefly driven by Lae C.

World	Name	AKA	Role
W1, HW203904	Perry Lee	Tristan	Dad to Billy Jay; formerly data scientist and inventor; son of Wilson Lee and Abigail Serrano Lee.
W1	Rat man	Roger Rathman	Colleague of Andre in Public Safety; in costume at *The Theme Park*.
W1	Sam	Sam Muller	Formerly unhoused; brother of Jo-Jo; college friend of Douglas Zynn.
W1	Sandy J	Sandy Jackson Malik	Child of Charly; born after house was rebuilt.
W1	Sarah Jones-Smith	née Sarah Jones	Mom of Jeremy; project manager at new Honus resort east of Sierras.
W1	Sergey	Sergio Carlos Hernandez	Groundskeeper of Rancho del Fuerte farm adjacent to the childhood homes of Billy Jay and Bella.
W1	Squeaky	The Squeaky Wheel	Voice commanding Tim regarding drug trafficking.
W1	Tim	Timothy Spencer	Construction supervisor; works for Squeaky
W1	Tristan	Perry Lee	DBI-assisted lawyer; brain interface cap assists memory and legal skills.
W1	Wesley		Friend of Sam and Jo-Jo; formerly unhoused; working at *The Theme Park*.

Guide to terms

Name	AKA	Role
Abbie	Uncommonly renamed by Abitat's inAbitant	Intelligent assistant based in an Abitat and dedicated to the well-being of its inabitant; unable to intentionally deceive.
Abbie-vetted	Guaranteed trustworthy	Data known to one Abbie and shared with others as completely trustworthy; for example, sensor data used in sharing road conditions or current planned route for coordinating travel, or videos taken by Abbie-controlled cameras certified to be unaltered and authentic; sometimes applied, incorrectly, to reliable information from other trusted sources.
Abitat	Various names	Autonomous Tiny Home Vehicle
AM Game	The game	Simulated worlds with autonomous characters that can be observed and influenced by players; typically, where Abitats are commonplace.
Amps	AM Points	Currency used in the AM Game and in the worlds that have adopted it.
DBI	Direct Brain Interface	Technology for direct transfer of sensory experience and knowledge or motor control to and from the brain by way of a headset.
Forgetdibles	Forgedibles	Drug with effects similar to, but milder than NeverMind; usually in gummy candy form; sometimes made from highly diluted NeverMind.
Inabitant	Resident	Person assigned to a specific Abitat
NeverMind		Mind-numbing drug with side-effect, or intended purpose, of erasing some memories for a period of time.
NCA	Nested Cellular Autonomy	A technique for recognizing (or generating) emergent intelligence from a hive of interacting components.

Name	AKA	Role
NPC	Non-Player Character	Worker at The Theme Park.
Player	Guest	Visitor to The Theme Park.
Reset	The Great Reset	At the implementation of AM Game rules as overriding law, people could assume identities from characters they played in game worlds merged into a new World One.
Theme	(italics required)	The non-profit tera-corporation that dominates technology and entertainment; a "tera-corporation" much bigger than mega or giga corporation but also focused on preserving the earth (terra) and other planets and their inhabitants.

Guide to Game Worlds

Name	Context	Role
HW203904	The ranch house private network	History world depicting the days in 2039 when Mara went missing and Billy Jay met Lae C and Javier.
QX2230	HW203904	Game world where Billy Jay had some early successes, before abandoning it; revisited to contact a private eye through Javier's access to Miguel.
QZ9301	HW203904	Lunar Resort World around 2093.
W1, World One		Projection of the real world used to communicate and do transactions using AM game points and tools; the world people think of as real.

Acknowledgements

Plots and characters have their own autonomy, discovered by authors as we write. But readers, like *players* in the AM Game, also participate in influencing the behavior of characters and the unfolding of the worlds of these stories, not only in their personal interpretations as they read, but also by sharing their reactions and participating in discussions with others that lead to a community of interpretation.

I acknowledge the valuable contributions of early readers who commented on these stories. Some drove the story with specific suggestions and words, and others with more subtle influences, questions, and reactions. All helped shape the story as it is today.

Most of all I appreciate my wife, Diane, who has been my partner for many years in raising our family and completing many adventures together. In her career as an art teacher she influenced the characters of hundreds of students as they discovered their own autonomy and talents under her guidance, and she has been the most important influence on my own character in the game world of our lives together.

This story depicts fictional characters dealing with various personal challenges. I take full responsibility for any shortcomings in my depictions of those struggles.

Questions and suggestions to feedback@auto-no-mo-us.com may influence future versions or expansions of these stories.

Books in the AUTONOMOUS Series
by Christopher L Truxaw

AutoNoMoUs

Part One

Friday, May 26, 2056

Struggles with memories, identity, and connection in an allegedly post-homelessness and post-disinformation world.

Part Two

Saturday, May 27, 2056

Life and death challenges.

Surprising choices and discoveries.

Part Three

Origins: Mara's Memories

Back story of the world of AutoNoMoUs.

Two bright young minds set out to fight negativity and disinformation.

See www.autonomousbooks.com